About the Author

Nick Bougas is passionate that teenagers learn more about, gain a deeper understanding of, and develop a strong desire to protect, our natural environment. With over fifteen years of experience working in tropical rain forests and drawing on many of his personal experiences, Nick is sharing his passion for the environment through his conservation themed adventure books for young adults.

I dedicate this book to my wonderful wife, Brigitte

Nicholas Bougas

BODHI AND THE LOST TEMPLE OF KING NANCHANCAAN

AUSTIN MACAULEY
PUBLISHERS LTD.

A CIP catalogue record for this title is available from the British Library.

ISBN 9781785543241 (Paperback)
ISBN 9781785543258 (Hardback)
ISBN 9781785543265 (E-Book)

www.austinmacauley.com

First Published (2015)
Austin Macauley Publishers Ltd.
25 Canada Square
Canary Wharf
London
E14 5LQ

Acknowledgements

This book would not have been possible without the wonderful support of our dear friends, Kevin and Effie Oates and their family. My eternal gratitude goes to them for their help, support, understanding and belief in "Bodhi".

I would also like to thank my parents, Efthemios and Marjorie Bougas from the bottom of my heart for all their support, without which this book would also certainly not have been possible.

Chapter One

A Night of Opportunities

Alex was more excited than he had even been. Not that in his short life he had lacked excitement. He had canoed down the Amazon in Brazil, he had played with orangutans in Sumatra, he had climbed to Base Camp on Everest. He had even helped capture poachers in the Serengeti in Africa. He loved that life in the wild, with his parents, moving from one tropical place to another, never knowing what tomorrow would bring. He loved learning how to survive in the jungle, how to hunt for food, which plants you could eat, which were deadly. He just loved everything about it. Yes, there had been plenty of excitement until it came to a sudden end two years ago. He would never forget the nightmare knock on the compound door outside Belmopan in Belize in Central America in the middle of the night. It was pouring with rain, monsoon style, and the police officer at the door was drenched, and he was whispering something to the housekeeper.

"What is it? What's happened?" asked Alex as he made his way to the door, not yet aware of the dour faces on the two people he was approaching. His parents had been killed in a road accident trying to avoid a jaguar and its cubs. They had lost control in the torrential rain and careered down a gorge. And just like that, with the tragic loss of his parents, the adventure came to an end. No more travelling the world to the harshest places on earth. No more home schooling from Mum with his desk a log and his shelter a tarpaulin between trees to prevent his books getting soaked. No more sitting exams at the nearest British Council in Delhi, or Santos, or Djakarta. Basically no more fun, excitement and thrills with his mum and dad, both of whom were environmental conservationists whose jobs were to travel the world and alert the authorities, when they wanted to hear about it that is, of danger to the flora and fauna in their country.

Shortly after the fateful night of the accident, Alex had been sent home to England, enrolled in a boarding school and had to go through the thoroughly difficult process of learning to sleep on a bed in a room with mod-cons like light switches and a soft mattress; of sitting with 20 other boys in a classroom to learn his lessons; of washing in a bathroom with hot water and showers. The call of the wild made it very difficult for Alex to settle in and he felt miserable.

Then two things slowly started to change everything. Although he loved the wild excitement of the jungle and the intensity of the beauty and the danger and the colour that every day had brought for 16 years, he had not had much company of his own age. At boarding school he started to make friends, real friends. The boys were fascinated by his stories of Africa and Brazil and Indonesia. He could entertain for hours and never got tired of answering questions and quenching the curiosity of boys his age who had never been further than a 100 miles from home, or if they had been abroad, it was only to a Spanish resort or a Greek island. Of course some of the boys were well travelled but only in conventional style – travel by airplane, living in luxury hotels, eating at posh restaurants. No jungle survival for them.

The girls were more interested in his long black hair, permanent tan, great physique. When he played rugby he had a fan club on the touch line. When he walked into the school dining room a dozen sets of eyes watched his every movement until he sat down with his mates, at the corner table.

Alex tried not to notice the attention, but nonetheless relished in being a popular pupil at school and it helped him to no end to settle in and work hard. He was equally interested in the experiences of the friends he made, supporting their football teams, discussing girls – wow – and taking part in team activities, especially rugby and cricket. His own favourite, however, was the Orienteering Club where he excelled with maps and compasses, hiking through bogs and forests, camping overnight in the cold and the wet. He almost felt back at home in the jungle – slightly colder of course, but in the wild and surviving using your intuition. He was a natural leader and often ran weekend trips for his fellow class mates. They loved it too and followed him with awe and respect. They loved the terror of being on a desolate moor in freezing temperatures, but in the presence of Alex Steele, who they trusted and with whom they believed they could survive, even Armageddon itself was no challenge.

Oh yes. School wasn't so bad after all.

The other thing which Alex relished and became familiar with was every form of computer technology he could lay his hands on, from laptops to smart phones to advanced technology walkie talkies. In his younger life his parents had used GPS and old style mobile phones to find their way around the jungle and stay in touch with their base camps, but here was a new world. Wikipedia, Facebook and Twitter, let alone Google Earth, brought everywhere and everyone within reach. There was nothing Alex could not find out from his own room. It was mesmerizing and Alex made full use of his time and interest to make sure he knew what the latest craze was and became part of it. He was a Twitter fan and had a following of several hundred, mostly from the school, but also his grandfather in Wales and some of his friends from his prior life trekking the jungles. He loved being able to stay in touch.

And Alex ultimately flourished at school, got over as best he could the loss of his parents, and passed his exams with flying colours, especially Geography and Environmental

Science. He was sure that he would pursue a career along the line of his father in trying to protect the environment and passing on the message of sustainable living methods. But now that he was finishing school he wasn't sure that he wanted to go straight to university. He needed to get back into nature, back to the wild. He needed to go back and make sure he could still survive without his mum and dad there to look after him. He needed an adventure. He needed a gap year.

The train pulled into the station in Llandovery and Alex jumped out onto the platform. He was getting more and more excited. He had been wondering what on earth to do during his gap year but his plans just didn't seem to be getting anywhere. He was at a loss and then his grandfather had summoned him to his cottage.

"A gap year," his Grandfather repeated to Alex. "You want to get back into the jungle do you? Well I have exactly what you are looking for. And this time, Alex my lad, you will be the leader."

Walking out of the station yard the excitement was building. Alex's grandfather had been a marine archaeologist. He too had travelled the world and he had been the influence who had gotten Alex's father interested. It was in the Steele family. But what can he have in mind, thought Alex. I am just eighteen. Is that old enough to lead an expedition? Where would I go? Who would be with me? Would it be dangerous? The thought of his parent's accident flashed through his mind.

Alex made his way up the country roads to his Grandfather's cottage. It was a good few miles but he liked the walk. He had done it countless times over the summer breaks when he had spent time here, away from his uncle's farm outside London. Eventually he could see the cosy slate roofed cottage in the distance. It was a familiar place. The smoke was billowing from the chimney; blossom was on the trees in the garden, a canopy of green behind on the gently sloping Welsh hills. It was a place in which he felt completely at home, almost as if his parents were still alive and just away on one of their adventures.

He ran the last few hundred yards and knocked on the heavy wooden door. In an instant, as if at that very moment he had been expected, the door opened and his Grandfather grinned and hugged his grandson. "Alex, it is so great to see you again. How have you been my lad?"

They were both equally delighted to be seeing each other and the two of them sat in comfortable armchairs laughing and chatting. Keeping the spring chill at bay, they huddled close to the roaring fireplace, sipping from large steaming mugs of tea. Alex's grandfather had the appearance of a wise, old professor, which is precisely what he was. His bi-focal glasses sat perched, precariously balanced, half way down his stately roman nose. Grey hair and a grey beard framed the visible portion of his face. Wrinkles and lines from a lifetime of experience and knowledge were etched deeply on to it. In contrast to his wizened old features, his Grandfather's indigo blue eyes twinkled with a bright and youthful energy.

He adjusted his position in the arm chair. His movement generated small sparks of static electricity which crackled on his heavy Aran sweater – the type North Sea Fishermen wear, with intricately knitted patterns. This very same sweater had in fact been through many a freezing storm, warming his Grandfather in his younger years on his sailing adventures leading expeditions retracing ancient Viking trade routes on the high seas of the North Atlantic.

"So Alex, what do you think, are we in for it tonight?" he said, his deep baritone voice booming. "My old bones tell me a big storm is approaching."

Alex stood up and wandered over to the window, his agile athletic frame moving lightly, without any wasted motion. He wore a wind-proof fleece, tough trekking trousers and sturdy waterproof hiking boots. He was fit and clean shaven and every part the handsome young man that his Grandfather knew was a credit to the Steele family.

Alex raised his left arm and pressed two buttons on his digital wristwatch. "Well Grandpa, my barometer tells me that the pressure is dropping, so I would say that your old bones are spot on. Good thing that we're squirrelled away in your stone cottage, warm and dry. My watch also tells me there is a full moon tonight. That'll be nice to see on my walk back to the train station later on."

"Yes," said his Grandfather, "it will be a total lunar eclipse tonight. That is, if the storm clouds don't prevent us from seeing the spectacle. It would be a shame not to see a full eclipse."

His Grandfather stood up, raising his mug in Alex's direction.

"Well, storm or no storm, my old bones are now instructing me to make another hot brew and get down to the business at hand. I didn't drag you all the way down here to hear your exam results or that you had just passed your driving test. No, no, no. I want to offer you a job to keep you busy during your gap year. Something to get you back to nature; to follow in your parents' footsteps. Something that would make them proud, and give you some more excitement in the jungle before you decide what you want to spend the rest of your life doing. It's all in there," said Grandfather gesturing at an old leather-bound folder which was lying on the small wooden table next to Alex's chair. "Why don't you take a look and I'll make the tea."

All his young life Alex had considered himself to be a happy wanderer, his family frequently moving from country to country, never settling anywhere for very long. This migratory lifestyle had become a pattern until the tragic accident. But even though he had learned to enjoy school and his friends, he had always longed for the day that he would be living again out of his backpack.

6

From his early exposure to different cultures, peoples and countries he had developed an ever questioning mind. He was constantly trying to understand and analyse why the world was the way it was; and why people did the things they did. He was never completely satisfied by the typical answers that were offered to his many questions.

Planning and running expeditions that supported scientific and conservation efforts around the world was what Alex wanted to do. It was so much better than the typical nine-to-five office life he had heard his friends at school talk about. They seemed quite resigned to such a life and in a way he felt slightly envious that so many people were destined to lead mundane, but routine and secure lives. But Alex could never do that. He wanted to arrange and lead nature conservation expeditions, something that would give him something truly worthwhile to do, work that he could actually, genuinely believe in. Having the sky as his roof, and being able to live and work in extremely remote regions suited the type and pace of life that he so cherished. He wanted again to be surrounded by forest. The often harsh and physically demanding expeditions were the perfect balm for his restless, free spirit.

As he gazed into the dancing flames of the cheerful fire he snapped himself out of his revere and opened the weather beaten leather document pouch. Inside it he found a neat bundle of papers, maps and photos. There was also a daily work log that was obviously very old. The beautifully scripted handwriting was faded but still perfectly legible, written with a fountain pen many decades previously. It was a timber merchant's log book and Alex took it all in. The merchant had been operating a lumber mill in a country called British Honduras and the logbook was dated 1802. Alex carefully scanned all the other documents and eventually focused on just one. It was titled 'ARACHNIS'.

He had just finished speed-reading it when his grandfather returned with more body-warming drinks.

"Well, what do you think?" he asked.

Alex separated three documents from the pile and said, "Okay, let me see if I'm clear about all this. From what I gather you have established a new organisation called ARACHNIS which has members all over the world and they're all teenagers. All the members share a common interest – nature conservation and scientific research. You have challenged the members to find and submit their own nature conservation project ideas from their countries. The projects must have a conservation and scientific basis and must also involve the local communities and cultures."

"Correct," said the old man. "And I want you to be the ARACHNIS Expedition Leader. You would plan, organise and lead expeditions to some of the most remote and interesting natural environments in the world. You would team up with members of ARACHNIS in their respective countries and make it possible for these young people to actively participate in the conservation projects that they themselves have put forward to me for approval and funding. How does that grab you?"

"Sounds great!" said Alex. "But I am only eighteen Grandpa. Do you think I can do this? Will people accept me as an expedition leader? Will they follow my instructions? Will they trust me?"

"Alex, when your father was only a young lad he travelled the world with me. He was independent from a young age, he earned the respect of people much older than himself because of his skills and knowledge and because he was a decent boy who was polite and proper. He earned the respect of others by respecting others. I know you are the same. Your mother and father were very proud of you. You lived for more than twelve years in harsh environments. You can look after yourself, you can handle difficult and sometimes dangerous situations. Your parents told me. Your school teachers have told me. You will be able to take charge of and lead others with complete competence. I have no doubt that you can handle this position. And you are the ideal candidate. ARACHNIS members are teenagers. They will only be a few years younger than you.

They will not only be your team members but also your friends."

"Wow," said Alex. "What a gap year this is going to be."

"I was also more than happy to hear you passed your driving test the other week. Not that you haven't been driving 4x4s in the jungle for years of course. But now that you are an expedition leader we have to be squeaky clean and above board. You'll need specialised transportation that will double as a mobile field base to live in and work out of. You remember the trips you made with your parents don't you, something similar."

"Dad always used a Land Rover. That would be my first choice too," said Alex, taking a big gulp from the heavy stone clay mug and putting the documents back down on the small table.

"Well, remember Alex. I will be there with you in spirit and contactable when you need me. I have transformed my small cottage into an operations centre of sorts. I have direct access to the best academic databases around the world, and I am networked to all the major conservation organisations worldwide. I am too old to be charging around in a jungle and saving the planet. That's your job. But I can stay involved through ARACHNIS. You know it was your dad's idea originally. Even when you were a young boy he saw the potential in you. You were a natural for this type of work. You understood the necessity of environmental balance, the human threat to natural ecosystems, how our flora and fauna is being eradicated through greed and malice. Yes, your father had the dream that you would follow in his footsteps and be a leader able to convince people to put the environment first. We were all going to be part of ARACHNIS. Now your dad isn't here, so it's just you and me and so many others out there who care but need help to make a difference."

Alex felt quite humbled. He felt the spirit of his mum and dad in the room. Right there, right then.

His Grandfather continued. "Young people are so full of energy and enthusiasm. Many of them feel the spirit of adventure calling them. So many are filled with a sense of wonder and awe for our wonderfully mysterious planet. There are still so many discoveries to be made, and these days protecting the natural environment isn't just an important issue, it's now an absolutely critical one – much, much more urgent work needs to be done. I want to be able to help as many of these teenagers get directly involved as I can, to support them and their ideas and to make it possible for them to make a difference. You are the front line in our offence. For your gap year at least!"

The Professor went on, "I am too old to be roving the globe but the members of ARACHNIS are not quite old enough to be hiring cars, or planning and executing these projects without some help. That's where you come in. You will bridge that gap and act as the catalyst that will allow them to participate in our world-wide conservation efforts! You will take them with you into your realm of expeditions and adventure! Teach them all you know. I am offering you this position because I know that you will also bring them back again, safe and sound and with all their various body parts still attached and in one piece!"

Grandfather stepped closer to Alex and looked him in the eye. "One other thing. The first expedition will take you back to Belize. Back to where your mum and dad died." Alex shuddered and felt a bit weak at the knees.

"I want it to be this way. I want you to experience the emotions and the tension of a difficult first assignment. If you can do this one, you will prove to me and to yourself that you are set for anything. In any case, you have lots of friends there and you know the place well from the year you were there. Another thing. When your dad was in Belize he was looking for a Mayan Temple that supposedly had treasures which were unique and would change our view of that ancient civilization. If the Temple truly does exist, it would be of immense importance to the international scientific and archaeological communities because of what may be hidden inside it. He was also undertaking some important jungle conservation work. You will be following in his footsteps – same undiscovered temple and same conservation work. The only difference is that you have the benefit of the maps and the diary you looked at before. These have been sent to us by a young ARACHNIS member."

"You mean I will be doing exactly what Dad was doing! Looking for what he was looking for! Oh man. This is just beyond belief," said Alex.

At that very moment and as if for natural emphasis, an enormous clap of thunder shook the small cottage. The strange ornaments on the mantelpiece above the fireplace jangled and rattled, and a wickedly barbed arrowhead fell off, burying itself in the polished wooden floor with a dull thunk. Alex bent over and began pulling the projectile point out, which took some effort. As he waggled it back and forth, his Grandfather noticed a small jewel-like orb drop out of Alex's collar. It dangled around Alex's neck from a loop of nylon parachute cord, the stone glowing magically in the firelight.

Alex followed the old man's gaze and said by way of explanation, "Something my dad always wore. It is from the Kanabo tribe in the Amazon. It was a parting gift to him and he was wearing it when he had the accident. Dad told me that they call it the "Seeing Stone" or "Looking Stone" – something like that. I never take it off."

Grandfather took the orb in his hand and studied it carefully.

"I have never noticed you wearing this before." He cradled it in his palm and saw that it was set into a narrow steel band with an eye welded to it for the parachute cord to go through. It was an almost perfectly spherical orb which shone a deep blue and flashed with all the colours of the rainbow in the flicker of the firelight.

"It's very unusual, I've never seen anything quite like it," said the old man. "The light seems to dance inside it, doesn't it? It has quite a hypnotic effect! It's wonderful."

"Yes, it's quite mysterious really, reminds me of a miniature full moon. I can stare into it for ages, and it brings back memories," said Alex as he watched the indigo blue stone flash unusually brightly this night.

Taking the talisman back, he tucked it into his shirt once more, "I've grown really attached to it – I never take it off. I like to think it brings me luck!"

Just then the wind began to howl and the first flashes of neon purple and electric blue lightning split the inky dark night. Like a giant flash bulb, it lit up the entire forest for an instant. The chickens in the coop began to squawk and cluck nervously.

"Wow," said Alex, "looks like we are going to have an enormous thunderstorm."

"Yes, it's going to be a bad storm," said Grandfather, "and my poor chickens don't seem to be at all happy about it! Now, let's talk for a moment about the vehicle you will need to conduct your expeditions…"

"Yes, about that," said Alex interrupting, "wouldn't it just be simpler and easier for me to hire off-road vehicles in the countries I am going to be working in?"

"Not at all. You are going to need not just any vehicle, you are going to need a very special vehicle to cope with the challenges that lie ahead of you. It will have to have certain modifications which you will need to make yourself. I will get you some help if you need it. You will also need to be able to fix it on your own too, which means you have to be totally familiar with it from bumper to bumper."

"In that case it will have to be a Land Rover then," said Alex. "I already know them inside out from all the years with Dad."

"It has to be totally reliable, especially as your small team will regularly be working in extremely remote areas. No, a hire car, even an off-road four wheel drive just wouldn't do. You'll have to buy one here and kit it out properly. It will need quite an array of scientific and expedition equipment. Besides, ARACHNIS is a registered not-for-profit organisation. Having that status means I am able to get some help from interested businesses and organizations. For example, a very good friend of mine from Scotland who works in international shipping has generously arranged for us to ship the vehicle on cargo ships to any corner of the earth at no charge. Isn't that marvellous? That's what makes it possible to invest time and effort in one special vehicle; we can send it wherever we need it. That is if you are interested in taking on the challenge Alex! What do you say? Do you accept my offer?"

A big smile spread across Alex's face, his eyes sparkled with excitement. He walked across and hugged his Grandfather.

"My answer is, yes, of course. I would be honoured to be part of ARACHNIS. Sign me up! And I promise I won't let you down and I will make Mum and Dad proud. And wait till I tell all my friends how I am going to spend my gap year!" said Alex.

"Well you don't have much time to go socializing and having fun with your friends. The first expedition is almost ready to go and we need you ready pretty soon, Land Rover and all," said Grandfather.

"I'd love to go through it in more detail tonight but I have to make a mad dash for the last train. I should also try and make it to the station before this storm really hits!" said Alex.

"Right you are," said Grandfather. "I'll come and see you next week and give you a full briefing pack. I am keen to visit your place anyway. I believe you have made some changes from your mum's interior decoration!"

"Yes, I don't live in the house anymore. I converted the barn down the road. You'll see!" said Alex draining the last dregs out of his mug.

Standing up he put on his waterproof jacket, slung his day pack over his shoulders and made his way to the door.

"It was so good to see you again Alex, and I am so glad that we will be working together on ARACHNIS, even though you will be having all the fun. Are you sure you don't want to stay over tonight? This storm is really becoming pretty fearsome!" the old man said, peering out of the window at the howling gale outside.

"I'd love to Grandfather, but I really do need to get the last train home tonight. I have to submit my outline presentation to the Royal Geographical Society, the deadline is tomorrow morning. I have been invited to give a talk there to the Young Geographers Club about tropical rainforest conservation," Alex said cracking the front door ajar.

"Like father, like son," answered the professor.

The strong wind pushed against the door, a cold blast threatening to blow it wide open. As Alex carefully opened it a bit wider they both heard a commotion that had nothing to do with the tempest raging outside and everything to do with panicked and terrified chickens.

Grandfather and Alex charged out of the cosy, warm cottage and into the cold wet wind. Running along the cottage wall they rushed around the corner into the back garden just in time to catch a glimpse of a big red vixen dashing along the top of the stone wall with her head held high and her neck straining with the weight of the plump, limp hen gripped firmly in her jaws. The vixen's sharp white teeth gave the appearance of a huge smile as the lightning lit her up like a paparazzi camera. In an instant she vanished into the dark, her image seared into the shocked eyeballs of the two observers.

"Blast! That vixen's at it again!" yelled the old man into the deafening wind.

"Anything I can do to help?" Alex shouted.

"No. Thank you Alex, you had better get moving or you'll miss your train. I'll go and find wherever she got in this time and block it up. See you soon!" Grandfather shouted, giving Alex a quick hug, the rain running down his face and dripping off his beard.

With that, Alex waved goodbye and began a slow trot out of the gate and down the path, pulling the jacket's hood over his head and stretching the elastic headband of his Petzl headlamp over it as he switched it on.

Piercing the darkness like a searchlight, the bright beam from the halogen bulb transformed the raindrops into a cascading shower of diamonds. His boots splashed through the muddy puddles, following the circle of light on the ground which was bobbing and jolting in front of him. With the rain pelting down, Alex increased his pace to a slow run.

He had learned to like running and now greatly valued his ability to keep up this pace for an hour at a time, walking fast between bouts of running. In this manner he was able to cover long distances. Apart from the physical benefits of running, Alex found that it cleared his mind and allowed him to focus on important issues, thinking them over while the miles passed under his feet.

As he ran through the wet, stormy night, he mulled over the new position he had just accepted. His enthusiasm and excitement grew and warmed him like the heat from the fire earlier on.

"Yes!" he yelled into the stormy night, "BRILLIANT!"

He was almost out of the narrow country lane. Stone walls covered in brambles stood on either side of him. He passed the odd turnstile and wooden gate and on his left and right stinging nettles and dock leaves crowded the drainage ditches next to the road. As Alex drew within sight of the main road he looked further ahead to the twinkling lights of the town of Llandovery, just two miles away.

Illuminating his watch face with the press of a button, he did a quick time-versus-distance calculation, confirming to himself that he would make it to the train station in time if he maintained his current pace. As his headlamp beam swung back to the lane he saw her.

The vixen was about twenty yards from him, the chicken lying on the ground. The vixen's mouth was agape, panting after the exertion of carrying her heavy prize. Just as the light lit up her fiery orange eyes for the second time that night, she snapped up the chicken and vanished.

Alex had noticed that her fur looked dense and healthy. He considered the fox's long standing distrust of people and thought it well justified. After all, humans had hunted them for their thick fur in the autumn since the dawn of time, never mind being hunted to this day for sport.

"Well, you're the hunter tonight," he thought, grinning, "enjoy your dinner!"

As he ran through the parking lot of Llandovery train station he contemplated the mysterious circle of life, and what all living things did in order to survive. A feeling of joy and satisfaction spread through him. He always considered it a privilege to see a wild animal following its instincts in its natural environment. He looked to the sky but there was no sign of an eclipse at the station platform, the clouds thick and twirling, dark with heavy rain. But he felt more than a little happy that he, too, had come away with a prize tonight.

He boarded the last train and settled into his seat for the trip back to London. What a day. What an adventure lay in store. But although elated, he also felt apprehensive. Yes, he had lived in jungle environments for most of his first sixteen years, but always with his mum and dad. Now he would be the leader and he would be responsible for the others with him. It would be completely different now. And going back to where his parents had been killed? How would he handle that? But his Grandfather had belief in him and he was sure that there would be help at hand if he needed it. And wow! Having a brand new Land Rover! He just couldn't wait. In fact he had to let someone else know right now so he took out his iPhone and tweeted:

"Best news. Gap year fixed. Back to the jungle!!!"

Within minutes he had responses from his friends:

"Good on you Tarzan," tweeted Johnny.

"Go save the world. I know you can," tweeted Ricky.

"Can I come with you. Love Jane," tweeted Jane.

And that last tweet certainly got Alex's heart racing even more.

.

Chapter Two

Storm of Life

The storm clouds rampaged wildly across the night sky in what one witness would later describe as an invocation of black dragons. Thick black tendrils twisted their way north-east, weaving a cloak over the sleeping English countryside below. The huge storm rolled along at great speed becoming an unstoppable airborne tidal wave of thunder, lightning and downpour, its strength building as it invaded. It passed over Hereford, and then Worcester, gaining power as its forward speed slowed down. It settled like a great dark blanket over the town of Solihull in the West Midlands.

In complete contrast to the storm raging on its surface, planet earth floated in the perfectly silent vacuum of space. The earth, timelessly travelling along its orbit, began to drift directly between its own natural satellite – the moon – and its life giving star – the sun. The earth's shadow finally touched the moon. The lunar eclipse had begun.

The instant this happened, a primordial life force bloomed out of the ether, flowing and swirling as it gathered. A whirlpool of cosmic power spiralled down from the universe, blending with the earth's atmosphere as it penetrated through its spinning layers, funnelling it directly into the centre of the storm far below.

Rain and wind battered the huge Land Rover vehicle manufacturing plant at Lode Lane. Sheets of rain swept over the large white factory buildings, flooding the huge fenced-in parking lots which were full of brand new vehicles. It's perfectly manicured and landscaped main entrance was completely drenched in flowing rainwater.

Rivulets cascaded down the shiny black granite slab on which stainless steel lettering announced: 'Welcome to Land Rover'. The hazy orange glow from the street lights in the car lot bleached out periodically in the blinding white flashes of the unending lightning.

The dark figure of a man ran across the car park's slippery flooded surface and threw open a large green metal door. He made a quick dash into the shelter of the huge factory.

"Have you seen what's going on outside?" panted the worker breathlessly as water ran off his waterproofs and pooled around his boots.

"That's one bloomin' wicked storm, I'll tell you!" he said, catching his breath. "How many more cars are left on the production line boss? I knock off in ten minutes."

The solidly built shift-foreman, wearing a Coniston Green polo shirt with a beige collar and stripe across the chest, looked down at his clipboard.

"Only one left on the line, Tony. She's finished and ready to park outside. Better get a move on though. As you say, the shift's nearly over, the buzzer will go any minute now," he said above the noise.

A loud hissing and electric hum came from the work floor. Giant orange mechanical robotic arms swung and spun all along the production line, hydraulic powered limbs picking up parts with precision and twirling, turning and stopping instantly in the perfect position. Showers of sparks sprayed from the electro-welders as smoke drifted up from the holes being drilled and cut into the metal bodywork of the skeletal vehicle chassis.

The engineers and machines worked in complete ergonomic synchronization. In unison, they smoothly installed seats, engines, lights and wiring. An orchestra of manufacturing that performed in perfect harmony.

Tony walked to the end of the production line where he could see that there was one last Land Rover waiting to be taken out of the factory. He loved his job and always wondered where all these vehicles would wind up and how they would be used. As he pondered this thought, there was an enormous and deafening bang and instantly the entire factory was plunged into complete darkness.

A second or two later, emergency lights blinked on all around the building, casting an eerie glow. The shadows of the now motionless robotic arms were cast up onto the ceiling like a giant shadow puppet show of futuristic techno-monsters as the emergency backup generators coughed into life.

"Great! A power failure! Well that does it!" the foreman exclaimed. "This storm is definitely one for the books."

"Tony!" he called loudly, his voice reverberating around the now much quieter factory, "You'll have to leave the last one on the line tonight, the holding clamps need full power to be released, so take her off in the morning when the power is up and running properly again, okay? It's so close to finishing time, let's call it a day."

"Right-oh," replied Tony as he headed for the staff room to change and go home.

The last of the Land Rover staff left the plant, thankful to be on their way to warm dry homes. They were amazed, and a little intimidated, by the light show they were subjected to as they left the factory and ran to their cars.

The night sky erupted with neon purple lightning bolts, electric blue and bright pink light waves. These bright colours were punctuated every few seconds by dazzling white magnesium flashes; blinding bursts of light that left imprints on the viewer's eyes afterwards and made it hard to see properly until they readjusted. No one could ever remember seeing anything quite like this. Some compared it to the aurora borealis that can be seen in the Arctic Circle. None of them had ever seen anything so spectacular here. It was a show they would never forget.

Inside the factory, the Land Rover Defendèr sat alone in the darkness, steel clamps holding it firmly onto the conveyor belt. A couple of electrical leads and some diagnostics wiring were still connected, forgotten by the line worker during the interruption caused by the blackout.

The storm raged outside the factory as the earth's shadow crept silently over the moon's surface. Already it covered half the glowing disc.

The metal in the factory began to hum as the ions in the atmosphere became supercharged. Small sparks jumped and crackled on the plastic covering of the brand new seats as the static electricity built up. The colourful light show in the sky above began to descend towards the ground below, directly over the factory.

Suddenly, the rain just stopped, as if a tap had been turned off. The wind died down and the entire atmosphere became electrically charged and expectant. The abrupt silence was broken only by the sound of tinkling and gurgling as rainwater flowed away. Then, an enormous clap of thunder split the air, a giant flash of light exploded from the sky blasting straight onto the factory roof. Power charged through every wire, surging into every piece of metal, and every machine, including the production line and its conveyor belt.

It flashed, sparked, crackled and banged as it raced along the conductive surfaces. Speeding down the line, the thunderbolt of power shot directly up and into the Land Rover still clamped to it. An aura of light lit up the entire vehicle. At first purple, then blue, red, green and yellow. The colours began to combine, forming a golden cocoon around it.

At this precise moment the moon's disc became black; the earth's shadow completely cloaking it. The lunar eclipse was now total. All the residual power from the huge blast trickled and ran up from the conveyor belt and into the vehicle. The glow around it intensified.

Deep within the engine, a tiny seed of consciousness came into being. It grew and expanded, pulsing outwards in all directions. Sensing... feeling... being. Awareness was gradually dawning. Blurred shapes were forming; muffled sounds filtering through into an emerging consciousness. Slowly, budding new senses became clearer and sharper. Steadily it began tuning in to its own self, its own being. The Land Rover began to transcend from a collection of inanimate pieces of machinery into a sentient being; a being that was gradually becoming self-aware.

Alive!

Steadily, it picked up on the surrounding environment, not yet knowing, or understanding – just sensing and intuitively assessing itself and its surroundings.

From the golden cocoon of light surrounding it, an intention took shape, becoming a thought. The thought formed, condensing and seeping into the Land Rover as an extrasensory communication – a message was being sent into every atom and electron of the vehicle. The message was:

"Awake!"

The Land Rover's very first thought began to distil and crystallize. It then popped into the golden glow like a blob rising in a lava lamp.

It asked, "What's happening to me? Who are you? Who am I?"

The golden cloud pulsed and throbbed as an answer was transmitted.

"Humans often call me Gaia, the Earth Mother," said a soft and gentle voice. "I have materialized tonight in order to infuse you with life force, so that you become self-aware. I have given you consciousness. I have given you a name, as you now exist as a conscious being. Your name is Bodhi. The reason that I give you this name is because, in one of the oldest human languages, Bodhi means 'awakened'. It is a fitting name as you were created by humans to serve their needs, however it is your destiny to fulfil a much higher purpose."

The cocoon glowed increasingly brighter as the message was absorbed into Bodhi's entire being.

Gaia continued, "There are human beings that need your help in order that they may, in turn, help me. Your combined energies, actions and efforts will create a positive, creative and protective force. This energy, your collective power, and the actions you will all take, will begin to restore natural balance to this world. Humans have allowed negative, destructive and chaotic forces to become too powerful. I am now out of balance. Consequently, the environment that supports human life is now endangered. The time has come for you to act as a catalyst for change. The humans you will be helping and influencing are young, but they hold the key! They alone have the power to make a lasting and real change in the balance, as they alone are the future of humankind, and it is humankind that has created the imbalance. Only they can rectify it. The young people you will help are a lot more powerful than they realize. Humanity's future well-being, the very survival of their species in time to come, rests in their young hands. I will always be here, they may not be."

Miniature, multi-coloured stars began to appear all over the golden cloud as Gaia infused Bodhi with more life force and information.

Gaia continued, "You will face many hardships and challenges, your journey will often be difficult and dangerous but you will never be alone. I will always be with you. As will two other powerful spirits that I have asked to help you whenever necessary. These two spirit guides will teach you and show you the way. Their names are Mezaferus and Andrasta; they too will visit you soon! Remember Bodhi, I am nature, I am everywhere!" Gaia proclaimed.

With that, the golden glow expanded, becoming bright red, then green, then blue and, finally, sliding into deeper and deeper hues of purple and indigo until darkness filled the now silent factory building.

Bright moonbeams began to pour their silvery blue light through the windows. The storm had passed and the moon was, once again, full and bright.

Chapter Three

Persuasive Passion

Alex stood at the front of the lecture room at the Royal Geographical Society in Kensington. His jungle trousers and khaki safari shirt were totally out of place in the swish lecture theatre, let alone his scuffed jungle boots which still had flakes of mud on them from some recent orienteering trip. This was who he truly was and how he felt comfortable. Alex always loved to have the opportunity to talk to his peers, which he did with authenticity and accurate hard facts. By just being himself, the audience easily recognised that he was the 'real McCoy', no pretence, no role playing – no need for him to be 'in character'. In a world crammed full of fakes and phonies it was a refreshing change for the young listeners. He was also comfortable talking in front of a room of people from his days at school in the Debating Club.

The President of the Young Geographers Club had introduced him as Alexander Steele, son of Peter and Sheila Steele who spent their lives working to protect the environment and assist people around the world to value and cherish their small part of paradise, and to stop big businesses from destroying and eradicating our precious flora and fauna. He also reminded the audience that Alex's parents were life-long members of the Geographical Society and that Alex had been given membership by his father on his sixth birthday.

"Alexander spent his first sixteen years travelling with his parents to many corners of the earth, experiencing the geographers dream, and we proudly call upon him to address you today."

Alex looked up from the podium and saw three hundred young faces eagerly waiting for his talk to begin. He was only a few years older than most of them, but he knew they all shared his passion for geography and the environment. Rather than speak, Alex firstly dimmed the lights, pressed a button on his laptop and began a slideshow of exquisite photographs of unbelievably beautiful, natural landscapes from the jungles of Central America and South-East Asia. Each new photo was more colourful and breathtaking than the last. Audible gasps, appreciative ooh's and aah's from the young audience, told Alex that he had their undivided attention. He smiled as he heard the quiet murmur of chatting as the members of the audience commented amongst themselves about the wonderful visuals they were seeing.

After thirty slides, the room lit up and Alex placed himself behind the lectern.

"As you've all probably gathered by now, I'm a jungle nut. I love the heat and the humidity, I love the animals, the trees and plants, and I even love the mud, snakes and bugs. To tell you the truth, I'd much rather be in a tropical jungle than outside this building on the overcrowded streets of London.

"And why, you may ask, am I fascinated with jungles and rainforests? Well, let me share a few startling facts with you all:

"Did you know that although tropical rainforests now only cover six per cent of the earth's surface, they are home to more than fifty per cent of all living plant and animal species?"

"Did you know that rainforests are the natural thermostat of the earth, to a large degree regulating temperatures and precipitation? Indeed, one fifth of the fresh water found on the entire earth, is in the Amazon Basin. For us humans to continue to have fresh water, the rainforests must survive.

"Rainforests once covered fourteen per cent of the Earth's land surface. As I just mentioned, they now cover a mere six per cent, but even this is being cut down and burnt at such a fast rate that I'm sorry to say that there is every likelihood that within our lifetimes," Alex continued, his hand scanning the room from left to right, "we will live to see the last rainforest tree cut down. That is unless we – yes, you, me and everyone you know and everyone they know, actively participate to change the current situation."

Alex continued with his factual assessment of the rainforests and their predicament. He told his audience how the U.S. National Cancer Institute has researched rainforest fauna and found that seventy per cent of all plants identified as useful in the treatment of cancer are only found in rainforests, an amazing two thousand plant species.

"Did you know that experts estimate that the earth is losing about one hundred and thirty seven species every single day due to rainforest deforestation? That equates to fifty thousand species a year, gone forever! As the rainforest species disappear, so do many possible cures for life-threatening diseases. Currently, one hundred and twenty one prescription drugs sold worldwide come from plant-derived sources. While twenty five per cent of Western pharmaceuticals are derived from rainforest ingredients, less than one per cent of these tropical trees and plants have been tested by scientists."

Alex continued his lecture. The audience was clearly very impressed, and paid close attention to what he was saying. Periodically he emphasized the points he made with slides, charts and graphs.

"Before ending I would just like to share a quotation with you and I hope that some of what I have said today will be meaningful and will lead you to better comprehend the problems facing our planet and, therefore, be better able to contribute in some way to their solution.

"Mr. Howard Zinn was quoted in the *Huffington Post* on January 28th 2010 as saying,

"What is called "apathy" is, I believe, a feeling of helplessness on the part of the ordinary citizen, a feeling of impotence in the face of enormous power. It's not that people are apathetic; they do care about what is going on, but don't know what to do about it, so they do nothing, and appear to be indifferent."

"Do not be apathetic about the problems being faced by the environment. You can all do something, whatever that something might be, to make this magical, mystical planet we live on cleaner, safer and more sustainable. Altogether, all the "somethings" that you, and millions of young people like you do, will make a difference!

"Our earth is an amazing place and we must do whatever we can to protect it and stop the damage being done to it. It is up to us all, but especially the youth of today, to organise a managed retreat from the cliff that we are all racing headlong towards and to try and rectify the environmental errors and thoughtless destruction of the earth by past generations of mankind. There can be no doubt that if we don't rectify the situation as fast as possible the earth will do it for us."

As Alex ended, a hand shot up from a young girl at the back. With an encouraging nod and smile from Alex the girl stood.

"You're clearly very passionate about rainforests and the environment. Your parents dedicated their careers to trying to save jungle environments and the flora and fauna that live in them. But in the lecture today you said that thousands of hectares are destroyed every day and hundreds of species of animal become extinct every year, many before they have even been discovered by man. The population of the earth continues to balloon and ever more of our finite resources are needed, so the destruction of the environment will inevitably continue won't it? Aren't you fighting a losing battle? Why go on? Is there any point?"

A melancholy silence fell over the audience. Three hundred faces slowly turned from the girl at the back to Alex at the front. An expectant hush awaited a response. Alex glanced down at his laptop and stayed in that position for a few seconds. He then slowly looked up, a huge smile on his face and walked round to the front of the lectern, raising his hands in the air, the khaki browns and battered jungle boots visible to the whole room.

"I am excited and enthusiastic, I am passionate and dedicated, I am certain and I am confident, because you are all here today listening to me! All of us are the future. What will happen to the earth next is up to us and our generation. Many of you may leave this lecture and say, "Hey, that was fun but not much I can do about it." Fair enough; but some of you may be touched by what I have said, mesmerized by the beauty and the magic of our planet. Some of you may just decide to do something about it. We can build awareness and influence others; we can sow the seeds of a global movement. If there are enough of us, we can make our governments and decision makers sit up and realise that what is happening to our planet is simply not sustainable. How humankind is treating nature is ultimately bad for us all. It is humans who are the "unbalancing factor" in all of nature; everything else is how it should be. We won't see change tomorrow, or next week or next month. This is a generational movement and we are that generation."

A round of applause exploded from the room. Alex, though slightly embarrassed, was thrilled. This was what he wanted to achieve; to get young people like himself on board with his mission. They were really the only ones who could actually make a difference and also see the benefit. He went back to his laptop and searched his files for a slide he had prepared as an aide-memoire for himself.

"A wise professor once told me that to be in this line of work you have to remember four words."

Alex pressed the arrow on the keyboard and the first word came up on the screen. Dedication.

"You must be dedicated to the mission. There is no point in being passionate about saving the jungle if you throw your litter out the car window in London."

He pressed the arrow again and the word 'Understanding' flashed up.

"To be dedicated you have to understand why you are doing it. Learn about the environment and how it interacts with your everyday life. Know why the protection of the rain forests is important. The third word is Devotion. You need to be devoted and think outside the box. You will not become rich being a conservationist, but you will realise that your efforts are actually much more necessary and self-rewarding than many others earning more than you."

Alex pressed the arrow again and the fourth word came up. Experience.

"With experience you become better acquainted with the mission at hand, better able to explain and debate the issues. More at peace with yourself that you are doing something entirely worthwhile and for the greater good."

A voice from the front shouted out, "Dude!"

"Excuse me?" said Alex, thinking he had not heard correctly.

"DUDE!" said the voice again. "Dedication, Understanding, Devotion, Experience. D.U.D.E. Dude."

Amazingly Alex had never noticed what the first letters of the four words spelled but he certainly knew now as the hall erupted into a chorus of "Alex is the Dude. Alex is the Dude."

Embarrassed but elated, Alex grinned and took a small bow. "Thank you very much. We can make a difference. "His last slide showed his twitter address and half the room seemed to take a second to write it down.

He gathered his things, packed up his laptop and with a bounce in his step, went to leave the hall together with the teenagers.

At the door, the girl who had asked the question drew near and said, "Have you got time for a coffee? My name is Jane."

Chapter Four

Alex and Jane

"Your soulmate can also be your downfall."
— Guillaume Musso

"Sure, that would be great!" Alex said with more confidence than he actually felt. He thought Jane was stunning and he felt himself becoming very self-conscious as he tried desperately not to stare into her blue-grey eyes, or at her long, wavy, auburn hair. The more he tried to avoid staring at her, the more awkward he felt. Alex always found it a constant source of frustration and irritation that this would happen to him whenever he was in the presence of attractive girls.

"Are you okay?" Jane asked smiling, "You seem a bit flustered!"

"No, no not at all!" said Alex, "come on let's go, I think there's a coffee shop down at the end of the block."

Walking side-by-side they exited through the main entrance of Lowther House, the magnificent redbrick building which houses the Royal Geographical Society. Alex was surprised to notice that Jane was almost as tall as he was. Glancing down he looked to see if she was wearing heels. She wasn't. She wore a pair of neat, flat, black leather pumps.

Black leggings showed off her very long, slim athletic legs which seemed to go on forever.

As was Alex's ritual whenever he left the Royal Geographical Society, when he reached a certain spot on the pavement he paused for a split second, looking up at a statue set into an enclave on the wall.

"Who's that?" asked Jane following his gaze to the figure of a powerful looking man dressed in an Arctic smock, his calm strong features looking out from the opening of a heavy woollen balaclava covering his head.

"That is Sir Earnest Shackleton, the famous explorer and expedition leader. One of my heroes, you could say," replied Alex as he cast his eyes up and down the street. He spotted the coffee shop and they made their way towards it.

Once inside they sat down on a small comfortable sofa seat as a waitress approached to take their order.

"Café latte please," said Jane

"A big mug of English breakfast tea for me please, with milk and sugar, thanks!"

"You're a very unusual guy Alex. You've had quite a life so far," said Jane settling back into the comfortable sofa.

"Well yes, I guess I have. Certainly I've had a very unusual upbringing, and that's paved the way for this next new phase of my life. Sometimes I'm envious of people who've had a more stable life. Today for example in the R.G.S., it was obvious that many of the people there were schoolmates and they've probably known each other throughout their high school life. It must be nice to have that sort of continuity. We moved from pillar to post all over the world and I guess that's probably why, although I do get along very well with most people, I am a bit of a loner. A happy wanderer!"

"In my own way I am a bit of a loner too. I like my own company, especially when I'm trying to recharge my batteries. I'm really enjoying your company now that I've got you all to myself! Tell me about the jungle, I've always wanted to visit tropical rainforests. What's it like to live in them for long periods?" asked Jane.

"Good," thought Alex to himself, "Familiar conversational territory, that'll help. That face, those legs..."

"Well, the jungle and tropical forests, are all really just that – forests. The big difference is that there are usually no dominant species. Pine forests, oak forests are all dominated by one species, tropical forests aren't, they're so diverse. Then there's the huge amount of rainfall and the enormous amount of life and biodiversity that they contain which is just staggering. I call it the 'fight for light', because all the plants and trees are striving to reach the sunlight. It's all just such a vibrantly green, pulsating, energy filled environment. I truly feel at home when I am under its canopy, and surrounded by trees, when I'm completely immersed in nature's life force."

Jane listened intently as Alex described some of his jungle experiences, and close encounters that he had had with various types of wildlife, including some near misses with venomous snakes and large predators. Alex started to get carried away and his natural enthusiasm and gift for storytelling held Jane entranced.

Alex suddenly realised that although he was really enjoying sharing his adventures and experiences he was also trying hard to impress this young woman. What was it about her that he found so mesmerizing? He was drawn to her charismatic and beautiful aura. Spellbound, he felt like a nervous wreck.

Suddenly he became very self-conscious again and the natural flow of his words became disrupted. He wound up his last story a lot more quickly, and a lot less smoothly than he would have liked.

"Enough about me!" said Alex, "tell me more about yourself, why did you come to the R.G.S. today?"

"Well, my dad's a scientist and an F.R.G.S., and he has been a huge influence on my life. I've also always been crazy about nature and the natural world. I just finished my A-levels and I'm taking a gap year before I go to university. I heard about you, and your unusual life story through the grapevine. Then I heard that you would be giving a presentation here today so I thought I would check you out for myself. I really enjoyed your presentation today by the way. It was very inspirational, it certainly motivated me to get off my backside and do more to help the environment!" Jane said laughing.

"Yes, we could all do so much more," Alex agreed.

"Where are you heading off to next?" asked Jane.

"Well it looks like I'll be heading to Central America. Back to Belize in fact..." said Alex, his eyes staring off blankly into the distance.

"Isn't that where... I mean, isn't Belize where...?" Jane struggled to finish her sentence.

"Yes, Belize is where my parents died," said Alex.

Jane saw the pained look in Alex's eyes and instinctively reached over and held his hand in hers.

"I'm sorry Alex. I didn't mean to bring that up..."

"No, don't be silly. It happened; it was a while ago now. It'll be good for me to go back there. Closure, I think they call it!" he said forcing a smile. His hand felt like it was on fire, an electrical current seemed to be pulsing between them.

Simultaneously they both became acutely aware of the chemistry between them and for several seconds they just sat in silence, until the silence started to become awkward.

Alex was the first to break contact making the excuse that he needed more sugar for his tea.

"Phwoar!" thought Jane watching him cross the floor towards the counter, "Those shoulders, that back! Very nice..."

Alex returned to the sofa and as he sat down he commented, "You seem as though you would be a sporty type of person, am I wrong?"

"No, you're right, I am. In fact I'm very active. I do orienteering and cross-country running. I play netball, hockey and lacrosse too," said Jane matter-of-factly.

"Lacrosse! That's a pretty hard-core game isn't it?" asked Alex.

"Originally yes. Now, not so much. It can get a bit rough sometimes though, but that's partly due to 'body checking' and partly because the players should aim to adopt the attitude and spirit of the warrior. After all the Iroquois tribe, the Native Americans, that invented it were all warriors. I love it, it's a lot of fun. Very competitive," said Jane.

Alex and Jane chatted for ages. Eventually night fell and they both realised that they should get going but neither of them wanted to end the great conversation they were having, nor did they want to part company just yet.

Alex really liked Jane a lot and he hoped she felt the same. He was quite surprised to feel a sharp pang of disappointment when he thought about the fact that he would be heading off to the other side of the world very soon and the chances of him seeing her again anytime soon was probably very slim.

"Get a grip of yourself man!" he scolded himself silently. "Nothing will come of it, don't get emotionally involved. You're heading off, she's heading off, that's it. That's all."

They settled the bill and left the warm cosy comfort of the coffee shop, stepping back out into the night and onto the cold London pavement. Walking shoulder to shoulder they headed for Knightsbridge tube station. They made the 15 minute walk last half an hour, chatting and laughing all the way down to the platforms. As they were heading in opposite directions, on opposing platforms, they had finally come to a parting of the ways.

"Well, it's been really wonderful chatting with you," said Alex.

"Yes, I've really enjoyed getting to know you a bit more too. We should get together again sometime," said Jane, a twinkle in her eye.

"That would be great! I'd love to!" said Alex enthusiastically.

"Great! Okay then, I'd best be off," said Jane.

"Okay! Good. Bye for now I guess. Wait, I don't know your name. I mean of course I know your name, what I meant was I don't know your full name. So that I can look you up I mean, so that we can keep in touch," said Alex tripping over his tongue.

"I've got your number silly! Remember? And it's Planchard. Jane Planchard!" Jane said as she smiled at his nervous floundering.

The way Jane smiled at him made him wish she wasn't going. She gave him a quick peck on the cheek and quickly turned and walked down the tunnel. He stood transfixed, watching her go. Just before she reached the corner at the end of the tunnel she turned around.

"On hundred and twelve centimetres!" Jane called out.

"What?" asked Alex totally confused.

"My legs! From my hips to my heels, they're one hundred and twelve centimetres, you've been staring at them all night! Naughty boy!" Jane said laughing, as she disappeared around the corner.

Alex's face and ears glowed red. "OK. Now I'm a total mess," he thought to himself.

Chapter Five

Kindred Spirits

The huge dog's eyes opened and it sniffed the air. Its large ears sprang up, the tops of which, however, remained flopped over. In an instant, it launched its heavy fawn coloured body off the sofa and made a beeline for the front door; deep, loud barks erupting from its maw. The dog's intelligent eyes looked quizzically at the door, tipping its wide head sideways in response to the scuffing and galumphing noises it was hearing outside.

"I'll be right there!" Alex said loudly.

Alex had been sitting on the floor unpacking boxes of equipment that had recently arrived. He rose from a cross legged position to standing in one quick fluid motion. As he reached the huge barn doors, he patted the enormous dog on its head and opened a smaller door set into one of the two much larger ones.

"Hi Grandpa, you're early!" said Alex.

"Yep. The traffic is better early morning so I set off at dawn to come and have breakfast with you," said the Professor, laughing. "I managed to avoid most of the lunatic drivers on the motorway. Only had one near miss with some damn idiot near here, still, no harm done.

"So, this is where you hide out when you're not at school!" Grandfather said, stepping through the doorway into the interior of the barn's open expanse.

"Yes," replied Alex, "I didn't want to live in the house with Uncle Thomas and Aunty Irene so they helped me to convert the barn into my own place. It's better here because I can have my own stuff where I want it and I leave them in peace and quiet.

"I used to play in this barn when I was young and back home for summer breaks with Mum and Dad so it's really great that I live here now" Alex said, leading the way into the huge old converted barn.

The Professor noticed the large dog giving him an evaluating and determined stare.

"Hercules over here actually belongs to my aunt and uncle but he likes to keep me company," said Alex, holding out a tennis ball. "Take this ball from me and give it to him. If I give you the ball and you give it to him, I'm telling him that you are a trusted friend. That's how he's been trained."

The Professor took the ball and gave it to Hercules. The dog took it gently in his teeth, sniffing the Professor's hand.

"He's rather big! I don't think I have ever seen this type of dog before."

"Hercules is a Boerboel breed. They're farm dogs, not bred to be aggressive, but they are naturally very protective. They're really smart, wonderful creatures. He looks after the place when I am not here," Alex said, giving Hercules' ears a scratch.

"I even built him his own private entrance. There's an oversized dog flap hidden in the wall at the back so he can come and go as he pleases. It's invisible from the outside!" he said ,pointing to the back corner of the building.

"You should see the welcome I get when I have been away for a while! He's like a bowling ball, I'm the skittles!"

"Well, I can see why you choose to live here," said the Professor, casting his intelligent eyes around and about, registering everything he saw.

"Yes," said Alex, "I really like having one huge, open space with a high ceiling so that I can swing things about without hitting anything!"

Pointing towards the far corner on his right, Alex added, "That small staircase leads up to the bedroom area. I built it up on that big wooden platform which used to be the hayloft, just under the roof. The whole ground floor is open plan – no interior walls! It gives me plenty of room to work and exercise and store all my gear. And now it is the ideal place to organize my first ARACHNIS expedition."

They walked over to the back half of the big barn.

"So I see," said Grandfather as he sat down in one of two big arm chairs.

Hercules had already claimed the entire sofa, his big head lolling on the soft armrest and his floppy pink tongue dangling down.

The old man looked around the comfortable seating area which was directly under the hayloft bedroom platform. He saw Hercules laying sprawled on the old sofa, the other arm chair and a recliner. In the opposite corner, he noticed large ceramic floor tiles demarcated the kitchen area from the otherwise wooden floors. Copper bottomed pots and pans hung from the walls on big iron hooks. An elbow of wooden counters simultaneously created a breakfast bar and kitchen work surfaces. A heavy, round wooden dining table and four chairs were situated in the middle of the tiled area, over which a wrought iron chandelier hung low.

The Professor thought the whole place felt very homely, practical and functional and, in his opinion, perfectly reflected

Alex's personality. He cast his gaze over to the front half of the barn.

Nearest the big double doors, there was an assortment of office furniture. A laptop and desktop computer sat side-by-side on a purpose built computer desk. A printer, scanner and the usual router and modem were positioned underneath it.

Next to this was a large writing desk with neatly organized files, maps and papers. Directly opposite this desk and along most of the adjacent wall was a series of cupboards and deep shelves which were packed with equipment stored and organized in labelled plastic crates. The Professor read some of them: Climbing Racks, Shell Clothing, Tents, Jungle Sleeping Units, Survival Kits, Emergency Rations. Several well packed rucksacks and coiled ropes were also visible.

Alex followed his gaze and said, "A lot of that stuff belonged to Dad and I have kept it all. It was shipped back from Belize and some of it was here all along. I hope I will be able to put some of it to good use soon."

In the dead centre of the floor was a collection of half unpacked cardboard boxes, many bearing yellow and red stickers that said 'FRAGILE, HANDLE WITH CARE' or 'THIS SIDE UP'. The packing material and plastic wrapping from the boxes was stuffed into a bulging blue rubbish bag for recycling, delivery invoices lying next to it.

"I see you've already received some of the kit and equipment that you said you'd ordered. Have you had any luck finding a vehicle to put it all into yet?" asked his grandfather rummaging through his battered briefcase which he had opened and set across his knees.

"Yes, as a matter of fact I'm cycling down to the local car dealer in a while to take a look. Trevor, the owner, told me that he has a great Land Rover which is fitted with some expedition accessories," said Alex.

"That's great," said the Professor. "You know Land Rovers have been around for well over sixty years now, since I was a young lad. Really shows how old I'm getting!"

"Yes," Alex added, "I loved going through marshes and rivers and thick forests with Dad in his Land Rovers. I can't wait to drive a brand new one. The ones we had had usually been to hell and back, and somehow were still running!"

"Which is precisely the point, isn't it," said Grandfather.

"Yep, certainly is. From Trevor's description over the phone, this one sounds like it will fit the bill nicely – can't wait to see it! Would you like to come and take a look at it with me?" asked Alex, looking at the pile of papers the Professor was stacking on the arm of his chair.

"I'd love to, but I'm afraid I have a meeting scheduled later. In any case I have spoken to Trevor also, and the car sounds great. This is your assignment, Alex, and you have to be the decision maker. If you like the car just sign and I will take care of payment. Make sure you drive carefully. You'll be driving her back here and we don't want you arrested first time out," said Grandpa.

"Wow. That's great Grandpa but it's a pity you can't come with me," said Alex.

"Don't worry, I'm not leaving any time soon. I want a good hearty English breakfast and we can go through the briefing notes I brought."

With that Alex and Grandpa went to the kitchen and started the exercise of making eggs and bacon, fried tomatoes, toast and tea. Both were more than familiar cooking for themselves and before long the spread was before them on the kitchen table, a veritable feast.

As they ate and chatted Grandpa brought the conversation back to the expedition. "As promised I brought your full briefing pack. It's over there by my bag. It details all the conservation projects you will be conducting. As you know you're heading off to Belize on the Caribbean coast of Central America. You will find your air tickets, travel and health insurance documents – which will cover yourself and your local contact – as well as maps, timings, risk assessments and the usual bumf. I wouldn't tell anyone about the archaeological aspects of this venture. It is very sensitive and no reason for anyone outside ARACHNIS to know yet. There are certain people in this world who don't have too many scruples about how they make their money, if you get my meaning."

"Wow, it all sounds pretty mysterious," said Alex.

"Yes, well, you'll understand my caution when you read about the Maya temple, and especially what may be hidden in it. It is a potentially incredibly important project. I must admit, I actually feel a bit envious of you. This trip promises to be a very exciting and interesting one; no doubt it will be very challenging too, but nothing you can't handle. I have every confidence in you, Alex, and like I said in Wales, if you can do this one then the world is your oyster.

"If you and the Land Rover are ready, we should aim to leave in two weeks' time. That should give you ample time to prepare."

"I can't wait to get going," said Alex.

"How was the lecture you gave, Alex? Entertain those young minds did you?" asked Grandfather.

"It was a great. I love speaking about my experiences and getting facts across to them. I'm hoping they'll all join ARACHNIS. They even called me a dude. Do you know what that is?" said Alex.

"Some kind of insult I guess, if the teenagers I know are anything to go by," replied the Professor.

"No, it means a cool guy. Someone who is "with it". Do you think I am a dude?"

"You may well be Alex but when you are knee deep in mud and sweating like a pig, being a 'cool dude' is not a likely characteristic!" laughed Grandpa.

"You know what else happened? I met a girl who is mad about the environment and conservation and everything that I love in fact."

"And is she good looking, my lad?"

"Good looking! She's gorgeous! Never met anyone that I thought was more stunning. Made my knees wobble in fact."

"And her name?"

"Her name is Jane Planchard."

"Planchard... rings a bell, that does. But can't quite place it. Anyway, Alex, for the next few weeks you will be busy swatting up this expedition and then completely off the beaten track so if you want to get into a romance, better to do it on Skype or Viber or something."

Grandpa stood up and patted Hercules' large head that had by now drifted into a deep sleep. His nose twitched and his legs quivered as he ran and played, enjoying the boundless freedoms of his dream.

"Thanks for breakfast, Alex, and great to see you. I won't see you again before you leave, so let me wish you good luck and a safe journey. I'm sorry I have to run, but I'm meeting a fellow academic who is on a very brief visit from Indonesia. He wants to pass on some information he has received from an ARACHNIS member on the island of Sumatra. He's had some very intriguing things to say on the phone, but he's flying back home to Jakarta tomorrow, so I must meet him today. We'll keep in touch via the usual means in case if you have any questions," Grandpa said, as he handed the sheaf of papers, documents and maps to Alex.

"Thank you for everything Grandpa. I'll keep you posted on my progress with the car and I will go through all this information you have given me. I will call or skype with any questions," said Alex as they both headed towards the door.

Alex walked his grandfather to his car, they hugged, and he waved him goodbye. He went back inside and put the documents into a plastic file folder.

"Bedtime reading. Right, I had better get to town and take a look at that Land Rover," he said to himself.

With that thought, he unhooked a thin rope from a cleat on the wall and, using a simple pulley system, he lowered his mountain bike from high up near the ceiling where he stored it. He grabbed a full water bottle, his wallet and keys and put them in his waterproofed daypack. Picking up his cycle helmet he wheeled his bike outside, locking his front door behind him. With a quick push and jump he landed on the saddle and set off. Hercules ran alongside him as far as the gate.

The winding country road soon joined a larger 'B' road. Several big green signs with white letters whizzed by, telling Alex what he already knew – that the town centre was twelve miles away. As his powerful legs propelled the pedals he thought about all the different qualities that Land Rovers possessed. Once he had customised it, he would be a completely self-sufficient, self-contained expedition unit, able to operate in remote areas for long periods of time. His excitement grew in direct proportion to his ever closer proximity to his destination.

Lost in thought, he suddenly found himself on the main road through the centre of town. Saturday morning shoppers were hustling and bustling in a steady stream along the pavement; clutching bags of shopping or small children in their hands. Traffic and noise filled his eyes and ears. The aroma of bakeries and coffee shops wafted up his nostrils on the chilly air, mixed with the smell of exhaust fumes.

In no time, he was locking his mountain bike to the railings on the pavement outside the big glass frontage of the car dealer.

He opened the glass door and entered the large, spotlessly clean, showroom. His eyes glanced over the shiny, brightly coloured sedans and SUV's with their chrome wheels and futuristic designs. As he turned his head to the left to look at the other half of the displayed vehicles he stopped dead in his tracks.

"There she is!" Alex thought looking at the brand new Land Rover Defender, excitement welling up and flooding him with a giant thrill.

"THERE YOU ARE!" he shouted out loud, unable to contain himself.

Shocked customers and sales staff looked at him as if he had a few screws loose and left them wondering how someone could get that worked up over what was essentially a tough work vehicle. With tunnel vision he walked straight over to it, ignoring the fancy, flashy cars that engrossed the other customers. To Alex she was the perfect vehicle.

He walked around the Land Rover slowly; this vehicle was all business. He would be installing plenty of scientific equipment but she already came fitted with more expedition accessories than he'd expected. A high air intake snorkel, vital when driving through deep water; winches back and front, and a pair of sand ladders attached to either side of a heavy duty roof rack. The sand ladders would help when crossing very soft sand. She also had flood lights, spot lights and a work light above the back door. There was a metal shield under the front bumper to protect the engine against rocks. Big, metal, twenty litre water and fuel containers were clamped onto the back and top, next to a pick and a shovel. She had the works!

For Alex, above all else, she was a Land Rover. He thought about the comment Grandpa had made at his barn. Land Rover Defenders had been the loyal companions of countless explorers, scientists and adventurers for over fifty years. They had been at the forefront of nearly every remote land-based scientific discovery made by man in the last half century, from deserts to the Arctic. They had been the vehicle trusted by his father.

Most television documentaries that took couch-bound viewers on adventures to the wildest places on earth had, no doubt, needed Land Rovers as an essential part of the production. Nearly all the international aid agencies, conservation organisations, the Red Cross and most of the armies of the world had made use of these pioneering vehicles at some time or another. Even Queen Elizabeth II enjoyed driving her Land Rover Defender on her estates in Scotland.

"BRILLIANT!" said Alex entirely too loudly, this time drawing the attention of the sales person who approached, wearing a bemused smile on his face.

"You have to be Alex!"

"Yes, guilty as charged," said Alex, grinning from ear to ear.

"Hi, I'm Trevor. You're younger than I expected. You've remembered to bring your license haven't you? Anyway let's take a closer look, shall we?" he said.

"Good to meet you Trevor! Yes, let's do that," said Alex, "but I think you are about to make the quickest sale you have ever made!"

After half an hour of paperwork and signatures the deed was done. The Land Rover Defender was moved out into the street. With a firm handshake Alex took the keys from Trevor, stowed his bicycle in the back of the vehicle and opened the driver's door. Hopping in, he put on his seat belt, adjusted the mirrors and the seat and put the keys into the ignition. The engine rumbled into life. Alex felt as though this vehicle had been custom built just for him. He felt so comfortable and at home in her.

"Wow," he said turning on the indicator and pulling out into the busy traffic, "this is it! A journey of a thousand miles begins with a single step or, in our case, a foot on the accelerator pedal!

"Don't mind me, okay?" he said to the steering wheel. "I talk to plants and animals, I sometimes talk to my toaster and I frequently yell at the television, lots of people do, you'll get used to it. Ha ha! Just listen to me; I think I've spent too long under the tropical sun! Well, you and I are going to become firm friends; you have no idea the amazing adventures we are going to share!"

"I have much more of an idea than you realize," thought Bodhi happily as they sped along the road back to Alex's converted barn.

Chapter Six

Opposing Forces

The wild raven flew on a north-westerly path over the City of London's famous East End. It was on its way to visit its captive and well fed, legendary cousins who all lived at the Tower of London. Shiny blue-black feathers fluttered in the wind, its wing tips bending and flexing in the slipstream of its flight. Gliding through the grey drizzle over Greenwich, its bright yellow eyes spied the tall masts of the famous tea clipper ship, the Cutty Sark, which was moored in her dry dock far below. Spiralling to the left, it soared along and then over the mighty river Thames. As it passed above Shadwell and Wapping, it focused on its next navigational landmark, the magnificent Tower Bridge which was followed a little further down on the right hand side by the Tower of London, home to the Crown Jewels.

At ground level, in the London Docklands, a completely different scene was unfolding. In a dark, dusty passageway of a disused warehouse, two very large and decidedly unfriendly looking men were dragging a third, very frightened one, between them.

The 'heavies' were both crammed into suits at least one size too small, the shiny cheap material stretched almost to breaking over steroid built muscles. In their vice-like grip the bedraggled victim had surrendered any thought of escape. Passing under the dingy yellow glow of low watt light bulbs which had corroded into their rusty tin ceiling cones, the menacing duo frog-marched the man to the door at the far end.

Kicking the warped wooden door open with a steel toe capped boot, the 'heavies' and their cargo entered a darkened, dusty office, the windows of which had long since been plastered over with ancient yellowed newspapers from another, happier era.

Dumping their small prisoner into a creaking wooden chair with a straight back, the two hulking oafs took up guard positions on either side.

An angle poise lamp clicked on, shining its bright light straight into the terrified man's face. All he could make out was a metal desk with a black silhouette of a man sitting behind it.

"Here he is Boss, he's a bit banged up but still in one piece," said one of the brutes in a deep nasal boom.

"So… you're my bad investment are you?" rasped the shadow in a very unfriendly tone.

"Look, I tried my best, honest Mister! I had a lot of bad luck, please…" squealed the captive.

"Save it!" the shadow exploded. "It was a simple job – run the old codger off the road, hit him on the head, steal the documents, and make the whole thing look like an accident. Not C-O-M-P-L-I-C-A-T-E-D," growled the shadow man.

"But the local copper was right there, appeared out of nowhere he did, just like that… it was just bad luck! Please…" the thief pleaded, peering into the shadows, trying to see his anonymous employer.

"I did the best I could at such short notice! These jobs need time to plan properly," he stammered.

A hard cuff to the side of his head, administered by the colossal yob on his right, silenced him.

"If you knew who I was, you would've made damn sure that you brought me those documents, even if you had to put your life on the line, or take someone else's to do it. Most people think I'm just a ruthless gangster. I'm not. I'm simply a ruthless businessman. I find unusual opportunities to make lots of money. But now, due to your incompetence, you're costing me money! I was told you'd be a useful asset, but you're not, are you? So I've reclassified you as a liability. Because you've screwed everything up, I'm going to have to phone my friends in Central America and ask them for a favour or two. I'm going to need their help to fix this mess and that's going to impact on my bottom line, they're not cheap. Having those documents would have stacked the deck in my favour. I won't have another chance to get hold of those documents for at least a couple of weeks and then I'll have to rely on other people, half way around the world to tell me what those documents say. I should have been reading them for myself in the comfort of my own home, TONIGHT!" the shadow boss yelled.

"You need to understand something," said the dark silhouette. "Only four things matter to me. One – is it a good opportunity, two – what's the risk, three – how much is it going to cost me, and lastly, how much and how quickly will I get a return on my investment. I've given my word to another 'businessman' that I will obtain a unique treasure for him and in return he's going to pay me an obscene amount of cash. My problem is that in order to do this I needed the information from the documents that I paid you to steal. You FAILED!!" the phantom bellowed slamming his fists down on the metal desk.

"As I've told you Sir, it was all done on such short notice. I wasn't expecting to have to find a barn in the middle of nowhere at night, or pick any locks, especially a really old fashioned one," the prisoner protested in a shaky voice, "and there wasn't no signs at all outside that he had a bleedin' great big dog neevah, woz there? No kennel, no food bowls – I checked! Honest guv, it's not my fault it didn't work out."

The forlorn prisoner heard the clink of a Zippo lighter opening followed by the rasp of flint against steel as an orange flame was lit. For a brief second, he caught a glimpse of the man's evil looking face glowering at him from across the old desk. He was shocked to see that his tormentor had two different coloured eyes, one ice blue, and the other dark brown, almost black. The evil looking apparition drew the flame onto the end of a cigarette, a glowing red ember appearing as he inhaled deeply. Slowly, he blew the smoke out in a rising cloud that gave the shadow man an even more demonic appearance. The deafening silence was broken only by the anxious scuffing of the thief's shoes on the floor as he fidgeted nervously, a cold sweat running down his underarms.

"Okay. Let's agree that it's not your fault," said the shadow man, finally breaking the silence, his bared teeth just visible. He grinned like a rabid hyena skulking in the dark. A brief look of redemption flashed across the thief's face. A crooked half smile almost started to appear on his thin pale lips.

"I think you'll also agree just as much as I do that what I am about to have done to you is not my fault either. But it is necessary so that you actually do become a useful asset to me and, unfortunately for you, the transformation process is going to hurt – really, really badly! But not for too long, I promise."

The expression on the thief's face went instantly from one of relief at the words he had at first taken to mean a reprieve, to one of sheer horror as he slowly comprehended that his fate was sealed. His lower lip began to quiver. These men were going to murder him.

"Ahhh… I see that you think my decision is so horribly unfair!" said the shadow man. "Life can be so cruel can't it? A baby deer gets eaten by a lion in the African savannah, who's to blame? These days we live in such a blame culture, everyone looking to blame anyone and everyone else for their total lack of personal responsibility. We live in a world of idiots who have lost any notion of the meaning of 'common sense'. Not me. I hold you personally responsible for your failure. In this life, you are either part of the pavement or part of the steamroller.

"To you, I AM the bleeding steamroller!" he yelled, hurling a heavy brass ashtray at the liability, hitting him square in the chest with a sickening thud.

"I'm going to do whatever I want to you, and do you know why? Because I CAN!" the shadow bellowed in megalomaniacal fury, looking impatiently at the dial of his solid gold, jewel encrusted Rolex.

"You've wasted my time. Time is money. You owe me and you're going to pay. You'll be praying for death."

"Please... please don't kill me, I'm begging you!" pleaded the thief. "I'll go back again and steal it, I'll do whatever it takes, please..."

"Too late for that now, those documents will have been hidden somewhere very safe," he hissed.

He did so enjoy playing God with his helpless victims, especially with the ones that begged and pleaded. The condemned man would never know that his murderer's name was Silus. All the members of Silus' gang knew he didn't accept or allow failure. Silus wanted what he wanted when he wanted it – no excuses. Who he crushed, and what he destroyed in the process didn't even register as a tiny blip on his morally barren radar. Silus considered compassion a serious error in critical thinking. He prided himself on having absolutely no conscience or feelings of guilt.

In his warped mind he felt truly free, unfettered by what he considered to be the self-imposed mental chains that most other people had binding and crushing their natural instincts. Silus had no such chains preventing him from acting on his socially unacceptable thoughts and impulses.

He considered himself to be a selfish winner and took great satisfaction bringing about the destruction and suffering of anyone or anything that he became fixated on. Money was his God, watching others suffer was his drug.

He gazed at the doomed thief, who sat, pitifully dejected, obviously frightened out of his mind. Slowly he exhaled a long stream of cigarette smoke and said, "Right then, we're wasting time and you're using up oxygen that belongs to other, more useful, people. My associates here are now going to take you away for an operation for which you won't be getting any anaesthetic. I'll leave you with a pearl of wisdom to contemplate in that moronic brain of yours: Ants shouldn't walk where elephants like to dance!" Silus sat back in his chair, gloating while the poor wretch was dragged, screaming, weeping and kicking out of the office.

As he drew the poisonous cigarette smoke deep into his black lungs, he savoured the burnt taste in his dry mouth, revelling in the man's terrified screams. He thought about how much money he would get selling the thief's organ on the black market. It would more than compensate for the additional expense he would have of tracking that bleeding-heart, tree-hugging, green-freak, expedition leader to the prize deep in the Central American jungles and stealing it from him.

"Yes," he thought to himself, "I know what you are looking for. I even know it's in Belize. I just don't know exactly where it is yet. Let that conservation fool do all the hard work for us, we will snatch it from him, like taking candy from a baby!"

Many kilometres to the north-west, Alex's boots crunched over the frost covered gravel drive as he carried the last of his equipment to his newly customised Land Rover. His breath looked like steam rising in the bitterly cold dawn air. He had set his alarm for five am and had started packing while it was still dark. He was carrying the last two plastic boxes full of gear.

The Land Rover was now filled with backpacks, ropes, various kits, assorted equipment, spares and parts for repairs. Lastly, he strapped a Canadian style open canoe onto the roof rack. Alex gave his barn a thorough once over to make sure it was all shuttered and locked up properly and patted Hercules on his enormous head. Waving goodbye to his uncle Thomas, who was perched on his tractor in the next field, he jumped into the driver's seat. Alex and Bodhi hit the road, zooming north along the M53 motorway for almost an hour, he then changed onto the M56 and again onto a smaller road. Being a novice driver Alex had opted for the more scenic, less busy route. He planned on crossing over the River Mersey using the beautiful Silver Jubilee Bridge which spanned the narrow gap between Runcorn and Wildness, rather than going under it through the busy Kingsway tunnel. Both routes lead to the same destination, the enormous and bustling Port of Liverpool.

Bodhi had had plenty of time to hone her very individual set of senses. In her own way, she could 'see', 'feel', 'taste' and 'smell', all of them working perfectly and she was now growing accustomed to her new-found 'self'.

As her front wheels touched the bridge over the ancient river Mersey, she heard its majestic 'voice' swiftly flowing up towards her. It greeted her and wished her well on her travels, its message washing over and through her.

"Bodhi, I have been looking forward to meeting you," the river swirled. "Remember, just as all the waters that run in me will eventually become one with the sea, perhaps eventually turning into ice in the Poles, or falling again as life giving rain on distant forests, so too will you find yourself always moving, always changing. We, the natural entities of mother earth – the rivers, the seas, the mountains, the trees and the air; we all wish you success in your quests; you give us all great hope that you will be able help shift Gaia's power back into balance. I will be waiting here to welcome you home again one day."

As her back tires left the bridge behind, Alex's mobile phone began to ring. Reaching over to the plastic housing that clipped it to the dashboard, he answered, pressing the speaker-phone button.

"Grandfather, good morning! It looks as though the cat is out of the bag," said Alex, checking his rear view mirror and changing lane.

"Yes indeed it does, doesn't it? I got your email with all the details of the attempted break-in," said the Professor in a sombre tone. "When I was run off the road, I had thought it was just your usual 'boy-racer' driving like a bloody lunatic. It's obvious now that he was after the expedition briefing pack."

"Clearly," said Alex.

"I'm quite baffled as to how word about the lost Maya temple has already reached the ears of the criminal underworld here in the UK. Only a handful of people here know about it and they all promised that they would keep it a secret. I'll have to start asking some questions. By the way, thanks for attaching the photos of all the additions to the Land Rover in your last email. She's looking marvellous. You've done an excellent job."

"Thanks," said Alex. "I wasn't sure I could do it all myself but memories of Dad fixing up his Land Rovers combined with all the IT and science lessons I have been having at school made it quite straightforward. And of course most of the gadgets have instruction leaflets!'"

"I'll make sure they crate her up properly. I wouldn't want her sliding around in her container during a mid-Atlantic storm, and there are bound to be a few brewing at this time of year."

"Right!" said Grandfather, "and while we are on the subject, I've arranged for my ARACHNIS project coordinator to meet you at the port. Her name is Jude. She lives in Liverpool and is a former student of mine. Jude will be waiting for you at the Sea Forth Dock, it's the biggest dock there, you can't miss it. Jude will walk you through everything with the Customs Broker and will make sure it all goes smoothly. All has been arranged! Well, I have to run; I have a Skype call coming in. Cheerio for now! And Alex, good luck!"

As the line went dead, Alex thought about how excited he was to be heading off on his first solo expedition. The planning, the organising, the research and the meticulous preparations, all building a sense of excitement as the date for the new adventure drew ever closer. Following the signs, he drove up to the dock and parked.

"We're here!" he said to the steering wheel. "Next stop for you, Big Creek Port, Belize, Central America! Soon we're going to be up to my knees and your wheel arches in mud, helping to preserve sub-tropical forests and wildlife.

"And then, there's the temple we have to get to, deep in the jungle. Not just any Maya temple mind you," he said, remembering all he had read and memorized. "The lost temple of a legendary Maya King – King Nanchancaan, no less!"

Bodhi listened intently. "So much to learn and experience," she thought. "Where is Belize? Where is Central America? What is a King? What is a temple? So many questions…"

Having watched Bodhi safely loaded into the metal shipping container, Alex completed the paperwork with the help of the friendly and very efficient Jude. He stayed on the dock until he had watched the crane lower the container into the hold of the ship.

His mind flashed back through the events of the previous few days. He had digitally scanned all the documents, put them into a heavily encrypted digital file and saved it on to a tiny Micro SD SIM card. Alex had put the SIM into a sealed, watertight, slim plastic pod which was in turn zipped into a hidden money pocket which ran all along the inside length of his trouser belt. It was one of Alex's favourite hiding places for extra cash and a few small, but essential, pieces of survival equipment.

As he hailed a taxi to the airport, he checked his plane tickets one more time. The ship carrying his Land Rover would take two weeks to complete the Atlantic crossing. Alex would spend those two weeks in Southern Florida, in the United States of America. It was convenient in Florida because it was a short one hour and forty five minute flight from Miami to Belize City. Also the climate there is quite similar to Belize, but not quite as hot and certainly not as harsh. It was just hot, humid and wet enough to make it the perfect place for him to re-acclimatise so that he would be able to work effectively in the Belizean jungle. Although he was fit, he needed to regain what his dad had always called 'bush fitness.' As Alex knew from his younger days, there was fit and then there was 'bush fit'. In order to accomplish this, he had volunteered with a Florida based conservation group that operated in the wild wetlands of the Florida Everglades. Much of the fauna and flora there was similar to that of Belize to some degree too, especially in the coastal areas. After two weeks of working in this environment, trekking for miles every day, with heavy packs and scientific equipment, he would be expedition fit – he would be ready.

Alex had planned it this way so that when he and his Land Rover got to Belize they would be able to hit the ground running, both of them up to full operational speed.

A day after leaving Bodhi in Liverpool Alex left Heathrow and headed west. Shortly after the jet plane roared into the sky, the seatbelt light above Alex's head blinked off. He reclined his seat back as far as it would go. He looked out of his window and down at the twinkling lights from the ships in the sea far below. He imagined his Land Rover stowed in its container on one of those ships, starting its long voyage.

"This is it," he thought. "Here we go – Action at last! I wonder what Jane is up to. I wish I could have seen her again."

Chapter Seven

Voyage of Discovery

For Bodhi, the two week crossing was not only going to be a physical journey across an ocean. It was also to be a journey that would take her deep into her conscious mind on a voyage of discovery. Soon after the huge red container ship left Liverpool port, Bodhi was visited by both her spirit guides in turn.

First to appear was Mezaferus.

Secured in the complete darkness of the shipping container, deep in the ship's cargo hold, Bodhi's newly acquired senses were reduced to 'hearing' distant clanging and booming sounds every now and again, and the continuous 'whump, whump, whump' of the ship's huge engines.

She experienced the weirdest sensations of rising and falling, of tipping slowly from one side to the other. She found it rather soothing, and given the fact that she was inside the pitch black container, it also put her into a very thoughtful mood.

As she remembered every minute of her new life, from the night of the storm, her mind played back the images of all she had seen and done since then, trying to make sense of it all. Her thoughts drifted and swam deeper and deeper into her mind until she entered a dreamlike state, somewhere between her conscious and subconscious, not awake, but not asleep either.

It was then that a bright green light appeared in her mind's eye. The green light came closer; it grew bigger and bigger and then the green haze condensed and took the form of a man.

The first feature Bodhi focused on was his striking eyes. They were a piercing golden yellow. She saw that his hair was long, raven black with ash grey streaks. His friendly face exuded a calm aura, his features were solid and strong. Bodhi realised that this must be Mezaferus coming to visit as promised.

He was dressed in heavy robes the colours of autumn leaves. He held a solid oak staff intricately carved with patterns and totems of animals. On a wide, thick belt, circling his waist and buckled in the centre of his stomach hung a golden sickle, a knife and a pouch.

Mezaferus' arms and legs were as thick and solid as an ancient tree. Slowly, he raised his left hand above his head, his enormous chest swelling as he inhaled. Looking up at the sky he let out a long and deep resonating call.

Bodhi watched in awe as thick mists formed around his feet and ankles, spreading quickly outwards. Dark forests sprang up from the mist. Shadows emerged from the forests taking form. A pair of timber wolves appeared, followed by a grizzly bear, then a succession of other forest animals materialized.

Badgers, pine martens, robins, foxes, weasels, squirrels, stoats, pheasants and nightjars all came into view. A huge owl landed on Mezaferus' shoulder. Bison, elk and deer, every creature great and small flowed out of the forest.

As quickly as this rich vision formed, it faded away leaving only Mezaferus in front of her.

"I am the spirit of the forest," he said smiling at Bodhi. "Humans have many different names for me, a different one for every type of forest in the world. Mezaferus is the name I am called by the people who dwell in the Taiga forest. This forest crowns the entire earth in the distant and frozen lands of the far north."

Mezaferus walked forward and slowly sat down cross - legged on the leafy floor, resting the staff across his thighs.

"Bodhi, you are now in a deep meditation, a trance-like state," said Mezaferus. "Some humans have discovered this method of gaining insight, however very few actually use meditation or realize its power for communicating knowledge and wisdom. The closer you are with nature, the more likely it is that that you can access these doorways into your subconscious, as you are doing now."

Mezaferus sat motionless with his back perfectly upright and his hands folded in his lap. He closed his eyes, speaking softly, "We are about to go on what people call a vision quest, some call it astral travelling. There is much to show you and tell you, much to learn, so let us begin."

Led by Mezaferus, Bodhi's consciousness floated out of the container ship but was still connected to her physical being with a thin, golden thread of light. Rising high through the sky, she looked down on the bright blue sphere of the earth floating in the unimaginably infinite universe. As she looked down on earth she was filled with a powerful and profound emotion. Being able to see the beautiful blue planet, she felt a change take place in her, knowing that she would never be the same again.

"I am here to teach you about nature's Circle of Life," Mezaferus said as they hung high above the earth's atmosphere, on the edge of space.

"It is a never ending cycle of change – birth, growth, decline and death," he explained, "These stages or states of being are reflected in all things. Whether it is a mouse, a river, a wild flower, a human or a mountain, it is always the same.

All that exists follows these cycles. On earth, the seasons are a good demonstration of these principles. It is a universal law. Spring represents birth and new life, summer brings growth and maturity, autumn leads the way to old age, decline and eventually death, represented by winter."

Bodhi listened intently as they travelled the world. She was able to witness this truth for herself as they passed through different climates, landscapes and environments. Gliding through glacial valleys, high over snow covered mountain peaks and low down into forest covered plains.

Deserts and jungles, oceans and islands passed beneath them. Often they stopped so that he could teach and explain. Mezaferus guided Bodhi on and on.

Mezaferus's voice was like a warm wind blowing through the leaves of a tree, "There are two 'Grand Cycles,' The Cycle of Creation and the Cycle of Destruction. Both are as important as each other, both are as powerful as each other. Often they appear to be the complete opposite of one another, and yet, at the same time, they always contain within them aspects of each other. They are like the spiralling galaxies you saw in space, Bodhi, forever spinning and circling, perpetually balancing each other. Darkness and Light. Positive and Negative."

Bodhi did not speak; instead she absorbed all the wisdom and knowledge like a sponge, eager to learn all she could about everything. They descended to Earth's surface many times, visiting, amongst other places, forests of all kinds where she could see and understand these principles in action. It did not matter which forest Mezaferus flew her to on the invisible winds of their minds' eyes, the processes she observed were always the same. The only difference was the speed at which the cycles of creation and destruction happened.

The hotter and wetter the forest or jungle, the faster it was, the colder they were, the slower the cycle completed. Bodhi realized Gaia's wisdom in sending Mezaferus, the spirit of the forests, to her first to teach her these lessons. Forests and jungles contained such an abundance of life in which the cycles were easier to observe as they occurred much faster than the growth and erosion of mountains or the changing courses of mighty rivers.

Bodhi saw seeds grow into saplings, become trees, age, produce seeds of their own and then die and decompose; becoming food and nutrients that in turn fed and nurtured new trees. She watched plants absorb the sun's energy and grow. She observed the animals and understood how those that ate plants were in turn often eaten by animals that could not absorb enough nutrients from plants alone and, therefore, had to consume the animals that could.

Bodhi also learned that the reason life existed on planet earth in its current form was because of the heat coming from the star that humans had named Sol, or the sun. Mezaferus explained that the sun and its solar system was part of a spinning spiral of about three hundred billion other stars which humans had named the Milky Way Galaxy. It was the sun that provided the energy so vital to all life on earth. The origin of all the cycles in nature which, in turn, created the Circle of Life, was the sun.

All plants and animals, seasons, winds and tides – everything – are directly linked to the fiery orange star. A star that very few humans ever pay any attention to on a daily basis, if at all, taking its very existence and life giving energy for granted.

"You see Bodhi," said Mezaferus, "the sun radiates abundant, but unrestrained energy. When the sun's rays collide with the earth, it is Gaia who regulates and controls how much of this powerful energy is absorbed, and it is because of this that life can exist. This is the great secret that a mere handful of humans are only now just beginning to discover. For billions of years Gaia has controlled the temperature of the earth's surface and its atmosphere in such a way that she creates the optimum climatic conditions that best supports whatever life forms currently inhabit it. Without the protection of Gaia's temperature regulation, the sun's fiery heat would not create life – it would destroy it. Gaia provides a cooling, nurturing shield, and her shield is becoming increasingly damaged. If humans can't correct this imbalance soon; if they can't halt and reverse this harm, Gaia will naturally take action herself. Gaia will increase the speed of her adjustments and this will lead to a great and rapid environmental change. Few, if any, of today's plants and animals will survive the changes in temperature and atmospheric conditions. Humans will have unintentionally brought about their own untimely extinction, exterminating most other species along with them. Gaia will have changed and adapted very rapidly, and those unable to change and adapt will die. Humans have still got a chance to prevent this change from happening prematurely, but only if they act globally and as fast as possible. The situation is extremely urgent; time is running out for mankind. Your mission is to help awaken this idea in humans all around the world, and from all walks of life. You're destined to be on the front lines, taking an active part in helping to restore the balance. You will be helping the younger human generation fight for their survival."

Bodhi listened and learned.

Mezaferus had watched Bodhi intently throughout their journey. A knowing smile had creased his face each time Bodhi had a revelation of insight, each time the significance of something she was seeing dawned on her and she understood yet another profound truth. The overwhelming beauty of what she saw made her spirit soar and emotions flood through her.

Finally Mezaferus's first lesson was at an end and they turned back, following the thin golden cord of light that stretched far away into the blue horizon. They floated along Bodhi's astral cord, high above the huge blue oceans waves beneath them. Eventually, the red cargo ship became visible. As they got closer, Bodhi watched the ship riding the mountainous mid-Atlantic ocean swells. White foam caps blew off the wave tops as they crashed against the bow of the ship. Cold, salty spray drenched the decks.

Passing an albatross perched high on one of the big deck cranes, they dropped down past rigging cables and the tower that housed the Captain's bridge. Finally, they descended below decks where Bodhi was reunited with her physical body inside the metal shipping container.

"Thank you Mezaferus, I am beginning to understand," said Bodhi with gratitude.

"It is my pleasure Bodhi. We will meet again when the need arises Remember Bodhi, we are all connected; all living things on earth look up at the same moon."

Mezaferus stood, using his staff to help him up. As he rose a bright green aura surrounded and then enveloped him completely. The green light shrank slowly until it was a tiny dot, then it vanished.

Bodhi's mind gradually emerged from its deep meditative state and became aware of a tickling sensation in the region of her radiator, next to the air filter housing underneath her bonnet. It was moving and scratching too. The tickling got worse. She laughed, at which point, all movement stopped. After a period of silence the moving and tickling began once more. Bodhi laughed again, and again, all movement stopped. A small muffled voice called out from under the bonnet, "Who's there?"

"My name is Bodhi," she said for the first time in her life.

"Where are you?" said the voice guardedly.

"I am the vehicle that you are sitting on the engine of," she replied.

"Ha! Don't try and fool me!" said the small voice. "Vehicles can't talk, I must be going mad, cooped up for too long on this giant rust bucket; that must be it!

"In fact, I think I must be going loopy, I don't think I'm hearing you with my ears...It's as if you are talking to me from inside my own head!

"POISON!!" the little voice shrieked in horror. "The cheese must have been poisoned, I'm hallucinating! Six years dodging ship's cats and I get nailed by poisoned cheese, LADIES SUSPENDERS!!!!"

"Don't panic," replied Bodhi in a calm and reassuring voice. "I really am the vehicle that you are in, and I really am talking to you, you aren't losing your mind, honestly!"

"Cats claws you are! If that's true, by rum, you had better give me some proof! I'm dying, I must be, oh what a way to go, in a dark container instead of in the fresh sea breeze, SCURVY SAUSAGES and DAMN IT!" the little voice cursed.

Bodhi could feel the small body rolling around frantically on the top of her engine block.

"I'm done for, finished, kaput, sayonara, ciao, salut, maboohai, selamat jalan, tot siens, asta nunca, goodbye, adieu... RAT POISON! I've seen it before, first the cramps, then the candy swirl eyes, then the foaming at the mouth AAAAAGGHHHHH!!! Noooooooo!" Its muffled scream ended in a soft splat as it rolled off Bodhi's cylinder head and landed on the floor of the container.

"Okay," said Bodhi, "you want proof, here it is!"

With the clicking of switches Bodhi turned on every light she had. Slowly, the small rodent's head appeared from under the front wheel arch, its shiny black eyes looking around and its pink nose sniffing and twitching, super sensitive whiskers curved forward in anticipation.

It quickly scampered up Bodhi's side and sat in the middle of the spare tire which was bolted flat onto the bonnet. The small grey rat looked at the front windshield.

"That's a huge relief!" it said.

"Who are you?" asked Bodhi turning off her lights again and plunging them back into darkness.

"I'm Sampan, Stowaway of the Seven Seas, Seafarer Extraordinaire. Ship's rat in other words," stated the rat.

"Sampan. That sounds like an unusual name," replied Bodhi.

"Well," said the rat in its squeaky voice, "I was born on a Chinese Junk in Hong Kong Harbour. It's the biggest in the world you know! I have never lived on land and the other animals started calling me Sampan, the name stuck I guess."

"I only travel long haul now though, tankers, container ships like this one and freighters. Less competition for food than living in harbours," Sampan said as he settled into a more comfortable position on the rubber of the spare wheel.

"I have sailed into every port there is," he said proudly, chatting away to his captive audience. "I've dodged pirate ships, cooks, drunken sailors and countless ship's cats which, by the way, is how I wound up in here with you. It's a good thing the metal grill in this container's ventilation hole has rusted through. I've just had a very narrow escape. This ship has a real killer cat onboard called 'Loose Cannon' because it likes to attack the sailors now and again for no apparent reason; biting, spitting and scratching them bloody like a cat-o-nine tails! You should see it launching itself – it's like heated shot and almost as dangerous. Ears back, tail all bushy, a psycho look in its mad staring eyes! Twenty small sharp claws and four teeth all sinking into the unsuspecting victim's leg or head! The Captain calls it the 'Furball of Fury' and makes 'Bruce Lee' noises when he sees it stalking someone. Of course, all the sailors think it's totally hilarious watching their mates fall victim to unprovoked surprise attacks. It's why he's still on board; I guess he breaks the monotony of long voyages. He's a mascot of sorts. They all wear Loose Cannon's battle scars like other sailors wear tattoos. All very amusing I'm sure, unless you are a rat sharing the same ship with a psychotic cat, even a ship as big as this one!"

"Speaking of which," Bodhi said butting in, "can you tell me more about this ship and where we are headed, if you don't mind?"

"Mind!" squeaked Sampan, "Of course I don't mind. I love a good yarn as much as the next old salt! Besides, I'm enjoying hearing your voice bouncing around inside my tiny brain, it's a novel experience!"

"Good," said Bodhi. "I am enjoying your company."

"Well," began Sampan, "you are on a container ship, a Panamax Class vessel to be precise, her name is *Carib Gypsy* and our destination is the port of Big Creek in Belize on the Caribbean coast of Central America."

The unlikely pair chatted for a long time about Belize and Sampan's adventures, while the *Carib Gypsy* rolled and crashed through the waves, now already halfway across the Atlantic. Eventually, Sampan settled down, curling up into a small ball on the wheel hub and falling into a deep safe sleep.

Bodhi, too, began to drift back into a deep, thoughtful mood and soon recognized the signs that she was entering a meditative state once again. She welcomed the now familiar feeling as the veil was drawn open on her mind's eye for the second time.

On this occasion, Bodhi's vision was a pure white, endless blank. A small speck appeared in the middle of this vast white emptiness. The speck seemed to be moving, slowly expanding, growing as it wobbled and jiggled in Bodhi's mind. The movements became rhythmic as the image got bigger and bigger. At last, Bodhi could make out what she was seeing in her vision.

A pale grey horse was galloping directly towards her, a rider on its back. It came thundering onwards, growing in size as it galloped at full tilt, its nostrils flaring and its mane shaking wildly as it ran. As it got within a short distance of Bodhi, the rider pulled up on its reigns. The huge horse came to a stop and reared up into the air, its front hooves kicking, shaking its head from side to side as it let out a loud neigh.

The warrior woman, mounted on the wild horse was a fearsome and spectacular sight. Dressed in shining steel armour, a mighty broadsword hung on her side and a battle helm was strapped to her saddle. Her long auburn hair cascaded from her head, curling over her steel clad shoulders and down her back. Her deep green eyes radiated a power that Bodhi could physically feel, her entire being emanating strength, pulsing with a force just waiting to be unleashed.

The lithe, armour clad figure dismounted smoothly and stood looking at Bodhi, holding the horse's reins in her left hand. Her face was beautiful but there was no doubt that she had forged her sleek muscled body in the fire of her will. She took two steps closer to Bodhi and spoke, her voice commanding and steady.

"I am the Warrior Andrasta, I am the spirit of the combatant that warriors through the ages have sought out and asked for guidance in battle. Often they call on me for deliverance in times of dire straits. When all seems lost and when all hope of victory or survival has been abandoned, they call my name," she announced.

Bodhi looked at the shining figure, amazed at the sheer force field of power that surrounded her. Andrasta's emerald green eyes were mesmerizing, her gaze almost hypnotizing in its intensity.

"Bodhi," Andrasta said in a commanding strong voice. "Gaia has asked me to teach you all I know about conflict. I will do so, to the best of my ability. The time will come when you will be confronted with darkness and destruction. If you find that you are faced with insurmountable odds or that the challenge you face is too great, call on me and I will help you.

"To begin then, it is necessary to learn that wherever there is life, there is conflict. Trees and plants struggle amongst themselves or with their environment to get enough light, nutrients and water. Animals get into conflicts over food and territories. Fights even occur within family groups to resolve who is the strongest or most dominant and the winner of those conflicts usually leads the rest of the family or group. Often, male animals fight each other over females. This is nature's way of ensuring that only the strongest, healthiest and most competent of the species continue to breed, continue to survive. Any and all conflicts revolve around one force trying to overcome the opposing force. Contemplate this thought," Andrasta said, letting the simple but profound statement sink in.

After a few seconds she began again.

"Nature, unlike humans, is impartial to the outcome of any conflict. This is a vital lesson to learn Bodhi. No matter who or what wins or loses in a conflict, the world will still turn, the sun will still rise and the omon will still look down on earth. The outcome is only of relevance to those who are directly affected by the conflict. To begin to understand humans you need to understand how conflict has shaped virtually every aspect of their history and cultures over the centuries. Nothing has changed since the dawn of human existence; the only difference is the level of sophistication. What started off by throwing rocks, then spears and arrows has now become highly advanced weapons systems that are much, much more destructive. The end result however is the same, although on a much larger scale. It has always been this way and it is so to this day," Andrasta said more softly, a look of sadness in her eyes.

Bodhi listened, making a point of remembering every word, every detail. Andrasta began again, her hands gesturing at intervals for emphasis.

"As emotional beings, we feel empathy and compassion for those that struggle to live and fail. It is very difficult for us to watch the weak and helpless lose this battle for survival. Many humans do all they can to preserve and cherish all life, weak or otherwise, but unfortunately, just as many humans do not. Each life is utterly unique and sacred and cannot be replaced, which is why the taking of a life is such a profoundly serious matter. All life, of course, does eventually end, changing into other states of existence and being. When we are in a position to help those who are suffering or are in need, it is the warrior's duty to do so."

She looked at her horse, smoothing her hand down its soft nose. Looking back at Bodhi she continued, "This is the way of the Warrior. True Warriors use their strength to protect the weak and defenceless; they stand against those who would abuse and manipulate power for selfish ends and those who would cause suffering and pain to others. The true warrior only resorts to physical fighting as a last resort to defend and protect against those who cannot, or will not, feel compassion for the vulnerable. Remember this Bodhi; the most skilful warrior wins conflicts without resorting to fighting. They see a potential conflict emerging and take the action necessary to try to prevent it. I will teach you these things and much more. There is a world of difference between a spiritual warrior and a soldier Bodhi; do not confuse the two. Soldiers give up their free will to become subservient to the will of others who tell them how to act and what to do... and who and how to kill. Their duty is to follow orders without question, with blind obedience.

"Spiritual warriors' use their free will to take actions that they, themselves, believe are correct and also take full responsibility for the outcomes of those actions, whatever they may be."

Andrasta drew her razor sharp broadsword out of its scabbard, holding it in front of her, "This sword is not only a weapon; it represents the strength of my will and the sharpness of my intentions."

Sheathing it again, she paced slowly up and down in front of her mount, gathering her thoughts before she started on another topic.

"Humans are unique in the entire animal kingdom," she began. "They have the most violent and most destructive conflicts of any of the animals on earth. This has developed as a result of them having evolved with almost no natural defences. No sharp claws, no huge teeth, they do not run exceptionally fast and they are not poisonous. There are two main reasons they have survived for so long: they have a large brain and they have opposing thumbs which has allowed them to use their hands to make and use tools…and weapons.

"When humans used their large brain to invent tools and weapons to compensate for what they naturally lacked in the way of defences, they soon found out that they were in a position to win most conflicts. They quickly became the dominant and most powerful species on earth. They also realized that weapons had other uses too. They could be used in conflicts with other members of their families or groups and with other tribes whom they wanted to dominate. War was the result.

"Humans become more powerful every day and as their power to create grows; their power to destroy grows to the same degree. Everything humans create, except their children, is made from something else that they have broken down or destroyed and transformed into something else. This is a very important point. Whatever humans make ultimately comes from, and is taken from the earth, and often this process is highly destructive.

"In fact, they have become so powerful that they now have the ability to totally destroy the very environment that supports them and almost all the other inhabitants of earth.

Humans are the only species on earth capable of bringing other forms of life to extinction, perhaps even including their own one day. This is why Gaia has such great concern for them.

"Bodhi, it is your destiny to become a peaceful warrior, a Warrior of Light. You are an instrument of the Creative Force, which will help to bring order and structure, birth and growth and which will help to redress the balance. The crafts of the Warrior are discipline, strategy, tactics, sacrifice, perseverance and fortitude. You must master the art of winning conflicts, mental and physical, to ensure that not only do you survive them, but that you leave the world a better place as a result of them. A warrior's place is at the forefront of the conflict. It is the combatants, in whatever shape or form they come in, that bring about the change that all conflict results in. Whether that change is positive or negative depends entirely on the strengths and weaknesses of the opposing forces. Let us begin, Bodhi; there is so much for you to learn, particularly about human conflict, and ways it can be resolved peacefully and with compassion."

After several days of instruction by Andrasta, Bodhi emerged from her deep meditative state and felt the scampering of small feet as Sampan scurried up onto his favourite spot on the spare tire.

"We're almost there now," he squeaked excitedly.

"We have passed through a cut in the barrier reef. This coral reef runs the entire length of Belize and I can see small islands and land in the distance! Fresh supplies! Oh how I have missed a nice plate of Creole rice and beans!! There are always plenty of leftovers in the bins here at the port, they make it with coconut milk you know, and it's delicious. I can't wait! Shore leave, hee hee," Sampan said happily, his small mouth-watering at the prospect.

"Most people haven't got much time for rats. We are only useful to them in laboratories because we are actually pretty clever, sometimes we are smarter than humans you know! For example, any rat worth his salt instinctively knows when to abandon ship long before it's about to sink, you show me any human who can do that!" he squeaked proudly sitting up on his haunches and preening his face and large pink-grey ears with his tiny front paws.

Suddenly the whumping of the engines stopped, followed by a prolonged and deafening metallic clanking and banging.

"Anchors away!" Sampan yelled in his tiny voice above the din. "We've arrived!"

Sampan jumped up, standing on his back legs, wiggling and shaking his tiny grey rear end and tail to the Belizean dancehall music that only he could hear in his head.

"Welcome to Beleeez, mon!" he eeked, making his voice as low as he could, putting on his best Creole accent that Charlie Price, a rat friend from Belize City, had taught him on a previous visit, "Evri'ting straight pan di dock, ready to Punta Rock!"

Chapter Eight

The Green Jewel

The red rectangular metal container swung over the side of the ship, suspended from the crane by four steel cables. It was lowered expertly onto the waiting bed of a truck and moved into the customs yard of Belize's second busiest port. Alex stood some distance away watching the dock workers unload the *Carib Gypsy* which was now securely moored to the dock with huge ropes. With the sub-tropical sun blazing down on him, Alex gazed at the port and the river that it was built on.

Big Creek's waters ran red-brown as a result of the mud and silt that had been washed into it from the inland Maya mountains and jungles during the long and wet rainy season that was just coming to an end. Occasionally, he spotted big semi-submerged logs; wooden flood victims drifting downstream. He hoped he would catch a glimpse of a crocodile swimming amongst the logs. Perhaps, he would spot one of the Belizean cousins to the American freshwater crocodile he had just finished studying in Florida or maybe one of its relatives, the Morlett's crocodile, native to Belize.

Alex's eyes scanned the tea coloured waterway which cut a wide path between the dense green vegetation on the banks either side of the river. The last time he had been here was with his mum and dad. How times had changed for him, but time had stood still for the port.

Palm trees of all kinds rose above broadleaf trees which were supported by wide triangular buttress roots. Vegetation of all types, bushes and spiny bamboo patches were all tangled and tied together with vines, lianas and creepers. This gallery forest formed a seemingly impenetrable wall of jungle vegetation overhanging the water's edge, so tightly packed together it looked as though it might fall in at any moment. Indeed, plenty of it was already dipping into the water and being dragged by the current.

Water birds of all shapes and colours flew from tree to tree and skimmed the river. A flight of pelicans were gliding in perfect 'V' formation across the mouth of the river, then suddenly, and in unison folded their wings and plunged into the water, scooping up beak-fulls of sardine-like sprats, emerging again to bob around on the surface.

Alex looked out further to the aquamarine blue of the Caribbean Sea. He saw dark green mangrove covered cayes forming a string of islands offshore; a long white line of waves crashing and breaking along the distant barrier reef way out to sea.

Moving into the shade of a small kiosk that sold snacks and soft drinks, Alex waited for the customs officers to break the seals on his container and inspect the contents. Sweat soaked his collar and underarms. His flight from Miami to Belize International Airport had been quick and smooth. He had spent the previous night on the coast in Belize City, in an area known as Fort George situated at the mouth of the Old Belize River.

He had checked into a comfortable, big old wooden house built in the colonial style which had been converted into a hotel in the early nineteen eighties. It was one block away from a local landmark, the Baron Bliss Lighthouse.

That evening, he had telephoned several contacts from his hotel and paid his respects to various Belizean officials who had been kind enough to issue him with all the permits and authorizations required in order for him to conduct his research in their country. The moment he mentioned his name, Alex Steele, everybody knew who he was and welcomed him with open arms. It was like a home-coming.

Belize is a small, jungle covered country known fondly to many as 'The Green Jewel'. Alex's permits had been issued on the understanding that he would submit full reports, and hand over and/or share all data, information, samples and artefacts he might have collected to the relevant government ministries upon his departure.

After touching base to let them know that he had arrived safely, he had made one last call to a young teenager whose name was Emiliano Guererro, Emil for short, who was from a small village in North Western Belize.

Emil was Alex's ARACHNIS contact and would be his assistant on this expedition. Emil had sounded full of life and energy and they arranged to meet at the main bus station in the coastal town of Dangriga late the following afternoon. It had been Emil's written proposal to the Professor about his discovery of the Maya temple that had resulted in this expedition.

Emil would accompany Alex on all the projects to gain experience at doing scientific and conservation research work in the field. The 'field' in this case meaning the steamy jungle. Alex and the Professor's plan was that all ARACHNIS assistants would be given a crash course in Tropical Expedition Skills which would also include conservation planning and management, training in first aid and survival where necessary and familiarization with technologies, including laptops, GPS communications and mission reporting. The aim was to teach Emil as much as possible so that when Alex and his ARACHNIS contact parted ways, the work of ARACHNIS would continue to blossom and grow.

Alex had arrived at Big Creek port mid-morning having caught the five am bus from downtown Belize City. As he patiently waited, he ran through his 'to-do' list for the day. He planned to make a stop on his way to meet Emil in Dangriga. Grandfather had asked him to pay a quick visit to the Cockscomb Basin Wildlife Sanctuary, also known as the Jaguar Preserve which he would be passing.

It was the only dedicated jaguar preserve in the world. The Professor had requested that he drop off several new digital trip cameras to the Belize Audubon Society Centre located deep in the jaguar's jungle sanctuary in the foothills of the Maya and Cockscomb mountain ranges.

The motion activated trip cameras had been donated by an organization that the Professor belonged to and which was dedicated solely to protecting big cats around the world. The spots on a particular jaguar's pelt are unique to that specific cat, so photos of jaguars allow the scientists to identify individual cats in much the same way that individual humans can be identified by their fingerprints.

As Alex worked on his list, a very smart looking customs agent walked over to him. He wore a blindingly white, perfectly ironed short sleeved shirt and navy blue trousers. He was holding a clipboard full of shipping invoices.

Taking off his sunglasses he glanced down at the name on the topmost customs form. Looking up again he spoke in a deep rich voice, "Good morning! Mr. Steele? My name is Mr. Palacio."

"Good to meet you Mr. Palacio, just call me Alex."

"Well, welcome to Belize Mr. Alex!" he looked Alex up and down, noticing that the legs of Alex's tough rip-stop cotton cargo pants were tucked into the tops of his well-worn jungle boots. He saw Alex's heavy duty, black nylon webbing belt with a multi-tool and other pouches strung onto it. The long sleeves of his tough cotton safari shirt were rolled up and buttoned under sleeve tabs.

"Bway," said the Customs Officer, "Unu look like yu redi foh tek bush!"

"What did you say?" asked Alex smiling back.

"Excuse, I was speaking Creole. I'm Garifuna though, I'm from down south, from Punta Gorda town – P.G. for short!" he laughed. "What I said was – you look seriously ready to go into the jungle!"

"Yes," Alex laughed "Wait until I show you what I have in the container! I am going to be doing a lot of work in the bush as you say."

"Very well," said Officer Palacio, "let us have a quick look. I see you are a registered N.G.O. so there will be no duty on your vehicle."

They walked over the gravelly road, sidestepping rainbow coloured puddles which had formed from oil that had been splashed off the undercarriages of the heavy trucks which were constantly flowing in and out of the customs compound.

"Goh tru! Open it up!" officer Palacio ordered the two dock workers who were waiting for them at the container.

The doors of the container opened and a wave of thick, heavy heat and humidity hit Bodhi as they undid the shipping straps. The two men undid the straps and removed all the wooden braces, then rolled and pushed her carefully out of the container.

Finally, Bodhi had arrived!

Bodhi's senses were bombarded with Caribbean scents, sounds and colours. Outside the compound on the main street, loud Punta Rock music blared from a taxi van parked next to a barrow selling coconuts, pineapples and bags of raw sugar cane sticks.

The moisture laden air was thick with the scent of tropical flowers mixed with diesel fumes. The smell of fish frying in coconut oil, and stewing pork wafted over to her from a small roadside diner. These smells mingled with the powerful odours of the dock, as well as freshly cut vegetation and spices.

Beyond the fence, Bodhi could see an open street market crowded with men and women, boys and girls of every shade of bronze, black and brown, all dressed in colourful loose fitting clothes; straw hats and bandanas, hair braids woven with coloured beads, baseball caps and head scarves. The milling crowds were all shopping for fresh produce, fish and household supplies. The lively locals were all laughing and joking, shouting and cursing in a multitude of languages – Garifuna, Creole, Spanish and Maya. Bodhi sensed the scene, mesmerized.

Alex and officer Palacio came around the door of the container and looked at Bodhi.

"Man!" said officer Palacio, "yu ready fuh tek bush for tru! That's one serious vehicle, bway! Okay, Mr. Alex, sign here, here and here and then you are free to go! Nice meeting you, I hope you have a great stay in our beautiful country!"

"Thanks very much," Alex replied. "I'm sure I will! See you again when we ship her out!"

As they shook hands, a small grey blur shot between Alex's legs making a dash for the diner, squeaking all the way. It reached the diner unnoticed, diving under the makeshift seating area made from old wooden shipping pallets which covered the drainage ditch and the muddy grass verge which passed for a sidewalk.

Directly above Sampan's new hiding place, a man sat on one of the diner's red plastic garden chairs preparing to eat his freshly served meal which had been set on a wobbly white plastic table in front of him. The plate was piled high with rice, beans and chicken that had been stewed in a cilantro and red ricardo gravy.

Crammed on the side of the plate was a large dollop of coleslaw and another of Creole potato salad. Lying on top of the food mountain were three slices of gooey banana-like plantain that had been fried in coconut oil. Next to his plate was a huge plastic glass filled with ice and freshly squeezed lime juice, condensation running down the outside, soaking the napkin underneath.

The man picked up an orange bottle of fiery hot pepper sauce and opened it, shaking at least a third of its contents over the huge pile of food. Grabbing his fork, he loaded as much as he could onto it and shovelled it into his mouth.

He chewed with his mouth open, some of its contents spilling out and onto the oversized vest that stretched over his deep bronze coloured pot belly. His face was wide and bloated, a wispy grey and black goatee surrounding his slack red lips. Two faded green prison tattoos, one of a scorpion and one of a cross, defaced the skin on the insides of each scarred forearm. A solid gold chain, thick and heavy, supporting a medallion, hung around his neck. Close cropped salt and pepper hair covered his big domed head in a brush cut that would rival any hedgehog's spines. His eyes were hidden by a pair of black lensed sunglasses. Picking up his cell phone in his sweaty, pudgy hand, he dialled a number.

Washing the overstuffed contents in his mouth down with a gulp of lime juice, he let out a disgustingly long and reverberating belch. He panted hot smelly breath onto the phone, waiting for it to answer.

For over an hour now he had been watching. His shielded eyes had been locked on the man behind the fence who now stood next to a Land Rover, following his every move.

Finally the person on the other end picked up.

"Aha? Tell me!" the voice on the other end answered.

"Boss, it's Gordo," he said wheezing. "I'm watching him now, he just got his vehicle out of customs, he's getting ready to go. Boss, you still want I should do the same plan?" he asked, eyeing the rest of the food on his plate greedily.

"Gordo, when I ketch up wi you again I gonna slap you upside yuh fat head, fool! You wanna dose people who need to feel to learn, I swear Bway! Listen to me noh, the plan noh change, you hear? An' I tell you, you betta no change it needah, you understand?" said the man on the other end.

"Roger that Boss, no worry! I got it, everything cool. My boys are ready. Three crews, one from Griga, another crew from P.G. ready to follow him right now, and one on standby from up North," he said picking his ear with the long pinkie nail on his right hand. "We will follow an' find out who his contact is, I'll call again inna while."

He pointed the cell phone at Alex and Bodhi, zoomed in as far as he could and snapped a couple of photos. After selecting several phone numbers on his screen he pressed 'send'. "Who he di call a fool?" he thought angrily to himself staring at the cell phone.

"Yes Boss, no Boss. One day that man's gonna learn that he's not the boss of me! I not no pot-licker street dog fool to be disrespected, that fool betta watch his back! He the damn fool," he deliberated, jamming his fork viciously into a chicken leg and raising it up to his slavering mouth.

Alex drove Bodhi out of the compound, splashing through water filled potholes as he rumbled up the road that would lead them onto the Southern Highway. He did not notice the big Pontiac saloon with tinted windows that had slid out of a side road and was now tailing him.

As they sped up the highway, crossing the boundary from the Southern district of Toledo into Stan Creek, Bodhi became aware that she was experiencing a creeping feeling of danger and apprehension that she had never felt before. Bodhi concentrated on it and decided it was not coming from the front or sides. It was lurking somewhere behind her.

Chapter Nine

Friends and Foes

Bodhi cruised along the Southern Highway sensing a dangerous presence in her wake. They were approaching a small village known as Maya Centre. That was where the main entrance of the Cockscomb Wildlife Sanctuary and Jaguar Preserve was. Alex turned left at the junction and stopped just short of the red and white striped metal barrier.

An official from the local community carefully wrote down Alex's details and Bodhi's license plate number on a clipboard. Smiling, he waved them through and dropped the metal pole barrier back into place behind them.

As this was happening, there was quite a commotion in the car that had been following and which had suddenly pulled into the shade of some trees near the entrance of the Maya Centre. The occupants of the car were in the middle of a heated debate.

"Mi noh know why he turned off into Cockscomb!" yelled the driver irritably.

"He meant to be going straight to Dangriga bus station to meet someone. Dat a da information I get from Gordo, so SHUT YOUR MOUTH!!" he yelled again, looking over his shoulder at one of the two young hoodlums in the back seat.

The four occupants of the car were all powerfully built, dressed in basketball vests, loose baggy cargo shorts and branded trainers. On their heads they wore bandanas with baseball caps perched at jaunty angles on top. Round their necks were ropes of gold chains and on their fingers, big and bulky gold rings. Their faces were hard. Their eyes looked yellow and bloodshot. The sullen gangster in the front seat made a phone call.

"Gordo, its Kiloboy. What's up with this gig man? The fool we're following just changed up the plan. He jus turn into Maya Centre. He goin' tru da barrier into the Cockscomb right now! What's up with that, G! You said dis a simple job, follow him to Dangriga Bus Station and getta I.D. on the contact he hooks up wi deh. Look like your info was wrong man! Wha' you wan' us to do?"

After listening for a minute he hung up and spoke to his sulking and brooding companions, "The Fat Man say for us to wait here. He knows we can't follow a Land Rover inna dis vehicle. No way it could mek it down dat mess' up road for two seconds. Anyhow, dem people over deh would see us and get suspicious."

"Shuks man!" said one hoodlum in the back sucking his teeth, "Cho! I no gonna sit here for noh laaang time, waitin' on that fool. Who knows how long he gonna be man. Us, all stuck here, inna dis HOT car, wi no dam A/C, no way, I not into that, you hear! Dis only becoming one LOUSY situation, I noh gets paid enough for this stoopidness man!"

"Cool it down back there!" said Kiloboy. "We will make a plan, no worry!"

As the gangsters argued, Alex cleared the barrier and was about to set off down the eight kilometre jungle track to the Belize Audubon Ranger Station when a mud spattered,

84

brightly painted bus pulled up on the highway. It spilled its passengers onto the road at the Maya Centre bus stop.

The throng of people pouring out of the bus all had strong Maya features and most were clutching bags of shopping, boxes, sacks of rice and other goods.

The men were mostly dressed in farm work clothes. The women, wearing brightly coloured dresses, were carrying local arts and crafts wrapped in hand woven shawls and blankets. Many of the women and girls had red-gold hoop earrings in their ears and most wore their long black hair rolled up into neat round buns on top of their heads.

Amongst the crowd, a teenage boy was straining and pushing to get through and around the back of the bus, his eyes glued to the Land Rover that was about to drive off into the jungle.

In one hand he clutched a big, bulging white rice sack that had been converted into an improvised backpack of sorts. Old car seat belts had been tied to the centre of the top and down to each corner of the sack, making strong and comfortable shoulder straps. In the other hand he held a long and heavy leather scabbard that sheathed his razor sharp machete.

He had jet black hair, cut short and neat on the sides, a little longer on the top, with a side parting on the right. His bronze face shone healthily. His features were sharp and well-proportioned and he had dark brown oval eyes. They shone with keen intelligence, lighting up his friendly young face.

Making a dash across the highway, he ran as fast as he could towards the barrier and the Land Rover that was moving off beyond it. His rubber boots galumphing, he shouted and waved as he tried to get Alex's attention.

Bodhi could sense a cheerful, youthful presence approaching from behind; it made a nice change from the ominous vibe she had been picking up all the way from Big Creek. She knew that whoever was behind her was friendly and trying to make contact.

As Alex changed from second to third gear, the clutch sprang back suddenly and the engine stalled, stuttered and then stopped. Surprised, Alex put it back into neutral and started it again.

Suddenly, a smiling face appeared at his side window and said, "Hi! Mr. Alex? I'm Emil Guerrero!"

"Emil! Good to meet you!" said Alex.

"What a nice surprise! I was expecting to meet you later in Dangriga! How did you find me?" he asked, looking at the fairly tall, well-built boy.

Emil wore strong work pants tucked into his rubber boots and a T-shirt with a picture of a local rock band. Over the T-shirt he wore a long sleeved olive green military surplus army shirt that was far too big around the chest for his wiry frame.

"Go round and jump in. Tell me all about it while we drive!" Alex said, pleased at the prospect of some company and excited to talk to Emil about what he had discovered.

"Chuck your gear in the back, there should be room somewhere!"

Emil's grin became a big smile; he ran round to the passenger's side, opened the door and jumped in, keeping his feet outside while he kicked his boots together to knock off the clumps of thick red mud before pulling them inside and closing the door. Twisting around, he pushed his sack into a gap behind the back of his seat, tucking his machete along the floor next to the door.

Alex and Emil zoomed off down the track and were soon driving through a green tunnel of thick jungle vegetation.

Back in the gangster car, Kiloboy and his crew had seen the boy from the bus, but assumed that he was probably just hitching a ride to the centre where he probably worked. In his mind, Kiloboy thought about how much money that brand new Land Rover would be worth broken down and sold as spare parts. If he sold it across the border there would be no connection to him or his crew. The more he thought about it the more he liked the nasty plan that was hatching in his dark and devious mind.

"Listen to me noh! I gotta plan to make us some pretty good cash from this change in plan...a lot more Chedah than Gordo is paying us to play 'Follow the Leedah!' and that fat fool won't be able to find out that it was us that did it needah," he said looking at his blood brothers in crime.

Predatory smiles spread across their faces as Kiloboy outlined his plot to the others.

Bouncing along the muddy track Emil explained his sudden appearance.

"I got into Dangriga early, so I texted the Professor on the mobile phone he had had sent to me. It was his idea for me to continue on down to Big Creek and meet you there. He said it would be valuable for me to see the Jaguar Sanctuary and meet the scientists and learn a bit about the research they're doing, seeing as I had the time. The Professor forwarded the picture of you with the Land Rover to me, the one you sent him before you left, so I would recognize you," Emil said as he flipped open the mobile phone and showed Alex the image taken at his converted loft.

"I would have made it too, but the bus got a flat tyre and that took a while to change. Luckily, I was keeping a good lookout along the way and I spotted you when you made the turn off the highway! We both tried phoning you on your mobile but couldn't get through to you."

"Well you managed to connect with me anyway, well done!" said Alex.

Soon they were driving down a small hill which led to a narrow river. There was no bridge over it, only a slime-covered reinforced cement ford which was submerged under the sparkling clear water about half a wheel's depth below it.

"Oh and by the way, plain Alex is fine with me, Emil; you can drop the Mr. part okay? I am only a few years older than you."

"Okay, I'll try Mr. Alex, but here in Belize it is very common to call anyone older than you Mr. or Ms. It's how we show respect."

"Well, whatever suits you Emil, I am easy either way!" Alex grinned. "Right, let's get to it; I am dying to hear the story about how you came across the lost temple. We have seven kilometres of bumpy road to drive, that should give us plenty of time!"

"Sure," said Emil. "It all started when my dad had his accident. He was in a sugar cane truck taking a load to the BSI sugar mill when the brakes failed. They had a really bad crash and my dad was badly injured. My mother went with my father to a very big hospital in Guatemala, the country next to us, where he is getting special medical treatment. My grandfather is visiting them at the moment. That's why we can only go looking for the temple after we finish all our other projects. He made me promise that I would wait for him to get back so that he could join us. He worries about me, and he also doesn't want to miss out on the adventure!"

Emil rummaged around in the pocket of his army shirt and pulled out his wallet. Opening it, he showed Alex a worn picture of his parents.

"Wow, I'm sorry to hear about your dad, is he going to be okay?" asked Alex.

"Yes, thanks," said Emil. "They say he will have a limp and some joint problems when he gets older but otherwise he'll be fine. They had to leave me here and I am staying at my grandfather's until they get back. My grandfather spent most of his life working as a Chiclero deep in the jungle. In fact, he was born in a Chiclero jungle camp. Chicleros used to search the jungle for Chicle trees. We are taught all about the history of it at school. They would climb right to the top of them using sharp metal foot spikes tied to their ankles and a rope waist loop wrapped around the trunk. Then, they would make V shaped cuts all the way down the tree using their machetes. At the bottom, they would make a thin cut into the bark and put in a leaf that would catch and funnel the sticky white sap into buckets. Once they had collected a big amount they would carry it back through the jungle to the camp. Then they boil it in big metal bowls until it's very thick, very sticky and brown. After that they would pack it into wooden moulds and shape it to look like bricks. They would sell the blocks to chewing gum makers. Chicle is the original chewing gum and it used to be a really big industry here in Belize, that and mahogany logging. I bet you didn't know that that's where chewing gum originally came from!" said Emil with a flourish.

'You're right. I had no idea! So how does that link in to you stumbling across King Nanchancaan's lost temple?" asked Alex, thoroughly enjoying listening to the story.

"Well, the Japanese like things to be original" said Emil, confusing Alex completely.

"Did you know that the Japanese will tow giant icebergs thousands of miles so that they can melt them, bottle the water and sell it for a lot of money? I saw it on TV! The reason people want to drink it is because the last time that ice was water was millions and millions of years ago. It's original, pure ancient water. Well it's the same with Chicle. The Japanese decided that they would like to be able to chew original chewing gum again, not the synthetic stuff we have today."

"Aha!" said Alex, realization suddenly dawning.

"So, your grandfather suddenly came out of retirement and took up his old profession again, is that it?" asked Alex.

"Yeah, and on weekends and holidays I started going with him into the jungle to learn the ways of a Chiclero and earn some pretty good pocket money to help my father and mother too," Emil said proudly.

"Two months ago, we were deep in the jungle looking for Chicle trees when we suddenly came across a big Maya site that my grandfather did not remember from his youth. It was a huge temple covered in trees and vegetation. We climbed to the top of it to have our lunch so we could catch some breeze and get a break from the mosquitoes lower down. As we climbed up the side, near the top, we saw something neither of us had seen before. Usually, the temples we have found have been much smaller and totally covered in bush and trees. Almost at the top of this one we found a big open doorway that had a really old looking piece of wood, like a beam, across the top of it, supporting the big stones on top. We chopped away the bush that was blocking it and went inside. We found a big square room with two kinda half rooms in the two corners at the back. The plaster on the walls is still in really good condition and they have a lot of paintings all over them! It was so exciting Mr. Alex! We only had a cigarette lighter with us to see everything the first time we went. I had to go back with a flash light and my camera which is how I got the photos that I sent to the Professor."

"You did a great job with those, by the way," Alex commented as he looked ahead at the jungle track. "The photos of the glyphs on the walls and the wall paintings of the King, High Priests, and other people depicted in it was what led the Professor to believe that you had indeed found the lost temple of King Nanchancaan."

Alex turned a muddy corner, straightening the wheel he changed gear and continued, "Most archaeologists don't believe it exists, they insist that it is mere myth and legend. When we showed your pictures to the Archaeological Institute of Belize they kindly agreed to let me and you visit the site again with our scientific instruments to gather more evidence, provided we do so very carefully. We'll be working in strict accordance to archaeological procedures and guidelines that they have laid out for us. If the evidence we find holds up, they will mount a full scale archaeological dig and that will require an enormous amount of money and skilled archaeologists. That's why we have to do the very best we can, given that we can only look and make notes, not touch or dig anything up."

Emil looked out of the front windshield, watching the red muddy water splashing onto it from the puddles they were driving through. Bodhi's windshield wipers were sweeping it away for a few seconds before another rust coloured splash showered over it again.

"If it is King Nanchancaan's Temple, why is this temple so important?" asked Emil. "The Professor wouldn't tell me. He said it was very important not to tell anyone else about what we had found. My grandfather and I agreed to keep it a secret. My grandfather told me that he remembers seeing men digging up a lot of old Maya things from many temples when he was a young Chiclero. He calls them 'Midnight Archaeologists'! He says that greed made them do it, digging up tombs and temples to rob them of their jade and other treasures to sell. He has a lot of stories, I love to hear them. When I told him about ARACHNIS and that I was a member he told me I should send my photos to them because they would know what to do. He was right!"

Rummaging around in the opposite pocket and pulling out a small plastic bag of sweets Emil said, "Would you like to try one of these sweets? They are called cuttabrut and are made from coconut and boiled sugar.''

"Sure" said Alex, taking one and popping it in his mouth.

As they drove past a sign that said they were only one kilometre from the Belize Audubon Ranger Station, Alex felt his foot pressing down on the brake pedal, - or was it the brake pedal going down by itself and his foot going with it? He couldn't be sure. In either case, he was sure that he could see a very large snake lying across their path directly in front of them. The huge Boa Constrictor was so long it touched either side of the road. They came to a stop only a couple of meters from it.

"Good eyes Mr. Alex!" said Emil craning his head out of the side window. "You would have run right over it!"

Alex could not remember seeing the snake before the braking started. He thought he must have registered it subconsciously, either way, he was happy not to have squashed it. So was Bodhi, who had known the snake was there and would not have been able to move off the road fast enough. Bodhi thought about the fact that she had just saved a life, a life she and Alex would otherwise have inadvertently taken, like the insects that kept hitting her windshield and the lines of ants they had already run over. It was something she decided to meditate on.

"Look at that!" said Alex.

"It's just eaten something pretty big, no wonder it's not able to move quickly," he said, looking at the large lump inside the Boa that stretched its scales so far apart the pink skin between them was visible.

"Come on Emil, let's get out and have a closer look. We have to make sure we don't scare it or it will bring its meal back up which would be a waste. Who knows how long it's waited to catch its prey?"

"Here we call them 'woawlah," said Emil. "What's it doing with its mouth? It looks like its yawning."

Emil stared at the giant snake as it opened its mouth as wide as it could and then closed it, moving each side of its lower jaw independently from side to side.

"It's resetting it jaw bones," answered Alex.

"Snakes can completely dislocate them so that they can open them wide enough to swallow prey that is much bigger than the size of their mouths. They also have two lungs, one large and one small. When they swallow their prey it completely blocks their breathing to the big lung. They have a snorkel-like adaptation under their tongues which lets them breathe into their small lung while they are eating. The small lung is only big enough to provide the minimum amount of oxygen to keep them alive. That is why, if you disturb them while they are eating they need to bring up the meal so they can breathe fast enough to escape from danger," Alex informed his young apprentice.

"Wow, that's cool," said Emil.

As they watched the Boa move very slowly across the road and into the safety of the dense bushes, Emil's sharp eyes noticed some depressions in the mud. A closer look revealed what they were.

"Mr. Alex, look, jaguar tracks! Big ones!" said Emil excitedly. "Fresh too!"

"Wow!" said Alex.

"There are more all the way down the road behind us, look!" Alex added, pointing back down the track.

"Yes, and more tracks further along it too," said Emil following the tracks past Bodhi.

"They lead into the jungle right here" said Emil, now standing several meters beyond the Land Rover.

"I think they're very fresh. In fact, I think the Jaguar heard us coming and only just jumped back in the jungle…it is probably watching us right now," Emil said excitedly.

Bodhi agreed with Emil, she could feel the big cat watching her from a distance. Bodhi also sensed another powerful emotion being directed to her from the jaguar hidden somewhere behind the tangled green vegetation. She felt its desperate need filtering through to her, its desperate cry for help. Something was terribly wrong.

Bodhi sent a powerful message in the direction of the hidden cat, "What's wrong, what's happened to you?

"I'm dying" the Jaguar replied. "I can't eat and all the animals are too scared of me to help me." The jaguar's message drifted back to Bodhi.

"Follow us," she said. "We will stop soon; I will make a plan to try and help you. It will be very difficult for you, I know, but you must trust me and trust the humans that I am with. We will do what we can to help you."

Alex and Emil both slammed their doors shut simultaneously and Alex fired up Bodhi's engine. While they drove the last kilometre to the Belize Audubon centre, Alex continued to answer Emil's earlier question.

"King Nanchancaan was a great king, by all accounts. At the time of his rule, Spain's Queen Isabella had ordered the ruthless plundering of gold from the 'New World'. The Maya king had heard that the Spanish conquistadores were destroying all the recorded wisdom and knowledge of the ancient Maya by burning all their libraries. The ancient Maya recorded their wisdom and knowledge using glyphs, a little bit like hieroglyphics. They drew these glyphs into 'books' made out of tree bark. Today, we call these 'books' codices. Only a few of these codices are known to have survived," said Alex.

"Legend tells us that when King Nanchancaan heard of the destruction of the sacred documents, he sent warriors and scribes, priests and shamans to secretly gather all the codices they could rescue and he supposedly hid them somewhere in what is now Belize. He knew the Spanish were unlikely to focus too heavily on Belize as it didn't have gold or silver like Mexico and Peru. After King Nanchancaan finally lost a great battle against the Spanish, the legends say he hid the Codices in a secret chamber deep in his temple."

"Really?" said Emil, fascinated.

"That's why the Professor didn't want us to tell anyone."

"Yes," said Alex, "they would be a priceless archaeological treasure.

"The Maya were able to build structures and theories that baffle modern scientists. They possessed mysterious astronomical and mathematical knowledge that enabled them to create the world's oldest and most accurate calendar. They had no telescopes, but they were still able to precisely calculate the time it takes for the planet Venus to orbit around the sun. They could also accurately predict the exact time of lunar and solar eclipses thousands of years into the future. Imagine being able to do that?! There are plenty of unsolved mysteries surrounding this fascinating ancient civilization."

Alex paused, seeing buildings appear around the corner.

"If those Codices are hidden in that temple Emil, we believe that they hold the key to unlocking all the ancient secrets of the Maya. Who knows what amazing knowledge they contain? It would be one of the most important discoveries ever made!" Alex said excitedly as they pulled into the parking lot of the Belize Audubon Outpost.

He parked Bodhi, her front bumper almost touching the thick jungle surrounding the parking lot. As Alex turned off the engine they could hear a distant but powerful roar coming from the jungle. It was a terrifying sound to those who did not know what was making it. It sounded like a combination of an angry lion and a Tyrannosaurus Rex.

"Howler monkeys!" they both said simultaneously, laughing.

"Who would think that a medium sized monkey could make such an enormous racket?" Alex added looking over to where the troop of monkeys was calling from.

They were perched at the very top of a huge strangler fig tree, way off in the distance. He knew they used this loud roar to communicate their position to other howler monkey troops. It was how they marked out their territorial boundaries which allowed the various troops that lived in the same area to space themselves out.

That way, they could avoid nasty physical fights that could lead to injuries or worse, given how easily bites and cuts became infected in the hot jungle. It was a clever system. The howl could easily be heard for a few kilometres. Alex also knew that the ancient Maya considered the howler monkeys to be the scribes and heralds of their mythological Gods, responsible for communicating messages.

"By the way, Emil, there is one more thing that legend says is supposed to be hidden in King Nanchancaan's temple," Alex said to Emil in a low voice as he opened the door of the Land Rover, "but I will have to tell you about that later. Give me a hand getting the boxes out of the back, would you? They contain motion activated cameras."

Alex and Emil had just finished unloading the boxes when the door to the main office building opened and a uniformed man emerged.

"Alex," shouted the station manager. "So glad to see you, and you have grown so much. Last time I saw you with your father you were just like your young friend here."

"Wow," said Alex. "I didn't even remember I had been here before."

Emil and Alex greeted the station manager and followed him through to the canteen where they were invited to lunch. They then spent the next couple of hours meeting some of the scientists and student volunteers doing research on jaguars, learning about their techniques and methodologies.

Meanwhile, the exhausted jaguar padded slowly through the jungle, its head and tail hung low, its normally shiny coat dirty, dull and unkempt. It cautiously made its way under the cover of the dense bush circling the parking lot and slowly approached Bodhi.

It got within a meter of Bodhi's front wheels and then collapsed, panting. Its balance was broken and the pupils of its eyes dilated wide and round. The big, male jaguar, normally huge and built of solid muscle was desperately thin. Its hip bones and ribs were visible through its loosely hanging skin, its face sprouting what resembled dozens of long, thick, black and white striped whiskers. They bristled out of his nose, lips, mouth and tongue; some were dangerously close to his eyes.

"What happened to you?" asked Bodhi.

The jaguar raised its painful, aching head and looked at Bodhi.

"I made the mistake of trying to catch a porcupine to eat. It fired all these quills into my face and I can't eat, I can barely drink. I have asked all the animals capable of pulling them out for help, but of course they are all too scared of me to try. My name is Balaam. Who are you?" asked the jaguar.

"I'm called Bodhi. But you must rest now, and listen to me. I can help you but you must do as I say, even if your instinct tells you to run or fight you must not. Here is what you must do..."

After a hearty lunch and fascinating discussion, Alex and Emil returned to the parking lot in the company of two scientists who had walked them back to Bodhi. They said goodbye, swapping contact information. Alex and Emil jumped into Bodhi.

As they reversed, saying a final farewell to the scientists, they all got a very big surprise. As Bodhi rolled backwards, they all saw it.

A jaguar! It was right there, less than two meters away from the scientists, lying on the ground where Bodhi had been parked. The scientists jumped back, and almost out of their skins; their instant reaction was to bolt and run, to get away to a safe distance.

Balaam sensed their panic and had the same reaction. The spotted cat sprang into a half crouch, unsteady and off balance from the raging fever and weak from starvation. He snarled and growled, baring his long teeth in warning. Alex and Emil looked through the windshield, their mouths hanging open in total disbelief.

"Stay calm Balaam, STAY CALM!" said Bodhi smoothly and steadily. "These humans will help you. You have to trust me. You have to lie down and stay still."

Balaam's eyes shone with menace, fever and fear, but they could not focus properly anymore. He felt death clouding his once bright eyes and so he decided to trust Bodhi; he had no other option. Balaam slumped back to the ground.

It took several seconds for Alex, Emil and the scientists to comprehend what they were seeing, and a few more to realize that the jaguar that they were looking at was in a very bad state. The adrenaline pumping through the scientists' veins subsided a fraction and their initial urge to run became instead a cautious retreat to safer distance.

"Balaam, what happens to you next will be strange, frightening and uncomfortable, but you must bear it," said Bodhi softly.

"You must stay calm and accept it all. These people will help you get better and when you are, they will release you back into your jungle."

"Thank you Bodhi," Balaam panted. "I hope we meet again. If I can help you in turn one day, if you ever need my help, send a message with the howler monkeys and I will come."

The small group assessed the situation and summed up what had happened to the jaguar very quickly. The scientists used a hypodermic tranquilizer dart fired from a metal blowpipe to sedate Balaam. Soon, the group became a busy crowd as students and researches all helped Alex and Emil keep the jaguar cool with ice and water, fanning it as they gently lifted and carried it under a small picnic shelter that was thatched with Kahune palm leaves.

The station manager sent an urgent message over the VHF radio to the Belize Audubon Office in Belize City to arrange for a vet to be sent as fast as possible to perform surgery to remove the porcupine quills from the jaguar.

Eight kilometres away, Kiloboy was on the mobile phone again talking to Gordo.

"Listen to me, noh! We noh gonna stay here all day an' all night for no kinda long time! We already getting funny looks from de people passing by," he winked at his fellow conspirators in the car, adding. "I already called the boys from Dangriga, they done inna position waiting at di bus stop. We gonna head down to P.G. When di man decide to leave Cockscomb, the Griga boys will be ready and waiting to I.D. the contact right there at di bus stop and follow them from there. It don't make no sense for us to hang around here attracting attention."

"Okay, go den," Gordo said in frustration, "but Treeways is di Boss an' he not gonna be happy about it at all, he wanted eyes on that Land Rover every step of di way."

"Well Treeways nevah had his information straight or correct! We should have already reached Dangriga long time ago and done finished with this job," remarked Kiloboy.

"Alright! I get it," fumed Gordo, "but I only gonna pay you boys half what we agreed upon, understand?"

"We can argue about dat later! Right now we got a few games of pool to shoot, an' some cold drinks waiting for us way down in P.G. Later Gordo!" he said, hanging up.

"Okay, we're on!" he said, grinning.

"We ambush dat fool on his way out. It will be dark in a couple of hours. We will stock up on snacks and drinks from that store over there for the wait," he said pointing at a small shack made of roughly cut planks and a thatched roof.

"Could be a long wait, den again, maybe not. We ambush him and take the Land Rover back in the dark. It will just disappear. Like magic, poof!" he said as they all burst out laughing.

Kiloboy sat back and silently contemplated what the fate of the driver should be.

By the time Bodhi, Alex and Emil were bouncing back down the jungle track towards the highway once again, the sun had become deep crimson ball, low on the horizon. Dark shadows began stretching across the road, the darkness of evening coming much faster under the jungle canopy.

Alex and Emil chatted excitedly about the amazing encounter with the wild jaguar and the journey they would be making across Belize. The happy trio rolled along the muddy road, Bodhi's headlights lighting up the way, her red tail lights glowing brightly behind.

All of a sudden Bodhi felt a wave pass over her. It was as if she had driven into an invisible dark cloud. It was the same bad feeling she had had earlier that day. Only this time it was coming from the front.

Chapter Ten

Highway Robbery

This was the third time Bodhi had sensed dånger lurking nearby. The first time had been on the night of the attempted break-in at Alex's converted barn. The second had been on the drive from Big Creek to the Maya Centre.

This time, the feeling was different. Bodhi could not only sense impending danger but also the presence of a person whose spirit was angry and full of murderous hatred. A person whose intention was to do physical harm. She felt this intention as a force. This was the force that Andrasta had so carefully described to her; the force of the killer. It was a premonition telling her that Alex and Emil were in mortal danger.

She listened to them chatting away inside her cab, blissfully unaware. They were the last people to leave the preserve and Alex watched the old Maya gatekeeper locking the barrier behind them in his rear view mirror.

They turned left at the junction, back onto the highway and headed north. This was Alex's kind of highway, only two lanes with almost no traffic – perfect. Once they had cleared the village of Maya Centre, not a person or building could be seen for miles.

"Dis da perfect place to take him! No witnesses," Kiloboy said to the two other street gangsters in the car as he looked at the desolate and lonely stretch of highway. No sooner had he spoken than his mobile rang.

"He's on his way Kiloboy," said the fourth 'hood', who had been stationed in the bushes at the junction to keep watch on the barrier for the Land Rover's return.

"It dark now but ee definitely di same Land Rover dat gone in and deh no one else commin' out behind dem, needah."

"Okay, good, Juni," said Kiloboy.

"We'll pick you up once the job is done and we head back down the road. Mek sure you stay outta site in dem bushes, got it?" he barked down the phone, hanging up.

Juni, whose real name was Kenrick Rogers Junior, was not enjoying the wait. He had had to walk through the sodden grass and mud to get into the cover of the tree line in his expensive flashy trainers, which were now soaking and covered in mud. The rest of his trendy clothes had not fared much better as he had to move into position without a light, so as not to be seen.

He had also not seen the rusty old barbed-wire fence which had sent him sprawling into the mud and crashing into a patch of Pokanoboy palms; the thin cane like stems of which were covered in thousands of long needle like spines.

The barbed wire had torn his shorts and the Pokanoboy spines had left his right hand and forearm looking like a pincushion. His favourite, most gangster-looking baseball cap had gone flying off his head and was now lost in the mud and darkness. To add to his misery the clouds of mosquitoes were savaging any exposed skin, of which there was much.

Juni kept telling himself that the money from this heist would make up for it all. He always got the worst jobs, but then again, he was still 'making his bones' with the gang. At fifteen, he was the youngest and newest member in Kiloboy's crew and only recently had been jumped in. As much as he was suffering, he would remain in his post until they picked him up again. He had seen what happened to people who disobeyed Kiloboy's orders.

"Here he comes!" said Kiloboy working himself into a vicious frame of mind, getting his blood up as he always did before he attacked people.

He reached behind his back, sliding his hand under his loose and baggy vest. Carefully, he drew a pistol out of his waistband. He hated anyone that had more than he did. Rich people, educated people that looked down on him because of the life he had chosen. He knew they all thought they were better than the poor street boy that had grown up to be a gangster.

There had been plenty of opportunities and offers for a different life and his mother had tried so hard to steer him down a more positive road through life but, to him, those offers had been boring. They required effort and hard work. That was for suckers and fools. He had chosen another, easier path to fast money; a path that came naturally to him, given his physical strength and a violent temper. People had learned to show him a form of respect now, the type that you get when you use violence and intimidation. The type of respect people have for those they fear.

Kiloboy's motto was 'when I see what I like, I'll take what I want!' and he liked the Land Rover that was fast approaching. He would have to get the driver out of the Land Rover first and then shoot him or else he would have a hole through that brand new windshield and it was worth almost six or seven hundred Belize dollars.

Alex saw the big saloon car pulling out of a side road right in front of him. "Idiot!" thought Alex, stamping his foot down on the brake pedal and skidding to a halt.

Their seat belts took the strain as they were flung forward by the sudden stop. As they rocked back to their upright position they saw the car in front had stopped right across the road, blocking both lanes.

Emil took one look at the three gangsters jumping out of the car and instantly dropped into the foot well.

"BAD GUYS! Mr. Alex! BAD GUYS!" he shouted and hid below the dashboard.

Bodhi's headlights lit up the three men who were moving fast. The leader, pointing a handgun directly at the driver's side of the windshield was yelling, "GET OUT! GET OUT OR I SHOOT!"

Alex instantly got out of the Land Rover, leaving the engine running and the gears in neutral. As soon as he got past the door, he was immediately set upon by the three highwaymen. The bandanas that had earlier been tied around their heads were now tied around the lower halves of their faces, bandit style. They grabbed hold of Alex, punching him savagely; blows raining down on his head and torso, until he dropped to the ground. Several hard kicks followed, knocking the wind out of him.

Although in pain, Alex was still able to think. He realised that because the headlights had been shining into their faces they had not seen Emil. If they had, they would have gone straight for him too.

Alex crawled away from the Land Rover towards the gangster's car to draw the aimed pistol away from the Land Rover and his young friend hiding inside.

The evil trio, now with their backs to Bodhi, strode up to Alex as he began to stand up. Kiloboy pointed the pistol directly at Alex's forehead and there was no mistaking what he was about to do next.

Alex had been in plenty of tight spots before, but he just could not see a way out of this one. Kiloboy's eyes narrowed and the muscles of his forearms twitched as he began to pull the trigger, taking up the slack, the barrel now only a few centimetres away from Alex's head.

Just as Alex thought his last moment on earth had arrived, Bodhi's lights went out. Alex instantly seized the moment, ducking as the gun fired. He dive-rolled to his left, lashing out with his legs as he hit the ground, sweeping Kiloboy off his feet.

Kiloboy fell heavily on top of Alex, winding him. Alex managed to grab his attacker's right arm and redirected the pistol just as it fired again, the muzzle flash burning his left ear, the deafening blast making both his ears ring. They both rolled over and over, until they were almost off the left side of the road. Instinctively, Alex applied a lock onto Kiloboy's wrist as they started scrambling to their feet in a desperate struggle to overpower each other.

Alex saw the other two assailants' shadows in the moonlight; they were still in front of the Land Rover, now moving straight for him.

Bodhi's engine revved in the darkness. She shot forward, knocking into the backs of the two gangsters and launching them through the air. They slammed forward hard onto the side of the saloon car. Howling in pain, they collapsed to the ground and then scrambled left and right to get out of the way of the Land Rover that was still rolling forward.

Alex's right hip made contact with Kiloboy's left hip, allowing him to steal his balance. With a hard tug of his arms and slam of his hips Alex hurled Kiloboy through the air. Alex heard cracks from the gangster's wrist which he still had a tight lock on.

Wrenching the gun from his grip, Alex snatched it away, hurling it as far as he could into the dark forest. As Kiloboy slammed into the ground head first, Alex made a dash for the Land Rover. Bodhi had by now hit the front right side of the saloon and was shunting the gangster's makeshift roadblock out of the way. Bodhi's left wheels were still on the road and her right wheels in the sticky red clay mud of the verge.

Reaching the driver's door, Alex wrenched it open. He felt an iron grip clamp down on his shoulder as the nearest gangster grabbed him. Holding onto the door with his left hand and grabbing the headrest of the front seat with his right, to give him extra balance and power, Alex launched a stomping back kick deep into the villain's solar plexus.

The gangster gasped, staggering backwards as if he had been kicked by a horse, his diaphragm spasming, unable to breathe. Alex quickly noticed that his Land Rover was in first gear and the handbrake was pulled up very slightly, allowing it to trundle forward without stalling.

He jumped in, gunning the engine and stamping down on the accelerator. Wheels spinning, it took off as fast as it could and within a few seconds was a couple of hundred meters away from the attackers.

"Well done Emil, are you okay?" Alex looked to his right at the passenger seat.

"EMIL!" he shouted in alarm. But Emil wasn't there!

Turning the lights of the Land Rover on again, Alex heard a banging on the roof and then saw a face, upside down looking in at him through the passenger window.

"Right here Mr. Alex!" he said, a huge smile across his face.

Alex stopped the Land Rover and Emil swung down from the roof rack and through the open window.

"Let's get out of here!" Alex said, looking in his rear view mirror at the attackers' headlights that were receding, but not nearly fast enough for his liking. He accelerated until his foot was flat on the floor.

"That's strange," said Alex, "they should be gaining on us by now, or at least keeping up."

"Well," said Emil, rummaging through one of his big shirt pockets and pulling something out, "they are going to have a hard time going anywhere with four slashed tires!"

Emil beamed from ear to ear as he held up his folding pocket knife for Alex to see.

"As soon as they grabbed you I snuck out so I wouldn't be trapped inside," Emil explained. "They were all busy with you."

"Well then why on earth did you get back in, turn the lights off and ram the two other carjackers? They didn't know you were there. You took a huge risk doing that. You saved my life so I am very grateful Emil, but still, you put yourself in extremely serious danger."

"But Mr. Alex, I didn't get back in, I don't know what happened! Suddenly the lights went out and I heard you struggling with the guy with the gun. That's when I snuck round the other side and slashed all the tires. I had just slashed the last one when the Land Rover ran into the back of the two others and then hit their car. As you drove passed me, I managed to grab the ladder on the back and climb up onto the roof rack so I wouldn't get left behind."

"But if you didn't put her into gear and run into those two carjackers, who did?" Alex asked perplexed.

"It couldn't just have happened by itself!" Alex said in astonishment.

"It's a mystery to me too," said Emil, "but however it happened, it saved your life!"

Alex didn't comment. They drove in silence for several minutes, thinking about what had just happened. It was unbelievable, all of it. Like a bad dream with a happy ending, impossible to comprehend.

"A mystery indeed," thought Alex to himself, "there's something strange about this Land Rover. First, the lights came on by themselves at my barn, the night of the attempted robbery. I am also sure I didn't see the Boa Constrictor and yet we stopped just in time, and now this. This was by far the strangest."

Turning to Emil, he said "Okay, I think we are far enough away to slow down and pull over for a minute. I need to call the police in Dangriga and let them know what's happened.

They may even be able to catch them thanks to your handiwork with the tyres. When we give our statements later, perhaps it might be better to leave out the part about the vehicle driving by itself! I still can't believe what happened, you must have somehow bumped the gear stick when you got out or maybe in my haste to get out I didn't put it into neutral properly and only half pulled the hand brake. That's probably it!" Though not convinced he felt better at having some explanation, even if it wasn't a very good one.

"After we make our stop at the police station in Dangriga, we'll press on to Gales Point," said Alex as he turned on the GPS navigation system. He checked the route, distance and most importantly the estimated time of arrival in Dangriga so that he could let the duty officer at the police station know what time to expect them.

Forty eight minutes and sixty two kilometres later, they arrived in Dangriga, gave their statements and were told that several units had been dispatched to the scene immediately after their phone call had been received.

The police were soon busy tracing the car which they had found abandoned. They had also immediately mobilized a unit of soldiers from the Belize Defence Force and were conducting a manhunt as they believed the carjackers were probably still hiding in the jungle. The police were sure that the soldiers would be able to follow their tracks as soon as it got light. This sort of carjacking incident was almost completely unheard of in Belize and the authorities took it extremely seriously. They were quick to allocate plenty of manpower and resources to track down the culprits. The police chief assured Alex that the guilty would swiftly be brought to justice and would feel the full weight of the law.

They left Dangriga late that night and drove passed the main bus station which had long since closed for the night, the last buses having arrived hours before. Alex and Emil didn't notice the car parked outside the bus station with two men sitting inside it in the dark. The two men in the car didn't notice the Land Rover pass right next to them either – they were both sound asleep.

Shortly after they left Dangriga, they arrived at a road junction. The GPS indicated that the Hummingbird Highway which lead directly to the capital city of Belmopan was dead ahead, the turning to the right being the rough dirt road known as the Coastal Road. This is the one they selected as it would take them North, all the way to the small and very picturesque town of Gales Point, located on a thin peninsula of land.

This thin strip of land stretched almost three kilometres into a large inland lagoon that was right on, and had a connection to, the coast. This big body of brackish water was known as Southern Lagoon. Bodhi would easily be able to handle the parts of the rough Coastal Road that were washed out, still under water or had been turned into slick slippery mud ruts by the heavy trucks that used this shortcut which linked the Western Highway to the Southern.

As they drove through the darkness, all three of them were in deep thought, reflecting on the very sobering close call that they had all had. As they passed the turnoff to the coastal village of Mullins River, Alex broke the silence. Rubbing the bruises and bumps on his head and face from the earlier assault, he concentrated on the plan for the next few days.

"Right Emil, let's talk about the plan for tomorrow," Alex said to Emil.

"We are going to spend a couple of days in Gales Point sorting out our base camp equipment and supplies and I also want to go through some training with you. You will need to know how all the gear works and the Standard Operating Procedures, or S.O.P.'s, we will be using once we get out into the field and we are on our own. Safety procedures, health and hygiene drills, navigation and route planning; radio procedures, communications and emergency procedures in case one of us has an accident. You are going to learn the whole works, my young friend! A crash course in expedition skills. There is a lot for you to learn, but I think you'll enjoy it. I call it 'Jungle Training'."

"I'm looking forward to it very much Mr. Alex!" said Emil excitedly. "I am so glad we are okay and that we still have everything."

"Too right my young friend, we were very lucky."

"Mr. Alex, how come you are so young but you know so much about the jungle and safety and all that."

"Well, it's a long story but this is not my first time in the jungle, or in Belize for that matter......" For the next few kilometres Alex filled Emil in on his background. Emil stared goggle eyed but exhilarated that someone so young but so experienced was his leader. It gave him huge confidence.

"Great! It looks like we have arrived," said Alex, seeing the sign for Gales Point. "I've booked us two rooms at a family run lodge near the end of the spit."

"I have heard about Gales Point!" said Emil excitedly. "This is where you can see Manatee! I haven't been to this part of the country before."

"Quite right!" said Alex.

"We'll take the canoe off the roof rack and go for a paddle tomorrow!" he said pulling into the sandy drive of the small lodge.

It wasn't long before they had settled in, eaten a very late dinner and crashed out in their beds, both quickly falling into a deep sleep. Now that the adrenaline from their earlier fight or flight reaction had worn off, it had left them both completely exhausted.

Outside, Bodhi was facing the lagoon, parked with her back bumper opposite the main entrance to the lodge. The moonlight sparkled on the water as tarpon and other big fish occasionally splashed the silvery surface. She did not need sleep; she would meditate on the teachings of Andrasta and Mezaferus and stand guard through the night, although the only feelings she picked up on now were peaceful and harmonious. Bodhi could sense the multitude of creatures on the land and in the water all around her, going about their lives, in balance.

Chapter Eleven

The Apprentice

Alex had woken up at dawn, at the usual time, but not in the usual manner. This morning he had woken up with a sudden jolt.

His eyes had sprung open to see the rising sun's rays lighting up the room. Horizontal orange bands shone between the gaps of the louvers of wooden plank shutters covering the window. He had left the shutters half open and a fresh easterly coastal breeze had been blowing across the lagoon all night. This, combined with the downdraft from his ceiling fan had allowed him to have a very deep sleep, in spite of the heat and humidity.

He had had a very strange dream, which was already becoming hazy and difficult to remember. He tried. In it, he recalled that his Land Rover had been trying to tell him something, but he could not remember anything it had said, or even if he had heard it properly. The Land Rover had become shrouded in a hazy white smoke; a strange but pleasant smelling incense.

A bronze skinned, muscular man had appeared. He had been standing on top of the roof rack. Alex had seen that he was dressed in the garb of the ancient Maya. The strange figure had had the appearance of a lord, or perhaps even a king. The dream was slowly coming back to him now. He closed his eyes and saw it all again in his mind's eye.

The Maya noble, standing on top of the Land Rover, had been dressed in jaguar skins. Green jade necklaces hung around his neck and he wore a splendid headdress made of coloured stones and long dazzling feathers. The part of the headdress surrounding his cheeks and forehead had been shaped to represent a fusion of animal faces: a jaguar's head morphed with an eagle's beak and a bat's face glaring out above them. The man held a war club in one hand and a sceptre denoting his high status in the other.

Chanting and dancing, he sang a strange and eerie song. The sound of his voice had an urgency about it as he sang and called out to Alex. His arms swung up to the star studded sky as his body span and danced, pointing to the constellation of the Big Dipper and the Pole Star.

His rhythmic chanting became louder and more insistent. His teeth were filed down to points. His ear lobes were stretched over big jade ear spools and his forehead was flat and misshapen. Bizarre looking tattoos covered his face and body and sharp white bone ornaments pierced his nose and lips. The regal figure beckoned Alex to follow him. Alex was drawn to the apparition's power. He could feel it pulling him. The ancient spirit from a bygone era, who had returned from the mists of time, was calling him.

Alex had got into the Land Rover which had still been trying to tell him something. They floated up into the air and flew through the darkness, following the running warrior king who led the way. In the dark distance, a huge, magnificent Maya temple appeared. It was covered in brightly coloured paintings and carvings; most of the temple was a deep red colour.

From far away, Alex had seen two figures high up on a large stone platform near the top of the main temple pyramid.

A tall standing figure had loomed menacingly over the other that was lying limp on the floor at its feet.

The warrior king had suddenly changed shape and become a jaguar. It bounded on, running in front of Alex who had suddenly found himself sitting on top of the bonnet of the Land Rover which was still flying along behind the big supernatural cat. As they drifted nearer, to his horror, he recognised the figure lying slumped on the platform. It was Emil!

A sinister looking man towered over Emil's unconscious body. The dark figure threw his head back, a maniacal laugh erupting from his sneering mouth and he held a large obsidian dagger in his hand. The man turned his evil scowling face and Alex saw that he had two different coloured eyes. One was ice blue, the other dark brown, almost black.

The running jaguar leapt in a giant arc, right over the temple and disappeared. Frantically, Alex had willed the Land Rover to close the gap so that he could reach Emil and save him from the figure that was now bending down slowly and raising the dagger over Emil's chest. The Land Rover had slowed to a stop, just out of reach.

It floated in the darkness, bobbing and rocking as Alex shifted his weight further and further forward reaching out to Emil. But a fathomless abyss separated Alex and the Land Rover from the Temple. Alex remembered the last fading images of the dream; he had stood up on the bonnet and jumped wildly into the void, trying to cross the gap. He shouted and yelled, but he made no sound at all. Then he felt the sensation of falling. He was falling, falling, falling, into blackness.

That was when he had woken up with a bang and a jolt. He felt as if he had actually fallen back onto his bed from a height, the sensation had been so realistic.

"Wow," thought Alex, "Intense! Haven't had one of those for a while!"

He thought about the strange dream which he was sure he had as a result of the nearly deadly encounter the previous evening. For years he had had a fear of heights and occasionally a bout of vertigo would still leave him gripped and frozen, holding onto whatever was nearest so tightly his knuckles would turn white. When the gangsters attacked the previous night he had been extremely concerned for Emil's as well as his own safety and thinking about how it could have all ended sent a cold chill up his spine, goosebumps appearing on his arms. Fear of heights, carjackers, the responsibility he had for Emil, sleeping in a strange bed, and the heat. He reconciled the strange dream to a combination of all of the aforementioned.

Alex rolled out of bed and looked out through the mosquito netting covering the window. The netting had its own covering of bloodthirsty mosquitoes looking back at him in hungry frustration. They whined away like a tiny, angry mob trying to break through, sensing the warm blood so close and yet out of their reach.

His eyes changed focus from near to far as he looked from the ravenous parasites to the beautiful Southern Lagoon which stretched way off into the distance vague memories of being here with his parents years ago floated hazily in his mind. He felt stiff and sore from the punches and kicks received in his fight for survival the night before. Bruises and lumps had appeared on his head and body overnight.

It already seemed like a crazy distant dream, and he could hardly believe how lucky he was to be able to see this new day, alive and relatively unharmed.

As the police had said the previous night, this sort of thing almost never happens in this small and very friendly country. It left Alex wondering if it had, in fact, been a random attack. He couldn't shake the feeling that they had been waiting specifically for him. He thought about the ambush as he put on his running shorts, vest and trainers.

After doing his morning warm-up exercises which included his own version of yoga and other warm-up stretches, he went outside. He walked along the veranda to Emil's room in order to wake him up. Looking at his Casio Pathfinder watch he saw it was 05:43 hrs. He would have liked to let Emil lie in, but expedition work always started at dawn and he would have to get used to that.

Alex heard footfalls running on the wooden veranda behind him and he was surprised by Emil's cheerful voice.

"Good morning Alex! Did you sleep well?" Emil said catching up to him.

"I'm surprised to see you up and ready for action so early Emil, good morning! Good to see you, especially after last night's drama! How are feeling you this morning?" Alex asked, smiling at his resilient companion, thinking how calm and quick thinking Emil had been during the highway hold up, and how quickly he had bounced back to his cheerful, helpful self.

"I feel great! We have to get up very early in our village up North too, usually just before sunrise," Emil said looking over the balcony railing at two stray dogs that were sharing some scraps from a polystyrene food container that had fallen off the top of a nearby garbage bin.

"I have to do a lot of work in our Milpa farm before I go to school, and my mother found a job in Belize City which is a long way to travel every day. She has to get the very first bus. Anyway, it gets so hot so quickly you have to get up early to have the cool. We all get up at the same time, put on some music and get ready together – the whole family. Actually, the whole village does the same so it's full of noise and music. It's the same as all the cockerels, wild birds and the parrots do every morning too! Big noise!"

"Aha! A dawn chorus to welcome the sun! Great!" said Alex with a chuckle.

"Well, seeing as you're up and raring to go already, I want you to read the expedition documents on my laptop while I go for a run. They will give you the outline of the projects we will be doing and give you some background information. Wait here for a minute."

Alex quickly popped back to his room, retrieved the SIM card from its hiding place in his money belt and grabbed his laptop. He returned to Emil, handing it all over to him and explaining which documents he should read first. He also gave him some brief instructions on operating his computer.

"Right, I'm off! See you in about fifty minutes," said Alex.

"Have a good run!" said Emil, grinning.

After spraying himself all over with his bug repellent, Alex trotted down the short flight of steps and began his morning jog.

The six kilometre run up and down the peninsula cleared Alex's mind and worked up his appetite. He showered, changed into his jungle clothes and boots, packed a large rucksack with several items and then met Emil in the restaurant as planned. They sat at a table that had a nice view of the lagoon.

"I read most of what you told me to. Now I know what the second thing is that you think might be hidden in the temple! Do you really think it's true that King Nanchancaan's death mask is made of a single piece of jade and hidden in the tomb?" said Emil lowering his voice to an excited whisper.

"Only time will tell, Emil. What I do know is that if it is true then it would be the only mask of its kind ever found. It would be absolutely priceless. If the Belizean government put it on display in a museum, visitors would come from all over the world to visit your country just to see it. Jade is the ninth hardest substance known to man, so to carve an entire mask out of one piece that long ago would have been a seemingly impossible task. We use diamond tipped saws and grinders to cut it these days and the Maya certainly didn't have those," Alex stated, continuing, "That's why it is so important to gather all the evidence we can to prove that it really is King

117

Nanchancaan's temple. I am hoping we will find conclusive proof. Perhaps paintings or carvings or glyphs that clearly show his name and dates that will hopefully correspond to when we know he ruled."

Alex thought back to his dream and wished they were able to go directly to the temple site, but they had agreed to wait for Emil's grandfather and, what's more, all the other conservation projects were en route. It made logical sense to do them in sequence on the drive north. Besides, what was the rush – even if they proved it was King Nanchancaan's temple it would still take many months for the authorities to organise a full scale archaeological excavation of the site. Still, there was something in the back of his mind nagging him about the mysterious temple hidden in the jungles of North Western Belize.

When breakfast arrived it was more like a feast than a meal and they both ate hungrily. Warm coconut tarts, Johnny cakes, fried jacks, frijoles which are also known as refried beans, and scrambled eggs. It was all homemade, fresh and served with a big warm smile from Ms. Prudence, the matronly Garifuna lady who owned the lodge.

"Good mornin', and ow are you all dis mornin'?" she asked setting down yet another tray, this one laden with jam, butter, honey, fresh pineapple and papaya.

Alex, Emil and the other guests washed the delicious breakfast down with Belizean coffee and fresh orange juice.

"We're okay now, thanks! That really hit the spot!" Alex said patting his stomach.

Alex turned to Emil and said, "Last night when we got into the hotel I phoned the Professor on my satellite phone and told him what happened. He was obviously very shocked and upset but also very relieved that we are okay. I then sent him a full Incident Report with every detail of what happened via email from my laptop. The Land Rover has its own satellite uplink for communication; internet, burst data transmission and the like. The reason I'm telling you all this, Emil, is that we'll be sending what is called Situation Reports, or SITREP's for short, back to the Professor at set times that we have both agreed on. Sometimes it will be every day, sometimes twice a day, sometimes only every few days. It all depends on where we are, what is happening and what we have arranged."

Emil sat quietly, listening intently, taking in every word.

"SITREPS are very important, Emil. If we fail to give a SITREP at the appointed time it will mean that we have a problem. The Professor would then immediately try and make contact with us to find out what had happened; if he is not able to contact us he would initiate a search and rescue effort. Sometimes, there is no news to report or receive but it is still vital to do the SITREP so that the Professor knows that we are okay. We will be in very remote areas all by ourselves and this is one of our lifelines."

Alex stood up and hoisted the large rucksack onto his back.

"Follow me Emil, I have asked Ms Prudence to allow us to use that big screened-in area under the red metal roof over there. They sometimes use it for parties because it has a large clear floor and roof and it's dry and free of mud and bugs. It will make a great place to spread out all the gear I have in the rucksack and practice skills like first aid. Your jungle training starts right now! Get ready to learn expedition skills!"

They walked down the red cement path towards the screened structure in the early morning sun, which was already blisteringly hot, breathing the thick steamy air. Both of them were already dripping with sweat. Alex wiped his forehead with the long cotton sweat rag he had around his neck. He took a few seconds to gaze out at the views over the huge lagoon; they were stunning.

Alex and Emil both sat on the clean smooth concrete floor, cross legged, facing each other. Alex opened the backpack and pulled out numerous items, arranging them around him in a certain order.

He picked up one of the items and handed it to Emil. It was a fairly thick, but practical sized book that was bound with a waterproof cover and printed on waterproof paper.

"What I am going to tell you today, Emil, was taught to me by my dad. He was a great teacher and I am going to do my best to pass on all I can to you. This is the first ARACHNIS expedition and I am determined to make Grand… I mean, the Professor, proud."

Emil stared back at Alex. "You mean the Professor is your grandfather?" he asked quietly.

"Yes Emil," said Alex. "I left that out of my story earlier to you yesterday. I thought it wasn't important, but now you know. I have a very close relationship to my grandfather, same as you have with yours. This expedition is the start of the rest of my life walking in the footsteps of my grandfather and my father. It is very important for me. And thank you Emil for being part of it."

Wiping a tear from his eye Alex arranged his equipment and started the lesson.

"This is your very own 'Jungle Aide Memoire' Emil. That's a fancy way of saying reference manual. Everything I'll show you or teach you from now on is in this book. Make sure you always keep it handy so that you can remind yourself of what we have covered and so that you can revise it now and again. After I leave, it will come in very handy when you continue your work for ARACHNIS here in Belize," Alex said as he handed Emil the manual.

Emil took the manual, opening it with excitement and read down the List of Contents.

"Wow! Thanks! I'll look after it. Thank you very much!"

"My pleasure! It contains the distilled wisdom of countless people who have, through trial and error, blood, sweat and tears, found the best, safest and most efficient way to live, work and operate in remote and extremely challenging environments. It also contains specific information about fauna, flora, survival and expedition techniques that work here in Belize which was written by my parents. Right, next is this," said Alex reaching for a wide webbing belt that had several pouches strung along it.

Emil noticed that it was similar to the one Alex had on, and had been wearing since they met. He had even worn it on his run.

"This is your jungle belt pack. The pouches contain all the essential pieces of equipment you need to make it easier for you to live in the jungle, especially in an emergency. If you should ever lose or get separated from your main backpack, myself or the Land Rover you would still have the basics to keep going. It contains all the essentials – bug repellent, water purification tablets, navigation equipment, twenty four hours' worth of food and much, much more. You must always wear it or keep it close enough to grab from now on, even, or I should rather say especially, at night too," Alex said, handing the belt over to Emil.

"Your jungle belt pack is your fourth most important piece of equipment, the first being full water bottles, the second being your machete, the third being your personal survival and first aid kits."

Alex picked up and handed Emil two small tins, sealed with waterproof gaffer tape.

"These you will keep in your pockets, so that if you are separated from your jungle belt pack and everything else, you will still have the basic items you need to survive."

Emil looked at the book, the belt pack and all the other equipment which he realized were all going to be given to him and felt honoured. He felt as if he was being initiated into a special group. A member of ARACHNIS, a group dedicated to helping nature and the environment, and now he was truly a part of it.

It reminded him of the time he had finally managed to persuade his grandfather to take him into the jungle and teach him the ways of the Chiclero that he had been learning so much about at school. On his first day, his grandfather had performed a small ceremony and then presented him with his machete and scabbard, a pair of metal tree-climbing ankle spikes, called spilones, and a hollow gourd filled with mashed corn and sugar water, the Chileros energy drink. The drinking hole at the gourd's top was plugged with a piece of corn cob; a shoulder strap, made from a thin but extremely strong length of Mahawa bark, tied around the middle of it. He had felt the same feeling then and it was exciting.

Alex smiled, looking at Emil's solemn and thoughtful expression.

"For the next two days you'll be learning a lot of theory in this makeshift classroom. We will have plenty of time to practice all the practical skills when we get into the bush, the day after tomorrow. But before we really get into the lessons, I've got a few more pieces of kit to give you. Here is your jungle sleeping unit, jungle boots, unless you prefer to use your rubber boots of course, work gloves, waterproof backpack liner and a few other bits and bobs," Alex said handing the remaining gear to Emil.

"Okay, the first subject for today is first aid. An easy way to remember the priorities you need to check for when you find someone that looks like they need first aid are the letters AABC. It is an acronym for: Area, Airway, Breathing, Circulation, and they are listed in order of importance. Make very sure that the area around the person is safe. Don't go rushing in. Make sure you can approach the person without becoming a casualty yourself. Call out to them, they may just be asleep or resting. If they don't respond then you check their airway. Is it clear of foreign objects?"

So began Emil's introduction to expedition skills and field work. He watched and listened, practised and learned; asking when he wasn't sure and guessing the answers when he thought he knew what they were.

Map reading and navigation, river crossing theory, route planning, how to use a GPS, correct radio procedure, environmental hazards of the jungle, health and hygiene, what to do in emergencies. Lesson after lesson, the hours flew by, Emil absorbing all he could like a sponge, his thirst for knowledge unquenchable and Alex's enthusiasm for passing on that knowledge equally boundless.

Soon, it was time to take a break and go for a paddle in the canoe and a swim. They walked over to Bodhi, stretching their legs.

"I'm really happy to see that you are a fast learner Emil, and it's great that you obviously already have plenty of skills that you have learnt growing up in Belize and going into the jungle with your grandfather. We are going to add to the skills you already have and give you a structured framework for them all," Alex said as he and Emil unstrapped and lifted the Canadian style open canoe off Bodhi's roof rack. Bodhi felt her suspension lift slightly.

Bodhi watched them walk into the shallow water of the lagoon's edge where they hopped into the wide two-seat canoe and started to paddle. As they drew further and further away, Bodhi suddenly felt a pang of an emotion she had not felt before. She realised that she wanted to go with them. She felt left out and the new feeling was one of melancholy. She felt sad.

For a second, she wondered how deep the water was and if she could follow. She realised that she needed some advice, and seeing as there was no conflict involved other than in her own mind, she decided to consult Mezaferus.

No sooner had her decision been made than she heard Mezaferus' deep, comforting voice.

"Bodhi, there is a way you can go with them. Remember what I taught you; if you wish to accompany your two friends, you must meditate on it. Use your desire to be with them to focus your intention. It will be a test of your progress. Let's see how much control you have developed over your mind." He paused for emphasis and then added, "Remember, you can only let certain humans know that you are alive, attempting to follow them would not have been wise. You are still outside the realm of understanding of most people; they would not easily be able to accept you as a conscious being. They could quite easily see you as a threat, something to be feared. Humans often destroy what they fear or can't understand. Eventually, Alex will know, but it would be too much for him to take in all at once. Now is not the time. Imagine his reaction if he had seen you driving into the lake as if by magic. He will need a gradual introduction to you and your unusual abilities. In the meantime, you will come across other, more enlightened, more perceptive humans, who will immediately sense your presence and make themselves known to you. Goodbye for now Bodhi, you are already making a difference in the world of mankind. Invisible wheels have been set in motion."

Bodhi reflected on all Mezaferus had said and the answer was crystal clear. She would meditate on Alex and Emil and join them in spirit. Quickly, Bodhi retreated deep into her subconscious, filling it with thoughts of Alex and Emil and willing her higher self to join them.

She felt her consciousness shift as her mind left her metal chassis. She drifted, disembodied in an opaque cloud which got darker and darker until she felt Alex's presence right next to her. Her surroundings were completely black; Bodhi could not 'see' anything but she was aware of Alex and Emil right beside her. She could hear them talking, but it was muffled.

"I see you are pretty good at paddling too!" said Alex, not that surprised that Emil was totally at home in the canoe.

124

"I've been using canoes in the rivers up in Orange Walk district, where I am from, since I was little!" he answered, continuing, "My dad has a dugout canoe made from a mahogany tree. It's very old but it's still good. It's not as wide as your canoe; we call them doreys here in Belize."

Alex's mind drifted along like the canoe. Subconsciously, his hand reached up towards his neck and he pulled on the cord around it. The small crystal orb popped out of his shirt and Bodhi's senses were suddenly filled with bright daylight, sights and sounds.

Bodhi looked out of the crystal orb and sensed Alex as he paddled absentmindedly, gazing at the fantastic scenery. She saw Emil sitting up at the front, with his back towards them. Bodhi's view was that of a fish looking out of a glass bowl, her vision was rounded at the edges like the view through a wide-angle camera lens.

A smooth gliding motion to their left caught all three's attention. A great blue heron soared gracefully through the air, its long neck stretched out with a slight 'S' shaped bend in it. Slender legs trailed behind, its slim feet and long toes neatly pulled together, dangling underneath it.

"That's more like it! I did it!" thought Bodhi happily.

The big water bird's elegant blue-grey wings hardly moved, soaring over the water and then flapping in great sweeping backstrokes as it slowed and landed on the branches of a dead tree at the water's edge.

Out of the corner of his eye, Alex noticed a big swirling in the water near them.

"Quick, Emil! Over there, lets paddle fast!" he said digging in with his paddle, swinging the canoe hard right, their arms moving swiftly in unison, pulling towards the undulating path of water he had spotted.

"Manatees, Emil! There they are!"

They drew up close to two huge grey shapes that were circling and rolling beneath the translucent green water of the lagoon. They could clearly make out the big faces of these gentle and docile mammals that were looking with curiosity at them with their small calm eyes. Bristly whiskers covered their top lips which, along with their nostrils, were the only parts of their bodies that broke the water's surface in order to breathe. To Alex, they always looked as if they were smiling a soft smile.

"You can see why people sometimes call them sea cows. These two are huge, they must weigh at least four or five hundred kilos each. Did you know that they are related to elephants and spend their whole lives in the water? Either in the sea, estuaries, rivers or inland lagoons like these ones. At rest, they can hold their breath for up to fifteen minutes. They are herbivores, feasting on water grasses, weeds and algae and can eat a tenth of their own weight in a day," Alex said, relaying all the facts he could remember about these wonderful creatures.

"They're great!" said Emil. "This is the closest I've ever been to them."

"Here's an interesting fact for you Emil. Did you know that manatees are the only mammals on earth whose teeth constantly replace themselves throughout their lives? As the ones in the front wear down, they fall out and are replaced by new ones that spring up at the back."

"Wow," said Emil, "I wish mine did that, I would never have to go to the dentist ever again! Think how much money and pain I would save myself!"

Alex laughed, looking at the huge, heavy round grey bodies of the manatees close by. And yet, they moved so gracefully and lightly beneath and around them. They were powered by the smooth, powerful strokes of their large, flat, leathery, paddle shaped tails. To steer themselves, they had two smaller paddle shaped flippers that resembled short flat arms protruding from either side of their body, up near the base of their necks.

"This area is the largest breeding area of the West Indian Manatee in the whole of the Caribbean Basin," Alex said as they paddled on and on.

Bodhi was enveloped by a feeling of immense satisfaction and contentment at being with her companions; watching and listening to them enjoying the simple pleasure of being surrounded by nature.

They eventually made it into the Manatee River. They paddled all the way to its mouth, appropriately named Manatee Bar, which was where its waters joined the Caribbean Sea.

After a swim in the sea and a late lunch on the beach they set back, arriving just before dark. They went to their rooms for a short rest, showered and changed into their evening wear and resumed the lectures and lessons in the screened building. They took a short break for dinner and then resumed the lessons again until they were both too tired to carry on, but had almost completed what Alex wanted to get through that day.

Late that night, they both fell fast asleep to the distant sound of drumming which the Garifuna people, especially at Gales Point, were famous for. The hypnotic pulsing rhythms drifted towards them on the warm Caribbean breeze, accompanied by women's voices singing beautiful harmonies in a soothing language that they could not understand.

The next day followed almost exactly the same pattern, minus the canoe trip. Emil's head was bursting with facts, figures, routines and procedures and, for the time being, had reached saturation point. Before they knew it, it was time to get Bodhi packed and ready for a dawn start the following day. Emil was glad of the break and Alex was very pleased at the amount of theory and information they had covered.

On their final night at Gales Point, Alex let Emil practice giving his first SITREP back to the Professor and he had done very well. Alex also checked his emails on his laptop via the Land Rover's own communications uplink and found one waiting for him from the Chief of Police from Stann Creek district.

The email informed him that a combined search party of BDF soldiers and police had managed to catch two of the three would-be car-jackers in just a few hours. They found them hiding in a mangrove swamp. They were covered in mosquito and sand fly bites and both had some injuries to the backs of their legs which is why they had had trouble getting away.

The search party had lost the trail of another set of footprints and they thought that the third accomplice had escaped, until they picked up a suspicious youth who had been hitchhiking down the highway, trying to get back to Punta Gorda. He was also dressed in trendy city clothes but covered in mud and was obviously the last of the gangster trio. Although he was clearly very young to be involved in something so serious, unlike the other two, he did not, up until now, have a record of arrest.

The email went on to say that they had not found the firearm yet, but it was just a matter of time. They had been questioning the three youths but none of them were talking. The police felt sure that they would get a confession soon and told Alex that they would keep him updated on the investigation.

Alex was just about to shut down when he clicked the Skype icon almost without thinking. He suddenly felt a strong urge to chat – to Jane. He did a search on the Skype name Jane had given him. It came up and he sent a contact request. He added a short message:

"Hi Jane! Yes, it's me – I was hoping you might be online for a quick chat but I guess you're still asleep. I just realized it's just before dawn in the UK. Anyway, drop me a line if you like. It would be nice to hear your news."

Alex quickly shut everything down and sat for a few minutes contemplating the fact that he felt surprisingly disappointed that he would not be able to chat with her.

A split second after he had signed out and eight and a half thousand kilometres away in an otherwise pitch black bedroom, the white blue glow of a mobilephone lit up the face of a sleepy Jane. She saw his status go from green to offline. Her loose hair falling around and over the touch screen, she squinted to focus as she re-read the message, her slender and lightning fast fingers had typed. It read:

"Hey jungle boy! I'm a GIRL, remember! I'm glued to my phone 24/7 you complete dingbat! LOL ;-D So you wake me up and then sign out, huh? Try again sometime! In the meantime I'll think of a way you can make it up to me. Bet you're head to toe in mud, bugs and bites. Send some pics ok? Stay safe."

Alex trudged off to his room feeling quite alone.

On the night of their botched car-jacking, Kiloboy had watched a long line of searchlights coming for them through the darkness. The manhunt stretched wide and he realised that the army was helping the police. That meant he was up against experienced jungle warfare trained soldiers. He had had no choice but to abandon his two injured companions. Their leg muscles had been pounded by the impact of the Land Rover and every step was agony for them.

Kiloboy had left them both with a few words of advice. It was very short and to the point.

"If unu boys say ONE WORD to the damn POLICE, I KILL YOU BOTH, unerstan'?"

They had both nodded sullenly in the dark, watching dejectedly as their leader abandoned them to their fate.

Kiloboy's anger grew into fury as he stumbled through the waist-deep water of the mangrove swamp. He saw a dim light of a small riverside shack and made his way to it. Stealing a small dorey that was tied to the rickety jetty, he made off. He paddled as fast as he could with his good arm. A small dog, that was chained up outside, had barked frantically, straining to break free and attack the thief.

Kiloboy made a vow to himself. He would take revenge on that boy, he owed him – big time – his wrist throbbed so badly he thought it was broken, or at least badly strained, and he had a gash on his forehead.

"That boy got some fancy tricks alright, but nothing a bullet between the eyes won't take care of. I gwanna blow his head off!" he fumed.

If only those idiots he had for a crew had acted faster. What had happened? He still couldn't understand it. The guy had to have had someone else in the Land Rover with him, but who? It didn't matter. They would both be top of his list now. He would need another gun, and he would have some explaining to do to Gordo.

News travelled fast and he was bound to have heard about the failed attempt and the abandoned car. He started thinking up plausible lies to tell the fat man. He had always been good at blending half-truths to sell his lies. He was a master liar.

Gordo had indeed heard, and he was purple with fury, swallowing antacid tablets like candy to fight the bile and heartburn raging like a furnace inside his huge stomach. The second crew had reported that the Land Rover had never shown up at the bus station in Dangriga and although they hadn't seen it, they had heard that it had been at the police station there later that night.

Gordo's lookouts in Belmopan and Le Democracia villages had not seen it pass by yet either. Those were the only two routes it could take to get to the Western and Northern highways. At this moment he had two teams out looking for it near Maya Centre where Kiloboy's car had been found abandoned by the police.

What had Kiloboy been up to? A double cross no doubt, but what had happened? And where was Kiloboy now? Did he have the boy and his Land Rover? What if he had hurt the boy, or worse? What if he could no longer lead them to what TreeWays, his boss, was looking for? It was a disaster. He would only find out when he could get to speak to Kiloboy's crew who were, at this moment in time, locked up in the Dangriga police station.

He made a call to his boss who he had known all his life only as TreeWays, a street name he had earned in his younger days by getting a reputation as a street brawler who would only hit you three ways – hard, fast and continually.

TreeWays, in turn, had to make an extremely unpleasant call to a certain, particularly nasty man in London who when hearing about the fiasco had a very short reply:

"SHUT IT! If you want something done properly you have to do it yourself! I'M COMING OVER THERE!"

Chapter Twelve

Hide and Seek

After leaving Gales Point, Alex drove Bodhi up the Coastal Road for an hour or so and then, following his GPS navigation, turned right, down an unmarked sandy track into an area known as the Jaguar Corridor Wildlife Sanctuary. This was part of a larger conservation area called the Central Belize Corridor.

It had recently been established by the Belizean Government to act as a corridor to enable all wildlife, but especially jaguars, to cross the different habitats. The creation of this corridor would ensure the continued free movement of animals from one area of the country to another into the future, just as they had been doing for thousands of years before roads, fences or buildings existed.

This wildlife corridor was absolutely vital for the long-term sustainability and survival of these beautiful spotted cats and many other species as well.

Bodhi bumped and rolled through the open savannah which was composed of a vast expanse of lowland areas covered in sedges and grasses. The white sandy road often became soft with thick water-logged mud. She meandered between swampy marshes as Alex carefully navigated along the boggy, sodden track scanning the flooded areas on either side of them for any signs of animals.

Caribbean pine trees and clumps of savannah palmettos dotted the otherwise flat savannah grasslands. Sunlight sparkled and flashed all over it, reflecting off the water which covered most of its surface.

In the distance, a formation of karst limestone hills rose out of the flat lands, a long chain of emerald green, jungle covered 'islands'. They crossed many fast flowing streams and, sometimes, the water got almost as high as the bonnet. Alex had to use Bodhi's winches, slings, and sand anchors to make it through the deep ruts and thick, sticky mud.

At last, Bodhi felt truly in her element. Every design feature on her was purpose built for exactly this sort of journey. She felt a wonderful sense of purpose. This was who she was. This was her world, in the midst of nature. She could cope with the worst driving conditions and still keep going in order that her passengers would safely arrive at their destination and achieve their objective.

The effort of winching, digging and pushing Bodhi deeper and deeper into this remote area would eventually be rewarded with plenty of wildlife sightings. Alex and Emil were now the only two people for many kilometres in any direction. They spotted a herd of white collared peccary rooting around the base of a hill. These animals looked very similar to pigs or miniature wild boar. Later, several whitetail deer broke cover from a small copse and ran, bounding and springing through the watery grasses. Multitudes of different birds were visible in all directions.

On several occasions, they drove close by freshwater crocodiles lying on the edges of the swamps while turtles sunned themselves on trunks of dead trees that had fallen and were now partially submerged in the flooded marsh pans.

Eventually, they came across something that always got Alex's adrenaline going, fresh jaguar tracks, and a few miles further on they found puma tracks too. There were no fences here: no gates. The big cats could be anywhere, perhaps hiding in a thicket of palmettos right next to them. Alex fervently hoped so. He would love to see one up close. Very few people actually got to see a wild jaguar, or a puma for that matter, in its natural environment.

Emil was having a blast helping Alex with the winches and straps whenever they needed to get through a particularly swampy area that offered no traction. Alex was having an equally fun time explaining how to do it properly. How far to wind out the winch cable, what angles the straps needed to be set at and how to place the mud anchors when there were no trees to strap on to. They were completely covered in mud, Bodhi most of all.

Alex would never have dreamt of attempting this journey in any other vehicle. He knew, and trusted in the ability of his Land Rover and its ability to 'self rescue' when crossing this type of terrain. He silently thanked his grandfather for sending him on the Land Rover Experience and off road driving courses as well as the patient Land Rover instructors, many of whom had known his parents, and who had passed down their unique and invaluable knowledge to him.

By mid-afternoon they finally arrived at the nearest big jungle covered hill. Alex planned to drive half way up it, along an old logging road he had seen marked on his map. Driving up it proved to be no joke though, as Emil had to lead the way on foot, swinging his machete to clear most of the deadfall and vines which were clogging the road with thorn covered jumbles of tangled vegetation. Many years had passed since the road had been used and it was now completely overgrown and blocked.

It was hot and hard work but Emil was no stranger to that, having grown up on a small farm. Stepping carefully in his new jungle boots and keeping a sharp lookout for poisonous snakes and hornet's nests, he used his razor-sharp machete expertly. Wielding it like a lightsabre, he created a tunnel big enough for Alex to drive Bodhi through. Alex, watching through the windshield, was impressed at Emil's skill with the blade which was almost a metre long.

An hour or so later they crossed a small freshwater spring that gurgled out from the side of the hill. Alex stopped, pulling up the handbrake and turning off the ignition.

Leaning out the driver's window he shouted to Emil, "This looks perfect, we'll make camp here!"

Easy access to good, fast flowing water made it an ideal spot to set up their base camp. It was also high enough so as not to flood in heavy rains.

Finding a level flat area, on top of a tree covered rocky outcrop that overlooked the savannah below, they got to work. They unpacked their jungle sleeping units from their backpacks. First, they each cleared an area between two trees and erected a lightweight, rectangular nylon tarpaulin, called a basha sheet, at about head height. They stretched the basha out until it was taut, with a slight pitch down the long sides, creating a roof shape so that rain could easily run off it. They secured it to the trees and surrounding vegetation using lengths of paracord attached to metal eyelets in each of the corners and at several points along the edges.

Next they strung their hammocks directly underneath the basha sheet and between the two main support trees. Finally, they hung their mosquito nets between the basha and the hammock, making sure there would be plenty of length to tuck the mosquito net into the hammock. The jungle sleeping units effectively created a bug proof, waterproof cocoon to sleep in. The hammocks were strung a good metre off the ground which would not only keep them far away from the wet mud but also out of the reach of snakes, tarantulas, scorpions, ants or any other hazardous wildlife that may live in the surrounding area. They also set up another, bigger tarpaulin in order to provide shelter over two camp chairs and a folding table.

"This will serve the dual purpose of work area and dining table!" said Alex.

Almost as soon as they had finished setting everything up, dark grey clouds gathered and it began to rain heavily. The sudden tropical downpour battered down on the tarpaulins, a deluge of huge drops giving the savannah far below the appearance of a watery blur in need of windshield wipers.

The jungle surrounding them and their base camp began to steam as white mist rose up through the canopy. Alex and Emil beat a hasty retreat under the big blue tarpaulin and sat at their table, talking loudly over the noise of the rain pelting the plastic sheeting. They discussed the three projects they would be working on here before going in search of the lost temple.

In the twilight of the early evening, Alex lit a hurricane lamp and laid out maps and documents on the table. He started by explaining the general importance of conservation work globally and then focused on Belize and how it fitted into the overall picture of conservation in Central America. Then he explained why the area they were in now was so important.

"So you see Emil, this place is the only corridor left that allows a connection between the habitats in the south to connect with those in the north and west. The jaguar is a great example of why these wildlife corridors are so important. Jaguars can cover huge distances in a day; they have very large territories, especially the males. They need to be able to move freely, and young jaguars need to be able to roam far and wide and find their own territories. This is what keeps their population healthy and strong. It's the same for all animals," said Alex.

Emil's interest was fired up and he asked dozens of questions which Alex was only too happy to answer in detail. They talked long into the night, until eventually the rain stopped.

Thousands of miles away, in a central London office, a discussion of another kind was taking place. Silus was speaking to a distinguished looking elderly man who sat behind a large desk. He wore a very expensive, tailor made Saville Row suit. His short grey hair was immaculately styled, his watchful grey eyes set into a hard face with chiselled features. His lips were thin and stiff.

"Yeah, it's a mess, I'll have to get down there and sort it out myself Dr. Planchard," said the man with the strange eyes as he slugged a mouthful of fiery whisky from a fine crystal tumbler.

He brought a cigarette up to his mouth and lit it.

"The guys I'm using need stronger motivation, the kind of leadership which I can provide. So far, it's been a bloody disaster from the get go, and we both want this venture to succeed. They're also not familiar with this type of job. It requires some patience and subtlety. They seem to be much more your standard 'Thuggery, Muggery, Theft and Violence' type hoodlums," he explained taking a drag of the acrid stinking cigarette.

Breathing out smoke he continued, "They're not taking the job as seriously as they should be. I guess it's to be expected. They've got no idea what the prize is really worth. Of course, I can't let them know either or they'd try and cut us out and go after it themselves. Not that they would have a clue who to sell that sort of treasure to for what it's actually worth. As far as they're concerned, I'm just a rich lad who wants to get hold of some Maya artefacts to add to my vault collections or sell. They're used to that kind of deal – that's why I'm using them."

"Very well, Silus, I trust your judgment on this and you haven't failed me … yet. It's why I always employ you and your special talents to get my dirty work done. I know you enjoy getting your hands dirty," Dr. Planchard replied in his well-educated accent as he leaned back in his very expensive, ergonomically designed leather armchair.

"There is one thing though," said Silus grinning. "Unlike my new associates in Central America, I'm very well aware of the value of the unique treasures that I'll be getting for you. I hear whispers on the wind of upward of one hundred million pounds being offered for the mask alone. My black market contacts tell me the old Maya books are apparently worth much, much more. I do like to get my hands dirty, you're right, but the dirtier they get, the bigger my percentage needs to be. When I go down there, a lot of people will see my face. I will have a lot of 'cleaning up' to do, if you get my meaning, and a lot of loose ends to tie up. Not to mention getting the treasures out of their country and into ours, past the customs agents. It won't be easy, a lot's changed in the world since the days of Lord Elgin.".

"What are you getting at?" said Dr. Planchard.

"We need to renegotiate my cut," came the reply.

"Always the businessman, Silus! What adjustment would you suggest? How much more do you want?" Dr. Planchard asked slowly, looking Silus in his unnerving eyes.

"No, no, Doctor. I believe that he who speaks first loses! Make me a suitable offer," he said smiling with all the warmth of a deadly reptile.

"Fair enough. Let's not beat around the bush. Big risks for a big return. I'll pay you ten million pounds, five up front before you go and five upon the successful completion of the task. I define that to mean the safe delivery of the mask and Maya codices directly into my hands from yours. That's a five hundred percent increase on our original deal."

"Done," said Silus stubbing out his cigarette in the solid silver ashtray on the desk and downing the remaining whisky in his glass.

"I'll leave as soon as the first half of the money arrives in my account" he said.

Silus left the office with a warm and greedy glow filling his entire evil body. He had known that Dr. Planchard wanted the artefacts badly, but what he had not known, until a few moments ago, was just how badly.

Ten million, just like that. No haggling, no bartering. Silus pondered his decision.

"I shouldn't have agreed so quickly, probably could've got more! Damn it!" he thought to himself.

"Still, didn't want him to change his mind. Ten MILLION! For some old Maya books and a stupid stone mask. Planchard will sell them for a hundred times that to some super rich idiots, just so they can hide it in their super private safes and gloat over it. They'll probably show them off to their super rich, idiot friends. Unimaginable amounts of money for some dusty old relics. What a bunch of super morons! I love it!" he thought as his driver opened the door to the Bentley.

Back in the Savannah, Alex and Emil were very busy. They gathered data on all the old Caribbean pine tree stumps they could find from the trees that had been cut down over the years, measuring the height and width so that they could estimate how tall the trees had once been. They determined the rough age of the trees by the number of growth rings. They were able to count these rings and make records of them by making rubbings with pencil and paper or by boring out core samples and taking digital photographs.

Once, a few decades earlier, this entire savannah had had a very healthy covering of pines which provided nesting habitat for the now endangered yellow headed parrot. In a mere twenty years, over ninety percent of the world's yellow headed parrot population had either been killed or captured and sold. They would be condemned to a life-sentence in a cage; just for the amusement of people who found this bird's ability to mimic human speech and other sounds entertaining.

Often, the whole tree would be cut down in order to kill the parents and steal the baby chicks from the nest, deep in the tree trunk.

It was a terrible fate indeed for a wild bird that usually mated for life, was naturally playful and gregarious and could live for up to fifty years. Many people that kept these birds as pets had no idea that they needed much more care, company, attention and stimulation than your average family dog. Very often they were left forgotten, hanging in a small cage, alone on a wall or stuck out on a balcony in some grey apartment building in a concrete city.

The data that Alex and Emil were collecting would help determine whether or not it would be possible to reforest this pine savannah with pine trees once again. Doing so would, in time, recreate a habitat in which scientists could re-establish colonies of the Yellow Headed parrots that used to abound in this area.

"Some friends of mine have yellow heads as pets," said Emil thoughtfully.

He now knew a lot more about the birds that he had barely noticed growing up and now viewed them differently, with more respect. Emil suddenly found himself filled with indignation.

"Parrots weren't created for entertaining humans," he said with passion.

"Well said my friend!" said Alex. "When you get back home you can teach your friends about parrots. Perhaps they won't take any more from the wild, and maybe they'll give the ones they already have a better life. Maybe, they'll entertain the parrots for a change!"

He laughed to lighten Emil's mood but he appreciated Emil's new found awareness of the plight of these feathered friends.

One of their tasks was to scout for locations on the tops of the hills that would make good sites to build lookout towers for forest rangers. It was a fairly simple, but very important project. Once built, these towers would enable scientists and rangers to monitor wildlife and spot fires in the savannah, which helped the fire-fighters respond more quickly. The savannah fires sometimes occurred naturally, but more often than not, were set by poachers.

Poachers would regularly set fire to the savannah in order to hunt the deer. The deer would come out at night to eat the new green shoots that sprang up after the blaze. The poachers would be waiting eagerly with spotlights and rifles.

Hunters and farmers usually set these fires in the dry season and they were incredibly destructive. At that time of year, the harder, drier ground allowed the poacher's vehicles easier access to the more remote areas, without getting stuck. Unfortunately, the dry season was when the birds usually had chicks in their nests. Many nesting sites had been incinerated – including several sites used by the enormous jabiru stork.

Standing almost one and a half meters high, the jabiru stork is the tallest flying bird in Central and South America. Its body is mostly white, its featherless head is black, and it has a large red expandable pouch at the base of its neck. Its enormous beak, about thirty centimetres long and its wingspan, almost an incredible three metres; second only to the mighty Condor in the Andes.

Alex and Emil criss-crossed the wet savannah in Bodhi, scouting hilltop after hilltop, recording the positions of ideal observation tower placements on their GPS while looking for jabiru nesting sites, of which they only found two. Emil loved this project; he was well practised at moving through the jungle looking for chicle trees, and this was similar but more exciting. The challenge now was to find the best spots on top of the hills, which also had the best views without having to cut down any trees. He also enjoyed working with the GPS and plotting the information onto the maps.

While they were exploring the hills, they came across plenty of caves in the limestone hills which they also recorded the locations of to report to the Belizean Ministry of Natural Resources. Alex had read that these caves were considered by the ancient Maya to be openings and entrances into their mythological underworld which they called Xibalba, pronounced Sheebulbah.

Often, the Maya would perform sacred rituals and blood sacrifices deep underground to ensure plentiful rains and bountiful crops. Every now and then, a truly terrible drought would hit the land, and when this happened, perhaps out of sheer desperation, like many other cultures at that time, the Maya would sometimes resort to performing human sacrifices in these pitch black underground caverns. As a result, many ancient artefacts were still regularly discovered inside them by archaeologists.

Alex and Emil sheltered in the entrances of several of these caves during heavy rainstorms and had seen pottery shards from broken Maya pots in quite a few of them. There were also more modern manmade vessels in the form of broken white clay tobacco pipes and old hand blown glass bottles that had once contained rum and brandy and which had been left behind by loggers and timber men who had sheltered in the very same caves over a hundred years previously.

Finally, they had covered all the areas and hills that they had been asked to investigate. As was usual at the end of every day of fieldwork they sorted out all their equipment, washed the dirt and sweat off themselves and their clothes next to the spring, and treated the minor cuts and scratches that had accumulated, removing the odd thorn or tick. They then changed out of their wet jungle clothes into their comfortable 'dry kit' for the evening and had dinner.

Over a dessert of hot tea and oatmeal biscuits they looked at all the new markings on the maps and discussed the best routes that would allow them to drive Bodhi and all her high-tech gear as close as possible to the area of King Nanchancaan's Temple site. They would need to do a lot of analysis using the instruments that were installed in Bodhi.

Later that night, sitting on the rock ledge of their base camp, overlooking the savannah, Emil had been scanning the open areas of sedges and grassland with a powerful pair of night vision binoculars. He had watched, fascinated, as a large male puma stalked and then ran down a big whitetail buck. He was amazed at the power and grace of the long sleek feline as its body bounded in powerful smooth strides, gaining rapidly on the deer that veered left and right, making lightning fast changes of direction in its attempt to evade the big red-brown cat.

With a mighty leap the puma sunk its front claws into the hindquarters of the deer, both tumbling to the ground, as the deer lost its balance. The puma, more agile than any human gymnast, regained its balance instantly and clamped its jaws down on the deer's windpipe in a final coup-de-gras.

Alex, meanwhile, sat inside the back of Bodhi, sending all the data, information and photographs to the Belizean Forestry Department, the park rangers at a station in a nearby 'private protected area', and a copy to his grandfather in Wales, together with the nightly SITREP.

This phase of their conservation work was now complete. They would break camp just before dawn and start heading north to the temple.

Alex thought about skyping Jane, but the time difference was once more against him. He'd read her message and had kicked himself for waking her up. Besides, Emil would be in earshot and he was already annoyingly nervous about calling her anyway.

"Best leave it for now. God, I must seem totally desperate!"

He smiled at the warmth he felt about the fact she had given him a nickname.

"Don't read anything into it," Alex admonished himself. "She probably gives all her friends nicknames."

As Alex shut down the communications and internet links he continued the conversation in his head.

"This time Alex, try not to stuff it all up by projecting all your baggage onto her. She's totally hot and gorgeous and she might actually be into you. Perhaps. If she is, then the question is can I let her 'in' to me? Listen to yourself, so deep and heavy and you don't even know her. Get a flippin' grip!" He was left with the thought "jungle boy'. "Why not? That's what I am."

As he stepped out of Bodhi he looked up at the night sky through a gap in the canopy. He noticed the plough, also known as the big dipper, a constellation which always pointed to the Pole Star, indicating true north. He remembered his very strange dream and wondered what it all meant.

Many kilometres to the north, in the large back room of a dirty, downtown bar in the roughest area of Belize City, Silus, TreeWays, Gordo and Kiloboy were all having their first meeting. Juni had been released from jail on bail which his long suffering and totally distraught mother had paid for. He stood guard outside on the street, watching for police or members of rival gangs.

Juni had not told Gordo anything other than that Kiloboy had left him at Maya Centre, knowing that to rat on Kiloboy would mean death, as would letting Gordo know that they had tried to highjack the Land Rover.

After making his getaway, Kiloboy had contacted Gordo by phone and told him that the Land Rover had, in fact, reappeared quickly after all, and they had decided to try and grab the guy and his Land Rover so that they could hand them over to Gordo.

Kiloboy had justified his actions by saying that "Who knows how many more stops and starts the man would make, surely it was better to grab him and make him tell them what Gordo wanted to know. Especially seeing as Gordo's information about the meeting at the bus stop was wrong."

It was a plausible story but Gordo had only half believed Kiloboy and had him beaten up by his bodyguard-enforcers for acting on his own and without Gordo's permission. He would deal with Kiloboy properly later. Right now he would be useful, at least for a while. Gordo had told Kiloboy that his informants in Dangriga had heard that there had been a young Mestizo looking teenager with the man when he had been at the police station.

Kiloboy guessed that it was the same boy they had seen getting into the Land Rover at Maya Centre. But surely that young boy couldn't be the contact? He wondered about it. It would explain the lights going out and the Land Rover ramming his two guys. Well he would be paying them both back soon enough.

The smoke-filled den had a pool table in the middle of it, with dozens of empty beer and stout bottles covering the tables, window sills and floor.

Silus began.

"Right, I'm bloody hot and bloody angry with you lot," he barked, fixing them all with his evil stare, daring any of them to talk back to him.

"I need to find the whereabouts of a certain expedition leader, his Land Rover and his passenger. I don't care if you hate my guts for being here or not. I come dangling a very big carrot and carrying a very large stick," he said mopping his forehead with a white silk handkerchief and swallowing a mouthful of local beer straight from its brown bottle.

"The carrot is this: I will pay you all ten times what we originally agreed. The stick however is this: if you mess this up, or decide to play your own games instead of mine, I will have a hit squad come over here from a neighbouring country and remove your heads. Are we all crystal clear?"

145

TreeWays was a very muscular Creole man who towered above Silus. He nodded but did not look intimidated. In his late thirties, he had a battle scarred face, and in this part of town it was he whom people were deathly afraid of. The Englishman with the strange eyes didn't scare him, but money was money and a deal was a deal – he had his reputation to think about. Gordo and Kiloboy were putting on brave faces, but both Silus and TreeWays had an unnerving, sinister presence which had them spooked. They nodded in unison, taking their lead from TreeWays, their boss, whether they liked it or not.

"Good. Now that we have an agreement, ideas please gentlemen," said Silus, slapping at a blood filled mosquito on his neck.

TreeWays spoke in a deep baritone voice, "Dis maan, dis Alex Steele, my people tell me that 'e spent some time in Gales Point den e lef', headed up the Coastal road towards La Democracia but 'e nevah got there. How come you think that is Mr. Silus?"

"Well he didn't come here with a fully kitted out Land Rover to go sightseeing did he? My guess is he's gone skipping off, wearing a sarong and sandals to hug some trees and knit some yogurt in the flaming jungle somewhere, saving small furry animals!" replied Silus, his voice heavy with sarcasm.

"Exactly correc' Mr. Silus," boomed TreeWays, his powerful muscled arms rippling as he picked up his beer bottle, draining the contents in two swallows.

"An' I have a good idea where someone with his interests would be going in dat area, and how we can find him too, but it gonna cost some money. Helicopter rental don't come cheap. Why did you want us to just follow him so close, why we couldn't jus' grab him when he arrived?" Treeways asked, intrigued by Silus's subtle approach as he was a man who clearly didn't mind ruthless alternatives.

"Well," said Silus choosing his words with care, "first we need the conservation idiot and his sidekick to lead us to where the artefacts that I want are buried. Second, I need the conservation idiot to use his knowledge and equipment to verify that the site where the artefacts are buried is actually the one we think it is. Once the enviro-clown and his assistant have done their work, they'll go home. They're only here to verify that the place is what they think it is, they aren't here to do any digging. They have to leave that to the professional archaeologists. That means, once they're gone it will be several weeks, if not months, before anyone goes back there again, giving me plenty of time to dig it all up in peace and quiet, without any nosey parkers interfering with us.

"The whole plan hinges on no one knowing that I am after the artefacts. If this Alex Steele guy realises then he will contact the local authorities here and they would put police and military guards on to the site," he said wondering if he had already said too much.

"It doesn't really matter," he thought to himself. He would be disposing of everyone in this room once he had what he had come for. He had absolutely no intention of paying any of the men as he certainly wasn't going to leave any witnesses that could identify him. No loose ends with a bonus: free labour, what could be better?

"So, what you are after is still buried somewhere in da big bad bush, an you gonna dig for your Maya artefacts!" said TreeWays laughing.

He continued in a more menacing tone, "If you want to waste your time and ours playing follow da leadah with dis guy I noh care, jus' as long as we get paid – in full, remember you not de only one who can chop heads. I'm sure you think dat what you are digging up is very valuable, but I try selling Maya tings before and dey not worth it, dey jus a real big hassle maan. But hey, it's your money right? Our job is to find him an' follow dis man all de way to where de stuff is buried, without him knowing. Den find out from him if it's de correc' place also without wi mek him know nuthin'. I can organize a crew dat can dig fast if you want me to, when de time comes; because as sure as dollar bills are green, none of us here in dis room are pickin' up no damn shovel on your behalf, straight? You feel me?"

"Agreed," said Silus. "I'll be with you all the way though, once we find him I want us to stick to him like glue."

"No worry maan," said TreeWays, "when we find him we'll be like a tick on a peccary's backside!"

Kiloboy sat in silence, going through the motions. He would bide his time patiently, but he had a 'beef' to settle. For now he would go along with it.

Gordo sat and nodded, playing along too but he didn't like the sound of this. The money would be very good, but he hated anything that involved heaving and humping his portly body anywhere that was not air conditioned. And helicopters – forget it!

"Okay Gentlemen, I think that about concludes things for this evening, we'll meet again first thing in the morning. Enjoy your drinks. They're on me!" said Silus, standing up and throwing a couple of hundred dollar bills on the table.

He couldn't wait to get back to the air conditioned comfort of his hotel room. It was as if he was sitting in a steam room, fully clothed and suffocating.

Alex and Emil finished packing up Bodhi and clearing up their base camp, leaving almost no trace that they had been there except tire tracks and footprints. Alex put his backpack in last. As he shut the back door of the Land Rover, a big black scorpion crept unnoticed out of a fold near one of the backpack's shoulder straps, crawling into the pocket on the back of the driver's seat.

Bodhi felt the creature's presence and decided to introduce herself. She found out that the scorpion's name was Terastus. In return for providing shelter, she made it promise that it would not sting her human passengers. Terastus agreed not to sting them unless he was about to be crushed.

As it got light enough to see without headlamps they made a final sweep of the area to check that it was all in order and then they left. By nine am the pine savannah was far behind them and they had already driven halfway through the dense karst limestone hill range known as the Peccary Hills. Thick, secondary jungle and lowland broadleaf forest surrounded them. The route that they were following on the GPS would eventually lead them to a small Creole community on the banks of the Sibun River where there was a road that would connect them to the Western Highway.

As they drove down a long open stretch of road, Bodhi began to feel the now familiar feeling of danger approaching, but this time it was not from behind or in front, this time it was from above.

"Hey, look!" said Emil, "a helicopter."

Alex stuck his head out of his window and, sure enough, there was a blue and white helicopter flying from right to left. As it was almost out of sight, hovering high above a ridge line, it turned, swooping in an arc and came flying down the road towards them and then buzzed over them. It made another low pass, circling slowly and then returned the way it had come, disappearing as quickly as it had arrived.

"Strange," said Alex as he looked at Emil, both of them overcome with an uneasy feeling.

In a short time they had crossed a very rickety, old wooden bridge over the Sibun River and were driving through the small community towards the Western Highway. Wooden houses built off the ground on heavy wooden posts came into view. Next to them were plantations of cassava, cocoa, banana and plantains and next to those, rows of corn and beans. The patches of crops were surrounded by barbed wire fences to prevent the big white Brahma cattle in the neighbouring fields from eating it.

Thirty kilometres away, the rental helicopter landed on its pad at its base. Silus, TreeWays and Kiloboy leaped out and walked fast to the waiting SUV which Gordo was sitting in, the engine running. They all jumped in and sped off.

"He either gonna go right or lef' when he gets to the junction on da highway. In any case, he eedah gonna pass us or we gonna catch up wi' him quickly."

Silus sat in the front passenger seat, air conditioning blowing in his face. He was starting to feel much better. He felt in control. Kiloboy sat directly behind him, fingering the new semi-automatic pistol he had got that morning through the fabric of his shirt, his wrist still aching and the gash on his forehead covered in a thick scab.

Chapter Thirteen

When The Going Gets Tough

Bodhi sensed danger and the feeling remained with her from the moment they got onto the Western Highway. They took a shortcut along a road called the 'Boom Cut Off' which led directly to the Northern Highway. Passing through village after village, eventually they crossed the New River at a small toll gate bridge before arriving in Orange Walk, the biggest town of the northern district of Belize.

They stopped and had lunch, unaware that they were being watched by Gordo, hidden behind the tinted windows of the powerful SUV. The rest of the gang were hurriedly buying machetes, water bottles, rubber boots, two small tents and other camping supplies. The gangsters would have to follow wherever their quarry went. Gordo was not a happy camper.

After lunch, Alex and his young companion took an hour to drive to Emil's village. They would spend the night at his grandfather's house and continue their journey the next day with him as guide.

As they entered the village, Alex looked out of the windows at the passing buildings. The school, the church and the community centre were built of cement block and brightly painted with corrugated metal sheet roofs. The rest of the houses in the village were made of rough wooden planks that were thatched with palm leaves.

Alex drove as far as he could and parked in the small main square. They then walked between the houses along a narrow path that led up the side of a small hill. A few minutes later, they arrived at a neat wooden house that had two dogs lying on the front step and some chickens scratching in the dirt nearby.

"Abuelo! Estamos aqui!" Emil called out, knocking on the door.

A slim and sprightly old man opened the door, smiling brightly. His hair was short and grey, his face weather-beaten from a lifetime of working outdoors under the fierce tropical sun. He wore a long sleeved shirt with a collar, the cuffs rolled back mid-way up his forearms, strong work pants and a pair of sandals. His wiry and hard muscled thin frame radiated health and strength.

"Como esta Abuelo?" Emil asked.

"Alex, this is my grandfather, Gilberto Guerrero."

"Muy bien, Emiliano! I'm very well! How is my adventurous grandson! Let's speak English so that your compañero here can understand us. You must be Alex Steele, mucho gusto! Pleased to meet you, please come in, welcome to my home! Where is your third companion?" he said, hugging Emil and shaking Alex's hand, ushering them inside.

"Thank you for your hospitality Don Gilberto. It will be good to sleep on a mattress for a night! And yes, my Spanish is a little rusty! It's a long time since I was able to practice. It's only myself and Emil, two of us," said Alex.

"Oh... I see, I had a strong feeling that there would be three of you visiting, no matter..." said Gilberto thoughtfully.

The trio walked into the small living room and Alex and Emil sat on the wooden couch with bright cushions while Emil's grandfather disappeared through a division in the house into what was presumably the kitchen. A moment later, he reappeared holding three glasses of water.

Handing cold glasses to Alex and Emil he announced, "Welcome Alex, to my home and to Orange Walk district, and welcome back Emil, my boy. I've missed you and your youthful energy. You know, Alex, I've worked the land in this area for more than fifty years and luckily I am still fit and healthy. Since Emil's father's accident, when Emil came to stay with me, I appreciate my health and the beauty of this jungle more than ever before. Taking Emil with me to gather Chicle keeps me young, especially as he values our traditions and wants to learn all about the forest. It's a joy sharing it all with him."

"Grandfather, I have so much to tell you about our expedition so far! But first, tell me how Dad is doing. Is he getting better? And how is mom? When did you get back?" Emil asked.

"Your father is doing a lot better Emiliano, but it will still be another two weeks until he can leave the hospital. Your mother is doing a wonderful job of helping him. They both send their love, and I was reminded that I should look after you to the best of my ability, which is why I'm very happy Alex waited for me to join you on this adventure. I'm sure you're really in a hurry to visit the temple," said Gilberto.

"You're right, I have been itching to get to the temple as soon as possible. But we've spent the last few days doing some important conservation work and Emil has enjoyed himself learning a bit about some jungle surveillance and survival techniques. At least I think you've been enjoying it," said Alex, grinning across at Emil.

"Enjoyed it! It's been the best few days ever," shouted Emil excitedly. "I love what we are doing and I want to learn more and more."

Gilberto indicated that they all sit at the small wooden table in the centre of the room.

"There is very good reason that I needed you to wait for me. Only myself and Emil know the way to the temple, and it is a complicated route. There are many old paths that can confuse you on the way, and even though Emil is becoming an excellent bushman, it'll be safer and quicker if I come too, to make sure that you get there and also to have another pair of hands in case we have any difficulties. I got back from Guatemala City yesterday and I am ready to go first thing tomorrow, as soon as the sun comes up," he said indicating a pile stacked up next to the door.

There, close to the entrance, was a fully packed flour sack makeshift backpack like Emil's, a machete in its scabbard, a pair of sturdy rubber boots, a calabash drink bottle and a brightly coloured square bag. The square bag lay on top of the pile; it looked hand woven with intricate designs and had a long thick shoulder strap. Emil noticed Alex looking at the bag.

"That's my grandfather's Koshta bag, he keeps all his bush medicines in it, my grandfather is a famous shaman! The bag was a present from another shaman of the Kekchi Maya people way down south in Toledo district!" he said with pride.

Before Alex could ask any questions, Gilberto quickly changed the subject.

Smiling at his lively grandson he asked, "So you've been enjoying all the project work so far?"

"It's been great!" replied Emil gleefully, a huge smile on his face.

"I've learned so many new things and everything I learned from you has come in very handy too!" said Emil as he launched into a fast paced account of all that had happened since he had left home.

As he recounted the attempted highway robbery, Emil's grandfather's face became dark with anger and concern which was eventually replaced with relief and pride as Alex interjected and recounted Emil's brave actions that night.

Gilberto stood up and walked over to a wooden counter fixed to the wall. He opened a plastic container and took out a large number of enchiladas, which are handmade corn tortillas rolled up and stuffed with strips of chicken, tomatoes, chillies and onions, covered in grated cheese. He put them in the centre of the table and sat down again.

"Now, let's eat. Why don't you tell me what all the mystery is about? What is this temple that we have found? It's not the first temple we've stumbled across, but your grandfather the Professor made us promise to keep it a secret. What's so special about this one?"

Alex explained in detail about the temple and the possibility of it containing a collection of codices preserving the ancient knowledge and teachings of the Maya that were saved from destruction and hidden by King Nanchancaan. He also told him about the legend of the King's unique jade death mask carved from one single piece of jade.

Gilberto listened intently until Alex finished.

"So now it all makes sense," said Gilberto, his eyes unfocused and seemingly staring far away to another time in his mind's eye.

He came out of his revere, a look of contentment on his face and spoke.

"Alex, as my grandson knows, I am very interested in the history and culture of my country and all its peoples; I have been since I was small. There are so many different languages spoken in our tiny country! Creole, Garifuna, Maya, English, Spanish and others too! Our country's entire population is only around three hundred thousand people, did you know that? It's quite remarkable.

"Here in the north of Belize most of us are Mestizo, descendants of the Yucateca Maya and the Spanish. Many of our people settled here as a result of the Caste Wars," he spoke with the practised, measured tones of a consummate storyteller.

"I want to tell you both a story that I think you will find very interesting considering what you have just told me about the temple we found and what it might contain."

He settled back into his chair and started, "This story begins in the year 1511, aboard a small, open Spanish caravel sailing vessel called the *Nina* that had set sail from Panama and was on its way to Santo Domingo. The crew of the ship were all Spanish soldier-sailors, men that we would call today marines, all experienced nautical warriors. The ship was caught in a terrible storm, probably a hurricane, somewhere off the coast of the Yucatan peninsula. The *Nina* sank and some of her crew managed to make it into a small wooden rowing boat. They were adrift at sea for days, some say two weeks. Eventually, strong currents pushed them past the coral reefs and onto the shore of the Yucatan peninsula. No sooner had they landed ashore than they were all captured by the local Maya, probably the Cocom tribe, and some of the survivors were immediately sacrificed in honour of the Maya gods. The rest of the survivors escaped from the cages they were being held in and made a run for it, only to be recaptured, this time by a Maya tribe called the Tutul Xiues, the sworn enemies of the Cocom. Of the remaining survivors only two of the Spaniards were spared. Their names were Geronimo de Aguilar and..." Gilberto paused for emphasis, "...Gonzalo Guerrero."

Gilberto looked at Emil and Alex's surprised faces, drank some water and continued, "At first Gonzalo was made a slave. He was a curiosity and a novelty. Perhaps they kept him alive because they hoped to find out more about the Spanish. If that was their reason, they succeeded. Gonzalo slowly learned to speak Maya, adopting the Maya way of life completely, including covering his face and body with sacred Maya scarring, tattoos and piercings. He gained the Maya's trust and eventually won his freedom. He used his skills as a soldier to fight alongside the Maya. He was a brave and charismatic man and quickly gained the title of War Leader and given command of hundreds of Maya warriors. During this time he also fell in love with a beautiful Maya princess named Zazil Ha, whom the King allowed him to marry. It was Princess Zazil Ha's father, this great Maya Lord – a powerful King – whom Gonzalo loyally served as War Leader. Her father was none other than King Nanchancaan!"

Gilberto paused again letting the impact of his story sink in to his very surprised audience.

"Princess Zazil Ha and Gonzalo's children were the first Mestizo people, they gave birth to our race, so even if we are not their direct descendants we are certainly descended from them. Gonzalo helped the Maya fight against the Spanish and won several decisive battles against his own countrymen, using his knowledge of their tactics and strategies against them. He eventually died in a great battle fighting against the Spanish, trying to stop them from invading and colonizing the Maya lands. I like to think that because we share the same surname that we are indeed direct descendants of this amazing man and his Maya princess."

"That's a fascinating story. Perhaps Gonzalo helped gather up the codices and hid them in the temple. He would certainly have been well aware that the Spanish Conquistadores would be determined to stamp out the Maya religious and cultural beliefs," Alex said, having gained a whole new perspective of this elderly man.

"That's true," commented Gilberto, "in fact, the drinking of our traditional blood-red coloured tea that we make from the tubes of the plant we call coxolmeca or Chinese Root was indeed outlawed for many decades due to its use in Maya religious rituals."

"I've got goose bumps thinking about the fact that we are also going to help protect the legacy of the Maya and that you both may in fact be related to the King whose temple you might have rediscovered! Let's hope we are correct and that it is King Nanchancaan's temple! What a coincidence it would be if it actually is!" Alex postulated, caught up in the story.

"Hmm, yes, coincidence…or perhaps we have all been on this journey for a lot longer than any of us realise!" said Gilberto quietly to himself.

The excitement in the small wooden house grew as they talked long into the night about the possibilities and the coming adventure. Eventually the flame in the small hurricane lamp on the table died down and the trio turned in for the night.

Several meters into the jungle, off a small muddy road just outside Emil's village, Silus and his band of brigands had hidden the SUV. Having camouflaged it with huge palm leaves, they were now all crammed into the two small cheap tents which they had hurriedly erected in their makeshift camp. The tents were not offering much protection from the mosquitoes or the wet, muddy forest floor. Water oozed through the leaky ground sheet and added to the already tense atmosphere and misery within. Curses flew and tempers flared as the band of thieves suffered in discomfort as the afternoon turned to evening and night set in.

After a couple of hours, Gordo and then Silus gave up and beat a hasty retreat, sloping off to shelter inside the SUV and leaving TreeWays and Kiloboy to tough it out in the tents. For a group that was short enough on patience already, they were all feeling the strain. The mood was distinctly hostile, their only common bond being a financial one and as their usual collective form of self-expression was, more often than not, violence, it was a recipe for disaster.

Silus thought that if he had been the captain of a pirate ship, this crew was just a few steps away from mutiny, which only the promise of money was preventing.

Silus' mind kept going over other possible alternatives to his plan, realising that this was just the beginning of what could be a very uncomfortable experience. Who knew how long it would take to get to the temple, and once there, how long would it take for them to figure out if it was indeed King Nanchancaan's? And how, short of beating it out of young Steele or the boy, would they find out the answer?

So many questions were flying through Silus' evil mind. Had they brought enough tinned food? How long could he bear eating it cold? Then, there was the time needed to dig the treasures up out of the temple – more time he would have to spend in this diabolical jungle. He decided that this whole thing sucked! There had to be an easier way. Why people ever wanted to work in these incredibly hot, sweaty, mosquito infested jungles, was beyond him.

"The sooner I get what I've come for and leave, the better! There has got to be a better, faster way," he thought to himself.

Earlier that day they had all groaned in frustration as they saw that the Land Rover and its passengers were going to stop, yet again!

"What NOW?" they had all thought.

As Gordo was the most Mestizo/Maya looking of all of them he had been elected to go and ask some questions at the small grocery shack in the village square. He bought lots of snacks and drinks and then started asking the store keeper some casual sounding questions about the fancy looking Land Rover parked in the square. He got some very interesting answers from the bored shop owner who was only too ready for a bit of a chat and some gossiping.

On his return, he was able to inform the gang that the boy was in fact from this village, his name was Emiliano Guerrero. He had been gone a couple of weeks and he had arrived back that day and was staying with his grandfather who had himself just got back from visiting his injured son in hospital in

Guatemala. The shopkeeper did not know how long he would be back for.

He told Gordo that they were always disappearing into the jungle, sometimes for days on end. The grandfather farmed now, but he used to be a Chiclero and had recently started doing that again. The shopkeeper also told him that the old man was the local shaman and if Gordo had any ailments or illnesses, the shopkeeper recommended that he pay him a visit and helpfully gave Gordo directions to the house. It was easy to find and had a big red water barrel next to the front door.

Silus mulled this new information over in his dark, conniving mind. The boy was obviously the 'ARACHNIS' contact, and he knew where the temple was. But if he did, then Silus had no doubt that the grandfather did also. That was the key to his new plan.

It had annoyed him that young Steele and the Belizean boy were clearly very well equipped, whereas he and his motley crew were almost completely lacking in proper equipment, supplies and jungle know-how. In this area they were weak, but what his crew did excel at was crime and violence. That was their strength and it was that strength that he had to use to gain the upper hand.

"Turn your liabilities into assets," he repeated to himself as he made futile attempts to get comfortable and fall asleep on the now fully reclined SUV passenger seat.

He started to recite his favourite saying, "Don't get mad, get even! Respond, don't react."

The conservation clown and the boy were at home in this environment, whereas he found it an uncomfortable hell. It was obvious to him that TreeWays and company clearly did not relish the thought of having to go trudging through the hot, snake infested and mosquito whining jungle. They were not real country boys. Every square inch of this damned jungle seemed to be covered in spines and thorns, and buzzing with blood sucking insects.

His original plan would involve a lot of really hard, uncomfortable work and there was just no way that they would be able to follow these two without being seen or heard. He had never imagined that this trip would be as remote or challenging. He hadn't even heard of Belize until this job had come up.

Silus had never been keen on the work thing. He had never wanted a job; he was all about finding and exploiting opportunities. He did not like the hand he had been dealt. The cards were stacked against him and whenever that happened, he always resorted to something he was naturally very good at – cheating. His new plan began to take form.

He had noticed how vast the jungles here were. To him, the jungle looked like a nasty, frightening, impenetrable mess. It also looked like a very easy place to get seriously lost, a place a person could disappear in completely – forever, never to be seen again.

This was something he had secretly been very worried about, as he did not have much faith in his gangster buddies' jungle abilities. Now he saw a way to make use of the jungle's remoteness and the inherent hazards together with Alex, Emil, and the old man's skills, knowledge and equipment. They would do all the work for him. Literally – all of it.

The patient wait-and-watch approach wasn't going to work. It had been great in theory but in practice it was time to make the best use of everyone's skills and bring everyone together. With this new information he could now do just that, without any fear of Alex alerting the authorities. He would have a brand new two tier team – masters and servants.

Within his sights, Silus now had what every businessman needs in order to gain the advantage in a deal – leverage! His new plan had a very neat and tidy ending too. He had once seen an Airborne Forces tee shirt that had said, "Kill them all, let God sort them out – Death from Above."

His t-shirt would read, "Kill them all, come back alone – Death from Within."

He chuckled to himself at his own private joke. No one knew about the special package that he had hidden in his small backpack. Guns had their uses but in a double cross, often subtler methods were called for. He was ready now. He felt so much better about everything.

Silus returned his seat to the upright position, flipped down the sun visor in front and above his head and turned on the small light built into it next to the vanity mirror. He looked with disgust at the large frame of the man in the driver's seat next to him.

Gordo's fat frame oozed over the sides and back of the heavily burdened, fully reclined driver seat. His head back, mouth open, he was snoring loudly enough to wobble his big double chin. Foul smelling breath filled the car and Silus had had enough.

"Time for a midnight meeting," he thought.

Reaching over the centre consul in the foot well with his boot, he gave Gordo a vicious kick in the calf to wake him out of his deep, comfortable looking sleep.

"Hey! FAT MAN! WAKE UP! Go get the others!" he barked at Gordo whose bleary, confused eyes had flown open in pained surprise.

"I am changing the plan," Silus yelled loudly right into Gordo's wax filled ear, "and tell Kiloboy to make a fire and make a big pot of strong coffee too, I want everyone wide awake."

Kiloboy's blood boiled like the coffee in the pot. While the other three big shots sat talking in the SUV, the engine running and air conditioning on, he was left standing in a cloud of smoke around his head and a cloud of mosquitoes around his feet and ankles. He really felt like killing something and stomped on any ant or bug within range of the firelight, mashing them to pulp, slapping and smashing at the mosquitoes with furious open handed blows until his fingers stung.

"Very soon!" he thought to himself, "blood gonna start flowin', very soon maan!"

The inky black jungle chirped and buzzed with life all around him. He could hear the crashing and snapping of foliage as animals went about their nightly journeys in search of food. Tree frogs began to croak and bawl and a nearby troop of howler monkeys fearsome roars rolled over the jungle canopy.

"Rain," thought Kiloboy gloomily, "heavy rain 'pan di way real soon."

Adding insult to injury, just at that moment Gordo pushed a button and wound down the car window calling over to Kiloboy with a smirk on his fat face.

"Hey Coffee-, I mean Kilo- boy! Hurry up! Mr Silus want you in here list'nin to the new plan too. We noh got all night to fool with, and make sure you put extra sugar in mines when you bring it, you hear?"

Finally, Kiloboy resentfully took the full steaming plastic cups to the SUV and got in, slamming the door shut as hard as he could in impotent rage, handing Gordo his cup, minus any sugar but with a crushed dead beetle sunk to the bottom instead, his eyes smouldering with hate.

Just as Gordo flew into a tirade about the lack of sugar, the skies opened up and heavy rain started to fall.

"Okay, everyone! SHUT UP and listen," Silus began, slurping the scalding hot coffee and lighting up a cigarette.

"Like my favourite, infamous, world heavyweight champion boxer once said, "everyone has a plan until they get punched in the face!" Well, I have just been punched in the face by the reality of our situation and I realize now that my original plan won't work. So, based on the new info we have, I have come up with a new one. Something that I think you will all find a lot more suited to your respective skill sets. I am now sure that we have two people who know the way to the temple, the boy and the grandfather. So that means no more having to follow! We're now in a position to take control and lead from now on. We are going to make this Alex guy do all the work for us because now we have a way of shutting him up and making sure he doesn't call the police. He is going to make our time in the jungle much more enjoyable, and when we are done you can have the pleasure of killing him and having the Land Rover and everything in it – think of it as a bonus. Just like everyone wanted to do in the first place, don't think I don't know," said Silus.

With that, Silus outlined his new skulduggery.

The village was now blanketed in complete darkness and all the villagers were fast asleep, the rain pouring down steadily. As Bodhi was already aware of the looming danger and had been present for many hours now, she did not notice any change as the two shadows slipped through the side streets, creeping past the main square through the pouring rain. The two figures slunk along dark paths between houses, the deluge muffling their footfalls. Up the hill they moved until they came to the house with a big water barrel, now overflowing, next to a front door. A quick flash from a torch revealed that the barrel was red.

Deep in sleep, Alex and Gilberto did not hear the muffled sound of dogs barking because of the heavy rain hitting the thatch with a deafening leafy clatter. They did not hear the footfalls of TreeWays and Kiloboy as the pair moved with the practised stealth of experienced burglars through the dark house until they found the sleeping form of young Emil.

As TreeWays bent over the sleeping boy, his massive hand clamped down over Emil's face stifling his outcry as they manhandled him as quietly as they could while he writhed and twisted, trying to free himself from their overpowering grip. In no time, he had been dragged off into the night; back to Silus who was patiently waiting.

Alex awoke with a sense of unease. The rain had stopped and the sun had just come up. He got up and found Gilberto looking at the floor in the main living room area, a quizzical expression on his face. Alex followed his gaze and saw huge muddy footprints tracked all over it. Gilberto looked up and their eyes met. Both of them instantly moved in the direction of Emil's room. Gilberto flung open the door open, shouting, "Emil!"

There, on the empty bed, lay Emil's cell phone with a folded piece of cardboard torn from a cigarette packet. Gilberto rushed over, picked it up, read it and handed it over to Alex. On it, in scruffy handwriting, was written:

"We have the boy. If you call the police or tell anyone – you will NEVER see him again. Call this number: 663 5497"

"Dios mio!!" gasped Gilberto in utter shock, "Someone has taken my grandson! Who would do such a thing?"

"I am really sorry Gilberto!" said Alex, overcoming his own shock and anger. "I don't know who, but I am sure I know why. We need to keep calm and make a plan. We will need to think fast and weigh up the situation before we go rushing around."

Alex took the liberty of going to the kitchen, putting the kettle on and making his proverbial cup of tea, his first act of rationality in any crisis situation where immediate action could not be taken.

"This whole expedition has become a complete nightmare! I've got to make the right decisions and come up with a sound plan – and fast!" he thought to himself. "My first expedition and my only expedition member, the only other person that I am responsible for, is kidnapped. KIDNAPPED! It's unbelievable. What if they harm him? What if they kill him?" Alex's mind was racing and he had to focus hard on his breathing to remain in control and fight the rising feeling of desperation.

"We need to call the police!" said Gilberto, deep concern etched into the lines of his face.

"Yes, of course, Don Gilberto," agreed Alex, "but I also suggest we need to buy some time from the kidnappers. How long would it take the police to get here?"

"Unfortunately, at least two hours," replied Gilberto, "and that's only if last night's rain hasn't caused the river to come up and flood over the wooden bridge! If it has, it could take a day or two or maybe more for it to become passable again! What am I going to do? He's my responsibility. My poor grandson."

"Well, we are all in this together," said Alex, "I think we should phone them first and see what it is they want. If I can give it to them I will immediately do so, whatever it is. Anything to get Emil back to us safely and as fast as possible."

"Yes, do it. Phone them right now. Give them whatever they want," said Gilberto

Alex picked up Emil's cell phone and dialled, putting it on speakerphone. It was answered immediately by a man with a London accent.

"Meet us on the road going north," said the cold hard voice. "You'll see a small fenced enclosure surrounding an electricity transformer and small substation visible above the jungle, just past the 153km highway marker. There is a solid road that takes you to a service clearing next to the transformer enclosure there. Remember, if you call the police or tell anyone you will never see the boy again. Do you understand?"

"Yes, I understand," replied Alex, "just tell me what you want and we'll give it to you if we can. Just don't hurt Emil. We want him back safe and unharmed."

"The boy's fine… for now. You can keep him that way if you do as you are told. What we want is you, the old man and the car. Meet us in half an hour and don't bring anyone else or the boy will die!"

Over a quick mug of tea, Alex and Gilberto took a few minutes to come up with a rough plan. They then gathered what they needed, including Emil's bush clothes and kit which had been left behind by the kidnappers. Alex opened up Emil's small personal survival kit and took out several items. He then took off his own belt, unzipped the hidden compartment and put several survival kit items into it, zipping it closed again when he had finished. He then took Emil's belt out of the boy's trousers and replaced it with his own, now packed with the hidden kit.

Next, they made a phone call to the police in Orange Walk and explained the situation. The police told them that they would send assistance as fast as possible, but the bridge was indeed flooded and two more had been washed out completely. They were also preparing for the arrival of a late tropical storm due to hit Northern Belize in the next couple of days which could delay them even further. They would do their best and in the meantime their advice was to comply with the kidnapper's demands until help could be provided. Alex agreed to phone the police again after they had met with the kidnappers and found out what their demands were. He had no doubt they were after what might be in the temple.

Next, Alex deleted the call history and turned the cell phone off. It wouldn't do for the police to phone him back right in the middle of the meeting or for the gangsters to find the number for the police as the last number dialled if they took the phone from him.

When Bodhi saw Alex and Gilberto rushing down the small hill, the thought formed in Bodhi's mind and popped out into the ether, "Where's Emil?!"

"He's been kidnapped!" came the immediate telepathic reply from the old man next to Alex.

Gilberto froze in his tracks and stared at the Land Rover, almost dropping the machete and baggage he was carrying.

"Who on earth? What on earth?" Gilberto asked silently. "Who are you? A forest spirit? Tata Duende? Who am I talking with?"

"My name is Bodhi, I am the Land Rover vehicle Alex drives," Bodhi said matter of factly, "But how is it we can communicate? You are the first human I have been able to contact like this. I can only contact Alex in his dreams and even then, not very well at all."

Gilberto could not believe what he was hearing. This was a first. Never before had he communicated with a car.

"Ahh, so you are the third companion I sensed yesterday. I am a shaman, my name is Gilberto, I talk to the wind, the stars, the trees and the animals, the rocks, water – everything. Sometimes they answer me. I have spent my whole life working in the jungle and in nature. I'm as much a part of it as it is a part of me. That's why we can talk to each other. I am close to the earth."

"Who has taken Emil?" Bodhi asked, deeply concerned.

"Bad men! Very bad men, no doubt – we don't know who yet, but we are about to go and meet them and then we will find out."

Alex turned round when he realized that Gilberto was no longer next to him. He saw that he was still only half way down the small hill above the main square. Gilberto was standing perfectly motionless, staring at the Land Rover.

"Come on Gilberto, we need to get going!" he called.

"Yes, of course," replied the shaman, "Right now! I'm coming"

They jumped into Bodhi and her engine rumbled into life. They drove out of the peaceful, picturesque village and headed north as instructed. Very soon, the razor wire topped enclosure was visible above the trees on the right. The turn off to it was almost invisible and Alex drove right past it. Gilberto had to stop him. They reversed and Gilberto pointed out the entrance and the fresh tire tracks that were visible in the mud.

The service road was more like a green tunnel, bullet-tree saplings and thorn covered vines tangled with basket tie-tie and pokanoboy palms. The springy vegetation pressed hard against Bodhi's sides as she squeezed through it.

Soon, they broke out into a small clearing, the centre of which was occupied by a square fenced enclosure. Inside it was a big electrical transformer and its small substation, the high voltage electricity making it hum. The sign on the fence said: Belize Electricity Limited, DO NOT ENTER – DANGER OF DEATH.

In front of the fence, a large gunmetal grey SUV with black tinted windows was parked. Alex stopped four or five meters from it and turned off Bodhi's engine. Gilberto and Alex got out of Bodhi and as they shut the doors behind them, all four of the SUV's doors opened in unison.

Alex and Gilberto sized up the four kidnappers, all of whom were wearing sunglasses. He didn't like that; it was always much harder to read what was going on in someone's mind if you could not see their eyes. They all had the aura and posture of dangerous, violent men, even the overweight one. Their body language was menacing. The small clearing had no shade and it was like a furnace, even though it was still only mid-morning. The humidity was in the high nineties and the temperature hovering at thirty-eight degrees Celsius. Everyone's shirts bloomed with dark patches of sweat almost immediately.

"Where is my grandson?!" demanded Gilberto, his expression strained and furious. "How dare you do this! How dare you come into my house in the middle of the night and KIDNAP MY GRANDSON!" he shouted, the outrage in his strong voice hitting out like an iron hammer.

"Try and stay calm, Gilberto," advised Alex quietly.

"That's right, Mr. Expedition-Save-The-World, you tell him! Cool your jets, Gramps! I don't like your tone," Silus ordered.

"We're not going to do anything at all until we see Emil!" said Alex equally forcefully.

"Gordo, get the boy!" said Silus.

Gordo lumbered to the back of the SUV and opened the boot. Reaching inside he dragged a kicking and wriggling Emil from inside it. Emil wore only the boxer shorts he had been sleeping in, his hands were tied tightly with strong cord, a piece of duct tape covered his mouth and a bandana blindfolded his eyes. His muffled yells were unintelligible. Dripping with sweat from being trapped in the oven-like boot he had several bruises on his arms and legs, no doubt from his attempts to escape his captors the previous night, but otherwise he seemed to be okay. Gordo took out a large folding knife, opened it and held it next to Emil's throat as he pushed him forward into full view of Alex and Gilberto. Gilberto struggled to contain his urge to rush over to him.

"Give him back his clothes! He needs protection from the insects and the sun. We have them right here in the Land Rover," demanded Alex.

"Really?" Silus enquired oozing venom. "You are actually trying to tell me what to do. REALLY!!"

He screamed in incredulous fury.

"It turns out that this insolent young smartmouth punk is as stupid as he looks! I tell you what to do you stupid MORON! You're like a disobedient dog I used to have, I beat it and beat it. No matter how hard I beat it it still didn't learn who its master was. One day I just had to beat it to death. Let's see if Steele is any different. Kiloboy, go and teach him who his master is."

Kiloboy took the pistol out of his waistband and handed it to TreeWays who levelled it at Alex's head. With savage glee he strode over to Alex and let fly, slamming his gold ring covered fists into Alex's face and midsection. Alex did not fight back and soon succumbed to the vicious attack.

"Okay! That's enough for now!" ordered Silus as Alex collapsed onto the ground. "We need him functioning, not crippled yet!"

Silus took a small pair of folding pliers from his pocket and walked over to Alex who was trying to breathe, his diaphragm having gone into spasms from the blows. Silus bent over and grabbed Alex by the hair, jerking his head back. Opening the small fine nose pliers he pushed them up Alex's nostrils squeezing hard as he dragged Alex back up into a standing position.

Excruciating pain exploded in his head and multi-coloured stars burst in Alex's brain. He yelled out, instinctively pulling away, which only made the pain ten times more agonizing.

"Who's your master!" Silus sneered, eye to eye with Alex, spittle flying into Alex face. "A-n-s-w-e-r me! WHO IS YOUR MASTER!"

"You are," Alex snorted furiously.

"You are, Mr. Silus, sir!" screamed the sadistic Silus. "SAY IT!"

Alex remained silent, the initial pain so powerful that it had become dulled through its intensity.

"SAY IT!" yelled Silus, squeezing the pliers harder, his face purple with rage, the veins on his forehead sticking out, a snarl-like grin on his face. He was obviously really enjoying himself, high on the power of domination.

Silus looked over to Kiloboy and then nodded his head towards Emil. Kiloboy's eyes lit up as he charged over and shoved the blindfolded Emil to the ground with all his might, knocking the wind out of him. Kiloboy's leg swung back in preparation to boot the defenceless Emil squarely in his ribs when Gilberto charged towards him. Two deafening explosions erupted as TreeWays fired two shots right at Gilberto's feet and Gordo yanked Emil back onto his feet, his sharp knife instantly pressed hard against Emil's neck.

Everyone froze.

Silus squeezed the pliers again – even harder. Alex's head jolted with the white hot pain screaming through his head and bright red blood ran out of his nose.

"We can do this ALL DAY, MORON!" Silus yelled. "ALL DAY! Until you learn your lesson!"

"You are the master, Mr. Silus, sir," said Alex, tears streaming down his face and defiant rage burning in his eyes.

"Again! Louder," hissed Silus.

"And correctly – you are MY master, Mr. Silus, Sir!"

"You are my master Mr. Silus, sir!" Alex said as loudly as he could, hoping Emil was okay.

Being blindfolded, Emil had had no warning that he was about to be pushed and Alex had seen his head rock back alarmingly by the force of the savage shove.

It was clear to Alex that he was dealing with a complete psychopath and a sadistic one too. Compliance was the only option for now. These men had no doubt murdered people before, and what was even more frightening was that they would obviously have thoroughly enjoyed it.

Gilberto stood shaking with rage. His eyes were like the eyes of a cornered jaguar ready to fight for its life.

Bodhi sat silently parked, also doing nothing for fear of endangering Emil, Alex and Gilberto. Instead she spoke to Gilberto.

"Gilberto, for Emil's sake, control your anger. You must outwit these men. Together we will prevail, but right now you are not in a position to fight back. You must help me be the link between myself, Alex and Emil. There is something familiar about this man Silus. I am sure I have felt this man's evil presence before. The one they call Kiloboy was one of the gangsters that tried to rob us on the highway, I know his presence. All of them have what my teacher Andrasta calls Seki – the force of the killer. They have all chosen the dark path of destruction, chaos and death."

"Yes Bodhi, you are right. They are the followers of the dark way, they have the auras of the followers of Ah Puch, the Maya God of Death. They are all on a journey, following Ah Puch to Mitnal, the lowest and most horrible of the nine levels of Hell. I will wait until we get a chance to turn the tables on these marras, these gangsters!" telepathed Gilberto, who barely managed to control his protective instincts and righteous fury at the kidnappers.

Alex's nose bled freely and his eyes were still streaming. He used the sweat rag around his neck to mop up the blood.

Silus put away his pliers after wiping them clean on Alex's shirt and spoke, "Good dog! I'll keep this short and to the point and there will be no need for anyone of you to comment. This is a one way transmission, not a conversation. Myself, the big man over there and Kiloboy are going to be joining you on your little adventure to this temple. You will go about your business as normal except for the additional work involved in keeping me and my men comfortable, safe and well fed. You will perform all the analysis and do all the tests necessary to confirm that this temple is King Nanchancaan's, and you better pray that it is! Once we are sure of our facts I will get a crew in to loot it. I'll, of course, be taking the artefacts that I've come for and you will be allowed to live. There will be no need for us to restrain you or watch you closely for one very simple reason. The fat man over there is going to take the boy somewhere very secluded. Once a day I will contact him using your communications equipment in the Land Rover and every day we will use a new code. The very first time I fail to do so, or the code is incorrect, your grandson will die, and just so that I am sure you have the right degree of motivation, I promise you it will be a very painful death that will be a long, long time in coming. Of course, if you decide to get smart and prevent, stop or delay what I am here to do, I can always contact Gordo and tell him to start the boy's journey to the next world at any time. So, in words that even you can understand, you work for me now!"

Silus stared hard at Alex and Gilberto and continued, "Make space for us on the bench seat behind the driver and passengers seats. Gordo, get the boy's clothes and get him dressed. You see how kind and merciful I am. Make sure all the pockets are empty, and keep him in the backseat from now on. He'll die of dehydration and heatstroke if you leave him in the boot. Tie his feet too and tie his neck to the head rest in the back while you're driving. Don't take any chances."

Silus walked over to Emil who now had several grazes to add to the bruises, breathing heavily through fear and anger and the tape over his mouth. Silus put his mouth close to Emil's ear and hissed, "Remember, don't try anything smart boy. If you escape or try and get help we will kill your grandfather and your friend and take our chances that the temple is the right one and dig it up anyway, do you understand?"

Emil nodded.

Gordo came back with Emil's clothes. He untied Emil's hands and let him dress. Emil noticed something unfamiliar about the belt in his trousers; it was a bit big and did not have the buckle he was used to. When he was dressed, Gordo tied his hands and feet very tightly again, sat him in the back seat and put a short noose round his neck and tied the end to the headrest.

Laughing, he looked at Emil trussed up like a turkey and said, "Oye, mi amigo! Don't struggle or that noose is going to strangle your skinny little chicken neck! Ha ha! You betta pray we don't have no traffic accident! Why don't you put on your seat belt? Oh yes, that's right, you can't! Ha ha ha. Don't worry, you've got a neck belt! HA. HA. HA!"

His slack greasy mouth broke into a lopsided smile as he chuckled and slammed the door shut. On Silus' signal he drove off.

Silus, Kiloboy and TreeWays got into the back seat of Bodhi. Alex and Gilberto took up their positions in the front seats. Bodhi's engine rumbled into life. Alex and Gilberto looked at each other and then they too set off, with their new passengers. No one spoke.

Chapter Fourteen

Improvise, Adapt and Overcome

Gordo stopped just short of the flooded river's edge. The bridge they had crossed the previous day was now submerged under several meters of rushing red water. Huge trees had washed downstream and were stacked up against the now invisible bridge, sticking up out of the water at odd angles. Gordo phoned TreeWays to tell him that it would be impossible to stash Emil in the gang's hideout on the outskirts of Orange Walk Town. Gordo found himself talking to Silus, who had snatched the phone from TreeWays.

"Use your imagination, be creative – find somewhere isolated, abandoned! Try and get the lard between your ears to function!" said Silus, his voice laced with contempt.

Gordo did just that, and after driving around for a couple of hours he found the perfect place to hide his captive. The old cement building was tucked away down a jungle track in the middle of nowhere, many kilometres from any other building. It was truly an isolated and lonely place that looked like it had been deserted. It was a small factory building of sorts and had the rusting hulk of an old cane truck parked next to it.

Upon closer inspection, Gordo found that it had several small rooms set off the main factory floor; no doubt they had been store rooms. Two of them had solid metal doors with sliding bolts that could be padlocked shut, the windows were small and high off the ground, improvised burglar guards had been installed using one centimetre thick construction iron. They were set into the cement window frame and, as hard as he tried, Gordo could not pull them out; they were solid. Each store room also had a square concrete pillar in the middle of the floor, supporting the roof. Having satisfied himself that this would be the best hiding place, he drove back the fifteen kilometres to the nearest village and found a small hardware store. There he bought four sturdy, hardened steel padlocks, a long length of chain, a metal bucket, a portable radio, two folding mattresses and various other bits and pieces.

Afterwards, he went to the local grocery store and stocked up on huge quantities of food, several five gallon bottles of water and various household items. As a treat, and knowing that many long boring days lay ahead, he also bought a case of rum and a case of Coca Cola and several cartons of cigarettes.

Returning to the building-come-hideout he slung the tied and bound Emil over his shoulder and dumped him in the nearest store room. He wrapped a couple of turns of chain around the cement pillar and secured it with a padlock. He then put the other end around Emil's neck and fastened it with the second padlock. He untied Emil's hands and feet, ripped off the tape across his mouth and pulled the bandana blindfold down.

Emil blinked his eyes until they became accustomed to the gloom. Gordo then put a five gallon container of water into the room together with the big metal bucket.

"This bucket's your new toilet, so don't ask me to go outside, dat no gonna happin, hear? You gonna stay locked in dis here room, I'll give you food once a day, at six o'clock da night, that's it, no more!" said Gordo.

Gordo threw the folding mattress into one of the corners, where it landed on an old wooden pallet, and slammed the metal door shut, locking Emil in. Emil heard the bolts slide home on the outside and the remaining two padlocks click shut.

It was now late afternoon and Emil took in his new surroundings. He was scared, but angry too.

Suddenly, he felt a cold shiver of panic run up his spine, an overwhelming fear that he had never felt before. What was he thinking? These men were murderers; they may well kill him, his grandfather and Alex. This wasn't a TV show, this was actually happening – to him!

Emil felt dread and terror rising, the chain around his neck suddenly making him feel trapped, suffocated and claustrophobic! He had to get out of this prison; he had to get this chain off his neck! He walked the length of the chain which restrained him a metre from the door and the walls. Tears welled up in his eyes as he frantically struggled to pull it over his head. Emil became more and more frenzied with fear and panic as the reality of his situation hit home.

He was trapped! He was locked up in a cement box at the complete mercy of that fat slug, Gordo. He started to shout, to curse, to threaten, to plead and to reason with his captor, struggling against the chain which bit into his neck. It was not all that heavy, but there was no way he could snap it.

Gordo sat on a makeshift chair constructed of wooden pallets, with his mattress as cushioning for the 'seat' and 'backrest'.

"Quiese!! Shut up buay!" Gordo laughed, cracking open a bottle of rum, "Or I'll come in there and cut your tongue out. You can live without it, I'm sure!"

Emil thought about his parents, his grandfather and Alex. What could he do? He had to live; he had to escape, but how? He was determined to survive this ordeal.

And then it came to him, survive, of course, that was it!

He remembered what Alex had taught him about survival at Gales Point. He had listened to the lesson intently but only now began to understand what Alex had been talking about.

The lesson had been about what to do when you got lost in the jungle, or whenever you found yourself in a survival situation. At the time, he had thought that it was extremely unlikely he would ever get lost in the jungle but had paid attention anyway out of respect for Alex. It all came back to his young bright mind.

Alex had taught him that when people got truly lost or wound up in a survival situation there was always an overwhelming urge to panic and run blindly around. He had warned Emil that this blind panic could exaggerate a situation or even be fatal. In this type of situation, Alex had said that provided you were not in imminent physical danger, it was best to physically stop your legs from moving by sitting down. STOP was the first survival watchword Alex had taught him.

Emil did just that. He stopped and sat down. He calmly remembered Alex's words, "Emil, your life and death is your breath! If you can control your breath you can control your mind and body!"

Emil closed his mouth and breathed in slowly through his nose, counting to five. He then held his breath for a count of four, then breathed out silently from his mouth for a count of six. He repeated this for a couple of minutes, focusing only on his breathing. It was working, his pulse was slowing down, his hammering heart was now beating slower and the panic and fear were subsiding. He was regaining control, just as Alex said would happen.

THINK was the next of Alex's survival watchwords. Emil thought hard, remembering all he could about his kidnapping, the meeting and the drive to this, his prison. He remembered Alex telling him about the Five Fears.

Fear of the unknown, fear of discomfort, fear of personal weakness, fear of injury and death and fear of loneliness and isolation.

Alex had said, "The way to combat these fears is to maintain a state of preparedness and plan as much as you can. To combat the fear of the unknown you should do research and learn all you can about the environment you are in and have the right equipment and clothing to cope with it."

Well, Emil knew a lot! He knew the jungle and he knew what was going on! What he did not know was what would happen next. He was scared of being hurt again or being killed. That thought was truly terrifying. He was all alone too and he did feel that he was weak, chained up and locked in this cement box, but he told himself that he was young and fit and still able to function well. There was hope indeed, and Alex had said that no matter how bad a situation was and no matter what you did or did not have, the number one most important key to surviving was mental attitude and the will to live. Never, never, EVER, give up or stop trying – EVER!

He had done his best to keep track of the number of left and right turns they had made on the road and had tried to guess how many kilometres they had travelled and how long it had taken, but with all the circling around and double backing Gordo had made, it was impossible for him to have an accurate idea. If only they had gone straight from the meeting spot to the house near Orange Walk he may have had a chance.

"Never mind," thought Emil. "What was the third survival watchword? Oh yes, ORGANISE!"

Emil looked around him, making note of every single thing on him and in the room. He had one pair of pants, one shirt, one belt, one metal bucket, one chain, two padlocks, one mattress, one wooden pallet and there was one barred window high up on the outside wall. Emil started to organise his mind and assessed what resources he had available to him.

Alex had said that in order to maintain a positive mental state, you should try and keep your thoughts practical and logical and try not to let your emotional side of your mind dominate. The best way to achieve this, according to Alex, was to keep active. In the jungle that would mean improving your survival shelter, foraging for food or firewood or purifying water to drink. Here in his cell it meant looking closely at all he had and organising the next step. This brought him to the last of Alex's survival watchwords – PLAN. The watch words for survival gave Emil something to focus on – S.T.O.P. – Stop, Think, Organise and Plan.

He thought about Silus' last words to him, "If you try to escape we will kill your grandfather and Alex."

"What should I do?" thought Emil. "Well for starters, I need to make another hole in this belt! Why didn't Alex just give me mine?"

Emil undid the belt and slid it out of the loops of his trousers, wondering if he would be strong enough to push the buckle pin through the fabric and, thereby, make another hole. There would be no other way to do it; there were no old nails or pieces of wire on the floor. As Emil laid the belt on the floor, he noticed the hidden zip all along its length making his heart leap into his mouth with excitement.

"A secret compartment!" he thought, thrilled.

Just then he heard the padlocks opening and Gordo's heavy breathing outside. Maybe he would be able to smash the metal bucket over Gordo's head and grab the keys from him! The door flew open just as Emil got the belt through the last trouser loop. Gordo looked at Emil, metal bucket in one hand, belt undone and the other hand holding up his trousers.

"Ha, ha, ha!!!" Gordo said looking at Emil and then roared with laughter.

"Look at you…Ha ha ha!!" he guffawed drunkenly, the strong sickly sweet smell of fiery neat rum blasting from his great maw.

"Didn't think we had scared you DAT badly, HA, HA, HA!!" slurred Gordo.

Emil's face flushed red with embarrassment and anger. He mentally willed Gordo to move his head within range of the heavy metal bucket, but as drunk as he was, Gordo stayed well away from Emil, tossing a plastic pack of tortillas, a can of frijoles and a can of spam at him.

"Here you are chicken poop, here's your dinner! Watta waste a food, I only gonna end up killn' you anyways. I jus' waitin' on dah Boss to tell me to get to work on you. No one will hear your screams from here, it is the most outta da way place I seen in a good while. I really gonna have a lot of fun with you bway!"

Hurling a few more slurred obscenities at Emil he backed out of the room, slamming the metal door and locking it.

Emil pulled the mattress off the wooden pallet and sat on it. He heard loud ranchero music blasting out of the portable radio and Gordo wailing along to it karaoke style.

"Good," he thought, "Now let's see what we have here!"

He slid the belt out of the loops once more and laid it in front of him. Keeping his back to the door, he unzipped the belt and took out its hidden contents. There was a fifteen centimetre length of metal hacksaw blade with one end sharpened to a point so it could cut like a knife or be used to make holes. There was also a fire making flint, a brass button escape compass, a long commando wire saw for cutting wood, bone and plastic, a small pair of tweezers, some waterproof lifeboat matches and a dozen water purifying tablets. Ten twenty dollar bills and four fifty dollar bills had also been neatly folded in three, lengthwise. Lastly, there was a piece of waterproof paper with a message from Alex written on it and a thin plastic laminated 'flap card' with emergency contact numbers and other information printed on it.

He read the message:

"Emil, if you manage to find this, we hope that you are okay. Your grandfather and I both agree that you must try and escape, but only if you can do so without the risk of being discovered. Do not worry about us, we will be fine. Make no mistake, if they catch you trying to escape things will be very bad for you, so be extremely careful. If you get an opportunity to escape safely, head to the nearest police station and tell them who you are. We have already informed the Orange Walk police but as the bridges have all been flooded or washed out it will take them some time for them to respond. Then try and make contact with my grandfather and let him know where you are, give him a full SITREP. Also, be advised that there is a tropical storm due to hit Belize within the next 48 to 72 hours. Look for signs of its approach and make sure you find adequate shelter. We are as certain as we can be that the men who are doing this want what we believe is hidden in the temple you found. Remember, stay strong, be brave, make the best plan you can and then stick to it. Good luck and we will see you again soon! Alex and your loving grandfather."

Emil was able to read between the lines. The chance of anyone coming to his rescue was virtually none. No one except Gordo knew where they were, for starters. Alex and his grandfather had three dangerous gangsters watching them.

"No," he finally decided, "it's up to me to get out of here on my own."

The music outside suddenly stopped. Emil froze and then with lightning speed grabbed up all the contents of the belt and crammed them into his shirt pocket. He listened intently and could just make out Gordo's voice.

"Yes boss, everytin' straight! No way can he escape – he locked inna cement room with a metal door wid two locks 'pan it. He got a chain padlocked round e nek too, and dat chain up to one big pillah in di middle ah da room. Yes, we inna da middle ah di bush right in dah hamadoolahs, di middlah nowhere man. I not even zackly sure where di hell I am needah! No worry, okay speak to you in di mornin'. Laters."

The ranchero music instantly started blaring again, only louder. Emil made a plan. He took the short piece of hacksaw blade from his pocket. Taking off the bandana from around his neck, he wound the corner of it round the last two centimetres of the blade. Now he was able to grip it fairly well.

Once, when he and his grandfather had been sharpening their machetes, he had explained to Emil that metal files and hacksaw blades only cut in one direction so you should only put pressure onto them on the pushing or forward stroke, not the pulling or return stroke. This makes sure the hacksaw blade or file stays sharp for much, much longer.

Emil walked over to the padlock on the pillar and tried making an impression on the padlock's 'U' shaped shackle, but it just slid over its hardened surface without making a scratch. He then pushed the blade over one of the chain links next to the padlock. Fine metal filings fell to the floor and Emil realised that he would eventually be able to cut through. He wanted to whoop with joy, his excitement growing as he realised that he had a real chance to escape.

He pushed, lifted, pulled back and pushed, on and on. His hand cramped up just like it did when he was filing an edge onto a brand new machete. He was so thankful that his hand muscles were used to this sort of work but an hour later he had blisters on his fingers and his hand muscles were burning. Finally, the link fell to the ground and the chain separated – he was free of the pillar! Emil punched the air with excitement at his victory.

Gathering up the chain, he put the loose end into his pocket. Now he was free to move around the whole room. He reached up to the window but it was out of reach. Picking up the metal bucket, he turned it upside down and stood on it, but still he was not high enough to saw at the bars easily. He looked over to the wooden pallet. Dragging it over to the window he propped it up against the wall. Its planks of wood acting like a ladder he cautiously climbed up, hoping it would not slide away from the wall and collapse. Gingerly shifting his weight from one foot to the other, he slowly climbed half way and then, with more confidence, all the way to the top. Reaching up, he could hold onto one of the three window bars with his left hand and saw at them with his right.

He sized up the window. If he could hacksaw the bottom of the thin bars he was sure he would be able to bend them all outwards, at least enough to be able to squeeze through. But what if Gordo checked on him before he was finished sawing through them all? He realized that he would have to cut through all three before he bent any of them out so as not to give the game away and he would also need an early warning system if Gordo was to open the door while Emil's back was towards it, cutting the bars.

Emil jumped lightly down from the pallet and picked up the big metal bucket. He placed it about fifteen centimetres from the metal door which, luckily, opened inwards. Now, if Gordo did open it, the door would clang against the bucket and hopefully give Emil time to jump down, sit by the pillar and hide the cut section of chain.

The ranchero music increased in volume, matched by an increase in Gordo's tone deaf caterwauling. Emil sawed and sawed at the bars. As it got dark it became harder to see his progress, or the bloodied state of his fingers. They were numb from pain and the burning cramp was unbearable. Several times he jumped down to take a break only to have to fight back tears of frustration and despair. He had to make it! He just had to! His life was hanging in the balance. He climbed up again and carried on. Three hours later he had cut through the bottom of two of them and there was no stopping Emil now – he was on a mission.

The hacksaw blade was inevitably becoming dull and each subsequent bar was harder to cut through than the last. Emil could not bear to think of the consequences should this small piece of hacksaw blade wear out before he had finished the last bar.

"If only Alex had put two of them in the belt," Emil thought to himself.

But normally the reason they were included in the personal survival kits in the first place was because the hacksaw blades made a wonderfully effective striking tool to scrape down a fire, making flint to create a shower of hot sparks. Of course, they were also very useful for cutting notches in wood or sawing pieces of bone into shapes for hooks or to make arrow heads too, but they were not usually included with this type of job in mind.

Suddenly, and to Emil's sheer joy and utter relief, the final millimetres of the last bar disappeared and he was through!

He stopped, had a break, drank a full litre and a half of water and then soaked the bandana in the cool liquid, wrapping his burning, aching and bleeding fingers up in it.

When he had somewhat recovered, he climbed back up onto the pallet and heaved with all his strength; the first, second and third bars all bent outward without too much of a problem. The gap was just wide enough for the slim and agile Emil to squeeze through.

Hauling himself up and into the window opening, he dragged himself over the short stubs of the metal bars, grazing his skin painfully. Gritting his teeth he swung out and lowered himself down as far as possible, unable to see what was below him or how far from the ground he was.

Emil took a deep breath and dropped, his bare feet landing on hard rocks, thorns and building debris. He lowered himself quickly onto the sharp, hard ground and clenched his mouth shut, fighting the pain in his feet. He ran his hands over the soles of his feet feeling for any foreign objects that were embedded in them. Carefully he pulled out what he could feel and stood up. Testing the ground with his feet before putting his weight down, he moved slowly along the back wall to the side wall and then on to the front.

Going into a very low crouch, just as he had seen action heroes do in the movies, he peeked around the corner. He could see light coming from the main doorway to the building and he heard the music still blaring away.

He stood up and moved quickly and quietly towards the yellow patch of light. When he reached the doorway he again went into a low crouch and peeped carefully around it. Inside the main factory room he saw Gordo's large form slumped on the makeshift pallet seat. Two rum bottles stood ready, within easy reach of the unconscious man, but with nothing left to offer – they were both empty.

Emil moved as quietly as he could, looking for the keys to the padlocks. He couldn't see them anywhere obvious. He moved closer to Gordo, focusing on him. There was a thin chain clipped to his belt that disappeared into his pocket. Sweating and holding his breath, Emil went over to Gordo. Gingerly pinching the chain between his fingers he began to pull it out of the pocket ever so slowly. The first several centimetres came out freely and easily but then it didn't budge any further.

Emil pulled harder. The lump on the end of the chain slid a little, but with much more resistance. Gordo twitched. Emil froze.

Gordo settled down again and Emil began pulling again, harder. After what seemed like forever, the lump started to become visible and popped out of Gordo's pocket; it was a large bunch of keys. Emil unclipped them from Gordo's pants. Moving quietly over to the big metal door, he tried the keys in the two padlocks until he was able to find the correct ones. With a turn of the keys the padlocks opened, Emil holding them tightly so that they would not fall to the ground.

Feeling for the opening to the keyhole of the padlock around his neck and using his other hand to guide the remaining two sets of keys into it, he found the right one and removed that lock too. Taking the long length of chain out of his pocket, he moved as quickly as he dared to one of the cement pillars nearest Gordo, whose mouth was wide open, snoring loudly in his drunken stupor.

Emil wrapped the chain around the pillar, padlocked it, and then tiptoed back over to Gordo. The next part of his plan would have to be executed swiftly, boldly and in one go. In a lightning quick motion, he put the chain around Gordo's neck and padlocked it shut. It was secured tightly around it under his double chin. There was no way Gordo would be able to pull it off over his head. Just as the padlock snapped shut, Gordo's bloodshot eyes flew open. He took in the situation in an instant and made a wild grab for Emil, who only just managed to spring out of range in time.

Gordo hauled his huge frame up and ran at Emil. The chain became taught and he was jerked clean off his feet, landing heavily on the ground.

"Well," thought Emil, "at least the chain is strong enough to hold him."

Gordo cursed and swore, bellowing in fury.

"You're DEAD, BOY! You hear me, DEAD!" he yelled.

"I'm not dead yet!" said Emil in defiance, "But you will end up that way unless you do as I say! Like you said yesterday, this place is far away from anywhere. Shout all you want. No one will hear you! In three or four days you will die of thirst. But if I roll all those five gallon water bottles closer you will have enough to last a week."

"You're not thinking my clever little Hombre, when I tell Silus and TreeWays that you have escaped they will kill your grandfather and your friend! Then what?" said Gordo wheezing.

"You're the one who's not thinking. You're not going to tell them. You're going to tell them that everything is fine, that I am still locked up," Emil replied confidently.

"Oh yeah?! And why would I tell them that?!" Gordo growled.

"Because," explained Emil, "I am the only one who will know exactly where this place is. How are you going to tell them over that old cell phone where you are; you said you weren't even really sure yourself. How good do you think your directions are going to be? You think they would be able to find you before you die of thirst? And even better – how hard do you think your friends will look for you after you tell

188

them that I escaped? You will have totally messed up; you'll be no more use to them. I'm sure your friends would leave you here to rot. No, I am your only hope of survival now. You know I'm right. I'll bring the police back here with me as soon as I know my grandfather and Alex are safe. It's better than dying of thirst all alone here, even though you deserve it. What do you say?"

Gordo shouted and yelled and pulled and jerked at the chain to no avail, it was solid. He was not going anywhere.

Emil rolled several of the five gallon barrels of water over to Gordo, staying well out of reach. The food and the rest of the rum were too far for Gordo to get to. Emil threw some of the food over to him too.

"If you tell them I've got away they'll kill my grandfather and Alex, but you will die then too, because if they die, I will forget where you are. Do you understand?" Emil commanded

Gordo looked at Emil with furious anger but nodded.

"Good," said Emil. "You better pray we all get out of this alive and in one piece. Now you can see what it's like to have a chain around your neck!"

Emil made sure that there was nothing lying around that Gordo could use to cut the chain. Leaving the building, he rolled the heavy iron door of the factory closed and used the third padlock to lock it.

He opened the SUV, and found his rubber boots. Using the tweezers he had taken out of the belt pocket he pulled out the thorns from his feet which he had got from his drop from the window, and then put on the boots.

Getting in the driver's seat, Emil decided that getting caught driving a car without a license was the least of his problems at that moment. It was an automatic vehicle which would make it easier to drive, more like his cousin's go-cart he had driven a few times, just a lot bigger. He would take it slow and hope for the best.

"Just put the lever in 'D' for drive and then it's just a simple matter of 'stop pedal' and 'go pedal,'" he said to himself. "Just take it nice and slow."

The note had instructed him to get to a police station and get in touch with the Professor. He would do his best to do so.

"Okay," thought Emil feeling a mixture of relief and joy at having succeeded in escaping, "let me get out of here!"

Chapter Fifteen

The Temple and the King

Bodhi rolled slowly down the steep muddy slope in low four-wheel drive, dense jungle surrounding her on all sides. No vehicles had driven down this old logging road for years. They were now a long, long way down it. Gilberto had been walking ahead of Bodhi, clearing the way of the fallen logs, vines and other vegetation that were blocking the road with his machete. When they reached the river bank at the bottom of the slope, Gilberto got back into Bodhi and spoke to Alex.

"The river is up pretty high, but we are lucky, the current's not that strong. We should be able to drive through it as long as we can stay on the old road's surface, it's good and hard. It should only be about a meter deep but the drop off on both sides is very deep so we must stay on it. The crossing isn't straight either; there is a bit of a curve to the right. I will tell you how much to turn and when, okay? I would walk in front to guide you but the current is too strong for a person to wade across. It would wash me away. The Land Rover, especially with the weight of three other men, should have no problem as long as we don't slip off the edge. I have been across this river hundreds of times; I will get you across," said Gilberto.

"Bodhi, please let me know if we are getting close to the edges. I have been across this river many times but I'll need you to guide me so that I can guide Alex," Gilberto communicated to Bodhi telepathically.

"Of course I will, but it's still going to be risky," answered Bodhi, getting ready for her swim.

Alex looked across the river to where Gilberto was pointing but could not see an obvious exit point.

"Okay Gilberto, I'm ready. We're in your hands," said Alex.

Looking around at his passengers he added, "Right everyone, seat belts off and roll the windows down in case we capsize and have to swim for it. Okay Gilberto, here we go, nice and steady, just let me know when to start turning so we stay on course."

Bodhi's wheels turned and she entered the water, washing away the thick red mud, sticks and branches that had accumulated in her undercarriage on the rough thirty kilometres she had just covered. The river was soon up to, and then past, the wheel arches. The long snorkel extension on the air intake made it possible for her to drive through fairly deep water and still keep her engine running.

Alex concentrated hard, making sure not to stall the vehicle. If that were to happen, water would flood the exhaust pipe and damage Bodhi's engine, leaving them not only stranded in the middle of the river but also many kilometres deep into the jungle with no back up transport.

This was not just any piece of jungle they had journeyed into either, this was La Selva Maya, the Maya Forest. It was the largest continuous area of jungle north of the Amazon basin. It not only included many hundreds of thousands of acres in Belize, but millions of acres more in the neighbouring countries of Guatemala and Southern Mexico. Not the sort of place to get stranded or lost in. It was a truly huge green expanse, pulsating with life and energy; world famous for being one of the most challenging jungles in the world.

Bodhi directed Gilberto, who in turn passed on her careful guidance to Alex, who steered Bodhi slowly across the big river. On two occasions all the passengers could feel when the wheels on one side, and then the other, had veered too close to the drop on the edge of the road and she started to slowly slip off the side. Bodhi instantly, but very carefully, adjusted her directions to Gilberto, so as not to over correct and slip off completely, which would certainly mean rolling and sinking into the flooded river.

"Come on, that's the way! Easy does it!" Alex said to the steering wheel, as was now his unconscious habit.

As they entered the middle section of the river where the current was strongest, all of their hearts leapt into their mouths as they felt the upstream side of the Land Rover lift slightly upwards until only the two wheels on the downstream side were in contact with the submerged road surface.

"Everyone shift your weight over to upstream!" Alex ordered like a ship's captain.

Immediately Gilberto, Kiloboy, TreeWays and Silus obeyed, moving as far across as they could.

"That's my lady, settle down now! Settle down lass. That's the way!" Alex said coaxingly to the Land Rover as they all felt the wheels come back into contact with the river bottom and they passed the most dangerous mid-flow section of the river crossing.

There was an audible release of breath as everyone realized that the worst was, hopefully, over.

The three passengers in the back seat were silent and tense. None of them had ever done anything like this and for three men who were usually in full control of all they did, to have to sit passively in the backseat, their lives in the hands of someone else they did not know or trust, was proving to be quite a challenge. Beads of sweat formed on all of their brows and it was not from the humidity.

Now and again Alex looked at their sweaty faces in the rear view mirror. Faces full of tension, with tight jaw muscles trying hard not to show the fear they felt, sunglasses hiding their eyes; the windows to their twisted, dark souls.

Alex felt that there was something vaguely familiar about the younger Belizean, the one they called Kiloboy and the thug in charge, Silus, but he just could not put his finger on it. Bodhi picked up on Alex's thoughts. She knew where they had met Kiloboy before but could not place Silus either. As they motored on through the river both of them pondered this thought. Silus had such an ominous and foreboding energy. It was like sitting in a car with a bomb that could explode at any second.

Finally, they reached the other side. In a flash, Gilberto had slid out of the passenger window and moved to the front of the bonnet holding onto the foliage, cutting cables with his left hand and chopping at the thick vines and branches that had been washed across the exit point and which could easily hamper Bodhi's forward momentum.

In a matter of seconds, Gilberto's razor sharp machete had sliced the way clear. Alex accelerated to get up the steep bank and Bodhi broke free of the river, red muddy water gushing from her chassis onto the jungle floor.

Alex decided that they should take a break and stretch their legs. He looked into the rear view mirror and saw relief on all three faces. Silus mopped the sweat off his brow and then slowly took off his sunglasses.

Alex found himself staring straight into one cold, ice blue eye and one almost black eye that stared back, as lifeless as a shark's. Alex's skin crawled, a cold rush of adrenaline flooded through his being as realisation dawned.

The hairs on his arms and the back of his neck stood straight up and he felt as if he had ice water running down his spine. Now he knew where he had met this man before, and so did Bodhi. It was the man from his dream, a dream that was now becoming reality. The suddenness of the revelation led

Alex into letting his foot slip off Bodhi's clutch before she was in neutral. They shuddered to a halt as her engine sputtered out.

"Ha," said Silus contemptuously, "you can't even drive! It's a flippin' miracle we made it through the river! I'll drive on the way back."

"Not if I can help it," thought Bodhi, Alex and Gilberto simultaneously.

"We need to have a short break," said Alex looking at Silus. "I need to talk to Gilberto about the old logging camp and how far away from it the temple is. I also need to see whether we will be able to drive all the way there or, if we can't, how far away we will need to park the Land Rover. All the equipment for the analysis is installed in the back and powered by the Land Rover's engine and electrical system."

"Alright, we'll take a break, no need to bore me with the details," said Silus.

"Gilberto, can you hear me?" asked Bodhi silently.

"Yes, Bodhi, what is it?" replied Gilberto's mind.

"I need to share a vision with you. A while ago the spirit of King Nanchancaan led me on an astral journey to his temple. I was able to contact Alex in his dream state and take him with me. The king was warning me about this man Silus. That he possesses a deadly threat to you all, especially your grandson which is strange as he is not with us. It will become clear when I share the vision with you. Are you ready?"

"Yes," answered Gilberto. "I'm ready."

"Gilberto? Gilberto!" Alex said even louder, gently shaking him by the shoulder. "Are you okay? You've been staring into space for minutes now!"

Gilberto's eyes regained their focus and he looked at Alex, "Yes I'm fine Alex. I'm sorry, I was getting some information. I'm back now."

"Information? What are you talking about?" asked Alex.

Gilberto just gave a slight smile and shrugged, looking around at the three hoodlums who were all staring mockingly at him.

"Okay, never mind," said Alex, dismissing the strange behaviour and equally mysterious explanation. "Let's go over there and have a look at this map. I want you to try and show me where you think the logging camp is, the place where you found the box with the logger's daily work log book. Then I need you to show me where you think the temple is from there. That way I can look at the topography to see where the hills and valleys, swamps and boggy areas are on the map and plan our route and camp sites accordingly. Come, let's go over there into that clearing where that big amate strangler fig tree has fallen down. We can use the trunk as a table to put the map on it. It's a shame we don't have a GPS fix on both places, it would make it all a lot quicker."

Gilberto followed Alex into the steamy clearing, out of earshot of the three gangsters.

"Sorry, Gilberto," said Alex, "we are actually just going to keep following this logging track until we get to the old loggers camp like you told me back in your home that night. I just needed an excuse to talk to you alone."

"Good, me too," replied the old Chiclero.

"I have to tell you Alex, Kiloboy was one of the men that attacked you on the highway, and Silus is the man from the dream you had. I'm convinced he intends to kill us when he has the artefacts. He may even want to kill us as soon as we have led him to the temple. I truly believe he intends to kill everyone, including the two men with him and the fat man who has Emil. He has an evil and dark heart; he follows the Lords of Death, and is completely without compassion or pity."

Alex's jaw dropped and he stared at Gilberto dumbfounded.

"How on earth do you know about my dream?!" said Alex, totally incredulous. "Gilberto, I'm completely amazed!

How can you possibly know about my dream? Are you psychic?"

"Psychic? I don't know, maybe," said Gilberto, "but I am a shaman. I'm an old Chiclero, Alex, a Belizean bushman – but, I am also a shaman... I will tell you how I know these things, but now is not the right time."

"Okay, but you must tell me later. I agree with you, Silus is probably the most evil person I've ever met. He is obviously insane, a very dangerous homicidal maniac. Probably a sociopath," said Alex glancing over at the gang of three who were in various attitudes of repose, either in, or on, the Land Rover.

"We have to use all our skill and knowledge to get the better of these men," said Alex. "We need to do our best to turn the tables and put us back in control and in such a way that they keep Gordo from harming Emil. It's not going to be easy."

"Yes," said Gilberto, "We will need to plan very carefully, I'll do all I can, I'm ready to do whatever needs to be done, you can count on that. The logging camp is about another four hours away. You won't easily be able to drive the Land Rover to the temple itself, probably not without a couple of big chainsaws."

"Well I only have one chainsaw, and its medium sized, just for emergencies," said Alex.

"I don't want to use any chainsaws," said Gilberto. "The forest has had too many trees cut down for no good reason recently. Besides, even if we could drive, it's only about a fifteen minute walk to the temple from the old logging camp anyway."

"Okay, good," said Alex, "We will each come up with as many ideas as we can between here and the old logging camp and compare them when we get there, then make a plan."

"Alex, why do you talk to your Land Rover?" asked Gilberto out of the blue.

197

"What?" said Alex, not sure he had heard correctly.

"Your Land Rover, why do you talk to it?" asked Gilberto again.

"Oh, I don't know," said Alex, slightly embarrassed, "it's become a habit I guess. Much better than talking to myself! I'm often in the Land Rover for hours at a time on my own, so I guess it's a way of feeling that I have some company. Besides, I feel she has her own character and personality in my mind, sounds crazy doesn't it? But many people do the same with ships and boats, don't they, so I know I'm not completely loopy. I think people form bonds with any vehicle or vessel that they really, seriously, have to rely on to get them from A to B safely, especially when their very lives depend on it. Whether it's a captain of a ship hoping to cross an ocean safely; or just me, hoping to make it through a remote and hazardous jungle. When I get to my destination safely and in one piece I always feel a strong bond and connection with the vehicle and people that I shared the experience with."

"Doesn't sound at all crazy to me," said Gilberto, smiling, "but then I am a shaman."

"Talking to yourself is okay too, Alex. Just don't answer yourself – that's when your friends will call the men with the white jackets!" said Gilberto, smiling.

Alex laughed, appreciating Gilberto's upbeat attitude given the dire circumstances they were faced with.

"Bodhi," Gilberto suddenly said.

Alex looked up from the map he was putting away.

"What?" he asked.

"That's your Land Rover's name, Alex. Her name is Bodhi," Gilberto said, a twinkle in his eyes.

"Hah!" said Alex. "Really? Well that's a fitting name for her; it suits her! Okay Gilberto, Bodhi it is, if you say so – why not, I like it. Bodhi, so be it!"

"It's not up to you or me, Alex," thought Gilberto. "If only you knew!"

Just as Gilberto had predicted, almost exactly four hours later, the first of the big rusting shells of the antique logging machinery came into view. Overgrown with vegetation and with huge trees growing out of them they were now as much a part of the jungle scenery as the trees, vines and canopy above.

Old steam driven engines, with huge solid iron wheels sat silent and ghostly; the relics of a bygone era. The completely corroded and abandoned vehicles and machinery stood testament to man's ability to brave the harshest environments as long as there was money to be made. Bringing with him these immensely heavy and cumbersome inventions, only to abandon them once they had loyally performed their function and man had got what he had come for.

These were the remnants of the mahogany and logwood industries that had led to the settlement and development of Belize by people brought from the distant lands of Great Britain and Africa, some willingly, in the hope of making their fortunes, and others unwillingly, as slaves. A bygone era indeed, where different rules applied, and with a different set of values which were now part of history except for the pursuit of power and wealth; that had never changed and Alex thought probably never would.

They pulled up and stopped near one of the shadowy, rusting hulks, the outline of which was hard to make out, so completely had the jungle claimed its body.

It had been a hard two hours, stopping and starting as Gilberto's jungle trail, known locally as a 'piccardo', along the old logging road had been widened enough for the Land Rover to pass along it. On most occasions, Alex had joined Gilberto, both of them chopping hard and long at fallen trees and incredibly thick tangles of vines and vegetation. After a very short time white salt stains covered their sweat soaked shirts as they lost about a litre of sweat per hour together with minerals and essential salts which were contained in it.

Along the way, Gilberto had gone back to Bodhi to collect his Koshtal medicine bag which he slung over his shoulder. Every now and then he paused to pick a leafy herb, a piece of vine or a strip of bark. On one such occasion Gilberto was out of sight of the group on the other side of a fairly big fallen tree, so no one noticed when he made a quick grab and put something quite different into his bag. When he emerged a few minutes later, after he and Alex had cleared the way, Alex swore he saw Gilberto's bag move slightly, as if there were something alive inside it.

Silus, TreeWays and Kiloboy took great pleasure in watching young Steele and the old man sweating and hard at work; chopping, pushing, lifting and hauling the vegetation clear. None of them lifted a finger to help, but all of them took turns to make comments on how slow they were or what a bad job they were doing. Twice, the mud became so thick and so deep Alex used Bodhi's winch to get them through, attaching the long winch cable to big straps that were in turn wrapped around the thick trunks of big trees.

At one of the enforced stops, TreeWays had taken to entertaining himself by flinging lumps of mud at Alex and Gilberto, laughing at the irritation he was causing. All three hoodlums had sprayed each other down with Alex's insect repellent but had refused to let Alex and Gilberto use of any of it at all. Silus reasoned that they might run out of it and he and his men needed it more than the workers.

A lump of red clay mud hit Gilberto square in the back of his head. The three villains roared with laughter. Gilberto turned and glared at TreeWays and noticed that TreeWays was leaning against a tree that he had trimmed the lower branches of a few minutes earlier. The tree had bunches of small brown berries, its oval shaped leaves were crinkled around the edges and where Gilberto had cut the small branches, jet black sap was oozing out of the trunk. TreeWays hadn't noticed that he had now got a fair amount of the sap on his neck and arms.

Gilberto turned back to his job of cutting. Barely moving his lips he whispered to Alex, "When you can, take a good look at the tree that TreeWays is leaning against. It's called che chem negro, the black poisonwood tree. Make sure you do not go near it or touch it, okay?"

Alex casually looked around making note of it and saw TreeWays leaning against it.

"Thanks Don Gilberto. Duly noted," said Alex looking back at the wall of vegetation they were clearing.

Just then, a clog of red mud hit the back of his head followed by gales of laughter.

Gilberto looked back at TreeWays and said in Creole, "You shouldn't abuse us like this, Tata Duende is watching you. You betta mind he doesn't put Obia on you! You in di forest now bway, there are spirits here! You betta mine yo'self and have respec' for di forest and her spirits."

"What's he yakking on about?" asked Silus from his perch high up on top of Bodhi's roof rack, surveying his 'servants' working from the loftiest position he could find, smoking his cigarette leisurely.

"Ain't nuthin', just foolishness. No worry yourself 'bout it maan. Dis ol' man tink dat Tata Duende, some jungle boogieman is gonna put some curse on me! Fool!" he said throwing another mud clog hard at Gilberto.

Gilberto looked TreeWays dead in his eyes.

"Mind what you say about Tata Duende. He is the protector of the forest, not some childish boogieman. If he curses you it is because you deserve it!" said Gilberto with feeling.

"Alright, enough twaddle about flippin' mumbo jumbo voodoo, gramps!" growled Silus. "Shut your trap and get working. We haven't got all bleedin' day now have we!"

The presence of the noisy intruders had alerted and disturbed a large troop of howler monkeys that were nearby. Swinging gracefully through the trees they came to investigate the strangers. As soon as they were overhead they started their roaring howl. It was deafening. Silus had to resort to yelling into TreeWay's and Kiloboy's ears to make himself heard.

Silus could not believe that such an incredibly loud noise could be made by relatively small monkeys. He hated it.

Bodhi, on the other hand, was having a great conversation with the monkeys. She explained who they were and what they were doing here. The howlers welcomed Bodhi to their area of forest. Bodhi asked them if they had heard of a jaguar called Balaam. They replied that they had indeed heard of the mighty jaguar that roamed the Cockscomb basin and the ranges of the Maya mountains. She asked them if they would send him a message for her, to which the alpha male, the leader of the troop, agreed to do with pleasure.

The howlers peered at the group below through the canopy, their small primate faces looking down curiously at Kiloboy with eyes that challenged him. They were directly above where Silus and Kiloboy were now standing, shaking the tree branches hard with indignation, snapping the thinner ones off and hurling them down at their heads.

Kiloboy screamed and yelled back at them, goading the howlers into roaring louder and more insistently. Then something else began to rain down on them and it wasn't leaves and branches!

Bodhi's conversation was cut short as shots rang out.

"Monkey poop!" yelled Kiloboy. "They're pooping on us!"

Alex watched as Kiloboy, his baseball cap perched at a jaunty angle on his head, fired his pistol at the howler monkeys. Alex noted that he held the handgun side on, a typical gangster pose which did not allow the shooter to align the weapon's sights easily or quickly. The result made for very inaccurate shooting, which was a blessing for the howler monkeys that beat a hasty retreat, unharmed.

"Save your bullets!" ordered TreeWays, scratching his neck. "I hope you brought plenty."

"I got nuff bullets man! Why? You looking to borrow my little brother here?" answered Kiloboy irritated, waving the pistol around.

"Nah. I got my own an' I done got nuff bullets too! But I only tek my little brother out when he gonna actually shoot and kill something! I no play around like you. Gordo's correc', you full a yout'full pride an arrogance. You tink' you wah big man waving that gun around don't you?" TreeWays said, rubbing his arm which was beginning to tingle slightly.

Kiloboy sneered at TreeWays.

"I di future bredren! When you look pan me you looking at di future! You're 'ole school. Nuff respec' to you TreeWays, you da boss man, I no mek no mistake, you di boss but I; I di future man. An I mek those baboons shut up now too, didn't I?"

TreeWays laughed hard, scratching his face again, "You gotta be alive to have a future fool! How long you tink you gonna survive for, youth? How many brothers looking to give you payback for tings you done to dem? How many got a beef wid you? Enjoy di ride bway, it's gonna be a short one. How many of your crew been shot dead already. Look at me, you tink I can just give dis life up an goh home, retire and relax? No way, maan. As soon as I get too slow, too old or too weak to defend my territory I gonna get eaten! The second I relax I gonna ketch wah bullet from some old enemy or some young fool like you who wants to take over, or wanna say dat he de big man who tek out TreeWays. It's just like here in the jungle, zacktly di same ting. Da strong rule, the weak die! Same ting. Di law of di jungle, maan, you betta wise up fool. Your future short."

In response, Kiloboy just lifted up his baggy tee shirt, revealing his tattoo and scar covered torso. There was one huge tattoo that covered his entire chest with gruesome designs of skulls and scorpions. In big letters tattooed under the main design it read, 'Gangster For Life'.

"I done mek my choice!" Kiloboy said fiercely.

Alex and Gilberto had opened the back of the Land Rover and were packing two large expedition rucksacks. They packed extra rations and water for the three gangsters and added first aid kits, a long rope, extra radio batteries and other bits of kit and equipment. Very soon the backpacks weighed almost thirty kilos a piece, which was fifty percent heavier than was comfortable to carry through the hot humid jungle.

"Which way Gilberto?" asked Alex.

Gilberto pointed at a huge dark brown ball shaped object that surrounded the spine covered trunk of a give-and-take palm tree and said, "Right next to that palm with the termites nest on it is the start of the Sac Be, that's Maya for White Road."

Alex had read about Sac Be's. Most Maya temples had them. Sac Be's were raised causeways built of stone, usually a straight road along the top of an embankment which could be very long indeed. Alex had read that the Maya used to cover these stone causeways with white lime plaster that they would make by burning limestone. The result was a dazzling white, long and straight causeway road that was used by ceremonial processions and would always eventually lead into the lower plaza of the temple itself. The plazas were big, square, flat areas, like giant courtyards surrounded on three sides by pyramid temple structures or palace buildings which contained rooms for the high priests, nobles and warriors.

"Good. That's nice and straight forward," responded Alex, thankful that they would not have to do much route planning.

"We have all we need to make a camp there and although with all this extra weight it will probably take half an hour to get there, it'll only take fifteen to get back to the Land Rover whenever we need to do the analysis. I wonder how Emil is doing?"

"Me too!" said Gilberto. "I don't know what I'll do if anything happens to Emil."

"Let's hope he's managed to make a break for it. If he has, I doubt they will kill us right away, they still need us. They'll hide the fact from us so that we keep to doing what they want, but if he does escape they will want to move a lot more quickly in the hopes that they can get what they want before Emil has time to bring the police. Then they will surely kill us as soon as they can. We need to watch carefully for any signs that Emil has escaped or that they are about to get rid of us. If we could be sure that Emil has gotten away we could make a break for it and leave them right here. They're actually much more dependent on us than they realize. I'll need to send a SITREP to my grandfather before we leave the Land Rover," Alex added.

"Bodhi," corrected Gilberto.

"Ah yes! Sorry, before we leave Bodhi!" said Alex, smiling.

They walked back to Bodhi and her occupants.

"I have to send a message to a professor in the UK before we leave the Land Rover, and he may have information for me to download," Alex said looking at Silus.

"Okay," said Silus.

"And I have to get in touch with Gordo and tell him not to kill the boy yet – so it looks like we both need to communicate. You first. I'll be right next to you, so don't try anything," Silus added.

The two of them got into the back of Bodhi and Alex booted up the onboard computer and satellite communications uplink. It took a couple of minutes for it to make the connection because of the thick overhead canopy. Silus sat out of the way of the webcam so as not to be seen by the Professor.

Soon the Professor's wise face appeared on the screen and his deep measured tones boomed through the speaker system.

"Good to see you! What news?" he asked.

"Very good to see you too! We are approximately one kilometre away from the temple site which is due north of our current position. Our intention is to proceed to the temple on foot and establish a base camp in the plaza area of the main temple structure. Once we have done our initial survey we will upload photos, and put other samples into the digital spectrum analysis for your archaeologists to analyse. I will be taking the sat phone and the E.P.I.R.B. with me in case of emergencies and I'm carrying the usual first aid and other kit. Otherwise all is well," Alex reported.

"What do you have for me?"

"Well," said the Professor. "I need you to specifically look for two things which are hopefully still there. One is a large – between two to four meters long – smooth rectangular stone called a 'stele'. It may be standing upright or it may have fallen over, it will be about a meter or more wide and as much as half a metre thick, perhaps more. There should be carvings and Maya glyphs on one side of it. Steles would usually be located in the main plaza area, right near the base of the biggest temple pyramid. There could be several of these steles next to each other in a row. If you find these, send photos of the carvings and glyphs for us to analyse right away, and also send pictures of the wall paintings inside the room at the top of the pyramid again. Emil's photos were great but the camera you have is a professional one with a much higher resolution and X-Ray style features. Oh yes, one last thing, we've been analysing the old log book again that Emil discovered and we found something very interesting. The author mentions seeing a square stone with only two glyphs carved on it. From its description it's not a stele or standing stone, it sounds more like a paving stone of some sort. Unfortunately, there is no further information as to its precise location and although the author did attempt a drawing of the two glyphs, my Maya experts here and the experts in Belize can't be sure what they are meant to represent. Send photos of it, if you can find it, as this is an unusual anomaly."

"Will do, I'll send another SITREP with the results of our first efforts at the same time tomorrow."

"Great, thanks Alex. Please give my regards to Emil and his grandfather – there are a lot of very excited people waiting to see what you discover! It's a bit dark in that Land Rover Alex but it looks like you have a pretty nasty bruise on your jaw. Are you alright?" asked his grandfather with concern in his voice.

"Absolutely!" said Alex. "I just slipped and fell and hit the side of my face on a rock. I'm fine, really."

"Tut, tut, Alex, not like you to break standard operating procedures! You know any and all injuries must be reported in incident reports. Make sure you log it."

"Right! Apologies, it slipped my mind! Will do," he said glancing quickly at Silus who was glaring back at him.

"Okay, then. We'll chat again tomorrow. Good luck!"

Alex put the mouse cursor on the shutdown buttons, but not before he very quickly clicked the Synchronise/Update Stats" button that would transmit Bodhi's exact location to his grandfather. Silus did not notice and in the blink of an eye the connection was closed.

Alex passed the sat phone to Silus who called Gordo.

"Gordo! It's Silus, the code now is 47, give me your response," Silus barked.

"Good," said Silus hearing the correct response to the timings code that they had pre-arranged.

"Is the boy still secure? Fine, we are all okay too, so no need to get rid of the boy yet. I'll be in touch again same time tomorrow," Silus said, about to hang up.

"Wait!" insisted Alex. "How do I know that Emil is really okay? I want to speak to him myself to verify that he is still okay!"

Silus looked hard at Alex and extended his arm towards Alex's face, holding the Sat phone out to him, showing Alex the keypad. As Alex reached for it, Silus pressed the red 'end call' button.

"You'll take my word for it and LIKE it!" he sneered.

Without showing his ire so as not to concern Gilberto, Alex kept busy by turning on his handheld GPS and locking onto several satellite signals. He logged Bodhi's exact position and programmed it to automatically save waypoints every fifty meters. Next, he made ready his Silva type 54B sighting compass and his pace counting beads which were strung along a piece of parachute cord and tied to a D ring which was sewn inside the top pocket of his bush shirt.

After re-sharpening their machetes with their files, Gilberto and Alex helped each other strap on the heavily loaded backpacks and Alex told Silus and crew to follow them. They set off down the trail.

Alex had not given Silus & Co. the benefit of a safety briefing. Usually, he would always give one, explaining which hazards to look out for, the order of march and where and how to step so as to avoid danger and injury. Their ignorance was to Alex's advantage, perhaps one of them would step on a snake or some other jungle nasty. Instead, he had limited his brief talk to assuring them that they would not have to walk for more than half an hour and it would be a fairly slow pace.

TreeWays was now constantly scratching his arm, neck and face as the itch slowly spread. At the moment it was not much more than a slight discomfort, he hardly noticed his left hand unconsciously scratching away every few minutes.

Gilberto took point position at the front of the line and Alex took the second position, a couple of meters behind him so that he could help clear the way. The five men were strung out in single file which was the only way to travel down the narrow trail. Silus was third in line followed by TreeWays, with Kiloboy last. They marched along, the new rubber boots starting to rub and chafe the gangster's feet and ankles who were also wearing cotton socks which were by now already soggy with sweat.

As they moved up the wide, vegetation covered causeway, Alex looked left and right. If Gilberto had not pointed out what they were walking on Alex would have probably thought it was just a natural land feature, not a manmade structure that was hundreds of years old. He imagined what the ceremonial processions would have looked like passing along here in past centuries – Lords, high ranking nobles and priests wearing feather headdresses, highly decorated carved masks, the warriors escorting the procession armed with atlatls and stone war clubs made from intricately knapped flint. He felt honoured that he was now walking in their footsteps, along their sacred way.

They hiked through the shadow filled jungle, surrounded by a multitude of different species of plants. Alex remembered that the word 'jungle' itself originated from a Hindu word 'jangal', or 'jangala', which meant something like 'tangled mess'.

"That's the big difference," Alex thought to himself. "This isn't an oak forest like the one surrounding the cottage in Wales, or a pine forest. There are no dominant tree species here. A kahune palm tree grows next to a mahogany tree that grows next to a strangler fig. The strangler figs, in turn, semi-parasitically grow on other trees eventually killing them and absorbing their nutrients. That's what makes this a jungle. Diverse plants and trees all thrown together."

It was a wonderful and beautiful place. Now he truly felt back at home. If only Emil was safe and he and Gilberto were not here at the mercy of three cutthroats, it would be perfect.

The Sac Be rose more and more steeply until the line of men passed through a gap in a large leaf and tree covered mound that formed the outer perimeter wall of the temple. They had finally arrived. Alex made a conscious effort to burn the memory of his first steps onto the temple into his mind taking in every minute detail. He wanted to be able to remember this experience for the rest of his life, almost no one on earth would ever do what he was doing now. Here he was, actually setting foot onto an ancient Maya temple, lost in the jungle for centuries and more than likely belonging to an incredible historical figure – King Nanchancaan! Despite the circumstances, he was utterly overjoyed to finally be here.

"BRILLIANT!" he shouted in his head.

The group walked to the centre of the flat square area that formed the lower plaza and looked around. Behind them and to the South, the wall mound was fairly high, at least three meters, as were the wall mounds to the east and west on either side of them.

Directly in front of them, to the north, was a much larger wall mound that made up the top line of the square. It was at least twenty five metres high, with a huge dilapidated stone staircase going straight up the middle of it.

Alex and Gilberto shed the backpacks and all of them walked over to the leaf and dirt covered stone staircase and began to climb the big steps. Parts of the staircase had collapsed due to the pressure from roots that had pushed between cracks in the stone steps, forcing the big rectangular blocks of limestone apart. The angle of the stairs was deceptively steep and all of the men had to climb carefully on the slippery surface. At the top was a small square shaped landing. Along the crest of the mound to their left and right was a series of sixteen ruined and collapsed chambers, eight on either side of the landing.

They walked from the small landing into a smaller square that formed the upper plaza of the main temple area. There, directly in front of them rose the huge main pyramid structure of the temple. Alex had done his homework and knew that this main temple would have been dedicated to the sun, the top of it was so high that it broke out above the canopy. To their left and right rose two more, slightly smaller, but equally impressive pyramidal temples, the one on the right he knew would have been dedicated to the moon and the one on the left dedicated to the planet Venus. Some of the moulded plaster decorations were still visible on the walls, stylized masks representing jaguar faces on either side of another staircase that led up to the top of the structure. A large doorway was visible at the very top. In front of the doorway was a large stone platform. By now, Alex was not at all surprised to see that it looked like a ruined and leaf covered version of the one he had seen in his dream. Alex felt that there were strange forces at work here.

At the base of the main temple pyramid there was a line of five large rectangular stones. The two on each side were still standing; the biggest one in the middle had toppled over. Gilberto moved a short distance away from the others who were all silently taking in the majestic scene which, even though it was all leaf and tree covered, exuded an aura of power. Gilberto took a handful of small granules out of his Koshtal. He knelt down on the ground and in the blink of an eye had made a tiny fire onto which he sprinkled the contents of his hand. Dense, heavy, pure white smoke rose from the flames, the scent of the copal incense spreading quickly throughout the area. Gilberto rose to his feet and started chanting quietly, in a low voice. He turned to all four directions, ending by facing north towards the main pyramid. As he stopped, the loud warning call of a crested quan sounded near them. Gilberto looked up at the large jungle fowl; it was almost the size of a turkey but not nearly as fat, it had brown-black plumage with a buff, mottled breast and a red wattle under its chin. It was perched high up in the canopy and had been feeding on ramon tree berries.

"A warning call," thought Gilberto. "I hear you! I understand."

Alex's blood ran cold watching Gilberto. The sounds of the chanting and the smell of the incense were exactly the same as he had experienced in his dream. It was all over in a few minutes and Silus broke the spell.

"Stop that mumbo jumbo and start building me something I can relax in. I want to put my feet up and get the hell away from all these bugs that are pestering me! Now! Move!"

The group moved back to the lower plaza and Alex and Gilberto set up three jungle sleeping units that Alex had brought for himself, Gilberto and Emil. The three gangsters immediately shed their boots and lay back in the hammocks under the mosquito netting.

"Do we have any spare sleeping units?" Gilberto asked Alex.

"No, I'm sorry Gilberto. We'll have to rough it and build natural shelters for ourselves. I think 'A' frame shelters would be best," Alex replied.

Silus, overhearing the conversation, chimed in with a question.

"Do you play golf?"

"No," answered Alex irritated, not seeing the relevance of the question.

"I didn't think so. You're too busy running around saving the planet and hugging trees. Never the less, I'm sure you know what a handicap is, don't you?"

Alex didn't bother answering the rhetorical question.

"Well," continued the sadistic Silus. "There's a saying – misery loves company. I find this place miserable – you clearly don't. I don't like that, so I have decided that you two need to be given a handicap to even things up a bit and make me feel that your suffering is greater than mine. That would make me feel a whole lot better. So, from now on you are not allowed to use anything in your packs. No changes of clothes, no food, nothing unless I say so and now that we are here you are to leave your machetes with me. If you want to make some sort of shelter that's okay, but, you'll have to do it without your machetes. It will be entertaining watching you try. You only have a couple of hours before dark. Oh and make sure we get our dinner by seven pm, latest. Got it?"

Alex and Gilberto could only glare at Silus, while TreeWays and Kiloboy chuckled in their hammocks.

"I didn't hear you! Got it?" Silus asked again.

"Got it," said Alex taking his and Gilberto's machetes over to Silus.

Alex and Gilberto picked a spot out of earshot of the gangsters and to Silus' anger they quickly built two solid 'A' frame beds using trees as the main supports and a combination of long pieces of dead but solid branches for the rest of the structure. They then tied the frames together tightly using a combination of strong iguana tie-tie and coral vines. Winding and weaving long strips of bark from the Mahawa tree around the horizontal poles, they fashioned comfortable looking beds which they then padded with Kahune palm leaves as mattresses. Next, they broke off several dozen bay leaf palm leaves, their huge fan shape and long stems making them perfectly suited to act as waterproof covers over their A-frame shelters. Lastly, Alex prepared a fireplace and built a thatched shelter over it as well in case it should rain.

He added a heat reflector behind it in the shape of a wall of logs, which served the dual purpose of drying out wet wood and reflecting heat into the shelters. The reflected heat was necessary to ward off the chilly and damp drafts that often gusted from two am to sunrise.

Gilberto collected several large pieces of dead, dry termite nests which he would later use to make a smudge fire. The termite's nests, once set on fire, would smoulder slowly, all night long, producing a thick aromatic smoke that would keep the mosquitoes away, allowing them to sleep comfortably even without the benefit of mosquito nets.

Later that evening, when Alex delivered the evening meal to Silus and company, he overheard Silus and TreeWays discussing how they could get a looting crew organized. TreeWays obviously had some experience with this type of thievery and he told Silus that a team of ten strong men could dig a vertical slit trench right through the main temple structure, from top to bottom in as little as four days if they took shifts and dug day and night.

He informed Silus that their best bet was to dig sideways through the temple, cutting into the east and west flanks. This, he assured him, would be the fastest way as the Maya used to build the doorways to the inner chambers of the temple on these sides. When a king died, the Maya would bury him under the floor of one of these chambers and then block up the doorway with plaster and rocks. The blocked doorways were much easier to break through than trying to cut through the gigantic solid stone blocks that made up the temple walls. Finding the old doorways was the key to a speedy operation.

TreeWays had instructed Kiloboy to organize the team and have them equipped, ready and on standby in the gang's Orange Walk hide out. He told him to make sure they would be ready to meet them at the turn off to the old logger's road as soon as the rivers and bridges were passable again. Each man would receive three thousand dollars pay.

Kiloboy used Alex's satellite phone to call Junior in Punta Gorda and made the arrangements. Many of Kiloboy's gang had in the past worked as labourers, digging trenches to lay water pipes for the municipality. For this they were paid two dollars a metre and many were capable of earning eighty to a hundred dollars a day, every day. This was an incredible rate of work as the trenches had to be sixty centimetres wide by a metre deep.

Several of his gangsters had also previously worked digging river sand for sale to the construction industry. These young men were amazingly strong and worked like machines. A three man team could load a twenty ton dump truck in three hours, digging by hand with shovels, throwing the heavy wet sand over the high sides of the truck. They could load three trucks in a day's work. Unfortunately, as impressive as this was, the relatively low pay received for such arduous labour had caused many of these strong young men to seek the much more lucrative, but illegal, employment offered by gang leaders like TreeWays and Kiloboy.

Alex and Gilberto lay under the palm thatch roofs of their improvised shelters and discussed their options. Bodhi listened in; her consciousness nestled contentedly in the gem-like orb tucked under Alex's shirt.

"Tomorrow at first light we should get samples, photos etc. and get them off to my grandfather as soon as we can. I will also work out how I can get a cryptic message to him about our situation. I don't think we have very long before Silus decides to get rid of us, perhaps two days at most. I need my grandfather to delay the findings and results of the analyses; that might buy us some time. Remember, we are due to get hit by that tropical storm soon too. We are way inland but it will still be pretty powerful and might even help us. If it drops a lot of rain it will further delay the police search for us, but it will also delay TreeWays looting team too," said Alex, looking over at Gilberto whose face flickered in the candlelight. Slius had refused them the use of their confiscated flashlights.

"Yes Alex, true," said Gilberto, "and TreeWays is not going to be happy in the morning. That poison wood sap will take full effect tonight, especially as I set up his hammock between two more poison wood trees!"

"You didn't! That's BRILLIANT!" laughed Alex.

"Okay, let's think, they only communicate with Gordo once a day. That means if we make our escape and take the communications with us we would have, at most, twenty four hours before Gordo realized something was wrong. The problem with that plan is that it would probably take us longer than twenty four hours to find Emil, and then we would also have to be in a position to rescue him before Gordo had a chance to hurt him. That plan won't work, it's too risky. I'm also sure Silus will make Treeways and Kiloboy take turns keeping watch on us tonight so that we don't try and make a trip back to the... back to Bodhi," said Alex.

"Alex knows my name!" thought Bodhi excitedly. "Gilberto must have told him!"

"Now that we have stopped for the day, we need to think about everything we have at our disposal and make a plan. Then we'll be able to act when an opportunity presents itself. What can you tell me about the layout of this temple from your previous visits?" asked Alex.

"Well, you know about the room at the top of the main temple, then there's an aguade at the back of the temple complex. The Maya used to dig huge ponds that would collect the rainwater runoff from the temple. They would channel it through cleverly angled grooves and pipes made of clay. The water in the aguade reservoir would be used in dry season, I've made use of them many times myself. Many still hold water. Then there is a Chel Tun about four or five meters away from the left side of the Sac Be, just before you reach the outer wall of the temple complex. A Chel Tun is a storage chamber that the Maya carved into the limestone bedrock. They have a small opening, only big enough for one person to go into at a time but the chamber opens up into a big circular storage room. Usually they stored food in them," Gilberto explained.

"Great," said Alex, "that might make a really useful hiding place. They could decide to kill us at any minute so we need to be ready to make a break for it at all times. Let's agree on some emergency rendezvous points that we can fall back to or meet up at, should we get separated. Let's make the first one the Chel Tun storage chamber, we can call it position yellow. The second can be the jungle area around Bodhi. We will call that one position red. Third, and furthest away, will be the junction of the road and the river where we crossed it, that will be position blue. If we get separated we will meet up again at one of those three points, starting with the first and closest, okay?"

"Yes, that sounds good. The last time Emil and I were here I cut big notches into a long tree trunk which I used as a ladder to climb down into the Chel Tun. It's still there," said Gilberto, "but remember, if you climb into it they better not find the entrance, there is no other way out. We could get trapped in it."

"Good point. I'll bear that in mind," Alex said sombrely.

"Gilberto, if the worst happens and they come for us, I plan on fighting like ten tigers. I'm sure you feel the same. We are not going to let these thugs kill us. I will not be going quietly."

"Es cierto, mi amigo! I agree, fight to the death!" said Gilberto.

"Right!" said Alex. "Let's get our heads down, tomorrow will be a long day!"

"Goodnight my friend!" said Gilberto blowing out the candle.

Alex watched the red ember on the wick slowly die out and listened to the noises of the jungle night which quickly serenaded him to sleep.

Bodhi listened to their rhythmic breathing for a while, contemplating the awful predicament they were in and tried to come up with ways to help them. Bodhi herself drifted off eventually, gliding silently through the inky black jungle back to her metal body parked in the small clearing.

Alex and Gilberto rose just before dawn to an assortment of bird calls. First, were the chachalacas, shortly followed by the screeches and squawks of the red lored parrots and then the sing-song, watery gargling whistle of the montezuma oropendolas. The oropendolas flipped completely upside down while calling, holding onto the thin branches high in the tree tops and opening their bright yellow tails like folding fans.

The criminal trio had not slept well at all.

Kiloboy and TreeWays had taken turns doing guard duty. TreeWays' itching had become worse and worse, until it was totally unbearable. He could not believe how itchy he was. He raked at his arm, neck and face with his nails, gaining some temporary relief which was immediately followed by an even greater fiery itch.

He felt as if his skin was burning and his arm was badly swollen. His face felt very bloated too and his eyes were half closed and very puffed up. It reminded him of how he used to feel in the mornings after the bare knuckle fights he had taken part in during his youth. Thousands of tiny blisters had formed all over his arm, neck and face, and every time he moved they burst, a clear yellow serum running out of them and spreading the fiery itch further and further over his body.

Silus was sitting with his feet hanging over the edge of his hammock, looking dejectedly at his soggy cotton socks. With a sigh of resignation, he pulled them onto his soft, blistered feet. No sooner had he stepped out from under the basha sheet tarpaulin than the rain started to pour down.

"This place is total crap!" Silus thought angrily.

Jumping back under shelter, he yelled breakfast orders at Alex and when he saw the state of TreeWays he ordered his two prisoners over.

"What the hell happened to him?" he demanded, angling his head towards TreeWays, who was sitting on the edge of one of the requisitioned hammocks.

"Tata Duende!" said Gilberto. "I warned him, but he didn't listen!"

"Don't try and frighten ME with your voodoo mumbo jumbo! That's a pile of bull. You!" he shouted at Alex, "Whatever it is, get your medical kit and make it go away."

"You put Obia on me!" said TreeWays looking at Gilberto, the deep seated superstitions from childhood stories told by his grandparents flooding back to him.

"You a witch doctor!"

Gilberto just glared at TreeWays.

"Let me kill him now," said Kiloboy taking out his gun. "We done got here, we no need this ol' man no more! The other fool can get all a da knowledge about this temple. Why wi need the old man? Mek I blast him!"

"True," said Silus, "but if that river is still up on the way back out of here, I'm going to need a guide."

"Don't you mean we will need a guide?" said TreeWays.

"Of course I meant we!" barked the irritated Silus.

Alex trudged off through the rain over to the backpacks, which Kiloboy had stowed next to the jungle sleeping unit he was using. He returned with a bottle of calamine lotion and some antihistamine tablets.

"Spread this lotion over the blisters and take two of these tablets," he said, handing the bottle and pills to TreeWays.

"No need to kill either of us," said Alex looking icily at Kiloboy.

After delivering coffee and breakfast to the gang, Alex told Silus that he would need the camera, flashlights and other equipment in order to start work on the identification process for the temple. Silus allowed them to take everything Alex asked for and they stowed it all into two waterproof Ortlieb dry bags; the type canoeist's use. They then packed the dry bags into two daysacks which he and Gilberto slung onto their backs. The duo headed in the direction of the stairway leading up to the main plaza. Silus ordered Kiloboy to go with them and keep an eye on all they did. Kiloboy reluctantly threw on the waterproof poncho that he had taken from Alex's backpack and trudged along behind them.

Gilberto and Alex started their investigation. Kiloboy watched them from a distance, taking shelter under a large kahune palm tree which acted like a giant umbrella. They started with the five stele stones at the base of the main temple. The four that remained standing had been badly eroded by hundreds of years of rainfall, and eaten away by acidic secretions from lichens and mosses.

The fifth and largest stele was lying on the ground. It was much too heavy for the two men to lift, and they knew they would not receive any help from Silus & Co. Alex used his long rope, some pulleys and climbing carabiner to rig up a 'Z' drag and pig haul system that they tied over the corners of the stone on one side. This block and tackle type arrangement allowed them to increase their leverage greatly, thereby, lifting the heavy stone with ease. As the stone came up onto its side at right angles to the ground, Alex and Gilberto could see that it was covered in intricately carved glyphs and images, which had all been perfectly preserved, having been lying face down on the ground for hundreds of years.

"Perfect!" said Alex, bending over the stone, examining the inscriptions.

Bodhi also studied the beautifully carved surface through the rounded view offered from inside the crystal orb which now swung back and forth, dangling from Alex's neck.

It took two hours of painstaking work for them to clean the mud, stones and roots from all the crevices and cracks in the proper manner so as not to damage the fragile surface. Finally, it was ready to photograph. After erecting a rough shelter over it, made from large hand shaped juano palm leaves, to protect it from the rain, Alex took dozens of photos at various angles, using the shadows cast by shining their flashlights at oblique angles to the carving to highlight the relief of the shapes and designs to the best advantage.

Once they had completed the work on the stele, they lowered it gently back down into its original position. They then climbed the steep staircase to the top of the main pyramid, arriving at the platform that lay in front of the doorway to the ceremonial chamber. Kiloboy wasn't about to climb up the slippery stairs after them in the pouring rain and instead chose to laze against the base of the kahune palm, smoking a long thick cigarette, watching the rain pour down.

Right in the centre of the platform lay a big round stone disk about thirty centimetres thick and a meter and a half wide. Both Alex and Gilberto looked down at it and a chill ran up their spines. Both remembered it from the dream-vision. It was such an innocent looking stone and yet, how many blood sacrifices, animals and human, had been performed on its surface through the ages of the Maya civilization?

Alex had always been fascinated by man's perceived need to spill blood to appease the gods. The ancient Greeks, Romans, Mongolians, Indians, Babylonians and Egyptians had all done just that. So many great cultures and civilizations all had this common link to a darker side of their different histories.

Alex and Gilberto passed through the doorway. They moved into the big interior of the chamber, looking up at its vaulted stone ceiling. The room had an antechamber at the back with walls that separated it from the front chamber.

All the walls were covered in beautiful, colourful paintings. Alex adjusted the settings of the camera to cope with the dark surroundings and took several dozen high resolution photographs of all the paintings. They moved into the dark antechamber and shone their torches onto the walls where they discovered yet more paintings, but these were much fainter, hardly visible in fact.

Alex changed the camera setting to one that used a penetrative laser and infrared beams which could scan through the layer of dirt and mould, seeking out the paint molecules, producing an x-ray like view of the image hidden underneath. It was a similar technology that crime scene investigators were using to pick up chemical and biological traces that were invisible to the naked eye.

As the camera gave off its electronic whining buzz-click and the bright green laser beam scanned the wall, a creature the size of a short, small, dog bolted from the darkened back corner and shot out of the entrance, disappearing in a flash.

Alex and Gilberto nearly jumped out of their skins with fright, Alex almost dropping his camera.

"Gibnut!" exclaimed Gilberto.

"I am sure you have seen similar animals Alex. It's a huge tropical rodent that can grow to be about ten kilos, you know, like an agouti or a paca. It must have a den in the corner over there."

Gilberto shone his torch into the corner and corrected himself, "No, not a den, but a big food cache. Do you see all those big kahune nuts piled up over there?"

Alex looked over into the corner and saw the pile of nuts, each the size and shape of a hen's egg. The outer shells of many had been stripped off by the big rodent's sharp teeth.

"Here in Belize, gibnuts are hunted as a game meat. The bushmeat markets sell it as a delicacy, in fact it's nickname is 'The Royal Rat' because it was served to Queen Elizabeth II on a visit to Belize in nineteen eighty five, four years after our nation gained its independ–" Gilberto suddenly stopped his history lesson short; he stood absolutely still, staring at the corner of the room.

"Gilberto? Are you alright? What's the matter?" asked Alex.

"King Nanchancaan," stammered Gilberto, "He's in here with us. He's standing in the corner; I mean his spirit is… I can see him, he's watching us!"

"What's he doing?" asked Alex in a hushed voice, knowing better than to doubt the word of this strange and mysterious old shaman.

"He's holding his arms out to us and beckoning us to come closer," said Gilberto absently, his whole focus aimed at the corner in which Alex could see nothing but shadows and darkness.

"Well," said Alex, "let's not keep His Majesty waiting."

Taking a hold of Gilberto's arm, he walked them both in the direction of the corner.

As they started stepping onto the kahune nuts and the stripped outer shells that littered the corner Gilberto spoke again, "He's fading, he's disappearing! He's gone."

They stood for a second or two looking at the corner and then up at the ceiling. Clearly the spirit was trying to tell them something.

Gilberto started to scuff away at the leaves and nuts exposing the floor beneath, "Here! Look at this!"

"What is it?" enquired Alex looking down at where Gilberto was pointing.

Gilberto was using the inside of his right foot like a broom, sweeping away at the debris and clearing the floor.

"It's the paving stone my grandfather told me to look for!" said Alex excitedly. "The one I read about in the old logger's diary. See? There are the two glyphs next to each other! Gilberto, shine your flashlight over it at ground level so the shadows clearly show up the carvings."

Gilberto did as Alex asked and no sooner had Alex snapped several pictures than Kiloboy's voice yelled at them from the main doorway, "Wah di gian ahn in here? Wha' unu two bways up to, you been in here too long!"

"Quick," whispered Alex. "I'll go out. You cover it back up and follow me in a few seconds."

Without waiting for a response, Alex stuck his head around the wall separating the two halves of the chamber and said, "We're taking the photos we need. It takes time."

Just then, Gilberto appeared at Alex's side. Alex wondered what had inspired Kiloboy to make the climb up the stairs, and then he noticed that the rain had stopped. That, and idle curiosity, no doubt.

Alex shone his torch around the front portion of the chamber. He spotted three fragments of broken pottery. Alex placed small numbered marker cards, which had a scale rule down the sides, next to each. He photographed them in situ to record their exact positions and then carefully picked them up and gently wrapped the shards in his cotton bandana, stowing it in his day sack.

"We're finished in here for now," he said to Kiloboy.

Kiloboy had been watching Alex's careful actions with the collection of the pottery shards.

"Yeah right!" he said, walking over to several other pieces of broken pottery and stamping on them as hard as he could crushing the finely painted fragments into dust. "Now, we done here for true, les' goh!"

Upon their descent back to the campsite, Alex and Gilberto saw that TreeWays' eyes were now completely swollen and his arm was now three times its normal size.

"As much as he deserves to suffer, if that swelling doesn't come down he could be in real danger. The circulation to his fingers could get cut off. Not to mention, the possibility of him going into anaphylactic shock from the severe allergic reaction he is having," said Alex as they arrived back at camp.

"I'll need to put up a drip line and give him hydrocortisone steroids intravenously. I'll inject it into a bag of saline," said Alex looking at the huge man lying quietly, suffering in his hammock.

"I think he has been neutralized as a threat for now. He's effectively blind, and his arm is no good to him. I'll dose him up with antihistamine tablets too; they will make him very drowsy. He'll be out for the count. One down, two to go!"

"When you go and do the SITREP I will stay behind with him and help him too. Do you see that tree over there Alex, the red one with the peeling paper looking bark?" asked Gilberto, pointing it out to him, "It's called the gumbo limbo tree, or cha-ka tree in Maya. We also call it the tourist tree because it looks like a sunburned tourist whose skin is peeling! Well, the bark and leaves of that tree are a natural antidote to the poisonwood tree. I'll prepare bark poultices and a wash from the leaves which will clear up the burns and blisters. But you're right; he's no longer a real threat."

"That's a good tree to know! Similar to the dock leaves that always grow near stinging nettles back home in the UK," said Alex intrigued.

"I'll go and tell Silus that we are going to help his man. I'll need access to my medical pack," Alex added.

After running up the drip for TreeWays, the party of three set off down the jungle track to Bodhi, leaving Gilberto and TreeWays behind. Gilberto started putting the soothing bark poultices on TreeWays' arm.

"Witch Doctor, why you di help me? You poisoning me? I noh trust you!"

"Tata Duende is punishing you! You are a wicked evil man! But it is my duty as a healer and a shaman to help even the likes of you, even though you don't deserve it. I follow the path of light," said Gilberto, wrapping the bark poultice in place.

"You have given your heart to the path of darkness and death. I can't say what I will do if you or your friends harm my grandson. Protecting the young and innocent from evil or harm can sometimes mean the taking of life, if the Great Power decides that it must be so. For now, I will help you; tomorrow, I cannot say. Our paths are linked; the outcome of our fates is still to be decided," proclaimed Gilberto.

Silus and Kiloboy followed Alex along the trail back to the Land Rover. Once they had all settled back into Bodhi, Alex fired up the computers and the satellite uplink. After uploading all the photos he had taken that morning he began selecting the clearest images. He paused to look at the pictures he had taken with the laser-scan setting. What had just been the faintest of images on the wall, were now as clear as if it had been painted yesterday.

The laser was capable of differentiating between the different chemical and biological compounds that had been used in the making of the paint pigments and the different hues of colour that each combination represented.

The result was a very impressive and equally intriguing painting. There, in what appeared to be a long wooden dugout war canoe, sat a group of figures. The one in the middle was obviously the king, judging by his headdress and regalia, holding a sceptre of sorts and cloaked in a jaguar pelt. Four animals sat with the king in the war canoe. In the back of the canoe was a howler monkey, sitting behind an iguana that was, in turn, sitting behind the king.

In front of the king sat a peccary and in the prow of the canoe, sat a strange animal that seemed to be part bat, part jaguar and part crocodile. All the animals were holding their paws, hooves or feet up to their foreheads and weeping, crying and mourning. Alex thought it one of the strangest paintings he had ever seen. The king in the canoe bore a striking resemblance to the one in his dream.

"If this isn't King Nanchancaan's temple, I'll be a monkey's uncle," thought Alex, loading the pottery samples he had collected into a three dimensional digital scanner.

Once all the information was ready, he called his grandfather. Silus sat watching him like a hawk. Kiloboy had sprawled out, slouching in the passenger seat behind the driver's, looking bored and surly, picking at his teeth with a match stick, chewing a wad of gum. Both of them were careful to avoid being in view of the webcam.

The Professor's face quickly appeared.

"Well hello again Alex, good to see you! So, how did it go?"

"Good to see you again too. Well we hit the jackpot!" replied Alex.

"The main stele had fallen over so all the carvings on it were intact, another four stele were still standing, but completely weather eroded. The photos came out perfectly; I'm uploading them as we speak. Keep a lookout, especially for the photo of a painting of a war canoe. It's very unusual, and we found the stone with the two glyphs you mentioned. I've put everything into a zipped file and I'm sending it in an encrypted burst data transmission. You should receive it any second now. Otherwise all is well this end, do you have anything for me?" asked Alex.

"Well done! Yes, your file has just come through, it's downloading. It's already midnight over here but we're all very excited about looking at your findings so I see plenty of cups of tea and a long night ahead. We'll analyse as much as we can and let you know the results. Let's have another SITREP at six am your time tomorrow. We should have plenty of information for you by then. Have you done an M.R.I. scan of the structures yet?"

"M.R.I. scan…? No, no, not yet," said Alex slowly. "We are going to do that tomorrow. I'm going to take that equipment in with me right now."

"Good, make sure you do," boomed the Professor's voice. "I only have one more thing for you to check on if you find the time. It's a list of plants. I was wondering if you could verify that these species are growing in that area. I know you know your plants but I'm going to give you their common and scientific names just so there is no confusion. Get a pen and paper handy so you can write it all down."

Alex wrote down all the names of the plants onto his waterproof notebook paper with his pen followed by their scientific names.

"But…" Alex began, "These plants? These scientific names…"

"Just bear with me Alex," interrupted the Professor hastily.

"I know they are all extremely rare, but you'll do your best, won't you?"

"Of course," said Alex, now realizing what his grandfather was up to. "I'll take a good look for them."

Excitement was building in Alex's mind.

"He knows something!" thought Alex keeping his face an expressionless mask. "All the plants he's asking about are as common as they come and the scientific names make absolutely no sense at all. Could Emil have escaped? It certainly seems so!"

Once he was finished he buttoned the notebook back into his top pocket.

"Right then Alex, I'll let you go. Do try and find the time to check on those plants for me," said his grandfather winking.

Signing off, Alex shutdown the computer. Silus produced the sat-phone and dialled Gordo.

"Hello Gordo. The code is now 68. Good, so everything is okay? Good, make sure you keep it that way! What the hell's wrong with your voice? What do you mean you hurt your throat? Don't play the fool you fat buffoon! Just do your job!" said Silus, his voice full of venom.

Alex could see that Silus was about to hang up, "Wait! Make Gordo put Emil on the phone. I'm not doing anything more until I have spoken to Emil myself and I am convinced that he is okay!"

"Really? Giving orders again are we?" Silus said, pressing the red "end call" button again and nodding to Kiloboy.

With sheer unbridled delight, Kiloboy leaned over the back seat and punched Alex hard in the back of his head.

"Terastus," said Bodhi, "would you mind doing the honours? I've had just about enough of this. I believe it's time to even up the score a bit."

"It would be my pleasure!" said the big black scorpion.

Sliding out of his den, he quickly made his way unseen up the back of Kiloboy's tee-shirt.

"You are stubborn!" said Silus, leering at Alex, "But I like that. I like people that fight back. It's so much more fun breaking them. Watching them get all angry, so full of righteous indignation! Like you now. It's only when they finally realize that they are powerless to stop me, does the begging and pleading begin. Weak people start blubbering and crying straight away. No fun in that. You had better make me very happy or I'll phone Gordo back and tell him to do something really nasty to the boy. I'll ask him to give the boy a handicap too, but one that will last a lifetime… perhaps, his eyes."

"Okay, you've proven your point," Alex said rubbing the big lump that was forming on the back of his head.

Silus looked over at Kiloboy who was clearly revelling in playing his part. Just then, Silus' eyes grew wide; the sadistic grin disappearing as his mouth opened. He lifted his hand and pointed at Kiloboy, at his neck, to be more precise. Kiloboy stared back dumbly at Silus, a frown creasing his brow.

"Wat di matter wi' you? Why you lookin' at me funny?"

Kiloboy suddenly felt the light, slightly scratchy feel of tiny hard legs crawling on his neck.

"SCORPION!" yelled Silus.

He watched, horrified, as the scorpion's long tail whipped over its head and in one one hundredth of a second, jammed the sharp curved tip of its hypodermic stinger deep into Kiloboy's flesh. Terastus grabbed the skin on Kiloboy's neck with both its small pincers for better purchase, and jammed its tail straight forward again and again, pumping in its excruciatingly agonising venom.

Terastus then dropped to Bodhi's floor and vanished.

"Nicely done," said Bodhi, "thank you!"

"You got it Bodhi! Anytime my friend!" came the reply from under the cover of the battery housing, beneath Alex's seat.

Kiloboy screamed in sheer agony and terror, tearing his shirt over his head and slapping frantically at his neck and back, the ghost sensation of the scorpions prickly legs making Kiloboy convinced it was still on him.

"GET IT OFF! GET IT OFF! GET IT OFF!" he screamed holding his neck, the neuron blocking toxin now taking immediate effect.

"AAAAAAAAAAAAAAGGGGGGHHHHH!!!"   he screamed, the veins in his neck and face popping out. He rolled frantically around the back seat, scrambling for the door handle, desperate to escape.

"OOOOOOOWWWWWWWW!!!!!" he screamed again. "I gotta get out!"

But the door wouldn't open. His terror increased, knowing that the scorpion was on the loose and close to him.

Silus launched himself at the back door, but that, too would not open. He looked frantically at the seat, the floor and his clothing dreading he would see the scorpion near, or on him. Kiloboy howled and cried like a baby, the stings, so close to his central nervous system, were excruciatingly painful. In desperation, he wound down his window and launched himself out, landing on the muddy jungle floor, of which he was totally oblivious, so completely overcome by the indescribable pain that made him thrash around on the ground, rolling and writhing, screaming and crying.

Silus yanked and pulled at the back door handle but the door refused to open. In a lesser vehicle than the solidly built Land Rover he would have wrenched it completely off. Giving up, he followed Kiloboy's example. Struggling past Alex, he squeezed over the back seat and hurriedly exited the open window. Safely out of the Land Rover, he quickly inspected his clothes and patted himself down to make sure the scorpion was not crawling on him, paranoia having set in.

Alex tried the back door handle which opened at his first try.

"Funny how panic can make doing the simplest things seemingly impossible," Alex thought to himself. "No wonder blind panic can get you killed. S.T.O.P. is a great watch word. Too bad you can't sit still when you have been stung on the neck by a scorpion! Oh well, I suppose that's what they mean by karma. Couldn't have happened to a nicer fellow."

Alex caught himself feeling slightly guilty that he was thoroughly enjoying seeing the heartless gangster getting a taste of his own medicine.

Bodhi was enjoying the spectacle just as much.

"What goes around comes around, that's the circle of life!" she thought, satisfied that the defensive response had been at an appropriate level.

Chapter Sixteen

Living with the Enemy

"Do something!" shouted Silus at Alex.

Kiloboy was now in a low crouch holding his neck and gritting his teeth so hard they looked like they would shatter. His flashy baseball cap lay squashed in the red clay mud which he too was completely covered in. Kiloboy's gun had fallen out of his sagging waistband and lay partially covered in the red goop and leaves. He picked it up but was in too much agony to bother wiping it clean. He shoved it carelessly back into the top of his trousers and stood up. His face was a mask of pain.

"There isn't much I can do for scorpion stings except give him painkillers. I could give him a local anaesthetic injection, but it's all back at camp," answered Alex.

"He's just going to have to bear it until we get back. The scorpions here are not deadly, they just hurt really badly. His glands may come up and he might get a fever, but that should be the worst of it. He's a tough guy, he'll be fine."

"Well, is that so smart arse? In that case, shut up and get moving! Both of you," shouted Silus angrily.

Alex grabbed some large, heavy pieces of equipment out of the Bodhi and strapped them onto an external backpack frame which he heaved onto his back.

When they returned to the camp in the lower plaza, Alex found Gilberto preparing firewood and stacking it near their improvised shelters. Using a technique known as battoning, he split the logs lengthwise with his machete to get to the dry inner core. Alex put the heavy scientific equipment that he had brought back with him in a safe and dry place under his kahune palm stretcher bed.

"Hey you! Come here and sort out the painkillers for Kiloboy!" yelled Silus.

"What happened?" Gilberto enquired.

"Scorpion stung him right on the neck!" said Alex.

"Hah! Serves him right! Tata Duende has cursed all of you!" Gilberto said loudly looking at the three villains. "He's coming for you all!"

"Shhh," said Alex. "No need to stir up a hornets' nest by antagonizing them."

"Alex, if people intentionally do bad things, negative things, destructive things, and go out of their way to cause others harm and suffering; then the consequences of those actions are always negative," Gilberto said quietly to Alex. "Bodhi and I had a long conversation about it."

"Steady now Gilberto!" laughed Alex. "I'm the one who talks to the… to Bodhi, remember!"

"Hah, my friend! Just wait until she starts talking back to you!" Gilberto chuckled knowingly.

"Well if that happens, you better buy me one of those jackets with the sleeves that do up round the back!" Alex continued the banter, his spirit buoyed by the knowledge that his grandfather had seemed to know of their predicament and, with any luck, that information had come from Emil.

Now free of the cumbersome equipment, Alex went over to the packs and took out what he needed for Kiloboy and a bottle of antihistamine tablets for TreeWays. He took it over to them both and dispensed the tablets, putting the bottle back in his pocket. As he turned to leave he was hit in the side of his head by Silus' soggy and very smelly socks.

"Wash them and have them dry for me by morning!" Silus growled. "And come over here, I have questions I want you to answer. You better answer them all or I am going to let Kiloboy here share his pain with you."

Alex stood in front of Silus who reclined back in the hammock, sticking his head and shoulders out from under the mosquito netting that was draped over him.

"What is this M.R.I equipment and what does it do?" he asked.

"It stands for Magnetic Resonance Imaging. It's used for lots of things but archaeologists have started using it for a technique called non-invasive archaeology," Alex explained.

"And this is helpful how?" asked Silus.

"Well, it means I can scan things like sealed pots and jars, to get an image of what might be inside them, without risking damage to them by opening them. They have recently used it to study Egyptian mummies without having to take off the mummy's bandages. I haven't found anything worth scanning yet but I still have a lot of investigation to do. Funding an archaeological dig on a scale big enough to really investigate a temple site this large costs a huge amount of money and can tie up archaeological specialists and their teams for months, if not years. They'll need to be absolutely convinced that we have found something really worthwhile. This may not even be the temple everyone hopes it is. After all, Belize is literally covered in Maya ruins and temples. They estimate that almost a million Maya used to inhabit this area alone," said Alex.

"Well, they're not here now, are they!" laughed Silus. "You had better pray this is the temple we are looking for! Tell me, will what you have sent the Professor today be enough to prove it is the temple of this King Nachican, Nanchun, Nacho Cheese Dip, whatever-his-face is called?"

"Perhaps," answered Alex cautiously. "We'll have to see what the results say tomorrow morning."

After a moment Alex added, "If it is, what do you intend to do with us?"

"Well now," said Silus, "I'm asking the questions, not you. As long as you do what I tell you, the boy will be unharmed. That's all you need to know. Now go and wash my socks and then go find something to scan."

Alex walked back to Gilberto and started helping him split the wood.

"I see that Treeways has given us back our machetes," said Alex.

"Only until dark, and only for preparing the firewood. I told TreeWays that I needed to boil cha ca leaves so he can bathe his burns and blisters," replied Gilberto using one log to tap the slim, long machete blade through another thicker log, vertically from end to end.

"Here," said Gilberto, handing Alex a bunch of small green plants that had reddish tops. "They won't let us have clean socks or foot powder so squeeze the juice of this plant on your feet. It has antifungal power that will help prevent infection. We use it for all sorts of fungal infections from athlete's foot to ringworm and that sort of thing."

"Thanks Gilberto, what's it called?" asked Alex.

"In Maya it's called ixcanan, which means goddess of the forest."

"What's that equipment you have there?" Gilberto asked looking at the pile under Alex's jungle bed.

"Well Silus thinks it's a magnetic resonance image scanner because that's what the my grandfather suggested, but it's actually a G.P.R unit – ground penetrating radar – archaeologists use G.P.Rs to help them find building features that are buried underground without having to disturb anything by digging. It can show you where walls, doors and other features are, like hidden cavities and hollows. In our case it will help us find burial tombs or chambers hidden in the temple!" Alex said excitedly.

"And Gilberto, my grandfather knows something about our situation. It's highly possible Emil might have escaped!" Alex whispered.

Gilberto's head snapped around and he looked at Alex with an expression of joy and hope.

"Really?!" he exclaimed.

"Yes," continued Alex. "my grandfather also gave me a list of plants to try and find for him, only the plants are all the most common jungle plants in the country, and the scientific names are nothing of the sort! I'm sure it is a coded message. I am going to have a look at it right now."

Alex took his waterproof notebook out of his pocket and looked at the list. The supposed scientific names were a combination of Latin and Greek words which Alex was able to translate. He walked around the site making a big show of comparing the list to various plants, shaking his head or nodding and pretending to make more notes about what he had found. He grew more and more excited as the meaning of the message became clearer until he could barely contain himself and had to control his walk back to Gilberto who was underneath their natural shelter. Making the walk back as seemingly casual as he could was difficult, he wanted to run over and clap Gilberto on his back and give him the good news.

The wind started to pick up and Alex checked the barometer on his watch. The pressure was falling; the tropical storm front was on its way and as if to confirm this it started to rain again.

"Tell me what the message says! Quickly!" said Gilberto impatiently as soon as Alex was within ear shot.

"Okay, let me read my rough translation to you. The boy is free. Pegasus cannot fly the· soldiers through the storm – which obviously is referring to a winged horse and soldiers which, in modern terms, must mean airborne cavalry. So the army helicopter with the police or soldiers can't come to our rescue as they are grounded due to the storm. Then it says – seek the books of knowledge and face of Agamemnon with the blessings of the senate and deliver it from the hands of evil men, take heed not to fall prey to them. Agamemnon was a famous ancient king of the Mycenaeans, in what is now Greece. He was buried with a mask made of solid gold. I take this to mean that senate represents the Belize Government or authorities and they have given us permission to try and retrieve and save the codices and King Nanchancaan's jade mask, if we are able to do so without getting ourselves killed."

"Well, I'm sorry to say that that doesn't seem possible Alex," said Gilberto. "We don't have the time or equipment to think about trying to find the books or mask. Also, they're probably going to want to get rid of us fairly soon. If Emil has escaped, I hope he has been able to make it back to the village across the rivers, or at least found somewhere safe to hide from the coming storm like we told him to do in the note. If he is free, we should try to make a break and get away from here tonight. There's no way we can dig up the temple, find the burial chamber and save the codices and mask ourselves. We need a crew of diggers, just like they do. I'm sorry Alex, but it would seem like a better idea for us just to escape and hopefully the police can stop them before they loot the temple."

"You're right Gilberto. We can't take a chance and hang around until Silus' looting crew have dug it all up. They could decide to kill us anytime. But, I don't think Silus is confident enough about getting out of here and back across the river without us at the moment. I agree that if Emil is out of their grasp, we should make a break for it. Let's make a plan for tonight."

"Hey! You two!" yelled Silus. "Get your pathetic backsides over here."

Alex and Gilberto reluctantly broke off their conversation and walked over to Silus who was in his usual position, swinging comfortably in the hammock. He held up the satellite phone.

"I've just turned this on to call Gordo to check in and I see this red light blinking – Why?" he asked, looking at Alex.

"That means there is a voicemail message waiting," answered Alex.

He hoped his grandfather had not left anything in the message that could give the game away to Silus. Or maybe it was from Emil! Emil had the sat-phone number on his flap card. What if he had called to say that he had escaped, they would be killed immediately. Alex's heart raced.

"Alright. I'm going to put it on speaker phone so we can all hear the message, and I had better like what I hear," Silus said, eventually finding the voicemail and speakerphone settings in the menu options.

The message started. Alex held his breath.

"Alex, hello! It's me," said the Professor's voice. "Just thought I would let you know that we got an immediate result on the two glyphs on the flat square stone. One is the Maya glyph Ak which represents a turtle and the other is the glyph Tun which represents stone. So it means stone turtle, apparently often used to represent Xibalba, if you get what I mean. Hope you find that interesting, perhaps this temple has a lot in common with the temple at Copan. Well cheerio for now, looking forward to letting you know more in the morning."

The voicemail ended.

"Exactly what does all that mean?" asked Silus.

"It means that the big temple over there was dedicated to a giant stone turtle god that carried the earth on its back around the sun, just like the temple of Copan," said Alex quickly without missing a beat.

Gilberto suddenly had a loud coughing fit.

"What's your problem?!" demanded Silus.

"Noth… ing, just… a bug, flew into my mouth… stuck in my throat," he gasped between coughing.

"Nice," said Silus. "Maybe you'll cough your stupid lungs up! That would be entertaining!"

He dialled a number on the sat phone and Gordo's voice came on the line, it was still on speaker phone. He sounded tired and strained.

"The code now is 92," said Silus.

"Uh, okay, the answer is 116," said Gordo.

"Okay, good. So everything is fine? The boy still locked in his concrete box, yeah?" asked Silus cruelly, looking at Gilberto and Alex's faces enjoying thinking about how they must be suffering.

"Well, yes Mr. Silus. Everting' okay, just as you say," panted Gordo in his usual thick tongued manner.

"Good! Keep it that way, you're the best paid babysitter in the world, and don't you forget it!" barked Silus, hanging up.

"Okay, you're dismissed," said Silus waving them away.

When Alex and Gilberto were out of earshot, Gilberto looked at Alex and said in a whispered hiss, "They still have him! You must be wrong about the code, it must mean something else."

"It's very strange Gilberto. If Emil hasn't escaped, then how does my grandfather know about our predicament? Ah, the police must have contacted him after we made the phone call to them and they didn't hear back from us," concluded Alex.

"Yes," Gilberto agreed, "that will be it. We will need to hope the police get here before they kill us. We can't leave now, they would kill Emil."

"Back to square one!" said Alex frustrated.

"And now we have an even bigger problem. If the police do manage to get here in time and rescue us, none of those three know exactly where Gordo is holding Emil, and I can't see them co-operating with the police. If they clam up and refuse to help, then as soon as Gordo doesn't hear from them Emil is done for! This is a very tricky situation."

"What was that back there Gilberto, did you really swallow a bug?"

"No, at the time I was so happy thinking that Emil had escaped, that when you made up that total 'basura' – rubbish – about the stone turtle god, and so smooth, you caught me off guard and I was actually trying not to laugh my cabeza, my head off! That was quick thinking – great story! But after hearing what Gordo said, I don't feel like laughing no more, my poor grandson!"

"Yes, me neither," replied Alex as they walked back to their shelter.

"You're right, we have to stay here for now. Let's run over what facts we have got again. Ak Tun, Stone Turtle, and Copan, why was my grandfather making reference to that particular Maya temple. Especially as Copan is in Honduras; another country, hundreds of kilometres away. What could the two temples have in common?"

"Certainly not your imaginary giant flying stone turtle god!" said Gilberto, regaining some of his sense of humour as he settled himself onto his stretcher bed of palm leaves.

"I did read up a bit on Maya mythology when I was preparing for this trip, but what can you tell me about the reference my grandfather made to Xibalba, the Maya's mythological underworld?" asked Alex.

"Xibalba," answered Gilberto. "It means the 'place of fright', a dark and terrifying place inhabited by the lords of the night, the lords of death and the Gods of the underworld, including Cha'ak the rain god. That's why the Maya would make sacrifices deep underground in caves. To the Maya, caves represented this underworld. Ak Tun is also the Maya word for cave. The most famous cave in our country is called Aktun Tunichil Muknal, which more or less means the cave of the crystal sepulchre. Ak Tun usually means they are talking about an entrance to the underworld."

"That's it!" exclaimed Alex in hushed excitement. "Well done Gilberto! That's it! I have been wracking my brains trying to figure out what the connection is to my grandfather's reference to the temple at Copan in Honduras. I've just remembered! That temple has crypts! The secret crypts of Copan! I read about them in a *National Geographic* magazine! It's one of the only Maya temples I have heard of where they discovered secret tunnels and passageways, leading directly into the burial chambers! Gilberto, do you see! You saw King Nanchancan standing on the entrance to his underworld! He left those two glyphs on that paving slab as a clue for those who could read them! That's why the Professor wanted me to bring the G.P.R equipment, so that we could be sure there was a tunnel under it before we lift it up! BRILLIANT!

"If that slab really is the entrance to the crypt, we could get in without these gangsters seeing us, and remove the codices and the mask. We can't escape while they are still holding Emil, but if we take what they want out of the tomb and hide it somewhere we would be in a position to bargain! We would have leverage, and be able to turn the tables on them!"

"Yes!" Gilberto agreed, "We would! But we would also need to be far away from them. After what he did to you with those pliers I'm sure he would have other, worse ways of finding out where we had hidden the treasures. We would have to be out of his reach and use the treasures to make sure he doesn't hurt Emil. But it's a good plan! We need to find out if that secret tunnel is really there!"

"I'll put the G.P.R equipment together right away. This unit has its own onboard computer so we can analyse its results without having to return to Bodhi. Let's get moving," said Alex, reaching for the bags under his stretcher bed.

Silus watched the two men leave their survival shelter, pulling what looked like a modified baby's stroller behind them through the pouring rain. It had three large wheels and a lot of technical equipment covered by a rainproof cowling.

"Kiloboy!" said Silus. "Go and keep an eye on those two. I don't believe a word they're telling me. Tell me what they do. Make sure you remember every detail!"

"Cho!" said Kiloboy sucking his teeth. "You tink I gonna walk around dis stinking bush, in dis here heavy rain with my head dat feel like it gonna bust clean open from de sting I jus' got? You crazy! I sick maan. Noh, I noh going nowhere. I HATE di bush! I no deh pan DAT!"

"You only got some serious bad style, rude bway! You gonna do zackly as di man say!" bellowed TreeWays.

"You hear me?! You gonna do anyting' an everyting' Mr. Silus di say, or you gonna have ME to deal wid! Dis whole ting ain't no foolin' matter bway! Sting or no sting! You goh! Dat di deal, you getting' paid real good money for dis and you workin' foh ME! My eyes closed right now from di allergy, or whatever it is but, notin' wrong wid my mind or my ears. You knoh you nevah wah cross me my bwah. Now go do as di man say!" Treeways ordered.

Kiloboy reluctantly dragged himself out of the hammock, making a big show of holding his neck, muttering and cursing under his breath. Donning Alex's poncho, he followed the two figures who were splashing their way through the puddles, drenched by the dripping understory of vegetation, as they moved slowly towards the main temple mound.

Silus made a mental note to phone Dr. Planchard in London later to let him know what was happening and ask him some questions.

It was fairly late in the afternoon and Alex and Gilberto, having observed Kiloboy following them, made sure they took the most difficult route up the steepest side of the temple, pretending to take measurements, tests and calculations as they went. They all slipped and slid, trying to keep their balance as they slowly made their way further and further up the side. Eventually, they reached the platform at the top, all three now quite tired from the exertions.

"Let's take a break for a half hour or so," said Alex casually as they all finally stood on the flat level surface. "We can take shelter inside the big chamber for a while, get out of the rain."

"And it's time for you to take some more pills for that sting too," said Alex, looking at Kiloboy.

"I done tek di pills you gave me a while back! What you di mean more pills?" he asked suspiciously.

"Well, the sting isn't going to kill you but you could still die from it if you have a bad allergic reaction. To stop that happening you need more pills," Alex said convincingly.

"Why are you bothering to help him Alex?" said Gilberto. "I hope he does have a bad reaction! He deserves to! Don't give him the pills."

"Shut up 'ol man. Gimme di damn pills," said Kiloboy reaching out.

Alex placed four pills in his hand which he threw into his mouth and swallowed.

"Right," said Alex. "Let's take a seat in the dry and get our strength back before we start again."

They all moved into the main ceremonial chamber out of the rain. Alex and Gilberto sat together with their backs leaning up against one wall, while Kiloboy sat across from them with his back up against the opposite one. They all looked out of the open doorway which framed the jungle canopy like a Carolyn Carr painting, the rain falling steadily. It had a hypnotic effect on the three of them watching as it fell.

Kiloboy sat huddled under the warm poncho. The exertions of climbing the hill and the natural adrenaline crash that he was experiencing as a result of being stung that morning would have been enough to send anyone into a fairly deep sleep. The combination of all that plus the overdose of antihistamine tablets would have knocked out an elephant. The label on the bottle warned that one of the main side effects of the pills was extreme drowsiness. After sitting in silence for a quarter of an hour, they noticed Kiloboy's head flop forward.

"He's out," whispered Alex softly. "Keep an eye on him, I'll go and scan the paving slab with the glyphs."

Silently, Alex rose in one fluid motion. He wheeled the G.P.R machine soundlessly into the antechamber and scanned all the big square paving slabs that made up the floors surface, starting with the one with the glyphs. As soon as he was finished he had a look at the readout on the small computer screen. Whereas the rest of the floor showed a dense grey-white solid mass, the area under the paving stone with glyphs showed a light orange square which quickly faded into a large black square, indicating a hollow cavity beneath.

"Bingo!" shouted Alex in his head. "Xibalba!"

After fifteen minutes, Alex returned to find Gilberto and Kiloboy in exactly the same position as he had left them. Kiloboy was snoring loudly, saliva drooling out of the corner of his mouth.

He looked over at Gilberto and silently mouthed; "There's a tunnel!" giving him a huge smile, his thumbs up.

"Hey! Wake up! SCORPION!" Alex yelled.

Kiloboy jumped as his eyes flew open.

"Only joking, we're leaving now," Alex said flatly wheeling the G.P.R unit back out into the rain.

Kiloboy gave Alex a murderous glare, "Hey, funnyman, I really gonna enjoy killing you!"

The wind was definitely picking up now, the odd dry branch snapping and falling, crashing to the ground below. It was also much darker than it should be for that time in the afternoon due to the buildup of thick storm clouds.

Alex checked his barometer; the atmospheric pressure had dropped even lower.

"Storm's on its way!" thought Alex as the trio scrambled and slid down the temple's steep staircase.

Chapter Seventeen

Actions Speak Louder

Emil had been having quite an adventure since his escape. He had steeled his nerves and worked his courage up, knowing that he would need to be brave, just as Alex had said. He had managed to break out of his jail and escape his captor and he was proud that he had managed to do so. It had not been easy, and failure would have meant death.

Now he understood what Alex meant when he had stressed the importance of personal fortitude, self-disciple, strength of will and resolving that, no matter how bad things appeared to be, that you must never, ever give up. These lessons were no longer theory. Emil had tried and tested them, clinging on to what he had been taught when all hope seemed lost and when his bleeding fingers had screamed to him to stop, he had carried on.

It had taken several kilometres for him to get used to driving the large SUV. He was thankful that he had learned to operate his father's tractor in the fields from a young age. He was also thankful that the SUV had automatic transmission. It meant that he could use one foot for the accelerator and brake, and the other to try and get some leverage on the floor of the car to pull his body up and get a better view out of the windscreen. He had almost lost control a couple of times when he had taken corners too fast. Now he noticed that the vehicle was running dangerously low on petrol, the fuel indicator was already way into the red reserve area. Passing through a small village, he pulled into the tiny gas station and popped the small lever under the dashboard that opened the gas tank.

To avoid suspicion, after he had parked up, he climbed into the back seat, exiting the vehicle from the back passenger door and pretending to talk to the driver as he did so.

"Okay, I'll phone and pay the man for the gas!" he said loudly slamming the door shut, the heavily tinted windows hiding the interior.

He bought phone cards and used the pay phone to call the police first and then the Professor, using the numbers he found on the flap card. Paying for the calls and the fuel with the cash Alex had also hidden in the belt, Emil opened the back door to the car, jumped in, slammed the door behind him, and manoeuvred back over into the driver's seat. Putting the transmission back in 'D', he continued on his journey.

"Grandfather, you're just going to have to forgive me. I am not going home quietly to see if this all works out. I want to help and I'm going to," he said with iron determination.

After a few hours, he had successfully managed to drive all the way down the old logging road that he and his grandfather had walked along many times before. Suddenly, he was going down the steep slope that led to the river. Slamming on his brakes he skidded to a halt just as the front wheels touched the swiftly moving water.

"What now?" thought Emil.

"They must have made it across; there is only one set of tracks going in. How am I going to get to the other side?"

He looked at the raging red water flowing past him, knowing that he would surely drown if he attempted to swim it.

He applied his S.T.O.P. watch-word to his predicament. He saw no reason it wouldn't help him find a solution to this problem too.

"Well," he reasoned, "I am stopped, and I am thinking. ORGANISE is next. Let's see what I have available to me."

He searched the trunk of the car and found the rest of the length of rope that he had been tied up with. It was at least twenty metres long. During his rummage around, he found his folding knife and small personal survival kit locked up in the glove compartment. He looked long and hard at the vehicle and finally came up with a plan.

First, he removed the spare tyre from the SUV and then cut out all five seat belts, tying them together end to end and then knotting the end of the seat belts to the long length of rope. He then secured the end of the rope through the wheel rim of the spare tyre. Next, he removed the big metal cross-wrench from its clip near the spare wheel housing and tied that to the seat belt end of his, by now, very long line.

He tested the spare tyre to check that it would float – it did, but with just a few centimetres sticking out of the water. It would have to do. Climbing up onto the bonnet of the SUV he dangled the cross wrench about a meter below his right hand. Swinging his arm up and around next to him in circles, he built up momentum, spinning the cross-wrench until it was a blur. As the cross-wrench's arc drew level with his chest he released his line in an underarm toss.

The cross-wrench sailed up in an arc over the raging river. Neat coils of the line that Emil had carefully laid out snapping taught as it stretched and stretched, until it reached its full length, dropping right into the dense tangled vines and lianas that were growing on the opposite riverbank. This extremely thick vegetation formed the understory of the gallery forest which lined either side of the river.

Jumping down from the hood, Emil tugged on the line as hard as he could and checked that the metal cross-wrench was as solidly set as any grappling hook. Pulling and tugging with all his might, it did not come loose.

Satisfied, he pushed the heavy spare tire into the river and waded with it until the current took his legs from under him. Suddenly, he swung out into the flow with no hope of going back. He clung onto the wheel which tipped sideways and span over, twisting Emil under the raging water. Still, he clung on as the river pulled at his body with incredible force threatening to rip him away from his makeshift raft and on to a watery grave.

Emil's head was submerged, and his need to breathe was becoming absolutely desperate. Still he dared not let go with either hand to try and rectify his position for fear of losing his grip on the tyre. He swung like a giant pendulum across the river, just as he had planned.

After what seemed like an eternity, and with his lungs burning for breath, he felt the terrific force of water on his body subside enough for him to risk grabbing the other side of the tyre, flipping himself and the tyre over. Gasping for breath, he could see that he was now only about five metres from swinging into the opposite bank.

To his horror, he realized that he was about to swing into a tangle of spiny bamboo and thorn covered basket tie-tie vines tangled with branches and floating logs.

It was a death-trap!

Emil knew that the moment he got tangled up in it, the force of the current would pin him against the bamboo spines and thorns. He would never have enough strength to fight the hundreds of tons of water that would be pushing him into the tangle of vines and debris. As this terrifying thought flashed through his mind, he saw his only escape route. There, above him was a low hanging tree branch, just above his head. Agonisingly close but just out of reach.

With seconds to spare, Emil scrambled onto the twisting bobbing tyre as best he could, launching himself up into the air and forcing the tyre down into the water, his wet slippery hands just managing to gain purchase on the rough tree bark. The branch began to dip low towards the rushing river which was still snatching at Emil's legs, all the way to his waist.

Emil gave a mighty heave and with strength he had tapped into through raw, primal fear, he hauled himself onto the branch and clung onto it for dear life. His knuckles going white with the exertion, he swung one leg up and over the branch. Once he had recovered his balance, and a bit of energy, he shimmied along it and up it towards the trunk, praying that it would not snap off under his weight.

Climbing shakily down the tree trunk and stepping back onto solid ground, he collapsed in a heap, breathing heavily. His legs felt like jelly.

"That was close, Emil" he thought to himself.

Taking a few minutes to recover, he emptied the water from his rubber boots and set off down the jungle track with nothing more than the clothes on his back, his survival tin and his folding knife. His grandfather's trail was now much wider and easy to move along fast, the passage of the Land Rover having cleared the way.

As he walked, he was suddenly overcome with the feeling that he was not alone. He sensed eyes watching him. Now and again when he was taking a five minute break he would hear a faint rustle close by, or a twig snap. The hairs on his neck stood up.

He cut himself a long, very solid stick, which made him feel a lot better. So did the reassuring weight of his survival tin and folding knife in his pockets; knowing that he had all he needed to make shelter, fire and find food. As his grandfather always told him, the jungle was his friend and he had nothing to fear, except fear itself. His grandfather and Alex were his goal. He was going to help them.

Still, he was sure he felt something had been watching him, was watching him. He quickened his pace, determined to reach the old logging camp before nightfall. Moving around the jungle at night without a flashlight was very risky.

Amongst other hazards, most of the poisonous snakes in the jungle were on the move at night, hunting. Accidentally stepping on one could mean getting bitten. If that happened at night, all alone and on foot, in a remote area far from help, the consequences could easily be fatal. The stakes were high.

After all, this forest was home to the fearsome fer-de-lance, a highly venomous pit viper that could grow to two metres in length, making it one of the biggest in the world. His grandfather had told him stories of Chicleros working deep in the jungle and days away from help who had been badly bitten by these pit vipers. They would have no choice but to tie a tight tourniquet above the bite and immediately have their friends amputate the affected limb – by chopping it off with a machete. It was either that, or die a slow agonising death.

A couple of hours into his walk, the wind picked up and the rain started falling hard. Eventually, the worn out boy reached the edge of the old logger's camp. Realizing that he had finally arrived at his destination, he suddenly felt utterly exhausted.

Emil cautiously crept forward through the shadowy jungle and saw the first of the old rusting iron hulks. When he spotted the Land Rover, in the last glimmer of twilight, his heart leapt into his mouth and he immediately hid. As he crouched motionless in the growing darkness, he listened and watched. The minutes ticked by slowly.

The only sounds and movements were those of the steady rainfall and the jungle, there was no one at the Land Rover. Still he approached very cautiously. Once he reached Bodhi he gently opened the door and the lights went on. He slipped inside, out of the drenching downpour and shut the door quickly again, for fear of being spotted by someone. He suddenly felt completely safe again, cocooned in the familiar and friendly vehicle.

"I better make another plan!" Emil thought to himself as his heavy eyelids closed involuntarily.

Emil dozed off, curled up on the front passenger's seat in the dark dry shelter of Bodhi's interior. He instantly sank into a deep, dreamless sleep.

"Were you with him all the way?" asked Bodhi.

"I picked up his scent just past the river crossing. He's brave that boy, determined too. It's very good to see you again Bodhi."

"It's very good to see you too, Balaam, my friend, thank you for coming. You're looking well," said Bodhi, sensing the huge cat's powerful presence next to her.

Balaam had recovered completely. His muscles rippled under his spotted coat as he took up guard position next to Bodhi, under a kahune palm. The unusual pair of sentinels watched over the sleeping boy. Bodhi told Balaam their tale of woe.

Chapter Eighteen

Destinies Collide

Thunder rumbled over the jungle canopy, rain lashing down, trees and branches swaying in the strong winds. Lightning flashed randomly and continuously all along the storm front.

In the late afternoon, Alex and Gilberto had made their plan of escape. The storm's intensity was steadily increasing and it had given Alex an idea.

Alex and Gilberto made their way through the downpour over to the villains' enclave of hijacked jungle sleeping units.

"Gilberto and I are going to sleep up in the chamber at the top of the main temple tonight. Our natural shelter can't deal with this storm, it's leaking like a sieve. We need a torch to see where we are going, the wind's too strong for candles, and we've only got one candle left anyway," Alex stated.

"What are you telling me? Scared of the dark are we? Your shelter-building skills not so good are they? Some jungle men you pair are! Hah! I don't give a damn where you sleep. I'd prefer it if you slept in the rain and mud, and no you can't have a flashlight, stumble around all night, just be back here in the morning for your call to the Professor or the boy won't see tomorrow's sunset," barked Silus.

Gilberto and Alex walked back to their shelter and started to gather the few things they had.

"I didn't expect to get the flashlight; we will have to improvise," said Alex, "but at least now they won't become suspicious when we leave and go up to the chamber in the main temple."

"Yes, and I also made some preparations earlier while I had my machete for cutting the firewood," said Gilberto.

Very carefully, Gilberto opened his colourfully woven koshtal bag and reached inside. He pulled out a large bunch of square edged sticks, each about twenty centimetres long and about one centimetre square. Next, he pulled out a large bunch of what looked like cotton wool.

"We call this candle wood, it burns nearly as good as pine. This should be enough for us to have enough light to search the secret passages and any tomb they may lead to. And this, this is a type of cotton. Actually, it's called kapok, from the seedpod of the cottonwood tree; in Maya we call this tree the yaxche or the ceiba tree. It is the sacred tree of the Maya. Now all we need is a spark to get it going," Gilberto explained.

"Well, they have taken away my survival kit and belt kit," said Alex.

Thinking for a moment while he looked around, he suddenly had an idea.

"I know, we can take the battery and some wires from the G.P.R unit, it's a twelve volt battery. If we connect two wires to the battery terminals and touch the ends of the wires together it will produce all the sparks we need to light the kapok!"

"Good idea, but how are we going to lift up the paving slab?" asked Gilberto.

"Well, we do have the rope and pulleys that we used to lift the stele," suggested Alex.

"Yes, and we could dismantle the G.P.R machine and use some of the metal frame poles as crow bars to help us pry it up," added Gilberto.

"Great idea," Alex agreed. "They're aluminium so they're not too strong but they should work well enough for us to be able to slip the rope under the corners, just like we did with the stele, and I doubt the paving slab is anything near as heavy as that stele was."

"Okay, good. That's a plan then. We'll make dinner and then head off. I noticed that TreeWays' eyes are open enough to see again," Alex said.

"Yes, I think I helped him a bit too much. But his arm is still really swollen and although the burns and blisters have stopped spreading he must still be suffering very badly. The burning and itching from che chen is really terrible. I doubt he's had any sleep at all since it happened. His arm, neck and head literally get stuck to the hammock. He might be able to see a bit more but he is still in a miserable condition," Gilberto informed Alex.

Alex picked up the bundle of candlewood sticks and kapok and began putting them back into Gilberto's koshtal bag.

"Stop!" shouted Gilberto, "don't move!"

Alex froze and Gilberto gently moved the bag away from Alex's hand.

"What is it?" Alex asked.

"Well," said Gilberto, carefully opening the bag. "It's something I found on the trail on the way in. Have a look."

Gilberto gingerly pulled out a smaller cloth bag, the top of which was tied up. Undoing the string at the top he slowly opened it and they both looked inside.

"Meet my friend, Babar Amarillo. That's its Spanish name; in Creole we call this fellow tommygoff and you would know it as the fer-de-lance."

There, curled up at the bottom of the cloth bag was a juvenile pit viper, and it looked every bit as fearsome and deadly as it was. Alex could clearly see the yellow lines that looked like eyebrows above the elliptical pupils of its eyes, and the yellow bottom of its jaw from which it derived its Spanish name.

The rest of its lithe, slim, scaled reptilian body was covered in triangular dark brown, light brown and beige markings – a perfect camouflage pattern that made it practically invisible when hidden amongst the leaf litter of the forest floor. It was second only to the fearsome bushmaster pit viper that was found in countries further south. The fer-de-lance was one of the most feared snakes of the new world.

"You never know when this little fellow may come in handy. Many of my countrymen are terrified of this snake in particular, due to the devastating effect that its venom can have. Of course, this snake, like all snakes, doesn't go out of its way to bite people; it just wants to be left in peace. But if you hurt it by stepping on it, it will naturally react aggressively, and this snake can be super aggressive. These baby tommygoff's will give you all the venom they have and are very dangerous."

Gilberto justified his new, improvised biological weapon, "These men have put our lives in danger, and they intend to kill us. Under these circumstances, self-defence is justified my friend. We need all the help we can get."

"I can see why you have to be so careful putting your hand in the bag; the snake can use its heat sensors to 'see' you through the material, just like an infrared camera. It could accurately target any body part that was within range and bite it right through the cloth bag you've got it in! You had better be very careful with that," said Alex.

Gilberto nodded, "We need to put this kapok in a waterproof container; it'll be useless if it gets wet, even if it gets damp it will be hard to light. I left this bunch on a warm rock near the fire so it's really dry at the moment."

.

"Okay, I'll put the kapok tinder and the candlewood sticks in one of the big waterproof bags that the G.P.R equipment came packed in. In fact, I'll take all three waterproof bags; they are very well padded too. We can put the codices and the jade mask into them if we actually find them."

"That sounds good!" said Gilberto. "Let's get their dinner over to them and then we need to get moving. The sooner we do this, the sooner we have a chance of getting Emil back. I can't wait to turn the tables on these gangsters."

Dinner was served to the three vicious thugs. Alex and Gilberto left the camp with their gear in their backpacks. In the blue-grey shadows of the last fading light they made their way through the rain and wind battered jungle to the main temple.

Water cascaded down the temple's steep stairway like a small waterfall. They climbed the slippery broken stone staircase and reached the top platform with its circular sacrificial stone in pitch darkness. They could not even see their hands in front of their faces. Rumbling thunder boomed through the jungle. Flashes of lightning had provided them with snapshot images which helped them move in the right direction. Finally, they reached the chamber and hurried inside, out of the rain. Inside the chamber it was remarkably dry and much quieter, the thick stone temple walls providing solid insulation from the tempest outside.

After a couple of minutes of fumbling around, orange sparks crackled from the wires Alex was holding and the kapok tinder caught fire. They lit the ends of several of the candlewood sticks, the friendly orange-yellow flames casting flickering shadows onto the wall paintings, making the figures in the paintings appear to move and dance.

Quickly, they made their way to the antechamber and the carved paving stone in the far corner. Gilberto gathered up a pile of kahune palm nut debris and made another small fire.

"Alex, I must do a small ceremony before we start," said Gilberto. "Once, long ago, this was a sacred site and in a way, to me, it still is. We are about to open a door which probably leads to a burial chamber of a Maya King. The door we are opening is the door to his underworld. Before we descend into Xibalba we need to ask for the blessing of the spirits of this place, out of respect for my ancestors, their ancient culture and ways. I must follow the old ways so that the echoes of the past may be carried into the future. It is only proper that we do so."

"Of course. I understand, Gilberto, please go ahead," said Alex.

Gilberto sprinkled copal incense onto the small fire and then went back out of the main doorway, returning almost immediately with some rain soaked leaves. Chanting in a low voice, Gilberto sprinkled the rainwater onto the paving slab, moving his hand in a square and then circular manner. After a couple of minutes he concluded the small ceremony by clasping his hands together, leaves between his palms, closing his eyes. He then stooped down and placed the leaves onto the small fire, the wet green leaves snapping and popping as they scorched, blackened and eventually burnt, releasing thick white smoke.

The pair then set to work, clearing the dirt and mortar around the edges of the stone slab, carefully chipping it away with the flattened ends of the metal poles they had brought with them. Once they had cleared the edges round the entire slab, they placed the flat ends of the poles upright in the crack on one side. Together, they gently applied pressure and the heavy stone slab started to lift. Once they had pushed both of the poles flat to the floor, they were able to lever them underneath the slab. They then stepped on the poles with their feet to keep them in position while at the same time freeing their hands.

The slab was now raised open a crack the size of the aluminium poles along one side. Alex and Gilberto grabbed the rope and slipped a long section of it under each of the two exposed corners. Carefully, they both took up the strain and heaved. The heavy stone square lifted and they continued until it was past vertical. It then fell several centimetres, coming to rest against the wall. It now resembled a big open trapdoor.

They looked down into the square black hole, holding a couple of candlewood torches to light it up. What they saw was a dusty shaft, about a metre and a half square, that dropped straight down to another floor, three or four metres below them. Built into the side of the shaft were stone lined foot and hand holes.

"Let's tie the rope around the big round stone on the platform outside, I don't want to risk going down there without another way to get back up. Those holes in the side might not be too reliable, some look a bit crumbly. We can also use the rope to pull up the bags out of the shaft safely without worrying about dropping them," said Alex, inspecting the plastered walls of the shaft that had been painted a deep shade of terracotta red.

Once the thick rope had been wrapped around the big stone, they brought the rest of it back into the antechamber and dropped it down the shaft. Alex swung down into the shaft and was pleasantly surprised at how well preserved the foot and hand holds still were. Once he reached the bottom, Gilberto dropped him the bags and then came down himself.

They both looked at the secret tunnel in front of them; it had a triangular vaulted ceiling that was made of large rectangular blocks of limestone. A steep stone staircase led down deeper into the heart of the temple. They walked down the stairs to a square landing. Once they reached the landing, they turned the corner and saw yet another flight of steps descending at a steep angle once more.

"Alex, stop!" said Gilberto halfway down the passage.

Alex froze and felt something soft and silky moving along his neck on the collar of his shirt.

With a quick flick Gilberto knocked a hairy, black and red object which was the size of a man's hand off Alex's shoulder. It landed with a soft thud on the tunnel floor in front of Alex. There, in the light of the flickering flame, Alex saw a huge red-backed tarantula crouched on the floor. Its eight, thick, hairy legs began to undulate as it scuttled quickly across to the wall, disappearing down a web lined hole.

"It won't bite you unless you try to squash it," said Gilberto helpfully, "but the hairs can give you a bad rash and they can really irritate your nose and eyes too. Better not to let him crawl around on you."

"Thanks Gilberto! This place is certainly well named, Xibalba – the place of fright!" said Alex with a shiver running up his back.

When they finally reached the bottom of the staircase, they were faced with a wall that made a dead end. On the wall was a painting with an incredible amount of detail. It was another, more complicated rendition of the painting of the King in the war canoe with the animals lamenting and crying. Above the canoe was a stylised painting of an enormous bat.

Alex recognized the fearsome face as belonging to a huge species of bat called vampyrum spectrum which, in reality, actually did look like a demon from the underworld. These giant bat's wingspan could be almost a metre wide, their facial expression a permanent snarl, with a big mouth crammed full of sharp fangs.

The largest carnivorous bat in the world; it was a nocturnal terror that flew like a silent phantom, snapping sleeping doves off their perches, crunching up the small birds whole, or crawling on its elbows, wings folded, using its long sharp claws to help it creep through hollow logs, hunting down small rodents trying to hide within them. It was truly a very scary looking bat.

"This is the tomb!" said Gilberto in awe. "We have found it! Look, you see this painting, the King has died and he is journeying to Xibalba in his war canoe, the animals are lamenting, mourning and crying! We are here! The tomb is behind this painting!"

In the top left corner there was a carving of another glyph on a smaller square stone. They both studied the painting.

Alex whispered what they were both thinking, "Now what?"

"Well, I know what that glyph means, it's the glyph for Kin'Ich Ahau, the sun God. You see the jaguar in the painting over here on this wall, which is looking at the stone with Kin'Ich Ahau? Well in our Maya mythology, the jaguar, one of the Lords of the Night, would protect the sun on its nightly journey through Xibalba, the underworld, making sure that it survived all the trials and tribulations, so as to rise again the next day. The sun, disappearing into the underworld! Let's see, maybe if I just..." Gilberto reached up and pressed the large stone carving.

The stone glyph of the Sun God slid back, disappearing into the wall and a half second later, a loud muffled thump could be heard followed by silence.

"Well," said Alex, "it was worth a ..."

His voice trailed off as a neat and uniform crack appeared in the plaster around the rectangular edge of the entire painting, floor to ceiling, and down the walls on either side. A loud scraping sound filled the tunnel, and the painting started to swing away from them, opening up into a dark chamber behind it.

"Open sesame!" Alex whispered in awe.

The glow from the flickering orange flames of their candlewood torches was suddenly greatly amplified and the entire chamber beyond the hidden painted door, lit up brightly with a yellow-white light. Alex and Gilberto's shadows stretched long in front of them.

It took them both a second to realize that there was a powerful light source, coming from behind them!

They both spun round as the realization dawned on them that they were not alone!

They found themselves staring straight into the beam of a powerful headlamp that was being worn on the head of a black silhouette of a person, whom they could not identify, the beam shining blindingly, directly into their eyes.

"Grandfather! Alex! It's me, Emil!" said the figure ripping the headlamp off his head so they could see him.

"Emil!!" they both shouted, astounded.

"How... when..." said Gilberto, overcome.

He rushed down the passage and hugged his grandson, clapping him on the back.

"Oh, thank goodness you are alright! How did you find us?! You shouldn't be here; you should have gone to the village. We are still in grave danger," Gilberto said with a mixture of relief and panic.

"Emil!" said Alex. "Well done! You absolute star! You did it! It's so good to see you! But your grandfather's right, we are all still in mortal danger. Are you sure you weren't seen?"

"Yes, I am sure nobody saw me, the storm is really howling outside. I saw the three head torches of those evil marras gangsters, they're all awake, but they were all in the sleeping units. They're having a bad time of it. I think the wind has torn away at least one of their basha sheets. I could hear them yelling and cursing over the noise of the storm. Some big trees have come down with the wind. I found the outer embankment wall of the temple and followed it round in the dark until I came to the main temple structure; the lightning helped me find my way. I got this headlamp from the Land Rover but I didn't turn it on until I had followed the rope all the way to the hole in the floor," answered Emil, continuing with breathless excitement, "I fell asleep in the Land Rover and had a very strange dream. In it, you were both inside the temple. That's why I came straight here! When I got to the landing at the top I found the rope tied to the big round stone and followed from there."

"Well done Emil! Right everyone, we have some quick thinking to do," said Alex, an unmistakable air of urgency in his voice.

"Now that Emil is here we should just make good our escape and leave the rest to the police. I'm worried that those three cutthroats might now come looking for shelter here themselves at any moment. On the other hand we could try and save what we can from the tomb seeing as we are here and have come this far. Gilberto and Emil, our lives may hang in the balance. Delaying even for a few minutes could cost us our lives. What do you both think?"

"Well," said Gilberto, "let's not waste any more time. Let's see what we can save in two or three minutes and then let's make a run for Bodhi."

"I'm good with that. Emil?" asked Alex.

"I'm with you both. Let's have a very quick look at what we can save and get going! We'll be in a better position if we have what they want."

The trio walked through the stone doorway and into the tomb which hosted beautiful wall paintings depicting the story of King Nanchancaan's entire life story, for there was no longer the slightest doubt that the skeleton lying on the stone pedestal in the centre of the tomb could be none other than the great Maya king.

The king's death mask, covering the head of the skeleton was stunningly beautiful, carved out of one single piece of flawless jade and still in perfect position covering the face of the King. Thick necklaces of jade beads adorned the bare bones of his rib cage. Painted pottery and clay effigies were placed neatly around the last resting place of this amazing historical figure. In his skeletal right hand, he clutched a royal sceptre decorated with a feathered serpent head at either end. Next to his left hip lay a long black, obsidian bladed, double edged dagger with a handle made of deer horn and inset with jade.

On the right hand side of the chamber were three long wooden boxes, each about a half-metre long, twenty centimetres high and twenty wide. Emil gently lifted one of the lids of the boxes, the bark binding long since decayed. Inside, they could all see the folded codices covered in glyphs. These were the lost, sacred writings of this past civilization, full of ancient knowledge and wisdom.

Alex, Emil and Gilberto looked down at them in awe. Here were the original written records of one of the greatest civilizations on earth, preserved and intact, exactly as the scribes had written them. Rediscovered – at last!

Carefully and as quickly as they could, they gently packed the three wooden boxes into the biggest and most heavily padded waterproof bag.

Gilberto, with great reverence slowly lifted the jade mask off King Nanchancaan's skull, putting it into the second bag. The King's forehead had been unnaturally flattened from his birth to denote his noble status. The ends of his teeth had been filed into various shapes, and some of his teeth were inset with perfectly round pieces of jade. Gilberto placed the mask into the second of the padded waterproof bags. At the bottom of the stone plinth, at the great king's feet, lay a Spanish conquistadors sword.

"Right," said Alex. "Let's get out of here!"

Emil picked up the beautiful dagger, looking at its razor sharp obsidian blade, made from volcanic glass. He quickly put it into the empty third bag and followed Alex and Gilberto out of the tomb and back up the series of passages.

They dashed up the secret passage until they were all standing at the bottom of the straight shaft.

Alex proceeded to climb up and back into the antechamber. He reached the top of the shaft and hauled himself out. Gilberto was next to appear. They crouched beside each other in the dark, looking back down the shaft at Emil who was busy tying the handles of the bags to the rope, using his headlamp to see what he was doing. When they were all secure, he scaled the shaft with the quick agility of youth and popped out like a cork. They then all looked down the shaft as Gilberto gently raised the precious cargo up it.

In a few short moments, all three bags were safely landed on the floor next to them and Emil began undoing the knots. Once free of the bags, Alex started coiling the rope as the trio made their way into the main chamber. The storm was still raging outside.

A huge blue flash of lightning split the night, framing the doorway of the temple. It lit up the shapes of the three large men that stood silently in the dark, glowering at them, blocking the only exit.

Alex broke into a cold sweat. Gilberto moved his koshtal slightly behind his right hip. Emil opened the bag he was carrying and reached inside.

Three deafening shots exploded in the darkness, the bullets slamming into the wall above each of their heads.

"NOBODY MOVE!" screamed Silus, "Been having fun down there in the underworld have we? I know a thing or two about HELL!"

Three bright lights turned on, blinding Alex, Emil and Gilberto. They were caught like deer in the headlamps of a car.

"We are the wraiths of DEATH! We are the EATERS OF SOULS! And we have come for YOU!" Silus screamed hysterically, spittle flying from his furious face, veins standing out on his forehead, his unnatural gaze staring madly at the trio in front of him.

Kiloboy had his pistol still at the ready, his finger pressing on the trigger, his body shifting and moving in his excitement. TreeWay's huge frame stood as still as a mountain. He held his swollen, raw skinned right arm across his midsection, his blistered hand gripping the butt of his handgun which was still tucked into his waistband. The unholy looking trio did appear as if they had emerged straight from the bowels of hell.

Silus walked forward a few steps, careful to stay out of range of his prey. He calmed himself down enough to speak normally.

"Technology is a wonderful thing. A couple of quick calls on that sat phone and suddenly, as if by magic, I know so much more! You're not the only one with knowledgeable friends. Did you really think I would be so stupid as to believe your story about stone turtles without checking it? My friend in London told me all about Xibalba, and the temple at Copan. After that, it wasn't hard to figure out what you were up to. But you boy, you have me puzzled. That's quite some magic trick! Gordo's still telling me that you are safely locked up! You will have to tell me how you pulled that one off."

"He is the grandson of a shaman!" Gilberto yelled. "He is a wizard like me. He can disappear at will; walk through walls! He can cloud men's minds. You are all cursed by Tata Duende! You will not harm any of us. You have your prize, here it is!"

Gilberto picked up the two waterproof bags and held them in his left hand.

"You can take these and let us live. Besides, you need me to get you back across the river, and if you touch a hair on any of our heads I will not guide you, you can go straight back to your home in hell," said Gilberto.

"He's right," Alex reasoned. "You have the prize, the mask is in one bag, the codices are in the other, and you will need him to get out of here."

"Ahhh yes... The prize. So good of you to collect it for me, you really are pretty good servants. Now, gentlemen," said Silus, looking at TreeWays and Kiloboy while he took a small day sack off his back and unzipped it, "as we are all about to become very, very, wealthy, let's drink a toast to sweet victory! And Kiloboy, if anyone of these dung beetles so much as blinks, shoot them in the head."

Silus produced three miniature bottles of whiskey, the kind you find in a hotel mini bar. Cracking the tops open,

Silus handed one to each of the gangsters, keeping one for himself – the one that he had marked on the top. Laughing, the three men downed the contents in one fiery gulp.

"Bway, unu drink some serious fyaah waata! Dat stuff burn worse dan di roughest shek up," said Kiloboy coughing.

"Only the very best whiskey for you two!" said Silus smiling broadly at his two associates, his eyes as cold as a corpse.

"Yes, as I was saying," hissed Silus, "technology is a wonderful thing. We made a couple of phone calls when the storm hit; oh, and by the way, thank you so much for not letting us know that a storm was coming in advance.

"TreeWays phoned home to find out what the hell was happening. Not only did he get the weather forecast, he also found out that the word on the street was that a huge manhunt had been organized by the Belizean authorities. Fancy that! In fact, wouldn't you know, a military search and rescue team is on its way to save you as we speak. Helicopters can't fly due to the storm so they have sent a crack team, made up of some of their finest Jungle Warfare instructors, no less. Who knows, they could get here any time now!" Silus said with an evil sneer.

"Does that news give you hope? I love to give my victims hope. As we don't have time for games, I'll just say this. There is no hope. Chaos, yes. Evolution, certainly! But no hope, especially not for you. This storm has made the river truly impassable, and because the police and army are on their way here, that exit route is no longer any good to me. But you already knew that, didn't you! Tie them up! Start with him first," Silus ranted on, pointing at Alex.

Kiloboy cut three lengths of Alex's rope and proceeded to tie Alex's hands behind his back. Alex tensed all the muscles in his wrists and forearms, bunching his hands into fists. It was a trick he had once heard escape artists used. The theory was that once tied up, you then relax and the bonds become a bit slack, giving you some room to work on them, perhaps enough to wriggle free. Alex hoped it might actually work.

"You think you are so smart, don't you, barely a man and pouncing around like some grand important expedition leader, some leader you are dogboy," Silus snarled, watching Alex being bound. "I'll tell you another reason why technology is just so great. I am going to take your G.P.S unit. My friend in London, with the assistance of Google Earth, has found me a G.P.S location that we will head for. An open clearing in the jungle, a baccadero, I believe it's called. A big open space where loggers stack their logs before they are transported to sawmills. All my friends here and I have to do is make it to that clearing, guided by your G.P.S, and wait for the storm to pass in the next few hours. Then, a private helicopter has been chartered to pick us up. My friend in the UK arranged it so there will be no suspicions. He told the helicopter company that his VIP, oil executive friends got stranded in the jungle due to the storm and urgently needed a ride out. He agreed to triple their usual rate so that we would get priority top class service. So, I am delighted to tell you three that I no longer require your services and I can now torture you all to death immediately! How about that! You are all now classified as expendable assets, to be written off! So now let the fun begin!"

"Me and you," Silus said pointing at Emil. "I've got special plans for you. We are going to have a very personal conversation in a little while. I'll do the talking, you'll be doing all the screaming and crying. Shame I didn't bring my video camera; filming your last agonising minutes would have made a great souvenir of my holiday here. TreeWays, bring him over to me."

TreeWays was suddenly feeling revitalized and stronger than ever, but now had a raging thirst and his pulse was racing. He walked over and grabbed Emil's arm, dragging him over to Silus.

Gilberto glanced quickly at Alex and they saw the same message in each other's eyes: Do or die!

Gilberto reached behind him with his right hand, feeling around in his koshtal for the string of the cloth bag inside. He found it, pulled it, and felt the small viper slide over his fingers. He held the two bags with the artefacts out towards Silus in his left hand, hiding what his right hand was doing. He grabbed the snake and felt white hot pricks as its fangs sank into the web of skin between his thumb and forefinger.

Emil struggled in the big man's grip as his own hand gripped the handle of the obsidian dagger still hidden in the bag.

In a flash of movement, Gilberto's hand flew forward as he flung the deadly viper at Silus' face. Gilberto leapt forward, still clutching the two bags. Silus moved fast; his natural reaction was to grab at the incoming object and deflect it. Gilberto charged for the gap, counting on the distraction to gain vital hundredths of a second.

"Yellow!" yelled Gilberto as he flew past the door lintel and out onto the platform outside.

While TreeWays' swollen eyes tracked Gilberto's movements, Emil brought the stone dagger up and forward, jamming it into TreeWays' blister covered forearm which he was smoothly raising, lining his pistol sights up with the back of Gilberto's fast disappearing head.

"Run, Abuelo! RUN!" shouted Emil.

Emil watched in helpless horror as TreeWays fired, the bullet slamming into his grandfather's right shoulder blade, blood spraying from the impact, sending him tumbling down the side of the temple, into the black stormy night, but still clutching the bags with the priceless artefacts in his left hand. More gunfire rang out as Kiloboy joined TreeWays and fired a wild hail of bullets after Gilberto in the deluging rain and wind.

Bodhi listened and watched helplessly through the crystal orb.

Silus screamed as the bullets flew, shaking his hand wildly to get the fer-de-lance off it. The hypodermic fangs were working their way deeper into his little finger as the small snake pumped its venom into it. Silus grabbed the terrified and angry snake with his left hand, ripping it away and throwing it as far away as he could, leaving one fang snapped off in his finger. Alex saw his chance to act. Simultaneously swinging one leg up and out in front of him and collapsing the other supporting leg, he dropped vertically as fast as he could. As his seat made contact with the floor he twisted, spinning as fast and as hard as possible, slamming his shin across the backs of Kiloboy's knees and sticking his folded leg out in front of Kiloboy's ankles. The scissor-like sweeping action felled Kiloboy like a tree and he slammed face first into the floor. Kiloboy's headlamp flew off his head but he still had a firm grasp on his pistol.

Rolling on the floor, Alex's mind was frantically thinking about how to find hard cover as he disappeared into the shadows. His hands tied, he was in a very bad situation. He thought of the tarantula and how it had scuttled into the hole, its best defensive position. Easy to defend the opening, hidden in the dark, protected on all other fronts.

"That's it!" Alex thought as he sprang up and ran until he made it back into the darkness of the antechamber.

He sprinted along the wall, hearing Kiloboy quickly regaining his feet too and scrambling after him, his headlamp back in place.

Alex found the entrance to the secret passage and swung his legs over the edge, feeling for the first foot holes about a metre below. Unable to use his bound hands, he braced his back against the side of the shaft and pressed hard against the opposite wall with his feet. As fast as he could, he began to descend using a rock climbing technique called chimneying, dropping the last two metres or so to save precious milliseconds. Alex hit the bottom and instantly launched himself down the passage head first, using a forward dive roll that he was able to do without having to use his hands to break his fall. As he completed the roll he stayed low to the ground. Bullets ricocheted past him as Kiloboy fired blindly down the shaft, quickly descending himself in hot pursuit.

Back in the main chamber, a furious Emil pulled back the dagger and stabbed again, this time at TreeWay's chest and with all the force he could muster. Before the dagger could connect, TreeWays spun round from the doorway, slamming Emil off balance. The blow sent Emil reeling towards Silus, the deflected knife strike burying the razor sharp obsidian dagger deep into Silus' right thigh, just as TreeWays brought his pistol crashing down onto Emil's head. Emil collapsed unconscious onto the floor at Silus' feet.

Lightning split the night and thunder crashed down.

"GET HIM!" Silus bellowed hysterically at TreeWays.

Silus gawked in wide eyed disbelief at the dagger sticking out of his thigh. "STOP HIM! My leg... aaahhaa... AAAHHH MY LEG! DO NOT LET THAT OLD MAN GET AWAY! AAAAAAAGH, my bloody HAND! Make sure he's DEAD! KILL HIM, KILL HIM!"

"No worry, Silus! I done bus' a cap inna da man, I shot him, he noh gonna get far! No worry! I will kill dat ol' devil witch-doctor!" said TreeWays, adjusting his headlamp and heading out into the storm.

As TreeWays got to the first step, he turned and threw a bandana at Silus.

"Tie dat tight around your hand, and tie your belt around your leg! You no gonna die on me befoh I get mi money dem, you hear! Di tommygoff bite on yoh hand noh gonna kill you right away, we got some hours, but you gonna need da hospital. I goh find di 'ol man. Den I come back an' get you. You tek care a di boy, mek sure e dead. Kiloboy will kill the other one," said TreeWays looking at the blood dripping from the deep gash in his swollen arm.

TreeWays couldn't understand why he was so thirsty. His throat felt as if it had been sand blasted. He adjusted the headlamp and set off down the steep side of the temple where he had seen Gilberto tumble away.

The battle was raging at the temple and Bodhi was still parked in the clearing far away. She felt absolutely desperate. What should she do? What would be the best way to help her friends? Gilberto had picked up on Bodhi's thoughts.

"Bodhi, we need your help!" he telepathed, focusing all his thoughts on the Land Rover as powerfully as he could.

"I know that you're fighting for your lives Gilberto, but I don't know how best to help," answered Bodhi.

"We need you here, we can't make it all the way to you in time. That is how you can help, come to us, I will die if you cannot make it, Emil and Alex will too."

"I will do my best Gilberto," Bodhi telepathed.

"Andrasta, Mezaferus, I call on you to help me, to guide me! Hear me!" Bodhi's message reverberated through the jungle, every leaf and tree vibrating with the harmonic resonance of Bodhi's message.

Andrasta answered the call first, appearing in Bodhi's mind's eye immediately followed by Mezaferus.

"Bodhi, remember how to tap into Gaia's life force, remember the exercises I taught you. Remember how to channel the energy, to direct it! Do it! Do it now! This is your first real challenge, your first real test. You are new to this, but it will become easier as you gain experience," said Andrasta.

"Begin!" said Mezaferus. "Save your friends! They must live; their work on earth is far from complete. There is no time to waste. Hurry!"

Bodhi remembered.

Andrasta's and Mezaferus's lessons flooded back to her. During her training, Andrasta had taken Bodhi on a vision quest to watch Tibetan and Shaolin Monks and martial arts masters, all performing seemingly superhuman feats of strengths. Their bodies had been seemingly impervious to weapons. They had been able to jump great distances, to break piles of bricks with what looked like nothing more than a hard open handed slap. Bodhi had watched them balance and climb as if their feet were magnetic and as if they were free of the effects of gravity. Most impressive of all, they had been able to heal themselves and others merely by directing energy to the affected area.

She remembered Andrasta taking her to the scene of a traffic accident. A woman's baby was trapped under an overturned car. The woman had lifted the car off her child on her own with her bare hands.

Bodhi used the techniques that Andrasta had taught her that allowed her to tap into this force, this power. Andrasta had said that humans called it chi energy or prana or power. Those who practised these ancient secret exercises were able to build this force within their bodies.

Bodhi started her own special exercises; she grounded herself, sinking her life force energy into the earth through her tyres, sending energy roots deep into Gaia's body. She drew the earth's energy up these roots and into her until she felt the fusion of elemental power flowing through her entire being. The combined forces of the elements began surging through her. Earth, water, fire, wood, metal, and air; Bodhi was drawing on the power of all of them, building energy. Charging herself with it.

Next, she directed her intentions and energy up into the winds of the sky and beyond; out into the vast limitlessness silence of the great void, into space, into the universe. She gathered the astral energy radiated by a thousand trillion stars, the dust of which everything that exists is made up of. She drew this golden light of the heavens into her. The universal winds now merged with earth's elemental forces – the cosmic orbital energy circuit inside her was now complete. The connection had been made.

Bodhi's engine fired into life, revving.

Mezaferus held out his arms and a distant clacking noise started in the distance. The clacking grew louder and louder and the ground began to vibrate. The loud snapping and cracking sound was joined by a low rumbling, crashing and grunting noise. It approached like an invisible wave, moving through the jungle behind Bodhi.

"Follow them!" said Mezaferus as he and Andrasta slowly faded away, "They will lead you to your friends. They will show you the best way through the forest."

The enormous herd of white lipped peccary charged through the undergrowth and flowed past Bodhi on either side by the hundred. Their sharp white tusks were clacking noisily as a warning, loudly broadcasting to the other inhabitants of the forest that they should clear the way. The giant herd crashed through the understory like a cavalry charge. They had dark, wiry, bristled backs and small black eyes which were set into big powerful heads, giving them a primordial, wild look that matched the pungent sweet odour coming from the scent glands between their shoulders. The huge herd quickly passed Bodhi who charged along after them.

Back in the temple, Alex dashed down the dark passageway. Every split second counted. He made the landing to the second flight just as Kiloboy got to the bottom of the shaft. Bullets thudded into the wall where Alex's head had been moments before. He charged down the second flight of steps.

Running blind in the pitch dark, touching the wall for guidance, he ran straight into the burial chamber, crashing against the stone plinth. Dropping down, he felt around on the floor until his fingers found what he was looking for: the Conquistador's sword. The rope bindings around his wrists were still quite firmly bound. Quickly, he rubbed the rope along the Toledo steel blade; the rusty battle damaged edge was still sharp enough to cut through the bonds.

Back in the wet dark jungle, Gilberto had run for his life. He knew he was losing blood but he had enough experience to know that if the bullet had pierced his lung, he would be coughing up blood and he would be having trouble breathing. If he was lucky, the bullet may have passed clean through him. He was in agony, with a blinding pain in his shoulder. He knew it would not be long before he went into shock and his right arm flopped about at his side – completely useless. Still he ran, guided by instinct born of a lifetime of living and working in the jungle; his home.

As accurately as a tarantula hawk wasp dragging its paralysed prey backwards to its underground chamber, Gilberto unerringly arrived right at the Chel Tun. Ripping down a long length of iguana tie-tie vine dangling from a tree, he tied the two bags to the end and lowered them down into the Chel Tun. He tied the other end around a nearby tree trunk and covered the whole vine with leaves to hide it. He then lay down next to the Chel Tun and slowed his breathing as much as he could, lying as still as he could, in an unnatural way. To an observer, he would look for all the world as if he were dead.

In no time, TreeWays came bashing along through the thick wet vegetation, following the trail of bright red blood stains which glistened on the water covered leaves, betraying Gilberto's passage. As soon as Gilberto had been shot, he realized that it would be easy for anyone to track him and he had come up with a plan born out of desperation.

Deep inside the temple, Alex was making plans for his own survival just as quickly.

"If only I had echolocation like bats, I would be able to find my way around in here in the pitch black and plan an ambush!" Alex thought, remembering the image of the truly fearsome looking bat painted on the wall in King Nanchancaan's tomb.

It gave him an idea. He would have a few seconds to plan as Kiloboy would surely be quite cautious coming down passages he had never been down before. He would be using his headlamp too, which would warn Alex of his approach.

"I will become the bat!" Alex thought to himself.

Alex slid the sword through his belt and looked back up the stairwell. He could see the glow from the headlamp lighting up the landing, and he could hear Kiloboy reloading his pistol with another magazine.

Alex heard Kiloboy pull the pistol's slide back and then the unmistakable metallic sound that it made as it was released, slamming home and chambering a fresh round. Kiloboy would be around the corner soon! It was now or never!

In the jungle, Gilberto lay perfectly still. TreeWays scanned him with the head torch and raised his pistol up, aiming it at Gilberto's head, but his vision was blurred. Just then, he noticed the hole in the ground near Gilberto, with the tree trunk ladder sticking out of it. He looked down and saw the bags at the bottom of the stone chamber, a smile creeping across his otherwise agonised face. He felt light-headed and his muscles were cramping. His eyes were not focusing properly at all now, and he was so thirsty. He wondered if the ancient dagger had been poisoned. He gave Gilberto a kick, and bent over him, looking at the large bloody hole in the front of his shirt. He gave Gilberto another savage kick in the ribs. Nothing. No response at all. Satisfied that Gilberto was dead, TreeWays climbed down the tree trunk ladder to retrieve the two bags.

As he reached the bottom, he walked the few steps over to the bags and heard a sliding scraping noise behind him. He spun round to see the tree trunk ladder disappearing over the lip of the Chel Tun. He ran over to it and jumped into the air, reaching for the end that was still sticking over the edge. He jumped and jumped yelling and cursing and reaching for the end. Then he heard another scraping sound, again behind him. He spun round, just in time to see the two bags disappear over the lip of the Chel Tun on the other side. He screamed with rage, firing his pistol in the air. The end of the tree makeshift ladder that Gilberto had used as bait slowly slid out of view. TreeWays was hopelessly trapped.

Alex put his plan into action. He dashed out of the tomb and back into the narrow passage. For the second time in as many minutes, he used the chimneying technique, putting his back against one wall and his feet against the other passage wall. Now that his hands were free, he quickly shot up through the inky blackness, towards the vaulted stone ceiling, much more easily, and as fast as he could. Alex was banking on several suppositions.

First, Kiloboy would be expecting him to be hiding somewhere in the burial chamber as he would not see him in the straight and narrow passage. Second, Alex was counting on Kiloboy not looking up at the shadowy dark recesses way up in the passage ceiling as there was no obvious way to climb up to it, the walls being smoothly plastered. Lastly, the tomb would be the natural hiding place for Alex as it would provide the best and most logical position to attempt an ambush, because Kiloboy would have to enter through the narrow doorway.

Another advantage Alex knew he had in his favour was that headlamps and flashlights tended to make everything outside of the light beam very difficult to see. This was because the human eye needs time to adjust to low levels of light in order to see well. Bright light destroys night vision. Like a bat, Alex crammed himself as tightly and as high into the arched vaulted ceiling as he could. He was braced just outside and above the tomb's doorway.

Kiloboy turned the corner. The headlamp beam lit up the passageway. He held his pistol out in front of him, concentrating on the open door at the end of it and the dark chamber beyond. Kiloboy swallowed hard, he was desperately thirsty and his heart beat like a sledgehammer in his chest. He felt unusually strong, his senses heightened but his vision slightly blurred. He shook his head, blinked his eyes and carried on moving cautiously down the tunnel.

Twenty five meters above, Silus was now in great pain from the snakebite on his hand, which had begun to swell rapidly. In contrast, his leg felt numb, it did not want to work, and it kept collapsing on him. After a few minutes, he got enough nerve up to grasp the bloodied handle of the dagger with his good right hand. In a cold sweat, he pulled hard on the handle and the long sleek volcanic glass blade slipped gradually out of his leg muscle. He threw up and almost passed out. Once he had regained a bit of control over his quivering and damaged muscles, he hobbled over to Emil, who was still out cold. Sheathing the dagger under his belt, he grabbed Emil's shirt collar and dragged his limp body onto the platform outside.

He pulled Emil's form onto the big round stone. The rain had almost stopped and the wind was dropping.

"I'm told by my friend in London that this big round stone was used for sacrifices. I've often wondered what it would be like to be a surgeon. I have an overwhelming urge to show you some of your organs. Shame I won't be able to sell them, but after all the trouble you have given me, I'm really going to enjoy ripping your heart out and chopping you into little pieces!" Silus was angry at himself for having given the poisoned whiskey to TreeWays and Kiloboy a bit prematurely.

He hoped TreeWays would last long enough to kill the old man and bring the treasures back to him.

"Wake up!" Silus said, slapping Emil's face again and again as hard as he could "Wake up! I want you awake for this! Doctor Silus wants to start his vivisection! WAKE UP!"

Emil started to regain consciousness slowly. Silus bent over him, the dagger's black blade glinting in the beam of his headlamp.

Back in the passage, Alex was straining to keep the pressure up. Sweat running down his face, he managed to remain motionless until Kiloboy had passed under him and moved into the doorway of the tomb.

As soon as he did, Alex dropped down behind him. Drawing the sword from his belt, he brought the blade down towards the back of Kiloboy's head as hard and fast as possible. Kiloboy heard Alex land behind him and spun round in a flash, only just managing to dodge the blade. Kiloboy raised the pistol.

Alex spun the blade in a blindingly fast arc, the flat of the blade crashing onto the back of Kiloboy's gun hand. The pistol went off, the bullet searing past Alex's head. The gun fell to the floor from Kiloboy's shattered hand. Swerving his body round Kiloboy, Alex swung his arm around Kiloboy's neck, trapping Kiloboy's throat in the 'V' of his left arm between his forearm and bicep. Alex gripped his right bicep with his left hand, and used the palm of his right hand to force Kiloboy's head forward into the vice like 'V'.

A wild struggle began as Alex tried to hold onto Kiloboy long enough for the shime waza choke hold to make him pass out. But Kiloboy had poison charging through his veins that was giving him incredible, if temporary, strength. He smashed Alex hard against the wall, stepping on and crushing the headlamp, plunging the struggling pair into complete darkness.

Kiloboy broke the hold and turned, stealing Alex's balance, clawing at his face and slamming his head hard into the wall.

Suddenly, Kiloboy felt really weird, light headed and sick, his muscles starting to cramp. Alex, only aware that he had broken free of Kiloboy, made a scramble away from him. Lights bursting in his head from the blow, he too felt nauseous and faint but from physical damage, not chemical poisoning.

Alex stumbled and staggered up the passage, feeling his way along, running on pure adrenaline. His only thought was to get out of the secret tunnel, away from Kiloboy and his gun before he collapsed. He was soon at the shaft. As his strength was ebbing fast, Alex started the climb up and out. He reached the top of the shaft, scrambling out, and heaved on the heavy stone paving slab as hard as he could. His vision was blurring, his balance gone, he was about to pass out from the blow to his head. He had to seal the hole, he had to, or he was done for! He pulled again as hard as he could with his last bit of strength.

The big stone slab crashed down. At least Kiloboy was now contained, trapped. There was no way he would be able to lift the stone slab from below, and by himself.

Alex collapsed on the floor, stood up again, his ears ringing loudly, before falling once more. He crawled around the wall of the antechamber. In his blurred and fading vision, he saw Emil lying face up on the big circular stone, Silus bending over him, raising the long black dagger up high.

Emil was slowly lifting his arms, trying to lift his head, weakly shouting for help. Alex tried to lurch forward. In his mind he jumped, trying to get to Emil before it was too late. His eyes closed, his arms gave out, and as the dagger began to fall, Alex felt himself falling.

Falling… falling… falling… as the darkness rose to meet him.

Silus raised the dagger high in the air. The ecstasy of his bloodlust was reflected in his raving mad eyes; his nostrils flared in anticipation of the delightfully grisly bloodbath to come. He clutched Emil by the throat, pinning the struggling boy down by arching his back over the stone. Emil's arms and legs flailed and kicked, not able to make contact with anything but the air, not able to gain any purchase on anything at all. He was helpless. He was doomed.

"Now you DIE!" screamed Silus as he brought the dagger down in a powerful plunging motion.

A blindingly fast movement caught Silus's eye. He barely had time to comprehend what he was seeing in the headlamp beam before the giant cat slammed into him.

Balaam had sprung, sailing through the air with his huge paws splayed on his outstretched thick front legs, sharp long claws unsheathed, ears back, eyes ablaze, mouth agape in a fearsome snarl. The cat exploded onto Silus with all muscle, teeth and claws, attacking him with savage fury. With his top lip pulled back over his long pointed teeth, the big male jaguar slammed into Silus's body like a juggernaut, smashing him off his feet, and blasting him clean off the high platform.

Emil started to sit up on the big round wet stone, rubbing the egg sized lump on his head. He looked around the platform. There was no one. Faint fingers of dawn's light were breaking through the thick clouds above the jungle canopy. He stood up and walked over to a headlamp that was lying on the ground and picked up the long obsidian dagger. He shone the light into the chamber and saw a body lying on the floor, blood pooling around its head. It was Alex!

AABC, Emil remembered from his first aid lecture. Cautiously, Emil approached Alex, gripping the dagger, holding it ready. When he was sure there was no danger from Kiloboy, he checked that Alex was breathing, and performed the other checks in sequence. Ripping the sleeve off his shirt, he applied pressure to the cut on Alex's head. He fought his rising panic as he remembered all that had happened to his grandfather.

Alex stirred and started trying to talk.

"What did you say?" Emil asked.

"Yellow!" Alex said hoarsely. "It's a code word for the Chel Tun storage chamber near the Sac Be. Do you know where it is?"

"Yes," said Emil, his own head thumping with a headache.

"That's where your grandfather is either hiding or has hidden the artefacts. I think I'll be okay, go and help your grandfather if you can! Hurry!" Alex said before passing out again.

Emil moved as quickly as he dared. When he got to the Chel Tun he heard a faint voice calling him.

"Emil. Over here! Over here my boy!"

Emil saw his grandfather sitting propped up against a rock, his hand badly swollen and his shirt covered in blood.

"Emil, cut me some inner bark from a bull horn acacia tree. It will help to slow down my heart, which will help with the loss of blood and it will slow the spread of the snake venom too," said the old shaman.

Gilberto raised his torso up a bit more and spoke, "Emil, I have not got long my boy. If the worst should happen, remember I love you! Tell your mother and father that I love them and I'm truly sorry for all that has happened!"

"Tell them yourself!" Emil shouted. "You can't die! You mustn't give up! EVER! Fight grandfather, you're strong! Fight, don't give up! Please!"

"But Bodhi's so far away, too far to walk. Maybe if you and Alex made a stretcher... no my boy you couldn't make it in time, and then there's the river too..."

"Bodhi? Who's Bodhi?" asked Emil confused.

"Bodhi is Alex's Land Rover, Emil. And she's no ordinary Land Rover. Let me rest a minute. Do what you can for the bleeding and my shoulder, bind up my hand and get me the bark. Don't be scared if I don't speak or seem as if I have passed out. Just do what you can. I'll be back in a minute," Gilberto said weakly.

"Back in a minute! Back in a minute? What are you talking about, Abuelo? Stay with me! Don't give up!"

Gilberto closed his eyes and drifted off. Emil frantically ripped at what was left of his shirt and bound the gunshot wound as tightly as he could, applying pressure to stop the bleeding. Then he bound Gilberto's finger and hand in the way that Alex had taught him to do in the treatment of snakebites of this kind. He looked around and found a bull horn acacia tree. Ripping off some small young branches he stripped the inner bark, ignoring the bites and the stings of the ants that rained down on him from their homes in the acacia's hollow thorns.

Gilberto's eyes opened to see Emil's face looking at him, concern, fear and worry written all over it.

"Here, Grandfather, chew on the bark!" said Emil, giving Gilberto a teaspoon sized wad.

Gilberto started chewing it and drew Emil close, whispering in his ear.

"My boy, there are many, many things that we humans still do not know and can't explain. To the initiated, to shamans like me, they are known as the Mysteries. What you are about to see, what you are about to participate in, is a great mystery. Do not try and understand what is about to happen, just try to accept it. Do not be afraid. Play your part in this great story, this collision of fates, this meeting of destinies. Bodhi is here Emil! She has done it!"

"Don't talk Grandfather, save your strength," said Emil trying to decide what the best plan would be, knowing that nothing he could do would be fast enough.

Just then he heard the rumble. The clacking. He knew that sound, and knew what it meant – DANGER!

"Warrie!" he yelled as he dragged his grandfather behind a large mahogany tree, tucking him between two of its big flat buttress roots. Then he dashed over to an all spice tree and climbed up into it as fast as he could.

The peccaries started appearing. Power balls of energy, tightly packed muscular bodies, careening through the jungle. Emil had rarely seen a herd this big. They flowed onto the Sac Be about a hundred meters away, a river of rushing, grunting, clacking bodies. Then he heard something else. It was the noise of an engine that he had grown to know well.

He could not believe his eyes. The Land Rover was following the herd, steering and bouncing along between the trees. It drove up the steep embankment of the Sac Be and drove along it. Emil looked, and looked again. There was no one driving it!

Emil looked down at his grandfather, his eyes were closed, and he had a smile on his serene old face.

Bodhi stopped level with the Mahogany tree.

"Okay," said Emil to himself. "Okay, Okay, Okay. Just accept! Just accept!"

Now, his mind flashed with the possibilities as he climbed down from the tree listing the priorities. First, he must load his grandfather and the two waterproof bags into the... Bodhi. Next, pick up Alex and get to a hospital as fast as possible.

He didn't stop to think about how he would get Alex down off the temple, or how he would cross the flooded river, he didn't even think about how he would drive Bodhi.

He would take action, he would just trust completely and act. Now he had hope, and he truly believed that anything was possible!

Chapter Nineteen

Final SITREP

The red footed booby bird swooped and dived, evading the frigate bird's aggressive and persistent attempts to steal the fish it had just caught.

The booby's white-grey form swirled and stooped, rolled and span, until it forced the black plumed frigate bird to break off the contact. Snatching victory from the jaws of defeat, the booby flew in the direction of its home in the nesting colony on Half Moon Caye.

Way below the two competing marine birds, the Caribbean Sea sparkled and shone under the warm sub-tropical sun, the sea's azure and emerald hues slowly becoming aquamarine in the distance beyond the reef. As the sea became deeper, past the shallow reef waters, it reached the drop off and turned into the deep sapphire colour of what Belizeans call The Blue.

A dive boat bobbed at anchor just off the long coral barrier reef, which was visible as an extended white foaming line of breaking waves. Under the water three divers mingled with the abundant sea life.

Horse eyed jacks, yellow snappers, hawksbill turtles and mighty eagle rays glided up to them and flashed under, over and past them. A giant old grouper lay near the bottom in the shelter of a coral head, while a nurse shark scoured the sea bed for food.

Parrot fish and trigger fish, angel fish and moray eels hovered over and swam between the rainbow coloured corals. Amongst fan corals, brain corals, stag horn corals and fire corals, the three divers were suspended in a kaleidoscope of colours and vibrant sea life.

Surfacing, the divers swam over to and climbed back up the aluminium ladder into the boat. Under the shade of the boat's blue canvas bimini top, they shed their now cumbersome, heavy, air bottles and BCD's, which weighed nothing in the water and allowed them to be part of another world, if only for an hour or so.

The dive master, Alex and Emil laughed and joked with the jovial boat captain as he started the engines and his boat left the world famous Hol Chan Marine reserve and its neighbouring Shark and Ray Alley. They sped back towards the large island of Ambergris Caye. The main town of San Pedro came into view, coconut palms and beach resorts lining the shore. Mangroves still grew along the seafront in the less developed areas to the north and south.

"So Emil, you are now a qualified advanced open water diver! How do you feel?" asked Alex.

"It's great! I can't wait to show my parents and my grandfather my dive log! I've seen so much!" Emil said, grinning, the rushing air drying the salty water on his body as the boat sped along.

"I have been speaking to my grandfather every day while you were both in the hospital. He says you're a lousy patient, always trying to get up and move around. He says you were driving the doctor crazy asking when you could leave all the time," said Emil.

"Is that so! I don't think I was that bad, I always listen to what the doctor tells me, Emil!" said Alex.

"You were listening fine!" said Emil grinning. "You just weren't doing!"

"I'm so glad they released me from the hospital just in time to join you for your last qualifying dive! It's wonderful down there isn't it! I'm also really looking forward to chatting to you about what happened. I've got a lot of questions!" said Alex.

"Yes," said Emil knowingly. "But maybe my answers will leave you with more questions."

The boat turned, carving a smooth arc through the water, sliding up next to the large wooden dock.

"Well, here we are!" announced the dive master. "Enjoy the rest of your time on our beautiful island, La Isla Bonita!"

"Thanks!" chorused Alex and Emil simultaneously hopping up onto the dock.

"Surprise!" shouted Alex, the boat captain and the dive master in chorus, as Emil stood up straight and saw his grandfather standing in front of him.

"Abuelo!" shouted Emil delighted. "When did you get here?"

"Well," said Gilberto, embracing Emil with his good left arm, his right arm still heavily bandaged and splinted, "Alex and I escaped from the hospital at the same time and as he has so much more to learn about Maya traditions and shamanism I couldn't just leave him all alone. I'm joking of course! I couldn't wait to see my brave grandson again! Emil, I'm so very, very proud of you! We came out here together, but I wanted to surprise you. I have another surprise. You're parents are flying in to the island later on this afternoon!"

"Verdad? Bueno! That's great news!" said Emil, overjoyed.

They walked along the beach together until they reached their hotel. Gilberto excused himself and went to his room to lie down and save his strength for that evening.

Alex and Emil sat outside next to the swimming pool and ordered cool drinks.

"So, how are you Emil, honestly?" asked Alex.

"Good. Really, I'm fine. I haven't had any more nightmares about Silus and I have loved learning to dive every day. It will be a little while before I get back to normal completely I guess. I was a split second from being murdered! We all were! It's funny, I feel so full of life now, and I don't want to waste a second. I want to learn everything, I want to do everything!" said Emil with a huge smile.

"I'm very happy to hear it! We were all very lucky, and you were very brave Emil. Your grandfather told me about the jaguar attacking Silus. He's convinced it was the same jaguar that we helped down in the Cockscomb Wildlife and Jaguar preserve, but that seems very unlikely given the vast distance it would have had to travel over the Maya Mountains. It's unlikely it would have left its home territory like that either. And for a jaguar to help save a human, well that's truly one for the *Guinness Book of Records,* but I'm so happy it did!"

"Many, many strange things happened. When I have nightmares about all we have been through, the same jaguar always comes to save me," said Emil.

Emil's eyes stared off into the distance. Looking at Alex again he added, "I feel as though his spirit is with me all the time now. My grandfather says it is; that now we are connected forever."

"Tell me, how did you manage to get me down from the temple? I would have been a dead weight, unconscious as I was," asked Alex curiously.

"I tied a triple bowline knot like you showed me around you using the rope you had left up there," answered Emil, "and then I put a belay on that big round rock, pushed you off the temple and lowered you down to the plaza. Then I did the other one you taught me, the 'Z' drag, pig haul to pull you into Bodhi. My grandfather was able to walk a little, but I mostly carried him in the fireman's lift that you also showed me, and put him into Bodhi too. He's much lighter than you! I'm already taller than he is," Emil explained.

"How did you drive Bodhi?" Alex asked. "I can understand the automatic S.U.V. that has basically got stop and go pedals, but Bodhi has a manual transmission with a shift stick and a clutch."

"Well, if I told you, you wouldn't believe me," said Emil seriously, rummaging around in his day sack and handing Alex a sweet.

"Try me!" said Alex.

"Well, my grandfather relayed information from Bodhi to me about which pedals to press and how to move the shift stick but I'm sure you know it's not that easy," said Emil unwrapping the coconut sweet and putting it in his mouth.

"The answer is that although I was driving, I wasn't really driving. I know it doesn't make sense, but Bodhi was really driving herself."

Alex didn't speak for a second or two, trying to understand what he was hearing.

Eventually he said, "I'm sure you believe that Emil, but it is entirely possible that you are a natural and found it easier than most people do; people are capable of doing amazing things when they are under extreme stress.

"Your grandfather is a great teacher, and plenty of young people have put cushions on the front seats of vehicles to see and as long as they can reach the pedals they can manage. I'm sure you're in that category Emil," said Alex logically.

"No Alex, think about it. First of all, my grandfather has never driven a car in his life. The military search and rescue team found us after we had crossed the river. The river was twice as high as it was when I swam across it," said Emil.

"When we got to it, I was very scared; I didn't want to drive into it. My grandfather told me that Bodhi had asked the river to build up the rocks that were tumbling along the river bottom in the flood and make the causeway high enough for her, and us, to cross. I believed him and he was dying, I thought you were too, I had no choice. I went for it, I drove in and across."

"Well," said Alex, trying not to let his scepticism be heard in his voice. "Perhaps that was a natural result of the lower causeway blocking the material that was being washed downstream. It's entirely possible that enough boulders and tree trunks washed down and were trapped there to build it up high enough for us to cross. There could easily be a logical explanation."

"I guess," said Emil unconvinced.

"But then how did my grandfather know it was high enough for us to be able to drive over?" asked the young man.

"Well…" thought Alex, "your grandfather has got some uncanny abilities. He was able to tell me about a dream I had as if he had had the exact same dream, as if he was psychic. Perhaps that's how he knew."

"Alex, you must listen to me. Don't try and find explanations that fit what you know. This was different, Bodhi is different. I think your Land Rover is alive," said Emil earnestly.

"Yeah right, Emil! Your grandfather told me the same thing! Ha ha, I wish she was, but really, come on, that's impossible and you know it! You've got a wild imagination!" Alex laughed.

"Really? Do I?" said Emil slightly upset, "Okay, then how did Bodhi get to the temple? Answer that for me."

Alex began to answer immediately.

"You drove her of cour…" the sentence trailed off as the impossibility of that occurred to him.

There hadn't been time for Emil to run all the way back to the Land Rover and return, and without his grandfather with him to give him basic instructions, it would have been unfeasible. For a complete novice to navigate through and around all the jungle obstacles, off road, to get there, let alone back again, certainly seemed impossible too. Alex was stumped. It was a mystery.

"Okay, Emil," said Alex eventually. "I'm stumped. I'll think about what you've told me. That's enough questions for now. Thank you Emil, however you managed it, you saved our lives. Let's have a rest and get ready for the event tonight with your parents. I have to meet my grandfather in a few minutes too. I'm so happy that he set you up with the dive course!

"When my grandfather told me you were out here diving I came straight from the hospital to join you for your last dive and see you qualify."

"Yes, thanks for being here for that and the surprise! I love diving," said Emil, standing up. "I'm really looking forward to seeing my parents later this afternoon. What time are they coming in?"

"They're flying in on the last flight at five thirty with my grandfather and all the other guests that have been invited to the thank you dinner event that has been organised for this evening. Apparently, the local news media have heard of the discovery and it's been headline news for a few days now. They will no doubt want to interview you. Having the codices and the mask will be an enormous asset to Belize, its people and the Belizean tourism industry. People will come from all over the world just to see them and when they get here they will be amazed at how beautiful and fascinating this country is. That alone should raise plenty of funds to help support conservation efforts," said Alex.

Alex and Emil made their way to their respective rooms. When Alex got to his, he found his grandfather had already arrived and was waiting for him.

"Alex, how great to see you, my boy. And looking so well I would say."

"Grandpa, I am so glad you are here. I was expecting you later," said Alex, stepping forward to hug his grandfather.

"I caught an earlier flight. You left the hospital in such a rush we didn't have time to tell you. Let's have a chat though, there is so much to talk about. It'll be our final SITREP, but face to face, more of an expedition debriefing really

"Well, you have had quite an adventure with your first ARACHNIS project, haven't you! Congratulations, and I am happy that it all ended well, but I am so sorry that you were in such danger with those thugs," said the Professor.

They sat down in the comfort of the hotel room and ordered some tea. When the tea had arrived and it was poured and the sugar stirred in the Professor continued.

"Let's wrap up this expedition properly shall we?" said the Professor, picking up a sheaf of papers and casting his eyes down a list.

"I have taken care of your insurance and dealt with the medical bills. All the paperwork is waiting for you at the reception in the lobby. There's still quite a bit to do, signing off on various statements and paperwork for the Belizean Archaeological Institute and other government ministries that will need information from you. Hopefully, I have lessened the load.

"I also dropped your Land Rover back at Big Creek port into the very capable hands of Officer Palacio for shipping. You must have left some open food or something that attracts rodents inside the Land Rover. I looked high and low and I couldn't find anything, but I kept seeing a rat at the port running around the Land Rover trying to find a way in. Check it when you get it again. Funny little fellow really, looked as if he was dancing to the music that the dock workers were playing!

"Let's see now, what's next. The motion sensing trip cameras you delivered are producing fantastic results for the scientists studying the jaguars in the Cockscomb. Have a look at these photos later on. Next, the data on the pine forest in the savannah has come back. It is indeed viable to start a reforestation program in that area and scientists are looking at the best way to plan the re-population of yellow headed parrots there. Also, the jabiru stork nests you found have been included on the ranger patrol list to make sure they stay unmolested and protected from fires. A budget has been proposed for the construction of the towers that will serve the triple purposes of fire watch tower, scientific research observation posts and forest ranger outposts. The construction of the first five will start this February."

Raising his head and smiling, his grandfather continued, "Then there is this expedition's magnificent crowning glory, King Nanchancaan's tomb. Those artefacts will be studied and then put on display at the National Archaeological Museum of Belize. The world's best experts on the Maya will endeavour to unlock their secrets. Perhaps now we will finally be able to understand how they were able to know what they did, how they had such advanced astronomical, mathematical, engineering and agricultural knowledge. Some are even suggesting that these codices may, in fact, hold the key to understanding and harnessing a different form of energy. The hypothesis is that there is a limitless and powerful source of energy that the ancient civilizations were aware of that has since been lost. Something like an electromagnetic force field, generated by vibrations and resonance linked to what some quantum physicist researchers have found in subatomic particles. They claim that ancient civilizations like the Egyptians, Incas and Maya may have tapped into this energy. Who knows where this will all lead," said the Professor, pausing for breath having finished reading his list.

"That's absolutely fantastic news! Fascinating!" said Alex.

"We should probably start getting ready for the thank you dinner that I've arranged for all the official dignitaries and other people that helped us achieve all we have here in Belize. But before we do let me tell you what I found out about the criminals that were after you here. This Silus character was a real menace to society. Apparently, he has a thick Interpol file. He escaped from Ashworth high-security psychiatric hospital, a secure facility for the criminally insane in the UK. He had been institutionalised there, it was meant to be permanently, for the rest of his natural life. The doctors at Ashworth diagnosed him as being a homicidal sociopath, a paranoid delusional with extremely sadistic tendencies. For the last five years, since his escape, he has been a big player in the shadowy criminal underworld. A really nasty fellow, who ruled through terror. That gangster, TreeWays, survived the poison Silus gave him, but he may wish he hadn't, the docs tell me that he has permanent liver damage. The Belizean Defence Force went back for him and Emil led them to Gordo after they reached you. They're both looking at a life sentences for kidnapping and attempted murder. The other one, Kiloboy wasn't so lucky. By the time they got to him he was dead. Nasty poison too, relatively slow acting. Initially makes you feel great and then causes total paralysis followed by massive internal haemorrhaging and agonising pain. The soldiers searched the surrounding jungle for three days but did not find Silus' body, just a blood trail that eventually ended in a clearing."

"Well," said Alex "they all got what they deserved. I'm just so relieved that we all pulled through okay."

"Indeed, indeed!" said his grandfather. "Oh, and another thing, Emil mentioned that there is a small chance that he could be a distant descendant of King Nanchancaan, Princess Zazil-Ha and Gonzalo Guererro. I've spoken to the Archaeologists and they have agreed to see if they can find viable DNA from the King's skeleton. If they can, we might be able to see if Emil's DNA has any matches."

"Wow, that's really exciting," Alex said looking at the print of a painting of a Maya temple in his hotel room.

The brief pause was interrupted by the sound of the Professors cell phone ringing.

"Well hello there!" said the Professor, answering the call. "I'm afraid you've caught me at a bad time as I can't chat right now. Besides, I'm in Belize on roaming charges and it would cost an absolute fortune to chat to me here! Okay, good. I'll ring you when I get back to the UK. Cheerio for now."

"I hope that wasn't important," said Alex.

"No, not at all, that was Dr. Planchard, a colleague of mine. Well he's more an academic rival really; we've been sparring intellectually for many years now. He thinks he's smarter than I am. I usually win our debates, it drives him crazy. He's recently taken quite an interest in ARACHNIS and was curious about where our next project would take place."

Alex and his grandfather looked at each other as they both realised the connection. "Do you think Jane is related to Dr. Planchard?" said Alex. "Anyway... Whatever... Well, don't keep me in suspense. Where am I heading off to next?"

"Well after a short rest break back home you will be leading an expedition to Sumatra, Indonesia. I have very good reason to believe that there is something extremely rare and incredibly important to humanity hidden deep in the jungle, amongst all those volcanoes on that magical island. I'm very much hoping that you'll be able to find it."

Alex felt a rush of excitement and quickly grabbed his cell phone and tweeted:

"Hi all! AAS! Well, my Belizean adventure is over. I'm heading home to plan the next one!"

A couple of minutes later a text message appeared on his phone. It was from Jane:

"J4F, would Jungleboy like a lift home from the airport? iwtb 1st to hear yr adven. LMK."

He replied: "Does the sun shine! :-D Tk's, will send the details. CU soon!

Alex smiled to himself and shouted at the top of his voice "Brilliant!"

Postscript

As the tropical sun set over the Caribbean Sea, a cargo vessel pulled out of the port of Big Creek. It had a long, long way to go. Deep in its hold, in a container, a rat sat comfortably reclining in the spare wheel bolted to the bonnet of a Land Rover. The odd pair were happily chatting to each other.

"Yes! It is nice to have company on these long voyages isn't it!" said Sampan.

"First, let me tell you all about the Panama Canal, oh and the Pacific Ocean! And my favourite – the South China Seas! Oooh, Sumatra. There's a dish there called Nasi Goreng, it's served with a fried egg on top – such a shame you don't eat proper food. Never mind, I can't wait."

Bodhi listened contentedly to the excited chatter of her informative little friend.

Above decks, on the bridge, the ship's captain set his course and steered the mighty *Java Sun* into the rolling seas.